95 – L

A

RED WOLFF

NOVEL

K.T. MINCE

"95-L: A Red Wolff Novel," by K.T. Mince. ISBN 978-1-60264-563-9 (softcover); 978-1-60264-564-6 (ebook).

Published 2010 by Virtualbookworm.com Publishing Inc., P.O. Box 9949, College Station, TX 77842, US. ©2010, K.T. Mince. All rights reserved. No part of this publication may be reproduced, stored in a retrieval system, or transmitted in any form or by any means, electronic, mechanical, recording or otherwise, without the prior written permission of K.T. Mince.

Manufactured in the United States of America.

TO

Judy, wife, lover, and best friend,

TO

My fans, all six of them, who encouraged me to
write a second book,

TO

Good cops everywhere. Thanks for what you do.

AND ESPECIALLY
TO

Jill Angel, the real *RED WOLFF*

OTHER NOVELS BY

K.T. MINCE

RED WOLFF

And,
if necessary,
lay down my life rather than swerve from the
path of duty;

Excerpt from the
California Highway Patrol Code of Honor.

CHAPTER ONE

Looking over his shoulder, he glanced at the woman lying naked on his king-sized bed. She was pretty, maybe thirty-seven or forty years old, shoulder length, auburn colored hair, and a good body, too. She was also very dead.

He was in an almost trance like state as he stood naked in front of the open sliding glass door leading out to the upstairs balcony, smoking a cigarette. In his mind he could visualize his mother as he casually brought the cigarette back to his lips. It happened every time.

The sound of a dog barking in the distance snapped him back to the business at hand.

No hurry, he thought to himself, turning his attention back to the outside darkness. He knew how much time he needed as he watched the light rain continue to fall.

Below him the redwood and oak trees, mixed with the ferns and other vegetation, blocked his view of the house below on the terraced hillside. The same trees also blocked any nosey neighbors from seeing him. Not that he worried about it. With the bedroom blacked out, there was no backlight to silhouette him as he stood there.

Sniffing at the outside air he could detect its heavy, moisture-laden feel that muffled noise and caused all the plant life around the house to emit an odor that reminded him of mildew. He could also smell the smoke coming from the chimney as the woodstove downstairs slowly burned the logs he had added several hours ago. Seasoned oak firewood gave off a distinctive pleasing smell as it burned, he thought to himself.

Looking out over the landscape he could see the dim glow of lights from the town of Crescent City three miles to the south and the yellow flash of the beacon atop the Battery Point Lighthouse as it rotated in his direction every five seconds. In the valley below there were a few lights in the distance from other houses scattered north of town, and occasionally he could hear, but couldn't see, a big-rig truck as it drove by on U.S. Highway 101.

Echoing up the hillside he could hear the dog barking again, more urgent this time. With the rain, and the way the sound carried in the wet night air, it was hard to tell how far away the dog was, but the barking had the distinctive dual intonation of danger and warning.

1

Probably a raccoon rummaging around a trash can. He felt sorry for the dog. Some local schmuck would wake up in the morning to find a yard strewn with wet smelly rubbish, and the poor dog would get its butt whipped for letting it happen.

Shrugging his shoulders, he flipped the cigarette out the door, watching as the red tip glowed against the dark sky and arced out of sight. Turning back into the room, he looked at the dim red digital display of the radio alarm clock on the nightstand next to his bed. 12:18 he noted.

Walking away from the bed, he entered the bathroom, turned on the night light, and opened the bottom drawer of the vanity. It took his eyes a second to adjust to the small printing on the page as he checked the tide chart. "High tide in ninety minutes, no need to hurry," he murmured, sliding the drawer shut as he turned back to the bedroom.

"You ready?" he said to the woman, a slight chuckle in his voice, half-expecting an answer.

Through trial and error he had established a routine, a protocol for disposal for the woman's body, the set order of exactly what to do next and how much time it would take to accomplish each step.

Still naked, he first went to the nightstand on the right side of the bed and pulled out a pair of disposable latex medical gloves from the box in the bottom drawer. The non-powdered ones were best he had found from experience.

He also pulled out a hand-held programmable radio scanner. Rotating the power knob, the device clicked on. Adjusting the volume to mid-range, he set it on the nightstand. The device was silent, although the line of small red lights on top danced in sequence as the scanner began monitoring all the public safety radio frequencies in the county. Not unusual to hear nothing, he told himself. It was the late Monday night, early Tuesday morning shift, and he knew there just wouldn't be much going on.

He also knew there weren't very many cops working. Mentally he formed a picture, let's see, one Crescent City P.D. officer, one Del Norte County Sheriff's deputy, both working solo, and one California Highway Patrol two-man unit. "Four cops in three vehicles for the whole county, the odds are on my side," he muttered.

Step one, prepare the body. From the nightstand on the other side of the bed he removed the eight foot by eight foot sheet of three millimeter thick, clear plastic visquine he had pre-cut the day before. Building contractors bought the stuff by the roll, using it to protect their jobs from the elements, to cover window openings, and when they were doing roof repairs. He found the three millimeter thickness was just right for his purposes. Unfolding the visquine he laid it out on the bed next to the woman and rolled her lifeless body on to it so she was lying next to one edge.

Reaching into the same drawer he pulled out a small clear plastic sandwich bag and a brand new pair of hair scissors. Wrenching at her left hand, he managed to get her double wedding and engagement rings off. He dropped the rings in the bag, then using the scissors he snipped off a six inch lock of her hair and put it in the bag, also. With the hair and the rings inside, he slid his thumb and forefinger across the top to seal the bag shut. This was his fourth bag since moving here.

Unhurriedly, he put his latest souvenirs on the nightstand and turned his attention back to preparing the body.

He began by kneeling on the mattress, his knees at a right angle to the woman's head. He first removed the cloth sleep mask from her eyes, then turned his attention to the brightly colored scarf around her neck. His movements were almost reverent as he untied the knot and lifted her head to gently pull the scarf free. The scarf was almost three feet long, with a flower print design, the kind his mother liked. It was the type he always used.

Once the scarf was clear he could see, even in the faint light of his bedroom, the two burn marks on the nape of her neck. The marks, about two and a half inches apart, were several hours old now and had swollen as they turned a dark blue.

Taking one last look at the woman, unfeeling and uncaring, he rolled her over several times until she was wrapped in a plastic cocoon. Only a couple of wraps around her body would do it, any more than that, he had learned, made the body difficult to bend. Then, from his walk-in closet he retrieved, still in its sealed package, a black plastic raincoat. Opening the package, he laid the raincoat out on the bed, slid the visquine wrapped woman's body onto the raincoat, drew the sides together, and pulled the attached hood up over her head.

Carrying the body downstairs, he went through the kitchen into his attached, two-car garage, where he put the raincoat wrapped woman's body in the trunk of his vehicle and slammed the lid closed. Step one completed.

Still unhurried, but with purpose, he went back up the stairs to the bedroom where he methodically stripped the sheets off the bed, careful to fold them toward the middle of the bed so the sleep mask, any trace hair, skin cells, or body fluids would be trapped in the folds. He then stuffed them in a large heavy-duty, black plastic contractor's clean-up bag. Next, he carefully pulled the fitted edges of the rubber-coated bed pad off each corner of the mattress and folded it toward the center of the bed before putting it in the garbage bag, also.

As the last part of his cleanup, he vacuumed the carpet, careful to get under the bed with the hose attachment. When he finished he removed the disposable paper bag from the vacuum and put it in the bag with the sheets. Step two done.

Satisfied with his cleanup work, he headed for the shower. After showering he toweled the dampness out of his scalp and used the hair dryer to blow it completely dry. It took a minute or so for him to comb it into place and hit it with a couple of shots of hair spray. Three steps finished, and still time to spare.

His next to last step was to remake the bed. Back to the closet now where he paused for a second, looking at the six new sets of sheets and six new mattress pads on the shelf, still in their store packaging. They were all the same color, white. "Someday maybe I'll have to try some different color sheets," he said out loud, then quickly reminded himself that no, white was the best color as it made it easier to see blood stains.

It had gone almost textbook perfect from start to finish, he thought to himself, as he made the bed with the new white sheets. The flashlight had done its job well by taking any thoughts of resistance out of her mind. Once he had her handcuffed and gagged, she had not struggled again, almost if she was resigned to her fate.

The rage had been building in him for several weeks. He had fought down the rage and the urges it brought, by telling himself the conditions were not right. But when the images of his mother came in the night, waking him from a fitful sleep, he knew he could not resist much longer.

On Sunday, the urges had driven him almost mad. No, no he kept telling himself, only on a Monday or Tuesday, and then, only if the conditions were right. He was fighting a losing battle he knew. The urges needed satisfying.

Monday was a work day and he had gone looking for someone late that afternoon. His first step in the process was a stop at the local Wal-Mart where he spent nearly a half-hour choosing just the right scarf. Normally, he didn't shop for scarves from stores in Crescent City as he was fairly well known in town. The last thing he needed was to draw attention to himself. The urges he felt, however, fueled by the hate and rage built up over the last several months, were almost overwhelming. The images of his mother lent a sense of urgency to his task.

Don't forget, the flower print ones, like the ones you used to buy for her, he told himself as he pondered just the right scarf.

It was dark by 6:00, and the rain that started lightly about 2:30, had changed to a steady drizzle, keeping the roadways wet and reducing visibility. All the right conditions were starting to fall into place.

Driving his work vehicle, he'd stopped to get a cup of coffee at the mini-mart gas station about 7:00 that evening when he saw her pull in. Late model silver-blue BMW, 700 Series. Since it was a self-serve station, she had to do it herself. It did his heart good to see a rich bitch pumping her own gas. After filling her tank, she left her car at the pump and went into the market to get the key to the restroom. Arrogant rich bitch, he said to himself, don't inconvenience yourself by moving your car a few yards and parking. Go ahead, just leave your car where it is, and don't worry about anyone else who may want to gas up.

While she was in the restroom, he strolled casually across to the pump island and yanked a couple of blue paper towels from the dispenser next to the windshield washer bucket. The glittering silver license plate frame told him the rest of what he needed to know. BMW of Beverly Hills.

Yes, she would do nicely.

Pulling out of the station she turned right, heading north. Waiting a couple of seconds after she left, he headed northbound on U.S. 101 as well. He dared not let her get too far ahead lest he catch a stoplight and lose her, or she made an unexpected turn. She just needed to get a little ways down the road, out of the city limits, to a place where the traffic was always light.

Even though it was only a little after 7:00, there were very few other cars on the road and he kept her in view a couple hundred yards ahead. It was a typical dark, rainy, late winter evening in Crescent City. The town would close down early. Anyone still out would soon be wrapping up whatever business they had and heading home for the night.

He followed her for several miles as she drove north on 101, then took the turn to go north on Highway 199 toward Grants Pass, Oregon. In several places 199 had sharp curves with up and down hills as it roughly followed the Smith River into the mountains. He used his knowledge of the highway to close the distance until he was directly behind her.

Eyes on the road and her vehicle, now only a couple car lengths in front of him, he pulled the hand-held spotlight from underneath the driver's seat, plugging the cord into the cigarette lighter receptacle. The rich bitch probably didn't even notice him behind her until he pressed the switch on spotlight's handle. The inside of his vehicle glowed red as the powerful beam from the spotlight bathed her car in a deep magenta. And the rest was history, he said to himself.

———————

Standing back from the bed he scanned the entire room. Everything looked normal. As he smoothed a wrinkle on the bedspread, he glanced at the clock, 12:55. Need to pick it up a little and get going.

Retreating to his closet again, he grabbed a brand new pair of Levi blue jeans from the shelf. Giving them a quick once over, he assured himself all the tags were removed and slipped them on. He did the same thing with a hooded black pullover sweatshirt. Lastly he slipped on a new pair of socks.

From the top of the dresser in the closet, he grabbed his wallet, keys and a handful of change. The last thing he picked up was his five-shot, .38 caliber, Smith and Wesson, Chief's Special. He didn't bother to inspect the weapon to ensure it was loaded, it always was. Still snuggled in its soft pliable leather "inside the pants" holster he stuck the pistol inside the back waistband of his new blue jeans and made sure the spring retaining clip was on the outside. Satisfied the weapon was secure against the backside of his left hip, held in place by the spring clip on the holster and the tightness of the jeans, he reached back with his left hand and felt for the pistol grip. The grip was right where it was supposed to be, just above the waistband, easy to grab and draw. He pulled the bottom hem of the sweatshirt over the gun.

Grabbing the two plastic bags, one with the sheets, the other with the dead woman's clothes and purse, he hustled down the stairs in his stocking feet. He could feel himself moving faster now, something that happened every time after he had satisfied his urges. But he couldn't help himself. He stopped momentarily and contemplated throwing another piece of oak in the woodstove, thought better of it, and went out to the garage with the two garbage bags in tow.

Disposing of incriminating evidence, like disposing of common household trash in Del Norte County, he had discovered, was kind of a pain in the ass. There was nothing he could do about it tonight, but it would be first on his "to-do" list in the morning. Stashing the bags by trash cans in the garage was best for now.

On the shelf, just inside the roll-up garage door, he glanced at the row of muddy leather work boots, worn running shoes, and a pair of rubber, pullover muck boots. There were also two pairs of new, non-descript, no-name-brand tennis shoes, one pair was dark gray in color, the other black. Both pairs had different tread designs on the soles. The boxes he had long since discarded. Selecting one pair, he slipped them on and finished lacing up.

All steps now completed, he was ready to go. Glancing at his cell phone, as he didn't wear a watch, he saw the time. High tide was in twenty-five minutes, no problem.

———————

Driving down Highway 101, he headed south, back toward town. Because 101 runs through Crescent City, not around it, as it did many cities in the northern part of the state, he slowed from sixty-five to the posted thirty-five limit as he made his way into town. Amazing, he thought to himself, not another car on the road. "See, I told you we had to wait until the conditions were right," he said out loud, talking to himself.

He was headed to his usual spot near the village of Klamath to dump the body. It would take him about fifteen minutes to get there. The location was a small vista point just off Highway 101. It was the perfect location, about two hundred feet above the ocean, with a sheer drop to the water below. There were no sandy beaches within a mile either way for the body to wash up on, and as the high tide receded, it would suck the body out to sea and down into the frigid depths. From there, the currents would either push it southward toward the mouth of the Klamath River, or would pull it further out to sea. It would be better, he told himself, if the body drifted south toward the river mouth where sharks hunted the sea lions that were feasting on the salmon trying to get up river to spawn.

The ocean was the great ally he didn't have when he'd disposed of women's bodies at his previous jobs before coming to Crescent City, he thought to himself as he drove. Yes, there had been rivers, but about half the time the bodies floated to the surface and were recovered. And yes, there were forests and parks, just like here, but the bodies of women he left there always seemed to be discovered eventually.

But here things were different. Here, the ocean helped him. The ocean he found was not judgmental, it never closed, and so far, it had not given up any of the three women he had disposed of from the vista point since starting his new job here less than a year ago.

It was quiet as he drove, the only sound coming from the rhythmic movement of the windshield wipers and the hum of the tires on the wet asphalt. It was the quiet that caused him to realize he didn't have his scanner.

"Damn!" he said in a loud voice. He could picture the scanner sitting on the nightstand in the bedroom. He'd made a mental note to make sure to grab it when he was ready to leave. But in the rush he got going through the cleanup steps and preparing the woman's body for disposal, he had just plain forgotten it this time.

He quickly considered his options. There were only two. He could turn around, go back to his house, and retrieve the scanner, or he could continue on without it.

If he turned around, it would take him an hour to get back to the spot where he wanted to dump the body. Two bad things could happen if he chose that option; one, he might be spotted, or his car recognized by a local cop. Second, going back home would also mean he may lose the tide. He needed to dump the woman's corpse at just the right time after high tide to ensure the body would be carried out to sea. If he was too late getting the body in the water, it might float near the shore, where it could be spotted by a tourist at the vista point in the daylight.

His other option was to keep going. The downside of that option was without the scanner, he had absolutely no idea where the three cop cars were working in the county. While he knew it would only take a minute or so to dump the woman's body, and the odds were really long that a patrol unit would happen by at that precise moment, still it was risky.

He kept driving south.

CHAPTER TWO

"16-30, Humboldt, 16-30," the communications operator's voice had the tone of overwork as he called the field unit working U.S. Highway 101 near the city of Eureka. The radio crackled again as the comm-op dispatched the Humboldt CHP area unit to another accident. "16-30, 11-79, northbound 101 at Fields Landing. Overturned vehicle, possible victims trapped inside, Eureka Fire enroute."

Once unit 16-30 acknowledged their call, the comm-op at the Humboldt Communications Center in downtown Eureka, sat back in his swivel chair and stretched his back, then stood up to get the circulation going in his legs. Tethered by the six-foot-long, stretchable coiled cord from his headset to the dispatch console, he walked six to eight feet from the radio then back again several times.

Damn, he thought to himself, what a hectic night it had been.

Working alone in the dispatch center, he had started his eight hour shift at 10:00. Normally, Monday and Tuesday graveyard shifts were really slow and easy for a single communications operator to handle by themselves. It had been a fairly typical quiet Monday until just after midnight. The calls had been almost non-stop since then.

Fortunately for the comm-op he only had four field units to keep track of that night. Each of the units was identified by a radio prefix that corresponded to their assigned command. Tonight he had 105-Edward in the Garberville area, 16-30 and 16-50 were in the Humboldt CHP command, and 95-Edward in Crescent City.

Those three CHP areas the Humboldt Communications Center dispatched for, Garberville to the south, Humboldt in the middle, and Crescent City to the north, right up to the Oregon border, covered nearly two hundred fifty miles along the Highway 101 corridor, plus thousands of miles of other state highways and county roads.

Thanks to computer-aided dispatch technology, 9-1-1 call routing systems, mountain top repeaters which relayed radio signals over great distances, and a normally low volume of calls on Monday and Tuesday nights, an experienced comm-op could handle graveyard shift alone. Tonight was just one of those fluky times when everything happened at once.

A hundred miles to the north, the two-officer graveyard unit from the Crescent City Highway Patrol area rode in silence listening to the radio.

"The Humboldt County units are taking a beating tonight," the female officer said to her partner as he drove, "I think that's the fourth call they've had in two hours."

Almost as if to validate her statement, the radio blared again.

"16-50, Humboldt, 16-50, 11-83," there was a noticeable twinge of frustration now in the comm-op's voice.

When unit 16-50 responded they were dispatched to yet another collision.

"Now both of the units in Humboldt County are working crashes. Let's not say anything about how quiet it is tonight in Del Norte County so we don't jinx ourselves," the male officer said, taking his eyes off the road momentarily, as he turned his head to the right and looked at his female partner.

Like all California Highway Patrol units statewide, officers rode doubled up on "C" Watch, or graveyard shift, as the officers called it. It was almost 1:30 in the morning and the officers in unit 95-Edward were about halfway through their shift.

"105-Edward, Humboldt, 105-Edward," the exasperated voice of the male comm-op sounded even more gravelly than usual as he called the single graveyard unit assigned to the Garberville Highway Patrol area.

Two hundred miles north of Garberville, the Crescent City officers couldn't hear the unit from the CHP command that covered the northern part of Mendocino County and the southern part of Humboldt County respond to their call. They knew, however, the unit had answered as the communications operator's voice broke the silence giving the Garberville unit the particulars of their call, "105-Edward, disabled big-rig blocking northbound lane 101 at Piercy."

Four units, eight officers, to patrol such a vast geographical expanse didn't seem like very adequate coverage, especially on a night like tonight. Oh well, it will slow down soon and get back to normal, he said to himself as he sat back down at the console.

And just that quickly it did. The 9-1-1 calls stopped coming, the field units were working their incidents, and the radio was silent.

Sitting in front of the console, the overhead lights in the radio room off, the green lights from the computer screen were the only illumination. The comm-op let his mind drift.

He thought about only having four units working tonight and then about how the job of being a communications operator had changed in the past twenty years. In the '80s, when he transferred to this communications center from Los Angeles, the Highway Patrol didn't even provide twenty-four hour patrol on highways like 101 in rural locations. Back then, units worked until 11:00 by themselves, then one officer would take a patrol car home and be on-call. If something happened between eleven and six in the morning, like a stalled car, or a minor fender bender, the comm-op would request the local sheriff's department to handle the call. If there was no deputy available, or if the incident was more serious, the on-call officer would be contacted at home and respond from there.

That system worked fine for many years until the night a California state senator's daughter broke down on 101 south of Eureka. In an era before cell phones, in a remote area without emergency call-boxes, she had spent a cold, lonely, and scary night by herself in the middle of nowhere until the CHP day-shift officer stopped to check out her vehicle about 7:30 the next morning.

Two days later the Commissioner of the Highway Patrol found himself getting chewed out in the office of the girl's father at the state capitol in Sacramento. Out of that incident, the senator agreed to sponsor a bill to add two hundred new officers to the Highway Patrol, and the Commissioner agreed to deploy them on rural highways to provide twenty-four hour patrol services.

"Humboldt, 105-Edward, roadway clear, 10-98," the voice of the Garberville officer reporting they had removed the disabled truck and were available for another call, brought the comm-op back to the present.

"10-4, 105-Edward, roadway clear, 10-98," he responded.

The radio went quiet again.

Officer David Castle, Davy to his friends, steered the big Dodge SUV effortlessly through the curves on U.S. 101 as it headed south. Holding a steady sixty miles-per-hour, he scanned the road ahead as the windshield wipers kept a slow steady rhythm clearing the constant light rain from the windshield.

"Damn it's dark tonight," he said out loud, not expecting an answer from his partner. There was dark and then there was rural dark, he thought to himself. In the early part of his career he had worked in metropolitan Los Angeles. Night time there didn't always mean dark. With all the buildings, freeways, and millions of houses, there was always some illumination. But here, this was rural night time. Here dark meant dark. Without the constant traffic and only scattered small towns here and there, it could get really black out at night. Tonight, with the overcast and rain, was one of those nights.

Because he and his partner were the only CHP unit working in the county tonight, they had opted to use one of the three SUVs assigned to the Crescent City command, rather than a regular Ford Crown Victoria sedan patrol car.

It was late March and it was cold inland. Chances were good the rain would keep up all night. If the temperature dropped a couple of degrees, it could snow in the mountains. They'd need the four-wheel drive and big snow tires on the SUV if they got a call on Highway 199 as it snaked its way inland, up the Smith River gorge, and into the mountains toward the tunnel at the Oregon border.

Sitting on the passenger's side, his partner yawned. "Damn, will this night never end!" the officer exclaimed. The tone in her voice made her comment a statement, not a question. "Christ! We haven't seen another car on the road in almost a half-hour."

Dave Castle smiled at his partner and said, "We could be running our asses off, going from call to call like the guys in Humboldt and Garberville."

"Yeah, okay, I'll stop whining."

Few people have an appreciation of how vast and sparsely populated the northern part of California actually is. To most, Northern California means San Francisco. What they don't realize is over one-third of California is north of the Bay Area, but it contains less than fifteen percent of the state's population.

Del Norte County, with the Pacific Ocean to the west and Oregon to the north, is about the same size as Rhode Island. But, unlike "The Ocean State" with over a million people, California's northwestern most county had only 28,000 residents. With so few people, working graveyard in a place like Crescent City could get boring, especially late on a rainy Monday night and through the early morning hours of a dark, wet, and quiet Tuesday. There just wasn't much to do.

The few cars and trucks on the road were headed toward San Francisco, four hundred miles to the south, or north to Oregon. There wasn't much in the way of local traffic either by that time of night. The only places still open in the county were a handful of bars, a couple of all-night gas stations, two convenience marts, and the twenty-four hour Denny's restaurant in the center of Crescent City.

The female partner shifted to find a more comfortable position in the padded bucket seat of the patrol unit. Having promised not to whine, she settled for a disgruntled shrug and crossed her arms over her chest.

"I am seriously bored, and that's not whining, it's just a statement," she said.

"Patience Sweetie, a couple more hours and we're off for three days," her partner replied with a mock sympathetic tone in his voice.

Ordinarily it was taboo for partners of the opposite sex, well of the same sex for that matter, to use endearments like "Sweetie". Comments like that could well end up being the basis for a sexual harassment complaint and disciplinary action.

Officer Dave Castle didn't worry about the CHP policy implications of how he addressed his partner, and he didn't think it at all improper to call her "Sweetie".

His partner, Officer Jodie Castle, was his wife.

Married for eight years, they first met when they were both assigned to the South Los Angeles area. He had been one of Jodie's Field Training Officers when she reported to South L.A. after graduating from the academy in 1994.

He was a veteran with four years on the job when they first started working together. He was single, living in a bachelor pad near Redondo Beach, working graveyard, and knocking down huge monthly overtime checks from all the hours he spent in court as a result of his prowess in arresting drunk drivers.

Arresting people for DUI was not his only talent. A little over six feet tall, slim, and with skin that tanned easily, he had an air of casual self-assurance that accumulated a steady parade of beach bunnies who he charmed and bedded. Living in a beach town frequented by beautiful and fit, single women, mostly secretaries, nurses, and college girls, he was living a *Baywatch* lifestyle. For the women, what was not to like? He was handsome, funny, and made great money. Besides, he was a cop, so there was a good chance he was neither an ax-murderer, nor just another loser with no prospects who hung around the beaches of southern L.A. County.

Despite his reputation as a "player" among the troops in the South L.A. CHP squad, Davy Castle was a tough Field Training Officer as he took Jodie through the last fifteen days of her "break-in". He carefully explained and demonstrated how to do things, expecting performance pretty close to perfection when she had to perform the required job task like arresting a suspect, interviewing witnesses, or watching out for her own safety. He was as tough with Jodie as he was with any male trainee.

He explained it to all his trainees this way, "In less than fifteen days you're going to be out working by yourself on day or afternoon shift, or riding with another partner on graveyard. Either way, you have to be responsible for your own safety."

Then he would ask them this question, "When it comes to driving, safety tactics, dealing with suspects, investigating at the scene of an accident, or just talking to somebody you contact, how many times can you get away with making a mistake?"

He would let them think about his question for a few seconds, then answer it himself. "You can get away with making a mistake every time, except the last time," he told them. Then, pausing for a moment while his trainees contemplated that answer, he would continue.

"Think about it, something as routine as making a traffic stop. You've seen officers who make left side approaches when they make stops on the freeway. They know better, they know it's dangerous, and they know that someone driving along distracted by talking on a cell phone, or lighting a cigarette could accidently veer off and hit them. They know it's a mistake to approach a car on that side with traffic whipping by, but they do it anyway. Same thing with turning your back on traffic, or not doing a pat-down search on somebody, or any of the hundreds of things we do every day. So the answer is this, you can get away with making mistakes every time you do something, except the last time, 'cause that's the time the mistake will get you killed."

That little speech was usually met by silence from his trainee's while they thought about just how dangerous a job they had, and how some little mistake, a lapse in judgment, or letting their guard down for a moment, could get them killed.

Dave Castle was a tough training officer, and he gave his trainees a lot to think about. He also turned out really good, highly competent, safety conscious officers.

When he became her training officer, Jodie Castle was known as Jodie Hanson.

She was married when she took the test to become a CHP Officer. She had married a guy she met while attending Merced Community College, where she'd earned an Associate's Degree in marketing. Following their marriage, they moved to the California central valley town of Fresno. She found a job as a sales rep for one of the cell phone companies, supporting her husband while he attended Fresno State University. After graduation, he became a high school teacher, and the Hanson's settled into the lifestyle of a young couple building a life together in California in the early '90s. With two incomes, they bought a house in the suburbs, had two fancy cars, a ski-boat, and enough disposable cash to enjoy life. They'd mutually decided to hold off on kids for a couple more years.

Always an active outdoorsy person, working in sales was not something that Jodie Hanson found very exciting. Sure, it paid pretty well, and the hours were right, but it was less than fulfilling for her.

She'd seen the recruiting billboard advertisements all over town for the Fresno County Sheriff's Department and started to check out what the job of a sheriff's deputy entailed. She liked the prospect of working patrol, the specialized assignments in narcotics and vice, and the potential to promote, plus the salary was twice what she was making at the cell phone company. She'd almost signed up to take the entry examination when she learned that she would probably have to spend the first four years of her career as a deputy working in the jail. That part of the job turned her off on being a sheriff's deputy.

Two weeks later, on a weekend trip with the ski-boat, she saw the recruiting billboard for the California Highway Patrol on Highway 99. When they got back from their weekend outing, she did her research on the internet. The next week she called the local Fresno CHP office to see about doing a ride-along.

She did the ride-along with a Hispanic officer on the Saturday afternoon shift, one of the busiest days of the week for the CHP. Halfway through the shift, she was hooked. It was a different world, a world she did not know existed except for cop shows on television. The officer she rode with couldn't think of anything bad to say about the Highway Patrol, except maybe if she did become an officer, there was a good chance she would get assigned to Los Angeles.

The prospect of having a cop for a wife and her working in Los Angeles, didn't thrill Jodie's husband. Reluctantly though, he supported her decision, secretly hoping that her desire to become a California Highway Patrol Officer was just a passing fantasy.

It wasn't. She filed the application on-line and took the written test a month later. The seven steps in the testing process took almost nine months, but she stuck it out and received an appointment to the CHP Academy.

Their problems started almost as soon as she left for the academy in Sacramento, a four hour drive north from Fresno on Highway 99. Since it was a paramilitary, live-in academy, Jodie only got liberty on Wednesday nights for five hours, and from Friday night at five till Sunday night at midnight.

On those weekends when she could make it home or when her husband came to Sacramento, he found she was a different person. First of all she was always tired from the long training days at the academy, and she spent countless hours studying. She also constantly wanted to tell her husband about her training, something that was interesting, but not something he wanted to talk about or could really understand, especially after having not seen her for sometimes weeks at a time. After all, there were bills to pay, cars to get to the shop, chores to do around the house, all things her husband now grudgingly found that he had to do by himself.

Their real problems began six months later when Jodie graduated from the academy and was assigned to the South Los Angeles area.

Their initial plan was for her husband to keep teaching in Fresno. Jodie would get an apartment near where she worked and come home on her days off. That plan sounded workable, except Jodie Hanson, having no seniority, found herself working graveyard shift, with Tuesdays and Wednesdays off. So, after completing her shift at 6:00 on Tuesday morning, she would make the five hour drive up Interstate 5, over the Grapevine, and then take Highway 99 to Fresno. Exhausted, as soon as she got home she crashed for a few hours.

When her husband got home in the afternoon, she had that groggy, not-enough-sleep manner about her, while he was eager to talk, make love, and have her help him with all the things that needed to be done around the house. By 10:00 at night, her body clock was in the time to go to work mode, while his was ready for bed. It wasn't a good situation.

They might have made it through the distance separation if he had agreed to look for a teaching job in the L.A. basin, or she could get a transfer to a CHP area closer to Fresno. Her husband, however, was unwilling to give up his job and tenure in Fresno, and she couldn't even put in for a transfer until she completed her one year probation. To make matters worse, to actually get a transfer back to Fresno, she would need ten years seniority. In the end it wasn't the distance that broke them up, it was the job.

Police work takes its toll on relationships. While nationally about half the marriages end in divorce, for cops the divorce rate hovers around eighty percent.

Part of the reason undoubtedly involves the odd hours, working weekends and holidays, and the everyday stress and danger associated with the job. But mostly, it involves the type of people and situations cops deal with day-in and day-out.

Most people who become law enforcement officers come from average middle class backgrounds, have a desire to help people, and have a work ethic and value system that drives them to succeed. Most of them may have had only cursory contact with the police growing up, like a traffic ticket or a car accident. Their ideas about what police work is like came from television shows like *Law and Order,* or *CSI,* where detached cops unemotionally solve crime and deal with volatile people in a neatly packaged one hour program with time out for commercials.

Unfortunately, on a daily basis, most cops see people at their worst and are involved in situations that expose them to the life's seedier side. Working in that environment everyday starts to take its toll, especially if they can't vent their feelings to someone.

Venting takes different forms for different officers. Married male officers, at least early in their careers, tell their wives everything they did that day. For them it's exciting, and retelling the events of their shift, especially the dangerous situations they were in, is kind of a macho thing. Most single male and female officers, if they don't have a significant other, at least have other officers they can grab a beer with after work to decompress and talk. But married female officers, those not married to another cop, generally have no one.

Intuitively, a married female cop knew she couldn't go home and tell her non-cop husband about the day she had. She couldn't describe wrestling a suspect to the ground when she tried to arrest him. Nor could she tell him about the two year old baby girl who went through the windshield of a car in an accident because her stupid mother was in a hurry and didn't take the time to put the kid in a child seat. Surely, a non-cop husband could not visualize, and certainly couldn't identify with, the smell of what it was like going into a house where there was dog shit all over the floor and dirty dishes in the sink with maggots crawling on them.

Jodie Hanson couldn't tell her husband about these things because first of all they would become the subject of a fight. Then, during the fight, he would tell her being a cop was too dangerous and demand she quit.

But most of all, a female cop like Jodie Hanson, married to a civilian, didn't tell her husband about these things because he wouldn't understand them. In her husband's world, people didn't fight with cops, or fail to secure their babies in car seats, or live with dog shit and dirty dishes. These things didn't happen in his world, ever. They happened everyday in hers.

So it was with Officer Jodie Hanson. She did her job in South Los Angeles, made a ten hour round-trip drive on her days off, and grew steadily unhappier.

For the first three months after completing her break-in, she worked doubled up on graveyard shift with another officer. Their beat had responsibility for the Harbor Freeway right through the Watts District of south central Los Angeles.

Even though she was still the new kid, she was good at her job, David Castle's training had seen to that. Sure, there were things she needed help with from her more experienced partner, but for the most part everything she did was fairly routine, an accident investigation here, help out a stalled motorist there, arrest a drunk driver, back-up the L.A. Sheriff's Department at the scene of a gang shooting.

Getting off at 6:00 in the morning she headed to her apartment, took a shower to wash away the night's grime, fixed a snack, checked her e-mail, and watched T.V. for a couple of hours to unwind. Next night, same thing. When her days off rolled around, she made the long drive back to Fresno.

By her second month on graveyard shift she began to dread her days off. The drive was bad enough, but the fights with her husband were even worse. By the end of her third month, she started telling him she had court on her days off, or had to work a special overtime detail so she didn't have to drive to Fresno.

They both knew it was over. In fairness to him, she realized that she was as much to blame as he was. He had his career, she had hers, and they weren't compatible. They mutually agreed to the terms of the divorce. He got the ski-boat. Four months later she was single.

———

It quickly became common knowledge around the South L.A. CHP office that Jodie Hanson was now single. She had a constant stream of male officers asking her out, and even a few female officers too. Occasionally she did go on a date or for a beer after work, but for the most part, life was pretty much the same as before her divorce, except she didn't have to make the drive to Fresno on her days off.

A year later, still relegated to graveyard shift by her lack of seniority, she found herself partnered again with her former Field Training Officer, Dave Castle. Working with him as a full partner, not as his trainee, she began to see him in a different light. He had a serious and a funny side, he liked the same kind of music she did, and he took a no-nonsense, but even-tempered approach to his job.

For his part, Dave Castle found his former trainee a breath of fresh air to work with. Because he was good at being a trainer for new officers, he was tapped constantly to fulfill that role. It paid an extra sixty-five cents an hour, but it was stressful having to watch out for his safety, as well as that of an inexperienced trainee every night. Then there was reviewing their reports, explaining the same things over and over, and how hair-raising it was to put his life in a trainee's hands when they started to drive.

They never really formally dated, but there was no doubt in either of their minds that there was a mutual attraction between them. They had a standing practice of grabbing a beer after work every Saturday morning. They chose a bar near the harbor in San Pedro, close to the cruise ship terminal, that catered to cops and would each drive their own car to the location. It was usually only two beers, three if they had a lot to talk about. They were always conscious they had to work that night.

For Jodie Hanson, those Saturday morning beers with Dave Castle filled the void she had felt for the last year. It was good to have someone to talk with. With Dave Castle she could open up about the people they worked with, the things she saw and did every night, and the pent up emotions she felt about the job. He was easy to talk to, he had many of the same emotions, he understood.

It happened on a summer Saturday morning during their third month working as partners. Call it synchronicity, or happenstance, or maybe Dave Castle just got lucky.

The previous Thursday, Jodie Hanson started a DUI trial in the Long Beach Municipal Court. She'd worked Wednesday night, got off at 6:00, drove to court in her own car, and grabbed an hours sleep in the officer's waiting room. The trial started at 8:30. She spent all day in the courtroom, testifying for three hours, and the rest of the day sitting with the Deputy District Attorney, trying not to fall asleep, while other witnesses testified. By 3:30 the prosecution rested and the judge adjourned for the day, telling everyone to be back at 9:00 on Friday morning.

Sleepily, she drove home in the hot, smoggy, afternoon sun, through the already heavy stop-and-go commute traffic, up Interstate 405 to her apartment in Torrance. She got home at 5:15, set the alarm for 7:30 and crashed.

Groggy from lack of good sleep, she was back to work at 10:00 Thursday evening. Knowing what it was like to spend all day in court, Dave Castle drove that night. Jodie sleepily rode along, mostly awake, nodding off every once in awhile. It was a no big deal night, one arrest, two minor accidents, and lots of patrolling. Friday morning, Jodie Hanson repeated the previous day's events, spending all day again in court. The case went to the jury about 2:30, and she was home just before 4:00 in the afternoon.

By the start of her Friday night shift, she had slept about seven hours in the last three days. Normally, since her partner drove the night before, it was her night to drive. Dave Castle just grabbed the keys and told her not to sweat it. As tired as she was, she didn't argue with him.

Fridays are usually busy nights on graveyards in South L.A., and this night was no exception. They were busy, running from call to call, making two arrests and investigating one major accident. It made the night go by fast, and Jodie Hanson didn't have time to know she was exhausted.

About 4:15 they cleared their last call and headed to breakfast. On the way they spotted a disabled vehicle on the right shoulder of the freeway, four-way flashers blinking in the darkness. Dave Castle pulled to the shoulder behind the vehicle, and Jodie Hanson jumped out of the passenger side to check on the driver of the disabled vehicle. Dave Castle got out also and took up a position on the shoulder to watch his partner and traffic. The driver of the disabled vehicle was a nurse on her way to work who had run out of gas. She told Jodie she was fine and had used her cell phone to call her husband. Jodie gave her the standard "for her safety stay in her car" warning and headed back to the patrol unit.

The older model pickup truck was doing about sixty when the right side tires drifted out of the lane and three feet onto the right shoulder. At the speed it was travelling it would hit the rear of the patrol car in less than two seconds. Davy yelled at his partner.

Jodie Hanson looked up to see the truck closing on their unit. Standing where she was, between the rear of the disabled car and the front of the patrol vehicle, she knew when the pickup hit the patrol unit it would be pushed forward into the nurse's car, crushing her in the middle. Her instincts took over. Without thinking, she vaulted over the three foot high steel guard rail bordering the right shoulder.

Somehow the pickup truck avoided the patrol car, passing so close that its tires kicked up the loose gravel on the shoulder sending it showering like a blast of birdshot over Dave Castle and the side of the patrol vehicle.

After the narrow miss, Dave Castle didn't hesitate. His first instinct was to jump back in the patrol car and chase down the pickup truck. He knew more than likely it was a drunk driver. At the same time he was heading for the driver's door of their unit, he looked up to be sure his partner was coming. She was nowhere to be seen.

Because the freeway in this location was elevated about fifteen feet on a raised earthen berm, when she jumped the guardrail, Jodie Hanson tumbled down the embankment, through the weeds and plants, until she reached the bottom where she rolled to a stop among the empty beer cans, dirty diapers, and other trash motorists discarded along the freeway.

Dave Castle was there in an instant, the drunk in the pickup truck now the last thing on his mind. Jodie was okay. Her hair was disheveled and her uniform dirty, but otherwise she seemed fine.

They skipped going to breakfast and headed back to the office. By that time her back was starting to tighten up, and it was painful to walk. They reported what happened to their sergeant who did the required paperwork to document the incident as an industrial injury. The sergeant told her she ought to go to the emergency room to get checked out.

Jodie Hanson thought about it for a second, thought about sitting in the waiting room of an emergency hospital for several hours, probably with lots of screaming kids, and she thought about how tired she was. No thanks she told her sergeant, she'd just finish her reports and take a couple of Motrin when she got home. If she was still hurting after a couple of days, she added, she would go see her own doctor.

By the time they finished their reports, about 6:30, Jodie Hanson's back was killing her. It was Dave Castle who suggested they skip their Saturday morning beers.

"No way," she told him.

"Okay, I'm up for it, but here's an alternate plan," Davy told her. "You ride with me. We'll grab a six-pack and head to my place where there's a Jacuzzi and pool. The hot water will do your back good. We'll drink a couple of beers, and then I'll drive you home. It won't be a problem to pick you up on my way to work tonight."

She started to protest, it was out of his way, and besides she didn't have a suit. He would find something for her to wear he said, overriding her protests, besides he told her, it was the kind of thing you did for a good partner.

Within an hour they were in the Jacuzzi, Dave Castle having found a pair of running shorts and an old Tee-shirt for her to wear in the water.

The high pressure jets of the Jacuzzi, the one hundred-two degree water, and the two Tylenol he gave her loosened up her sore back muscles. The two beers helped also.

21

After forty-five minutes she said she was fine and wanted him to drive her home as planned. They both headed back to his apartment to change.

Jodie slipped into the bathroom to change back into her street clothes, then took a seat on the couch waiting for him to get dressed.

When Davy came out of his bedroom, he found her on the couch, dead asleep. She looked so peaceful he didn't have the heart to wake her, besides, he knew the best thing he could do was let her sleep. She also looked really good, he thought. Her damp hair covering half her face, and her shirt had ridden up above the waist of her jeans exposing a lot of soft white skin.

Dave Castle was a hound, but he wasn't a dog. He gently slipped off her running shoes, grabbed a spare blanket from the closet, covered her up and headed for his bedroom, leaving the door slightly ajar so he could hear her if she woke up.

The long night, the Jacuzzi, and the beers, all took their toll on Dave Castle, too. He was sound asleep and only woke up when she snuggled her naked body next to him. He was a little groggy when she kissed him, and he started to say something, almost in protest.

"Sssh Castle," she purred, "It's the kind of thing you do for a good partner."

Over the years they would laugh about how they came to be a couple, and Jodie would tell him she didn't know what came over her, maybe it was the beer, or maybe she was disoriented being in a strange place. In her heart, however, she knew. It had been almost a year since she had felt the warmth of a man next to her, someone to make her feel alive again. Or maybe, she laughed at herself, she just needed to get laid.

So Dave Castle and Jodie Hanson became a couple, they worked as partners, moved in together, and a year later were married. They continued to work in the South Los Angeles area for eight more years until they both had the seniority to transfer to Crescent City.

Working in Crescent City was a big change for both of them. The slow pace of working in a rural county was in stark contrast to the millions of people, hundreds of thousands of cars, non-stop radio calls, smog, and the constant on-the-go lifestyle of metropolitan Los Angeles.

That idyllic, small town, rural atmosphere had changed two years ago when the Islamic terrorists had invaded Crescent City during a Fourth of July celebration.

Jodie Hanson, now Jodie Castle, had seen her husband drive off that morning enroute to Sacramento to attend four days of "In-Service" training that was required of all officers every three years.

The eight to nine hour drive would put him at the academy by five in the afternoon, class started the next day.

She'd been on patrol around the town area later that same morning when she got involved in a pursuit with the Crescent City Police Department. Nobody knew it at the time, but the vehicle they were pursuing contained two Islamic terrorists who'd just torched a stolen fuel tanker truck north of town. The pursuit ended when the terrorist's vehicle hit another car and ground to a stop. A vicious firefight ensued, killing one of the Crescent City police officers. In the exchange of gunfire, Jodie Castle wounded one of the terrorist's with her shotgun, and when the other had tried to flee on foot, she had run over and killed him with her patrol car.

Later that same day, with the terrorists rampaging through town, killing and burning indiscriminately, she had shot and killed another with her service pistol as he took aim with an M-16 rifle at CHP Officer Ray Silva.

It took about eight months of therapy with a psychologist trained to deal with police related traumatic incidents for Jodie Castle to come to grips with the terrorist incident and people she had killed. Thanks, however, to the support and understanding she got from her husband and the help of her commander, Lieutenant Erin Wolff, she was dealing with it okay. The details of that day would never go completely away she knew, but the nightmares were less frequent now, and she had not woken in a cold sweat for several months.

"95-Edward, Humboldt."

"Humboldt, 95-Edward, southbound 101 at Elk Valley Road," Jodie Castle answered.

"95-Edward, assist the sheriff's deputy, 415 on the Greyhound bus, northbound 101 at the Klamath River Bridge. Driver reports two males involved. Deputy has ETA of ten," the coarse voice of the comm-op mechanically gave them the details of their call.

Both Dave and Jodie Castle knew 415 was the Penal Code section for Disturbing the Peace, and the call could be anything from two passengers yelling at each other, to a knock-down, drag-out fight. Since there was only one deputy working, the sheriff's dispatcher had requested CHP assistance.

"10-4 Humboldt, 95-Edward responding," Jodie Castle acknowledged the call.

It took them a little less than ten minutes to reach the location, arriving almost at the same time as the deputy. As Dave Castle pulled in behind the deputy's car, Jodie used the radio. "Humboldt, 95-Edward, 10-97," she called, reporting their arrival at the scene.

As they exited their unit they could see the bus driver talking to the deputy. Standing about ten yards away was a black male who looked to be somewhere in his early twenties.

Both the Castles recognized the deputy, although they didn't know him well. Like a lot of the people on the sheriff's department, he was new, hired in the last two years to refill the ranks after the terrorist attack had killed twelve of the seventeen deputies. They knew his name was Jason something, and he had formerly been a police officer in a small town in Idaho.

Dave Castle spoke first, "Hey Jason, what's going on?"

Deputy Jason Griffith nodded to the CHP officers and said, "The driver says a few miles back the black guy over there just started screaming at another passenger and began trying to hit him. The other guy ran to the front of the bus, the black guy chasing him. The driver pulled the bus over here and called 9-1-1."

"All the screaming and yelling scared me to death," the driver added. "Then all the other passengers started yelling, so I pulled over and stopped."

"Where's the other guy?" the deputy asked.

"Still on the bus, afraid to come off," the driver replied.

"Let's talk to the black guy," Dave Castle suggested, motioning for the young black man to join their conversation.

David Castle was a good street copper. As the young man started his way, he sized him up by the way he was dressed, the way he walked, his expression, and the jewelry he wore. Everything he saw told him this was an inner-city street kid. He didn't look like a "gang-banger", but a product of the "hood" nonetheless.

As soon as they were within a couple of feet of each other Dave Castle spoke, "Say Homes, whazz's up?" Without giving the man a chance to answer he immediately added, "You don't have any guns or knives on you, do you?"

The black man was starting to answer "No", but Dave Castle had already started giving him a cursory pat-down, feeling the pockets of his bulky coat, his pants, and around his waistband.

Nobody, especially a young black male, liked being "patted down" by the police. By the same token, most cops have a real big aversion to being killed. It was one of those inconvenient realities of police work, that in today's world, people carry concealed guns and knives. Given the circumstances of the call they were on, Disturbing the Peace, and the driver's version of what happened on the bus, good officer safety procedures dictated a pat-down.

"Say dawg, I done toldt joo I don't got nutt'n," the young black man protested.

For a lot of cops the young black man's use of the word "dawg" in addressing them would have evoked a sharp retort, something like, "I'm not a dog, you can call me officer". It would also set the contact between them on an adversarial course.

Dave Castle recognized the young black man was just addressing him as he would anyone else using the vernacular of his world and said, "Sorry, dude, just making sure. So what's going on here?"

"Maan, ah be sleep'n an ah feels dis mo' fuc'n wide boy grabin mah dic," the black man rapidly and excitedly told the officers. His street talk almost unrecognizable as English.

"What did he say?" the deputy asked with a quizzical inflection in his voice, looking to Dave Castle.

Davy Castle had a wicked sense of humor, and he had worked the predominately black South Central part of L.A. for thirteen years. In a voice, with the tone and resonance right out of the 'hood, Davy looked at the deputy and spoke, "He said, maan, ah be sleep'n an ah feels dis mo' fuc'n wide boy grabin mah dic."

Jodie Castle almost peed her pants. She turned her back on the group and began trying to choke down her laughter.

The deputy, who didn't get it, just looked at Dave Castle, then his partner. The bus driver had a blank look on his face, and the black man was nodding in agreement.

The joke over, Davy translated for everyone. "He said he was asleep when the white guy started to fondle him."

The deputy laughed, shook his head, and walked off to talk to the "alleged fondler".

While the deputy was gone, Dave Castle started a conversation with the young man, "Where do you live?" he asked.

"I stays in Oakland."

"Where you headed?"

"Po'tlan."

Even though it had been several years since he'd worked in Los Angeles, Dave Castle had no trouble understanding the young black man's conversation.

The deputy was back in a couple of minutes and spoke to the young man.

"Okay, I talked to the white dude. He denies he grabbed you. Look, how 'bout we handle this the easy way? The white guy is getting off in Brookings. It's in Oregon, about thirty miles up the road. The bus is only half-full. You grab a seat in the far back; I'll have the white guy sit behind the driver. Both of you agree to stay away from each other. Deal?"

"Yeah, okay wit me maan, but that sucka come near me again, I'm gonna go upside his hayd," he told the deputy.

Dave Castle glanced at the deputy with a look that asked "do you want me to translate".

"No, I'm picking up a word here and there," the deputy laughed. "I'm good."

Turning back to the young man, Dave Castle told him, "Nah, man, don't be do'n that. If you hit him you'll get arrested and end up in jail."

"Kay, long as that fool stay away from me!"

Satisfied, the black man jumped back on the bus. The driver said thanks, and within a minute the bus was gone.

The three cops stood on the right shoulder of 101 watching the bus as it rounded a curve and drove out of sight. It was quiet again, the light rain continuing to fall, and the only illumination coming from the headlights of the two police cars.

"Thanks for the help," the deputy said.

"No problem, it's been really slow for us tonight," Jodie told him.

"Yeah, I think we'll head toward town, it's almost 2:00, and the bars will be closing soon, maybe we can pop a deuce," Dave Castle chimed in.

"The codes and local cop jargon is still new to me," the deputy said, "Why do you call a drunk driver a "deuce" in California?"

Dave Castle answered his question, "Oh, it comes from the old Vehicle Code Section, 502. You know, deuce for the number two, like the Beach Boys song, *Little Deuce Coupe,* was about a '32 Ford, deuce for two, or like playing poker where they call a two a deuce. Even though the section numbers have changed several times over the years, the name stuck."

"Got it. Still have a lot to learn. Cops in California speak a different language than we did in Idaho. Anyway, thanks again for the backup, see ya later," the deputy said as he headed for his vehicle.

Back in their unit, Jodie Castle advised Humboldt they completed their call and were 10-98. Davy put the black and white SUV in gear and headed north.

"You crazy shit, you almost made me wet my pants with that stunt," she laughed as she punched him on the arm.

"Mo' fuc'n wide boy grabin mah dic," Dave Castle mumbled.

They were northbound 101, headed back toward Crescent City, when they both caught the silhouette of a car parked at the vista point next to the southbound lane. The car was facing south, its lights out, a lone male figure standing by the passenger's door.

"That car wasn't there fifteen minutes ago when we came south," Dave Castle said.

Slowing the big SUV patrol unit, Dave Castle started to turn across the undivided highway into the vista point. "Let's see if he's okay," he said to his partner.

As the patrol unit finished its turn and glided to a halt fifteen feet behind the stopped car, the headlights illuminated the vehicle and the man.

"Is that a cop car?" Jodie Castle said to her partner.

"Looks like one to me," he replied.

"And is that who I think it is?" Jodie Castle asked.

"Looks like."

"You ever talk with him?"

"Yeah, a couple times, he's not the friendliest guy in the world," Dave Castle said.

"How 'bout he has a personality like a wet dishrag," Jodie shot back.

"Okay, I agree, he is pretty high up on the strange duck scale," Davy chuckled.

"Wonder what the heck he's doing out here this time of night?" Jodie asked out loud.

Shifting the transmission into park and switching the headlights to high beam as he opened the driver's door Davy Castle said, "Let's find out."

CHAPTER THREE

The call came at 3:45.

California Highway Patrol Lieutenant Erin "Red" Wolff sat bolt upright in bed. She was a little disoriented. It was the darkness, the strange bed, in a strange house, she realized, as her brain processed the surroundings to get her bearings. Mentally, she had been expecting the sound of the clock radio on the nightstand to wake her, not the loud ring tone of her cell phone.

Swinging her legs out of bed, she did a quick scan around the room. Still sound asleep next to her in bed was her life partner and new spouse, Mary Jean Snider. Everything cleared up in an instant. It was two days after the wedding, and they were staying at Julie's house.

After rubbing her eyes for a moment, Red Wolff picked up the phone on the third ring. On the brightly lit digital display flip cover she saw a 707 area code. The rest of the number looked familiar, but she couldn't place it right off the bat.

As the commander of the Crescent City Area, she was on-call 24/7, even at times like this when she was on vacation. Calls in the middle of the night were never good news, she knew. She flipped the cover open, "Erin Wolff."

"Lieutenant, this is Humboldt Communications Center." Just by the formality in the comm-op's speech, she already knew it wasn't good. "There's been an incident. 95-S-1 is on-scene requesting you call him," the comm-op continued.

She could detect the stress in his voice as he rattled off a phone number. He had used the word "incident" not "accident". This was going to be bad, Erin Wolff knew.

"What's going on?" she queried.

There was along moment of silence on the other end of the line as the comm-op composed himself. Leonard Schmitt, "Smitty" to everyone who knew him, had been a CHP Communications Operator for nearly thirty-five years, going back to a time when they were called "dispatchers". Back to time before computers, before there were female officers, and before anyone dreamed of such a thing as a 9-1-1 system. When he first started, dispatchers hand wrote everything on IBM cards. Cards travelled along mini-conveyor belts from dispatcher to dispatcher depending on what type of assistance a field unit required. Over the course of his long career, he had made three other calls like this one. Having experience didn't make it any easier.

He'd met Lieutenant Erin Wolff on numerous occasions over the last couple of years, and he knew there were times when it was okay to be informal and use a first name, and there were other times that called for formality. This was one of those other times.

"Lieutenant, we have two officers down. The sergeant on-scene reports both are 11-44," Smitty related, using the radio code for dead when he referred to the officers. He'd also, without thinking about it, used the term "we" when referring to the officers. In his mind, every officer he dispatched for was "his" officer.

It took Red Wolff a second to fully comprehend what she had just been told. It was the call every police leader dreaded, the call informing them one of their officers had been killed in the line of duty. In this case, two officers.

"Who are the officers, and are they confirmed 11-44?" Red Wolff inquired, a somber tone in her voice.

"It's the Castles. S-1 confirms they are both dead," the same somber tone now in his voice.

It took a second for the terrible reality of his words to register. Taking a deep breath, she closed her eyes momentarily, until her mind shifted into procedural mode.

"Where and how long ago?" Red Wolff asked mechanically, as she was writing details on a piece of scratch paper.

Smitty related the information he had. "My last radio transmission from the Castles was when they cleared a call involving a Greyhound bus about 0145 in Klamath. I never heard from them after that. About 0225 I tried to dispatch them to a silent alarm call at the Department of Motor Vehicles office in Crescent City. I called them every ten minutes after that thinking they might be in a radio dead spot, or out of their unit. Then, just before 0300, I got a 9-1-1 call from a long-haul trucker who pulled into the vista point on Last Chance Grade to check his load. He saw the patrol unit sitting there with nobody around, looking abandoned. He walked over and found both officers on the ground. He used his cell phone and the call came to me. I rolled S-1 and Klamath Fire Rescue. S-1 got to the scene at 0340."

"Okay, 10-4, good job on your part Humboldt. Contact S-1 and tell him I'll call within a few minutes. Give him my cell number so he can contact me as well. I'll stand by on the line until you make contact."

"Alright lieutenant, stand by one."

Red Wolff could hear him on the radio calling her sergeant at the scene, "95-S-1, Humboldt."

Within a few seconds she heard the sound of her sergeant's voice talking over the radio, but couldn't quite make out what he was saying to the comm-op.

She did hear the message Smitty relayed to the sergeant, "S-1, 95-L has been contacted, and advises she will 10-21 you in the next few minutes."

The conversation on the radio concluded, and the comm-op was back on the phone to Red Wolff. Satisfied the sergeant on scene had her phone number and knew she would be calling him soon, she ended her conversation with the communications operator, "Thanks for your courtesy, Smitty."

"I'm sorry Red, really sorry," he replied. He didn't know what else to say.

Red was fully awake now slipping on the jeans she'd laid out the night before to wear on the airplane.

"Time to get up already?" she heard Mary Jean ask sleepily from the middle of the king-sized bed.

"Listen Hon, we've got a problem," she told Mary Jean Snider, who for the last two days was now legally, in the eyes of the State of California, Mary Jean Snider-Wolff.

"What?" Mary Jean asked, now also wide awake and alerted by the stress in Red's voice.

"The Castles have been killed; I need to get back up north right away. I'm gonna wake up Ray. Would you mind making some coffee?"

"Erin! Oh my God, Dave and Jodie dead! How did it happen? Where?" Mary Jean was up in a flash, pulling on some clothes, while peppering Red with questions.

She quickly gave her what little information she had, and asked again, "Please Babe, we're really going to need that coffee."

She walked out of the guest bedroom, down the hall to the master suite, turning on lights as she went, and knocked sharply on the closed door.

"Ray, wake-up, we've got a problem," she called, loud enough to ensure he could hear.

A few seconds later the door opened. Ray Silva stood there in a pair of faded blue jeans, no shirt, his almost totally silver, full head of hair tousled. He was remarkably alert, considering he'd been sound asleep thirty seconds ago.

She didn't wait for him to speak, "The Castles have both been murdered. S-1's on the scene. I'm going to call him now. We need to get back to Crescent City."

When Red Wolff told Ray Silva "we need to get back to Crescent City" she didn't stop to think that he, like her, was on vacation, had only been married for a little over two days, and they all had tickets to Cabo San Lucas for their joint honeymoons. She didn't have to pause, or even think about it. Having two officers killed trumped everything.

Ray Silva didn't say a word. As Red turned to walk away, he closed the bedroom door and turned on the lights.

Awake now, sitting up in bed, was his new wife, the former Julie Bradley, now Julie Silva. She'd heard the conversation at the door and small tears were running down her cheeks.

"Oh Ray," she said, her voice choked with emotion, "Those poor kids, dead."

"I know, Honey, but the only way we can help them now is to get back and find the bastards that did it."

Ray Silva's mind was racing. He was working out the logistics of what needed to be done. Obviously the double honeymoon in Mexico was off, and there was a four hundred mile drive back to Crescent City. It took him a couple of seconds to think it all though.

They were at his new wife's house in Tiburon, just a few miles north of the Golden Gate Bridge. The four of them had used the location as a base of operations for the last five days while they made arrangements for a double wedding in San Francisco and as a starting point to begin their honeymoon.

"Babe, Red and I will take my car and head back to Crescent City. You and Mary Jean see what you can do about the airline tickets and the hotel reservations in Cabo. When you get things squared away here, the two of you can drive up north in your car."

"Okay," Julie Silva told him, now completely dressed.

It took Red Wolff's cell phone a few extra seconds to connect after she dialed in her sergeant's number before she heard the first ring on the other end.

"Sergeant Huddleston," the senior CHP sergeant in the Crescent City Area answered.

Of the three sergeants who worked under her, Sergeant Dick Huddleston, 95-S-1, was probably the weakest when it came to being a strong supervisor and a good leader. He was an old-timer, what the new kids called a "mossback", somebody who had been in Crescent City too long. He had nearly thirty-one years on the CHP, seventeen of them as a sergeant. Because he was the senior sergeant in the

31

command, protocol and policy dictated that he was in charge when Red Wolff was out of the geographic area. Unfortunately, he was one of those sergeants who instead of having seventeen years experience as a supervisor, he had one year of experience seventeen times. At fifty-eight, he just did his job, handled his paperwork, and filled a position. As sergeants went, he was no ball of fire.

"Dick, this is Red, what happened?"

Over the next several minutes, Sergeant Dick Huddleston related what he knew about the deaths of the two officers, the location, and the evidence at the scene.

"Okay, the S.O. is gonna want to take the lead in the investigation, it's their jurisdiction," she told him. "But since two of our officers are the victims, we will insist on a concurrent investigation. Get whatever resources you need, call in everyone, and protect the scene. I'm enroute from Marin County with Ray Silva. I'll be making the notifications to division, and I'll get a shooting team there within five hours. Got it?"

On the other end of the line, 95-S-1, muttered an unconvincing affirmative answer.

Red Wolff could hear the uncertainty in her sergeant's voice.

She used an old technique Ray Silva had taught her when they worked together in L.A. so many years ago. She could picture him then, he was the veteran officer, she was a rookie, and she could still hear his voice as he gave her the lecture on swearing. "Never use profanity in your ordinary speech, or make it a part of how you communicate with people on a routine basis," he'd told her. "That way, when you do use it, people will realize you're dead-on serious, and what you are trying to communicate will have that much more impact."

People who knew her almost never heard her swear. On the rare occasion when she did, people listened.

"Look Dick, this is important. What happens in the next twenty-four hours is critical, starting with the investigation at the scene. I've got confidence in you. Don't fuck this up."

Ray Silva was behind the wheel of his car ten minutes after she woke him up, a travel mug of fresh coffee on the center console. She jumped in the passenger seat. It was 4:09 in the morning, the winter sky still dark, with low hanging clouds scudding over the hills of Tiburon and on across the bay toward San Francisco. Red plugged her cell phone charger into the receptacle under the radio and said, "Hit it, old man."

The car lunged forward as he turned the wheel to clear Julie's black Lexus SUV parked in the driveway, then reversing his turn, as the car bounced onto the deserted city streets of the high class, expensive neighborhood.

"How far to Klamath," she queried.

"Three hundred eighty miles, give or take," he said, his eyes not leaving the road, his right hand steadying his coffee mug.

"How long driving time?"

"Normally six hours plus. We'll be there in four and a half."

Red Wolff didn't reply, she knew he felt the same sense of helplessness being so far away, and the same sense of urgency to get back.

It took two or three minutes for Ray Silva to negotiate the city streets, stop signs, and the one or two other cars on the road that led to Highway 101. Reaching the northbound on-ramp, he punched the accelerator as he turned up the ramp, causing the rear wheels to lose traction. He gently eased up on the gas, counter-steered to control the skid, letting the tires regain friction on the pavement, and slammed his foot down on the accelerator. His right hand never left the coffee cup.

Traffic heading northbound on 101 was still light. On the southbound side it was significantly heavier, signaling the morning commute had already begun as hundreds of people who lived in the less expensive North Bay, made their way to the Golden Gate Bridge and across into San Francisco.

Red didn't need to glance over at the speedometer to know how fast they were going. By the sound of the tires on the pavement and the wind noise she knew it was close to ninety. Satisfied they were now well on their way, she pulled a two-by-three laminated phone number list out of her wallet. She needed to make notifications up-the-line and get resources rolling to Crescent City. Her first call was to the sector chief.

The Highway Patrol, because it has statewide responsibility, is geographically organized into eight divisions. Each division's area of responsibility roughly corresponds to its name. Border Division, for example, takes in the areas south of Los Angeles County down to the Mexican border and out into the desert to the Arizona state line. Golden Gate Division obviously takes in the greater San Francisco Bay Area.

Red Wolff's command, Crescent City, was one of fifteen CHP areas that make up Northern Division. The division headquarters is in

Redding, the largest city in the northern one third of California, with a population of 50,000 or so.

Red knew her sector chief would be sound asleep as she punched his number into her cell phone and hit the send button. She stared through the windshield while she waited for the phones to connect. The broken white lines that separated the two northbound lanes now looked like a solid white ribbon in the middle of the road as Ray Silva sped north.

"Hello," Red Wolff recognized the sleepy voice of her sector chief.

"Boss, Erin Wolff, sorry to wake you this time of the morning, but we've had an incident in Crescent City."

"Red, I thought you were on your honeymoon?"

"Well, we were supposed to leave for Mexico in a couple of hours, but the honeymoon will have to wait."

"What's up," he asked, knowing nobody called him at four in the morning unless it was something bad.

Red Wolff related to her superior the call she had received, her conversation with the sergeant on scene, and that she was responding from Marin County.

"Okay, I'll make the notifications, get the shooting team mobilized, and be enroute. Should take me less than five hours from Redding."

"Boss, can I get you to call the Critical Incident Response Team from headquarters, also? With two dead officers, my squad will need all the support they can get," she added.

"Right, I'll take care of it."

"Thanks, chief, I'll see you in a few hours," she ended the conversation.

Red Wolff exhaled deeply and sat back in the passenger's seat. The stress was already setting in, her shoulders ached, and she could feel the tension in her neck.

The big green mileage sign on the right shoulder of the freeway loomed ahead: Cloverdale 30 miles, Ukiah 45 miles, Crescent City 340 miles. She glanced at her watch, 4:37. Closing her eyes, she began to visualize what her sector chief was doing.

As an assistant chief, his first call would be to the deputy chief who commanded CHP Northern Division. The deputy chief would in turn call his boss, the Assistant Commissioner of Field Operations in Sacramento. That person would then notify the Commissioner of the Highway Patrol. The death of an officer was a big incident, and everyone needed to be in the loop.

After completing this call, Red Wolff's sector chief called the lieutenant in charge of the division's Officer Involved Shooting Team.

Because most of the fifteen CHP commands in the northern part of the state had less than twenty-five officers, and officer involved shootings were rare, it was not practical to have a shooting team in each command. So, in Northern Division there were two, on-call, four person teams drawn from personnel throughout that part of the state. The teams could be activated with a phone call. Every member of the team was assigned an unmarked patrol vehicle which allowed them to respond almost instantaneously to wherever they were needed.

The lieutenant in charge of the shooting team closest to Crescent City was assigned to the Ukiah CHP area, about three hundred miles away. As soon as he got the call from the sector chief, the lieutenant put in calls to the rest of his team. His sergeant was stationed in the Clearlake area, one officer was in the Humboldt CHP command, and the other in Yreka. He gave them all the same instruction, be in Crescent City as soon as possible.

The last call the sector chief made was to Sacramento, waking Captain Steffani Taylor, who ran the Critical Incident Response Team.

Like CHP personnel at all levels who got called in the middle of the night, she kept a pen and paper next to the phone in her bedroom. Jotting down the info she needed, asked the sector chief a few questions, and got the phone numbers of key personnel in Crescent City. The conversation lasted less than two minutes.

The Critical Incident Response Team, like the shooting teams, consisted of specialists who dealt with the aftermath of the traumatic incidents that go hand-in-hand with being a cop. On her team Steffani Taylor had a chaplain, who was also a CHP officer, a civilian who was a specialist in processing all the paperwork associated with line-of-duty deaths, and psychologist who provided counseling.

Because Sacramento is eight plus hours driving time from Crescent City, the first call she made was to the commander of CHP Air Operations to ensure the department's fixed wing plane was available.

Next, she called each of her team members and told them to be at the Sacramento Executive Airport in an hour. The two engine, Beechcraft King Air would have them in Crescent City by 9:30.

From Sacramento to Yreka, the resources Red Wolff would need were mobilizing. Interestingly, they all went through an almost identical process in preparing for their assignment. A quick shower, brush teeth, throw on travelling clothes, usually jeans, a fast explanation to spouse, and out the door. Even though they knew they were going on a multiple day assignment, none stopped to pack. In their cars, or in a closet, each had a "go" kit already packed with enough clothes, uniforms, and toiletries to last a week. They had all done this way too many times before.

Red Wolff popped open the flip cover of her cell phone to illuminate the digital display. It was almost 6:30, although the sky was still dark. They'd been on the road over two hours, and Ray Silva was still hauling ass. They had travelled far enough by this time that they began to encounter the rain that was falling all along the northwestern part of the state.

After passing through the dinky town of Laytonville, Highway 101 opened up into two lanes in each direction for almost forty miles. There was never much traffic along this stretch, and given the early morning hour, they had the whole road pretty much to themselves.

"The four lane section will end in Piercy," Ray said to her, "Then about ten miles of two lane road."

She just nodded, lost in her thoughts.

He picked up her head nod in his peripheral vision and spoke again, "It goes back to four lanes again at Benbow all the way to Eureka. Probably should stop in Garberville for gas. It's an easy off and right back on."

"Alright, whatever you think," she replied absentmindedly.

A few seconds later she spoke again, "How many times do you think you've made the drive from Crescent City to Marin?"

Ray Silva thought for a moment before he answered her question, "Damn, I don't know. At least once, sometimes twice a month for the last five years since I met Julie."

She didn't respond immediately, then said, "But you've made at least eight trips in the last two months. Why so many?"

"Ah, you know, the wedding, getting her house ready to sell, that sort of thing," Ray answered.

They'd known each other over twenty years, worked as partners in Los Angeles, and shared the same life or death situations when Islamic terrorists had attacked Crescent City two years ago. At any other time Red Wolff would have picked up on the way he answered her question. She would have also detected something not quite right in his tone. Today, her mind lost in thought about her two dead officers, she missed it.

As Ray Silva kept pushing hard, eating up the miles, Red Wolff's thoughts drifted off to the events of the past several days.

It started just before Thanksgiving. Ray and his longtime girlfriend, Julie Bradley, were at Red Wolff's house for dinner. Red's even longer time significant other, Mary Jean Snider, was in her glory, cooking.

Mary Jean, a former navy helicopter pilot, had taken up gourmet cooking after she and Erin had moved to Crescent City. The terrorist attack that left her severely wounded and the birth of their son, Raymond, had put a crimp in cooking for a while. Tonight, everyone could tell she was back in form by the delectable aromas coming from the kitchen.

They were all sitting in the living room around the blazing woodstove, watching the flames through the thick glass door. Like most homes in the county, it was the only source of heat in the house. Erin, Mary Jean, and Julie were sipping white wine, engaged in girl talk. Ray Silva, treating himself to bourbon on the rocks, had pretty much tuned them out.

"We have an announcement!" Ray proclaimed.

"Oooh, the great stone-face speaks," Mary Jean jibbed at him.

That got a laugh out of everyone, but Ray.

"You done?" he growled, giving them all the menacing glare he used on violators who gave him a hard time.

"Spare us Silva," Erin laughed, with her trademark half-smile, "That look won't work on us."

"Okay, okay," he shook his head, laughing at himself at the same time, knowing he was no match for the three women, "Julie and I are getting married!"

"What!" Erin and Mary Jean exclaimed in unison.

Without waiting for his reply, the room was suddenly a blur of girls hugging and multiple congratulations.

"It's about friggin time, Silva," Erin said, "This woman's much too good for you. I'm surprised she's waited so long for you to ask."

Over the next half-hour, Julie filled in Erin and Mary Jean with all the details of where and when. For his part, Ray Silva sat back on the couch sipping a drink, saying nothing. He'd known these three women long enough to know he was irrelevant to the conversation.

After the three-way conversation died down, Mary Jean went back to the kitchen to check on dinner, Erin trailing behind. On the couch, Julie snuggled under Ray Silva's arm as they watched Mary

Jean and Erin begin to serve up dinner while whispering back and forth.

Mary Jean's grilled fresh Halibut with Mango-Chutney sauce, spinach salad, and wild rice was every bit as delicious as it looked and smelled. Everyone agreed it was one of her best productions.

Over dessert, double fudge chocolate cake, Ray Silva's favorite, Mary Jean spoke up.

"Guys, fair is fair, we have something to tell you, also."

Everyone stopped eating and looked at her.

"We weren't going to tell anyone until just before we did it, but since you told us, we'll tell you. We're getting married, too!"

The same flurry of questions, congratulations, and happy conversation erupted among the three girls. Ray went back to his cake, trying to keep up with the discussion.

Mary Jean explained she and Erin had been thinking about getting married ever since the California Supreme Court struck down the ban on same sex marriages in May. They had worked out the details of getting a license and a ceremony in San Francisco, Erin's vacation schedule, and even grandparents to watch little Raymond while they honeymooned.

It was Julie who voiced the idea. "Let's make it a double ceremony. Our plans are flexible, we can find a date that works for all of us, and we could even go to Cabo together."

Ray Silva saw it coming and knew better than to get in the way. The conversation took on a frenzy as each of the girls added something, and the excitement grew exponentially. He did the only sensible thing, he made himself another drink.

Over the course of the next hour, almost every detail was discussed, travel plans agreed upon, and assignments of responsibility to handle items related to the weddings made.

Ray Silva found a football game on T.V. while his future was being planned.

Thanksgiving and Christmas came and went, and the plans for a double wedding, double honeymoon took shape and became more and more defined. Wisely, Ray stayed out of the planning. By February everything was pretty much set.

All the parents would fly into San Francisco on Thursday. They were on their own to find places to stay. Following the ceremony Mary Jean's parents would take little Raymond and head back to Crescent City where they would stay in Red and Mary Jean's house, and have a chance to spoil their grandson for a week while the two couples were in Mexico.

Ray, Mary Jean, and Erin would drive down from Crescent City together in his car on Thursday and stay at Julie's house in Marin County. They would pick up their marriage licenses at San Francisco City Hall on Friday and handle any last minute details.

One of the other people who would attend the ceremony was Ray's nephew, Ralph Silva. In keeping with the non-traditional nature of the double wedding, Ralph would be the best man for both couples.

In the year following the terrorist attack on Crescent City, he had applied to become a CHP officer and follow in his uncle's footsteps. On the day of the attack, Ralph, a member of the local National Guard unit, had been one of the heroes, personally killing five terrorists, saving the life of Red Wolff, who was a sergeant then, and being wounded himself.

It had taken him nearly a year to get an appointment to the CHP Academy, and he was now in his second month of the six month academy training program. He wouldn't have missed his uncle's wedding for the world, just as he knew Ray would be at the academy the day he graduated to pin on his badge.

Their appointment at the city clerk's office was at 11:15 on Saturday morning. San Francisco had been doing such a brisk business conducting marriage ceremonies that they were open on Saturdays, and an appointment was mandatory.

They all dressed for the occasion. Ray in a dark suit, Julie in a crème knit skirt and top. Mary Jean and Erin both opted for matching dress and jacket outfits in complementing shades of green. Even little Raymond was dressed up in a green and white outfit with a bow tie.

The clerk's office and the hallways were crowded with other couples, well-wishers, and family. The atmosphere was a combination of joy, celebration, and a carnival, all intertwined.

Although the four of them and the majority of the other couples waiting for their turn were dressed somewhat formally for the occasion, not everyone followed suit. Some were dressed in leather biker garb, others in wild looking hats. Lots of feather boas were present and many couples, both male and female, wore matching tuxedos. One couple showed up naked. That was quite a shock for Mary Jean's parents who were from North Dakota. Nobody else seemed to even notice.

The actual "I do's" took only ten minutes. It might have gone faster if the city clerk who was officiating hadn't kept eyeing Ray and Julie, trying to figure out what a straight looking couple was doing there with a gay couple and a baby.

Lots of congratulations and good lucks followed, then the two newly married couples, and assorted in-laws and relatives, headed off to a reception at the Fairmont Hotel.

The newlyweds walked four abreast out of city hall and down the building's broad staircase entrance toward the street. The morning sun was shining warmly, the fog had burned off, and the sky was a cloudless blue. It was one of those glorious winter days in the Bay Area.

"So, Silva, how does it feel to be married?" Erin asked Ray.

As they kept walking down the stairs, Ray Silva thought about it for a few seconds before he answered, a funny grin forming on his face.

"You know, I can't put my finger on it, but I have this overwhelming urge to sing *YMCA*, dress up like an Indian chief, and watch the Ellen DeGeneres Show."

"Hit him for me Julie," Erin said as they all laughed.

The change in the sound of the engine as Ray Silva slowed to take the Garberville off-ramp, snapped her back.

While Ray pumped gas, Red grabbed two cups of coffee from the mini-mart. They were back on 101 in less than six minutes.

CHAPTER FOUR

Ray Silva made it to the scene in less than five hours.

"Holy crap!" Red Wolff exclaimed as he nosed his vehicle into a small space at the extreme north end of the vista point.

Neither of them could believe what they saw. A quick glance told her there were at least twenty-five vehicles at the vista point and what looked to her to be a mob of thirty-five to forty people milling around. She could see marked law enforcement units from not only the Highway Patrol and the Del Norte County Sheriff's Office, but Crescent City Police Department, the National Park Service, California State Parks, Fish and Game, and the Yurok Indian Tribal Police. In addition to the marked units, there were at least a half-dozen unmarked cop cars and twice that number of ordinary civilian vehicles. People were wandering around a Highway Patrol SUV that was obviously the dead officers' vehicle, and others were staring down at the two shapes on the ground covered with Highway Patrol issue plastic yellow blankets.

Red Wolff had learned a term from her two years at the Air Force Academy to describe what she saw. The scene at the vista point was a "Cluster-fuck".

"This is going to get ugly," she told Ray as they approached the center of the vista point mess.

As they got closer, she could see yellow crime scene tape stretched in a small perimeter around the bodies of the officers on the ground and their vehicle. Inside the tape were six people. Three were uniformed sheriff's deputies, one person in civilian clothes who was also a deputy, and two individuals taking pictures who didn't look like cops. Outside the perimeter tape were another ten or twelve ordinary citizens taking pictures with digital cameras or cell phones.

She spotted her sergeant, Dick Huddleston, standing outside the tape barrier talking to a uniformed sheriff's deputy. As they stood talking, two people, one a tribal police officer, the other a fireman in turnout gear, walked right past Huddleston, ducked under the tape and toward the officers on the ground.

"Stop!" she yelled. "Out, get out of there now!" They stopped, looked directly at her, then resumed walking toward the bodies.

41

Ray Silva yelled next. "You, both of you, get the fuck out of there!"

This time they froze. Ray Silva and Red Wolff were at the perimeter tape in a flash.

Looking directly at the two, a stern expression on his face, Ray Silva spoke again, a menacing tone in his voice, "When my lieutenant tells you to get out of our crime scene, do it!"

Both men sheepishly turned around, went under the tape, and disappeared into the crowd.

"Red, I'll handle protecting the scene, you go do your commander thing," he told her.

She nodded and headed toward her sergeant.

"Dick, what the hell is going on here?" she demanded angrily, not trying to hide her displeasure at his failure to take charge of the scene.

"What do you mean lieutenant? I've got the scene taped off, and I'm working with the sheriffs."

"Damn-it, Dick, this whole vista point is the crime scene, not just the six feet around the bodies. And why are all these people inside the tape?"

"But they're cops or firemen, Boss," he protested.

"So what do the tribal police, park rangers, and fireman, have to do with the investigation? And who are all those civilians taking pictures of the bodies?"

"They're from the local paper, said they have a First Amendment right to take pictures," her sergeant nearly whined, his self-confidence fading quickly.

"They do have a right to take pictures, but not to enter a crime scene to do it!" Red Wolff was hot.

"Who's your scribe?" she questioned.

"My what?" her sergeant answered, the tone of his response indicating he had no idea what she was talking about.

"The scribe. Who's recording the names of everyone here, the names of anyone who went inside the crime scene tape, the time they entered, what they did?"

"I guess I forgot, lieutenant," he said in a low voice, his eyes looking at the ground. Dick Huddleston knew he'd fucked up.

By the time Red had finished taking her sergeant to task, Ray had cleared everyone from inside the perimeter tape, and stationed other CHP officers and deputies to prevent any more "Looky-Loos" from entering.

While the two of them were trying to bring some order to the scene, an unmarked police car pulled into the vista point. Behind the wheel was the Sheriff of Del Norte County.

Red Wolff saw him coming as he strode purposefully toward the scene. It flashed in her mind by the way he was walking he had the look of Jesus come to clear the temple. He was impeccably dressed she noted, three button wool blend suit, fashionable tie, and brightly shined shoes. He was perfectly dressed if this had been Los Angeles. He looked out of place in Del Norte County.

"Hold it right there lieutenant," he said, using his best official voice and tone.

He walked directly up to Red Wolff, stood with his feet apart and snarled, "Is there any doubt in your mind that this is my department's jurisdiction and our investigation?" By the way he said it, he was stating fact, not asking for the CHP lieutenant's opinion.

Red Wolff was pissed. She had two murdered officers, a sergeant who let the crime scene become contaminated, and now this pompous ass new sheriff. She snapped right back at him. "Is there any doubt in your mind whose department those dead officers belong to?"

Jerome Williamson wasn't used to people talking back to him. He had thirty-one years in law enforcement, all but the last fifteen months with the Los Angeles Police Department.

"My people are handling this," he stated.

"They're not doing a very good job so far!" Red Wolff retorted, the tone in her voice every bit as determined as his. "Your people have been here over four hours. There's no command post, nobody protecting evidence, nobody taking down the names of the people here, and dozens of others wandering through the crime scene. Yeah, your department is doing a great job." There was as much sarcasm in her voice as she could muster.

"My detective has it under control," the sheriff responded, pointing to a thirtyish looking man in civilian clothes standing next to him.

She looked at the young detective. He was a nice kid, she had known him for a couple of years. She then looked back at the sheriff. "No disrespect to him, but eighteen months ago he was working in the jail. He's only done about a year working on the street, and has probably never investigated a homicide before, have you?"

The deputy slowly shook his head no.

"This is our crime scene, our investigation, if you interfere you'll be making big trouble for yourself," Sheriff Jerome Williamson played the threat to her career card.

He was trying to intimidate the wrong person.

"What are you going to do, put a horse in my bed?" Red Wolff angrily shot back.

Jerome Williamson stood there in silence, fuming inside.

The Del Norte County Sheriff and the Commander of the Crescent City Highway Patrol Area stood face-to-face, staring at each other. It was coming down to a case of who had the biggest balls.

Legally, they both knew jurisdiction belonged to the sheriff's office, but they also knew his department didn't have the technical expertise to handle a double homicide of two cops. Likewise, they both also knew while the CHP didn't have jurisdiction, the victims were from her department, and she had access to investigators and resources far beyond those of the Del Norte County Sheriff's Office.

All of these factors flashed in Sheriff Jerome Williamson's mind as he stood toe-to-toe with this female Highway Patrol lieutenant at the vista point on a rainy Tuesday morning. His dapper suit was already looking soggy and had begun to take on the smell of wet wool.

They each had their own reasons for wanting to be the lead agency in the investigation of the murders of the two officers. Hers were personal. His were political.

In the months immediately following the terrorist attack two years ago, the entire governmental structure of Crescent City and Del Norte County had to be rebuilt, almost from scratch. A large percentage of the elected political leadership, as well as the appointed department heads, had been murdered, including the city's chief of police and the county's sheriff.

Statewide resources had been brought in to maintain critical governmental services. The National Guard and the Highway Patrol performed law enforcement duties, the Department of Corrections brought in personnel to incarcerate prisoners, and the California Department of Forestry handled fire protection.

While it was difficult providing essential services, recreating everyday governmental services was even more challenging. Judges had to be appointed, city and county councils elected, a district attorney hired, and a new sheriff found.

Jerome Williamson became the Sheriff of Del Norte County by being in the right place at the right time.

Recently retired Los Angeles Police Captain Jerry Williamson had moved to Crescent City three months before the terrorist attack.

He'd kept a pretty low profile after relocating there, and only a handful of people in the county knew he was a retired cop. He had flown back to L.A. to wrap up some personal business the day before the terrorists launched their suicide mission, consequently missing the whole incident.

Since the sheriff and twelve of the department's seventeen deputies had been killed during the attack, there was a massive void to fill in county law enforcement. After the immediate impacts of the terrorist attack had been mitigated, the interim county council went looking for trained people to fill key positions as department heads. Jerry Williamson threw his hat in the ring for sheriff. At the same time he stopped using Jerry as his first name. Jerome sounded more sheriff like.

On paper, he looked really good. Not that it mattered much. Only one other person with law enforcement experience, a deputy with two years seniority, put in for the job. The interim county council gave Jerome Williamson a two year contract as Acting Sheriff and marching orders to rebuild the Del Norte County Sheriff's Department.

For the first year of his contract as Acting Sheriff, Jerome Williamson found himself trying to rebuild the Del Norte County Sheriff's Department by enticing officers from other agencies to lateral transfer to his department.

When the word went out over the police grapevine that Del Norte Sheriff's was hiring, he got lots of inquiries from cops around California and from other states.

As many as thirty-five seasoned officers made the trip to Crescent City to check out the area, the cost of living, schools, and working conditions. A full third of those who made the trip didn't stay long after finding out how isolated the area was. For others, the over one hundred inches of rain a year was too high a price to pay to live in "God's Country". Even a larger percentage, those who didn't mind the rain, or the isolation, were turned off by the pay, which was sometlmes half of what they were making at their current departments.

Consequently, in his effort to find new deputies, Jerome Williamson found himself hiring almost all newly graduated officers from police academies around California. Four were from the academy at the College of the Redwoods in Eureka, two from a college academy in Sacramento, and a couple from Southern California. He was able to attract three new deputies with previous law enforcement experience, one from the Humboldt County

Sheriff's Department, one from state Fish and Game, and the last from a small police department in Idaho.

At some level he knew, given enough time, they would grow into effective cops and would do a good job protecting the people of the county. That would take time, however. Until the seasoning that came with experience set in, they would make rookie mistakes, drive too fast, crash patrol vehicles, make bad arrests, and generate a host of personnel problems.

None of these things made the prospect of being the Acting Sheriff of Del Norte County particularly attractive to Jerome Williamson. However, he had personal reasons for taking on the job. First, his law enforcement career at LAPD had been cut short, and second, he needed the money.

———————

Jerome Williamson wasn't a California native. After college and a couple years of living and working on the east coast, he'd migrated west and found the three hundred days of sunshine and easy relaxed lifestyle of Southern California to his liking. He had grown up in the late '60s watching *Dragnet* and *Adam-12* on television and figured being a cop was just as good as any other job.

Early in his career with LAPD, when he had been a patrol officer, he'd gone through an expensive divorce. Not making much money at the time, he'd agreed to a settlement giving his ex-wife a percentage of his pension when he retired. It was a pretty good decision at the time, as he saw himself working until he was well into his sixties. Less time, he told himself, for that bitch to get part of the retirement he'd earned.

That plan would have worked out fine except for a couple of little personality traits in Jerome Williamson's makeup.

Like most cops, or anybody for that matter, Jerry Williamson had his likes and dislikes. He also had his ups and downs at work and in his personal life. There were things that he accepted as the "way it was", and with others he vocally expressed his displeasure. Life was, what life was. Generally he dealt with these life issues as all adults do, by reasoning, coping, and self-control. In most respects, Jerry Williamson was a pretty normal guy and a pretty normal cop.

There were only two things he couldn't stand, Gays and Highway Patrol Officers.

His divorce had cost him dearly in attorney fees and he got whacked with paying alimony for two years. Both of these things cut deeply into his take home pay and disposable income. In order to get financially back on track, Jerry Williamson decided that promoting was the easiest way to increase his income. It took him a year and a half, but he made sergeant and was assigned to LAPD's Hollenbeck Division.

The pay increase as a sergeant and the sizable overtime checks from going to court, helped with his financial situation. He was still just getting by month-to-month, and there was little extra for a social life. At thirty-two years old, not having a social life meant not having much of a sex life either.

As a new sergeant, he worked the night shift from midnight to eight in the morning. Hollenbeck was a predominately Latino part of Los Angeles, lots of illegal's, several bad-ass street gangs, but for the most part hardworking people trying to raise families and live the American dream. He would spend several hours each night doing paperwork, hit the street for a couple of hours, then head back into the station for more paperwork.

While he would have much rather been out driving around on patrol, there was one benefit to being at the station, Nora Kendricks.

He'd met her his first night at Hollenbeck. As a civilian file clerk, in a time before desk top computers, Nora Kendricks typed reports, maintained logs by hand, filed arrest reports, and did all of the daily, never-ending, clerical chores that needed to be done at a busy police station. Talking to her, you could determine right away that she wasn't a rocket scientist, but she was a nice person and good at her job. She was about his age, a single mother with a two year old daughter. She liked working the night shift so she had time to spend with her child in the afternoon and early evening.

Nora Kendricks wasn't a striking beauty, but she had a body that stopped men cold. In the early '80s, when mini-skirts were still fashionable, she wore them skin tight and just long enough to cover her butt while she stood. She was never concerned about what showed when she bent over a desk, or reached down to put a report in the bottom drawer of a file cabinet. The mini-skirts, coupled with the form fitting sweaters she wore, showed off her body to anyone who cared to look. She didn't mind at all if they looked.

Her most striking feature, however, was something that many men missed. Nora Kendricks had expressive eyes. Dark brown, to match her hair. She could use them, when she wanted to, to say "I want to fuck you".

She didn't let her eyes say that to everybody, and sometimes when she did let them say it, men missed the signal. Jerry Williamson was really good at reading eyes.

47

On the first night he reported to Hollenbeck, he had to walk past Nora Kendrick's desk to meet the lieutenant watch commander. She smiled at him as he approached, and her eyes told him that his social life was about to get better.

By the end of his first month at Hollenbeck, Jerry Williamson was feeling pretty comfortable in his new job. It was early in the morning and pretty quiet around the station. The watch commander had headed off to breakfast, leaving him to run the station for an hour. Nora Kendricks, the only other person there, was busily handling her paperwork.

He'd just finished reviewing and signing off on an arrest report from one of his officers. The report needed to be copied and filed.

"Nora, can you process this for me?" he called to her as she sat across the room.

"Sure, sergeant, be right there," she replied, her always present smile flashing.

She stood at his desk as he finished signing an evidence tag and then looked up at her.

I want to fuck you, her eyes said.

Jerry Williamson's mind was racing. It had been what, eight months? He felt the stirring between his legs and was glad he was sitting down. Looking at her in that short, short skirt, and that tight, tight sweater, he got hard as a rock. No way, he told himself. Not here, not now. He quickly devised alternate plan "B".

"Nora, I love the skirts you always wear," he fumbled for something to say.

"Thanks, sergeant," she half-giggled in response, a big smile on her face, her eyes yelling at him.

"We're both off on Tuesday, you up for dinner?" he asked.

"Okay, I need to get back to you though. Have to make sure my mom can baby sit my daughter. I'll let you know tomorrow. If I can go to dinner, I'll wear a skirt, a short one."

Jesus Christ, Jerry Williamson exclaimed to himself, a short one. Could they get any shorter? He didn't know how prophetic his exclamation about God would prove to be.

He picked her up about 6:30 Tuesday evening. Dinner was a low budget affair in keeping with Jerry Williamson's finances. Not that dinner seemed to be of any great importance for either of them. It was kind of like foreplay and their mutual building of anticipation to the evening's main event. Somehow Nora Kendricks had worn an even shorter skirt that night, plus a form fitting, low cut pull-over sweater that showed off the cleavage between her almost perfectly shaped breasts.

They were back at her place before 9:00, ripping each other's clothes off almost as soon as the front door closed. All the way into her bedroom they discarded clothing, and she tore the bedspread and blanket back. Jerry Williamson was almost in heaven.

Almost, because at the height of his arousal and her seemingly unstoppable drive toward being fucked, with both of them naked, pressed against each other, hands clawing wildly, she pushed him away.

Rolling away from him, she pulled the sheet up to cover herself, then spoke, "This is wrong, God will punish us for this."

"What the hell are you talking about?" he asked in astonishment.

"This, this is wrong, having sex like animals to satisfy our lust," she pouted.

Jerry Williamson couldn't believe what was happening. Horny as he was, he was also not one to give up without a fight. Sitting up, he put his arms around her and pulled her close, holding her for a full minute, neither of them talking. Slowly he moved his mouth down to her neck and gently kissed the soft area just below her ear, moving down to her collarbone, and then back up under her chin. She started to respond almost as soon as his caresses began, her torso grinding into his, her hands groping for his body, her mouth slathering his with kisses.

He wasn't letting God get his way this time, or taking "no" for an answer, not that he had to.

Jerry Williamson was no stranger to sex, and he had been on one or two wild rides in his life, but nothing like what happened next. Nora Kendricks was like an unbroken mustang. Between her screaming that God would punish them and the violent arching of her back, he almost couldn't stay on top of her as she thrashed side-to-side in pleasure.

"On top, on top," she screamed, pushing against him with both hands to force him off her.

Locking his right arm behind her back, he rolled over pulling her on top of him. Now on top, she became even more vocal and more animated. Arms crossed over her head, she gyrated side-to-side, hips thrusting forward with a loud guttural grunt each time, mixed with pleadings to God to forgive her this terrible sin she was committing.

It flashed in Jerry Williamson's mind that if this were Disneyland, it would be an "E-ticket" ride.

Much of the rest of that night was a blur to him. After they made love, she cried for almost a half hour straight, sobbing about how what they did was wrong. He was really confused. Here this gorgeous, sexy creature, who dressed to show off her body, who had sent him all the right signals, who had been just as eager as he was to make love, and who could have been, quite possibility, the best fuck he ever had, was crying and asking God to forgive her.

His confusion persisted through two more lovemaking sessions that night followed by crying jags, and one more bout in the morning.

Jerry Williamson headed home well after the sun was up, having not slept a wink. His pelvic bone hurt like hell from her violent hip thrusts, but it was a good hurt.

They saw each other at work that night. Her demeanor was just as perky and normal as always, and nobody appeared any the wiser that they had gone out together. Business was brisk the next couple of nights so there was no opportunity to talk at work. Likewise, their days off didn't correspond for the next three weeks, so another date was out of the question.

They did manage to grab breakfast after work one morning.

Jerry Williamson was eager to spend time with her, anxious to get another opportunity for a date. No way, Nora Kendricks told him, her mini-skirted legs crossed under the table of the coffee shop, her breasts pushing hard against the sweater she wore.

"Why in the world not?" he asked.

"I'm really ashamed of what I did with you. I've asked God to forgive me and promised to only date good Christian men in the future," she told him.

Over the next ten minutes, Nora explained that she came from a small town in the mid-west, was raised in a Christian household, with Christian values, where sex, for the sake of sex, was a sin.

"So we can't date anymore?" he queried.

"You only want to date me so you can you know what," she ashamedly replied.

Yeah, that's true Jerry Williamson thought to himself.

"The only way we can keep going out is if you start going to church with me and accept Jesus Christ as your savior," she told him flat out.

Jerry Williamson thought about it for maybe a full two seconds. He wasn't a heathen, but he was a long way from being a good Christian. Raised in a Methodist household, he'd done the "go to church thing" every Sunday when he was a kid, said grace before eating, gave thanks for everything, and knew the Lord's Prayer. Going off to college when he was eighteen, he'd left almost all of his religious side at home.

In his mind, he rapidly calculated the last time he'd even been in a church. Six months ago he recalled, at the funeral for the LAPD motorcycle officer killed by a drunk driver. He also calculated his chances, given his financial situation, of hooking up in the near future with somebody like Nora Kendricks who could ride him into a lather.

"Okay, I could use some stability and meaning in my life, and I respect you as a person. I'll go to church with you and try to become a good Christian." He had a hard time getting the words out, as his thoughts were on her breasts.

Over the next five or six months, he and Nora went to church on Sundays, listened to sermons about the evils of society, a godless government, and the need to acknowledge Jesus Christ as Lord and Savior.

On the other days of the week, she fucked his brains out. Life was good for Jerry Williamson.

One of the unexpected things that happened to Jerry Williamson after he hooked up with Nora Kenricks was being drawn into a fellowship of other Christian police officers.

Nora had let it be known around the station that she and Jerry were an item, and he was living up to his word about becoming a good Christian. Through the church he and Nora attended, he met several other cops, some from LAPD, some from other police departments around Los Angeles. About two months later he was invited to a meeting of the Los Angeles County Christian Peace Officers Association.

Composed of cops of all ranks, from almost every police department, sheriffs, CHP, and dozens of other law enforcement agencies in the county, this group met twice a month. In order to accommodate officers with different work shifts, one meeting would be for breakfast, the second for dinner.

Jerry Williamson had never been a joiner, but surprisingly, he found much commonality with the other members of the association. He enjoyed the fellowship, the bible study, and the discussions which equated being a cop in Los Angeles in the '80s, to the biblical references about Centurions at the time of Christ.

One of the added benefits Jerry Williamson got from belonging to this group was a sponsor for his career.

There were eighteen or twenty other LAPD personnel in the countywide association, almost half of them were sergeants, lieutenants, captains, or deputy chiefs.

Three months after joining the countywide Christian Officers Association, he got a call from a captain who was also a member, inviting him to an informal meeting with some of the other LAPD officers who belonged to the association.

Jerry Williamson was kind of hesitant. Between work, Nora, and his twice monthly meetings with the countywide association, he didn't have a lot of spare time. The prospect of another obligation, especially one that involved religion, was not high on his priorities. In the end, however, he decided he didn't have a good reason not to attend the meeting and blow off the captain who invited him.

It was the best career decision Jerry Williamson ever made.

The group, all twelve of them, met in the early evening after normal working hours, in the office of a deputy chief at Parker Center, the administrative headquarters and main jail for LAPD. The meetings were not officially sanctioned by LAPD, but lots of groups within the department, the Latino Officers Association, the Black Officers Association, women officers groups, to name a few, were allowed to use city facilities to hold their meetings as long as they didn't disrupt normal police operations.

It didn't take Jerry Williamson long to realize that the goals of the LAPD Christian officers group were considerably different than those of the countywide association.

While the countywide association's aim was fellowship, community service, mutual support, and Bible study, the informal Los Angeles Police Department group had other objectives. Led by the deputy chief, this group's brand of Christian values involved sponsoring the careers of fellow members, preventing what they saw as the moral decay of the department, and inserting God back into police work.

Over the next year, Jerry Williamson's relationship with Nora started to cool, but his relationship with several of the Christian power brokers within LAPD was paying dividends for his career. Soon he found himself transferred to an 8 to 5 desk job at Parker Center, working for a captain with staunch LAPD Christian values. Within two years came a promotion to lieutenant.

In the early '80s, LAPD, like almost every other California law enforcement agency, was struggling with societal issues like women officers, gay officers, and minority hiring.

With the deputy chief providing direction and protection within Jerry Williamson's informal group of LAPD Christian cops, gay officers, especially female gay officers, became a cause. There was nothing official, of course, and when asked, nobody would even acknowledge that such a group existed. Sure, a few Christian officers got together once in a while to study the bible, but as far as a group determined to keep gays off LAPD or to impede the careers of gay officers, well, there was no such group.

Maybe not, but if you were a gay LAPD copper, you always knew which sergeant or lieutenant you didn't want to work for, or what your chances were of getting a special assignment based on who was making the selection. You also knew who would give you a good recommendation for promotion and who wouldn't. If you were gay, you knew that you might as well not even show up for a promotional interview if you drew one of the members of Jerry Williamson's group as head of the promotional panel.

By the '90s, Lieutenant Jerry Williamson was fully entrenched into disliking gays. He avoided the word hate, as he didn't hate them. They, after all, couldn't help themselves, they were sick. They'd lost their way, had rejected Jesus Christ and the word of God in the Holy Bible. No, he didn't hate them, but he didn't have to like them either.

To the people who knew him, the transformation in Jerry Williamson was astounding. In a matter of a couple of years he'd gone from being more-or-less apathetic toward gay cops, to becoming almost openly bigoted. Protected by his sponsor, who had now promoted to a three star assistant chief, he often made derogatory comments in front of subordinates about officers he knew or suspected were gay, and made no bones about giving preferential treatment to other Christian officers.

He even prided himself with the fact that he could spot gay female officers by the way they walked, their hairstyles, body shape, speech, or mannerisms.

With his sponsor guiding his career, Jerry Williamson made captain, and within two more years, got his first star when he was promoted to commander.

He'd heard Nora Kendricks married a good Christian man in 1986, a school teacher, and they'd moved shortly afterward to Colorado.

By 2004, Jerry Williamson was a power broker himself, helping out the careers of a select few Christian officers who shared his views and insidiously derailing the careers of gays.

But being a power broker on LAPD couldn't protect him from everything. And it didn't one night in October, 2007.

It had been a great retirement party. His number one sponsor was retiring after thirty-five years with LAPD. There were almost a thousand people at the Bonaventure Hotel for his retirement celebration that night, including the Mayor of Los Angeles, several state legislators, business and community leaders, and hundreds of cops. As they tended to be, it was a long drawn out affair, maybe a dozen speakers, lots of plaques, funny stories about his career, and gifts too numerous to count.

This is the way I want to go when my time comes, Jerry Williamson thought to himself. Over the course of the five hour event, he had five, maybe six cocktails, plus a couple of glasses of wine with dinner.

By the time it ended around 11:00, Jerry Williamson wasn't drunk, but he was right on the border line of being under the influence by legal standards. Because of his rank and responsibilities, he got an unmarked city car to drive, a big 2006 Ford Crown Victoria. Policy forbade operating a city vehicle any time alcohol had been consumed, but like a lot of police big-wigs in many agencies, not just LAPD, he routinely ignored that directive.

Jerry Williamson lived in the San Fernando Valley, twenty-five or so freeway miles from the Bonaventure Hotel which was right in the middle of downtown. He found the on-ramp to the northbound Harbor Freeway, then transitioned to the Hollywood Freeway heading toward the valley.

He was two-thirds of the way home when the red and blue revolving lights on the Highway Patrol car lit up the interior of his vehicle. He glanced at the speedometer, no, he wasn't speeding. I wonder what these fucking "Chippies" want, he said to himself, using the less than flattering name other cops called CHP officers.

Slowing, he looked for a spot on the right shoulder wide enough to stop safely, then heard the public address speaker on the Highway Patrol car telling him to take the next exit off the freeway. Continuing on as directed for a quarter mile, he took the off-ramp, stopped at the signal light, and turned right, stopping at the curb on the city street.

This was not the way to end a great night, he thought to himself, as he bounded out of his car. Besides, he was a commander on LAPD. He would straighten these Chippies away in a heartbeat.

The Highway Patrol officers were already out of their vehicle by the time he got out of his. The female officer driver met him at the rear of his car and asked that he step up on the sidewalk where her partner, another female, was waiting.

Son-of-a-bitch, Jerry Williamson exclaimed to himself, every damn where I go, gay females. One look at the officers and he had them pegged. One of them was tall, with short hair, swept back in that style "they" all wore. The other was stockier, close to being overweight, not at all pretty in his opinion, and she stood like a man.

"Good evening, sir," the stockier one greeted him. "We stopped you because you were weaving around a little on the freeway. Can I see your license and registration, please?"

He may not have been drunk, but Jerry Williamson had just enough alcohol in his system that he said one of the things that was guaranteed to piss off the officers.

"Don't you know who I am?" he said indignantly.

It was actually a stupid thing to say. Between LAPD, the Highway Patrol, L.A. Sheriff's Department, and the fifty or so other independent city police agencies, there were nearly twenty thousand cops in Los Angeles County. The chances that the two CHP officers would know a commander from LAPD were about nil.

"No, sir, I don't," the officer replied, her voice still calm. "Could I see your license please?"

"I'm Commander Williamson, LAPD, and I don't appreciate being stopped by you "Triple-A with a gun" cops from the Highway Patrol."

He'd just said another thing that was digging him deeper into a hole.

"That's fine commander," the officer answered, "Could I see your I.D card?"

Jerry Williamson made a big show of pulling out his badge case, flipping it open to reveal his LAPD badge, thrusting it up arrogantly in front of the officer.

By this time, both female officers had come to the conclusion that, LAPD commander or not, this guy was under the influence and shouldn't be driving. They didn't need to have him do Field Sobriety Tests, or blow into a hand-held alcohol tester, to know he'd had too much to drink. The smell of alcohol on his breath and his erratic driving, told them that.

Highway Patrol officers run across cops driving their personal cars, or unmarked police cars, all the time who are speeding, running stop signs, drinking beer in their vehicles, or violating any number of other traffic laws. If the errant cop gives an "I'm sorry", or some other sign acknowledging they were wrong, the whole incident generally ends with nothing more than a "see ya" from the Highway Patrol officer.

Cops under the influence pose a little trickier problem. The last thing in the world any Highway Patrol officer wants to do is arrest another cop for DUI. If the CHP officer thinks the cop can make it home okay, in most cases, they let them go. If they're really in too bad a shape to drive, the officer might even take the cop home, or call someone to pick them up.

Veteran CHP officers also knew never to call their sergeant when they had a drunk cop. Once a supervisor got involved, the whole incident would then become official, and the sergeant would direct the officers to make an arrest.

For Highway Patrol officers who, two-thirds of the time, are working by themselves miles from any back-up, it came down to never making an enemy of another cop on purpose.

At that point, Jerry Williamson, fellow cop, or Commander Williamson, LAPD, could have saved himself and his career, with a little courtesy. He chose instead to let his alligator mouth override his hummingbird ass.

"I don't have to show you my I.D. card, here, look at my badge," Jerry Williamson snarled, a slight slur to his words.

By that comment, he failed the most critical of all roadside tests administered by CHP officers, "The Attitude Test".

"Commander, let's do this the easy way, please show me your identification," the stocky female officer said politely, but with her patience running out, as the taller officer moved to position herself behind and slightly off to the side of Jerry Williamson.

"Fuck you, you fat dyke," he hissed at her, "I'm leaving."

With that, he turned and started walking back toward his car. He only got two steps before the stocky officer grabbed his arm, and the taller officer pushed him face down on the hood of the patrol car. They had his hands twisted behind his back in an instant, secured with handcuffs.

As the taller officer was putting him in the rear seat of the patrol car, her partner was just picking up the radio microphone to call their sergeant, when an LAPD two-officer unit drove past on the street. She signaled them to stop.

It took the two CHP officers a couple seconds to explain to their LAPD counterparts who they had and what had transpired. During the whole time, Jerry Williamson, handcuffed in the back seat of the Highway Patrol unit, was screaming about "Fucking Dykes," "Goddamn lesbian CHP officers," and "Fucking Chippies".

One of the LAPD officers sat in the front seat of the CHP car, turned so he could talk to Jerry Williamson in the back seat, trying to calm him down. The other LAPD officer called their watch commander.

The CHP sergeant and the LAPD lieutenant watch commander got to the scene about the same time. Both conferred with the female officers, and then the LAPD lieutenant tried to talk to Jerry Williamson. After a couple of minutes the LAPD lieutenant had not been able to calm him down. He had also been subjected to numerous threats to his own career by Commander Williamson.

Unable to pacify his irate superior, the LAPD lieutenant approached the Highway Patrol sergeant and stated, "Do you want to book this asshole, or do you want us to do it?"

In the end, LAPD Commander Jerome Williamson was led away in handcuffs by officers from his own agency.

His arrest made big news in the L.A. papers. LAPD's Internal Affairs Division conducted the investigation into the incident. There was nothing they could, or would do, about the DUI. Jerry Williamson had to face the music on that charge by himself.

From the legal system, he ended up getting two days in jail, a four thousand dollar fine, mandatory alcohol counseling, and a six month suspension of his driver's license. From LAPD, he got thirty days off without pay and a reduction in rank back to captain.

His career might have survived the arrest if it had not been for what happened next. Within a day and a half, his arrest became the talk of LAPD. A few days after that, the anonymous letters and e-mails about Jerry Williamson's anti-gay bias and the manipulation of promotional examinations by high-ranking Christian management personnel within LAPD, began to flood Internal Affairs.

The day he returned to duty after serving his thirty day suspension for DUI, Jerry Williamson was summoned to the Chief of Police's office. There he was advised of the results of the internal investigation into his conduct over the past twenty years, his anti-gay activities, and the favoritism he had shown other members of his Christian officers group.

Jerry Williamson was given the opportunity to retire, or face dismissal.

It wasn't much of a choice. Without his sponsor to run interference and provide protection, he had few options. Jerry Williamson's career was over. He never got the retirement party he wanted.

———

While Red Wolff and Jerome Williamson were about to come to blows over who would head the investigation, Ray Silva, with the help of several other CHP officers and sheriff's deputies, were trying to bring some semblance of order to the crime scene and the vista point. All non-essential people, cops, firemen, ambulance attendants, reporters, and about a dozen ordinary civilians, who just stopped to see what was going on, were ushered back to their cars and out of the vista point. A string of law enforcement vehicles were positioned next to the southbound lanes of Highway 101 to keep any unauthorized personnel out of the scene, and officers were stationed to check anybody who tried to gain access to the location.

Over the next twenty minutes, several members of the CHP shooting team arrived, as did Red Wolff's chief from Redding.

While the investigators from the shooting team gathered their equipment and prepared to begin their task, Highway Patrol Assistant Chief Vaughn O'Dell ambled toward Red Wolff and Jerome Williamson. He could hear them arguing and see him gesturing wildly. Vaughn O'Dell had never met the new sheriff, but he'd heard the stories about his career on LAPD from several sources.

"Calm down, everyone, calm down," he said as he reached the two protagonists.

Sheriff Jerome Williamson was about to say who the fuck are you, when O'Dell extended his hand and said with a smile, "Hi, I don't think we've met, I'm Lieutenant Wolff's chief, Vaughn O'Dell."

The friendly greeting and the firm handshake, took Jerome Williamson off-guard, completely disarming him. It wouldn't take him long to recover.

After the somewhat uncomfortable introductions, Vaughn O'Dell suggested the three of them move away from the crowd and discuss how best to proceed.

———

Vaughn O'Dell was legendary on the Highway Patrol. With thirty-six years on the job, he'd done just about everything. He would be forced into mandatory retirement in five months when he turned sixty. Even so, he still had the enthusiasm and kick-ass attitude of a rookie.

His career had maxed out six years ago, shortly after he made assistant chief. The end of his rise within the ranks came as a result of a comment he made at a statewide, all-commanders conference. These bi-annual meetings brought all CHP command level personnel, lieutenants, captains, assistant chiefs, deputy chiefs, and the four commissioners, together in Sacramento. There, marching orders were given, goals set and priorities discussed.

At these meetings the Commissioner always spoke first. After the usual one-handed clapping by the Commissioner about how great everyone was doing, he began discussing his philosophy of pushing decision-making down to the individual commanders and that, as commanders, they had the flexibility to run their operations as they deemed appropriate to accomplish the CHP's mission.

That statement, by the head of the Highway Patrol, hit Vaughn O'Dell wrong. Looking at the four executive managers of the Highway Patrol, the Commissioner, the deputy commissioner, and two assistant commissioners, he saw everything that was wrong with the department he loved. Each of them had almost thirty years on the job, but between them, only one had ever held a field command. The rest had flitted from one headquarters special assignment to another, always with a sponsor to promote their upwardly mobile careers, without the inconvenient necessity of going to the field to learn what the Highway Patrol was really all about.

Vaughn O'Dell's experiences as a field lieutenant, a field captain, and now as a field assistant chief, were directly opposite of the Commissioner's statement. His experience told him everything having to do with flexibility and decision making was tightly dictated by headquarters. Individual commander decisions were often overturned, usually by the Commissioner himself, especially if the union that represented the officers got involved.

When the Commissioner finished speaking, he asked if there were any questions or comments. The usual "kiss-ass" commanders jumped up and asked fluff questions, while others stood up to voice their support.

To his everlasting credit and immortality on the Highway Patrol, Vaughn O'Dell stood up and said what most commanders really felt.

"Commissioner, you say we have decision making ability, and you want us to be innovative, but from the field level, that just isn't so. A field commander on the Highway Patrol is a lot like being the captain on the jungle boat ride at Disneyland. We get to wear the captain's hat, we get a gun to shoot the Hippopotamus, we even get to turn the wheel and toot the whistle. But in truth, the boat is on a rail underwater, and it goes the same way, at the same speed, all day long, everyday."

The whole conference room erupted into applause and laughter.

Vaughn O'Dell had said what almost everyone in the room was afraid to say. He also sentenced himself to never getting promoted again.

Once the three of them had moved to a location where they could talk, Vaughn O'Dell spoke first.

"Look sheriff," he began, using Jerome Williamson's title instead his first name, as a calculated way of showing deference to his position.

"Don't look sheriff me," Jerome Williamson retorted curtly. "It's my county, my jurisdiction, my investigation. As I told your lieutenant, if you or any of your people interfere, or touch anything, I'll make trouble for the both of you."

"What are you going to do, put a horse in my bed?" Vaughn O'Dell snapped back.

"No, I'm going to call your Commissioner in Sacramento, then I'm going to arrest you, and any other of your "Triple A with a gun" highway cops who get in my way. And what the fuck is it with you chippies and horses in your bed?" Jerome Williamson ranted, a quizzical look on his face.

Red Wolff turned to her taller chief rising on her toes and spoke into his ear, "Boss, I already used the horse in the bed line with him."

Vaughn O'Dell chuckled, and then looked directly into the eyes of this sheriff who was quickly trying his patience. He didn't speak for a couple of seconds, then broke off his eye contact, turning left and right to survey the scene and the dozens of people milling around. His mind was carefully formulating what he was going to say next.

Without knowing it, Jerome Williamson had probably said the two worst things he could have. Had he tried, there was nothing he could have said that would have sent Vaughn O'Dell into more of a rage. By invoking the threat to call the Commissioner of the Highway Patrol, this jerk-off sheriff had only strengthened his resolve in terms of the shooting investigation. It was, however, his comment referring to CHP officers as "Triple A with a gun", insinuating that the only thing Highway Patrol officers did was handle traffic accidents and call tow trucks for disabled motorist's, that sent him over the top. Ten years ago, he'd buried his oldest son, a Highway Patrol officer, killed in the line of duty. He was shot by an ex-con driving a stolen car who had kidnapped and raped a woman. In a roadside shootout, his son had killed the man who mortally wounded him. The kidnapped woman in the stolen car didn't care that she had been saved by a Highway Patrolman. She was just as alive as if she'd been saved by the FBI. The bullet fired by the ex-con didn't care that his son was a Highway Patrol officer, rather than a sheriff's deputy or a city policeman. The bullet killed him just as dead, leaving him by the side of a dirty freeway to die alone.

"Red, could you excuse us for a minute," he said to his lieutenant.

Once Red Wolff walked away, Vaughn O'Dell turned back to Sheriff Jerome Williamson and spoke. The volume of his voice was low, his words slow and deliberate. "Okay, Jerry, have it your way," he began, dropping any pretense of deference and civility in how he addressed the sheriff standing in front of him.

"You're not from around here are you?" he began. Vaughn O'Dell had been a good street cop in his time, and he was a good chief and good law enforcement administrator now. He only asked questions he already knew the answer to. Not waiting for the sheriff to answer, he continued.

"Things happen a little different in small towns than they do in places like Los Angeles. Here most people know each other. Their kids go to school together, they go to the same churches, shop at the same stores, they go to the same parties. Here in the sticks, the Highway Patrol, by virtue of reputation and the type of officers we have, gets the top spot among law enforcement. Not taking anything away from local cops, people here just consider the Highway Patrol to be the best. The two kids lying over there have been part of this community for a long time. Did you know Dave Castle was an elder in his church and coached Little League even though he had no kids of his own? Jodie volunteered at the local hospice and tutored kids in reading at the elementary school. She also personally killed two terrorists, and wounded a third, when they took over Crescent City two years ago. Everyone in town loved her. Now, they're both dead, killed, no, murdered by someone. You want to make their murders into a political statement about what a red-hot crime fighter you are so you can get reelected next year. Well, you just might pull that off, if you, or your people, don't fuck up the investigation. However, you have nobody on your department who has ever done a murder investigation before, while I've got a team standing over there who are specialists in cop shootings. In the past year, they've investigated seven CHP shooting incidents, three in which the suspect was killed. They've also assisted six different sheriff's departments in the northern part of the state with officer-involved shootings. You can call the Commissioner if you want. He may be a political appointee and a weenie on some things, but when it comes to his officers being killed, he's still a cop at heart. He'll tell you to go pound sand up your hockey hole. Then he'll tell me to get our people busy doing the investigation. Once the investigation is over, he'll go to the state sheriff's association and tell the other fifty-seven county sheriffs what a jerk you were. After that, you won't get their endorsement for reelection. And, just so we're clear, let me tell you the same thing my old Marine Corps boot camp drill instructor used to tell us, it takes two to fuck. You try to arrest me, or any of my people, and I'll make sure everyone in this county knows that you, an outsider, the big-city cop from Los Angeles, fucked up the investigation and refused to cooperate with the Highway Patrol. I'll also tell enough of the right people about why you left LAPD two jumps ahead of getting fired. After all that's done, you'll have a better chance of winning the lottery than getting elected sheriff."

Jerome Williamson was fuming inside. He was a smart man, and he realized there was obviously a lot more to this old Highway Patrol chief than first met the eye. He'd hit just about every nerve he could in his lecture about small towns and the political realities of being sheriff.

In the end, Sheriff Jerome Williamson, Assistant Chief Vaughn O'Dell, and Lieutenant Erin "Red" Wolff, agreed to work together on the investigation. They'd pool their resources, with the sheriff's office being the lead agency by virtue of jurisdiction. The CHP would conduct a concurrent investigation because their officers were the victims. Both agencies would work together and share their investigative findings.

The Del Norte County Sheriff didn't like it one bit, but he knew the CHP chief and his faggotty-ass female lieutenant, had him over a barrel.

Standing about twenty feet away, Red Wolff couldn't hear what the two men were saying to each other, but at the conclusion of their discussion, she saw they shook hands and each went a different direction. Vaughn O'Dell walked toward her, while Jerome Williamson headed the opposite way, lighting a cigarette as he went.

"So, what do you think of our new sheriff?" Red asked her chief.

"Well, I learned a couple of things about him," Vaughn O'Dell replied. "First, he's a reasonable guy when you explain things to him in a language he can understand. Second, I know he's never seen *The Godfather*."

"How did you get him to agree on a joint investigation?" she asked.

"I made him an offer he couldn't refuse," Vaughn O'Dell told her, the expression on his face never changing.

CHAPTER FIVE

Over the course of the next hour, the remaining members of the CHP shooting team arrived at the vista point. Following quick introductions and a short briefing by Vaughn O'Dell, they got to work.

With the team leader lieutenant providing direction, they first expanded the taped off area to include all but the very northern end of the scenic outlook. This meant telling more people to leave the scene and parking all vehicles farther south on Highway 101, or on the shoulders.

With the scene now virtually cleared of vehicles and people, they did a slow walk around the entire area looking at the location of the officers' bodies and their vehicle from as many different angles as possible. Once they'd completed their walk-around, video and still cameras were employed to photograph and videotape the scene from a distance. Satisfied they had captured everything on film, they went about their individual tasks.

Each person on the team had a different function.

One of the officers set about marking, photographing, and collecting what little physical evidence there was to be found. While everyone had drawn a logical conclusion that there had been another vehicle involved, most likely one the dead officers had stopped or one they were checking out, there was no evidence to support that hypothesis. The vista point was asphalt paved so there were no convenient tire tread marks from which castings could be made. Like any paved portion of road, there was always a certain amount of loose gravel and dirt on the surface, but the constant drizzle had long since washed away any light tire impressions another vehicle might have left. Even if there had been some trace tire marks, the constant parade of people who had traipsed through the scene would have contaminated everything.

Diligently though, the officer scoured the scene, marking and bagging what he found. After he had collected everything, he checked the officers' vehicle. Because the SUV had been standing in the elements for almost eight hours, he knew there was little hope of finding any fingerprints. Nonetheless, he made arrangements to have it towed to the CHP office and secured inside a closed garage. Once the exterior dried, he would dust for fingerprints hoping the natural oils everyone has on their hands and fingers might have left something usable.

Lastly, he elicited the help of Ray Silva to assist him while he searched the narrow two foot space on the ocean side of the guardrail at the edge of the cliff. From the trunk of his unmarked Crown Victoria he retrieved his repelling gear. As part of his training as an Emergency Medical Technician, he had, early in his career, learned repelling as part of rescuing victims involved in accidents where vehicles had plunged off the roadway into canyons and river gorges.

After strapping himself into the repelling harness, he secured the ropes to the steel guardrail and with Ray Silva acting as his safety assistant, hopped over the barrier. He had no intent of repelling off the edge; the equipment was solely for safety if he slipped. Slowly the officer walked the uneven terrain, the wet slippery grass, and jagged rocks along the entire length of the vista point. Leaning out as far as he could, straining against the ropes, he was able look down the cliff face to the churning water below. As he got to the area close to where the officers lay on the other side of the guardrail, he slowed his pace and inched along looking for anything out of the ordinary.

He missed it the first time he'd scanned the very edge of the precipice. Something caused him to look back to the area he had already inspected. At just that instant, a sudden gust of wind blew the long strands of auburn hair embedded in the rocky ledge like a clump of tall grass. His peripheral vision caught the movement. Backing up two steps, he called for Ray to take up tension on the safety rope, and then squatted down to get a better look. There wasn't much, but it was something that didn't belong there. He first used his camera to take six photos from close-up, then another three from a distance to show perspective. Then, he carefully picked the fifteen or so strands of hair and bits of flesh from the rock, depositing them in an evidence envelope. Getting down on his knees, he could also see minute amounts of what looked to be blood around the surface of the rock where the hair was embedded.

He called the shooting team lieutenant over and told him what he'd found. The rock containing what they thought was blood, was part of the entire cliff face and way too large to remove. So they improvised. Ray Silva hustled over to the tow truck and had a quick conversation with the driver. Within a minute he was back with a short-handled, six pound sledge hammer, and a chisel. It took the officer in his repelling harness with Ray Silva holding tension on his rope, almost a half-hour to carefully chip out a six inch long, six inch wide section of the granite rock. Nobody knew if the strands of hair, tissue, and the trace blood stains on the rock had any significance to their investigation, but this was "family business", and everything was important.

While one of his officers was collecting evidence, and another was taking measurements and doing a diagram of the scene, the shooting team sergeant, accompanied by the Del Norte County Sheriff's detective, began the process of examining the bodies of the two dead officers where they had fallen.

The bodies were covered with what CHP officers called a "fatal blanket". Used primarily at the scene of traffic accidents to cover dead bodies, it was little more than a white paper shroud with a thin layer of bright yellow plastic on one side, similar to a throw away table cloth for a picnic table.

Pulling back the blanket covering Dave Castle's face and upper torso, he did a visual examination and took another dozen digital photographs. He noted the officer's face had a discolored bluish hue, caused, he knew, by the blunt force of the bullets that had exploded the thousands of capillaries and small blood vessels around his eye sockets and in his cheeks.

With his hands protected by disposable rubber gloves, he first did a close-up inspection of the officer's hands. Although they were both covered with dried blood, he could find no cuts or indications of defensive wounds that would tell him Dave Castle had tried to fend off his attacker. He would conduct a more thorough examination of both officers' hands at the autopsy where he had access to brighter lights and better working conditions. For now, procedure was to "bag the hands". With the deputy helping, he gently slipped a small brown paper bag, the size you might get if you bought a single beer from a liquor store, over Dave Castle's right hand and secured it to his wrist with a heavy duty rubber band. This, he had been trained, would protect the dead officer's hands from contamination and would allow the fingernails to be scraped for tissue during the autopsy. He repeated the process on the other hand.

It took over an hour for the sergeant and the deputy to examine and photograph the bodies of both officers. Satisfied there was nothing else they could glean from the officers, the bodies were ready to be removed from the scene.

The CHP sent their people to Homicide Investigators School and Officer Involved Shooting Training conducted by the FBI in Los Angeles. It had been great training, highly intensive, and the officers learned the step-by-step Federal Bureau of Investigation approach on how to investigate these types of incidents.

The FBI model, however, relied on using the vast resources that agency had at their disposal, on-staff forensic pathologists, crime scene technicians, DNA and fingerprint databases, and a multitude of electronic scientific instruments to analyze everything.

Many of the bigger and richer cities and counties in California had much of the same equipment, the same highly trained personnel on-staff, and a crime rate that justified expending tax revenues to maintain their own crime labs. For small cities, which far outnumbered the large ones and for rural less affluent counties, crime labs and fulltime pathologists were a luxury they could not afford. Consequently, there were regional satellite crime labs, run by the state, which handled the forensic analysis of evidence, blood typing, and bullet comparisons.

So, while the FBI Officer Involved Shooting Investigation Protocol worked really well in big cities, CHP investigators had to make adjustments to these procedures for investigations they conducted in rural locations. One of the biggest adjustments had to do with autopsies.

Most people outside of law enforcement and quite a few, who are actually in the business, have little idea of the complex legalities that surround an "unattended" death. These are deaths caused by an accident, or murder, or unusual circumstances where the deceased is not under the care of a physician.

In California, regardless of the circumstances, at the moment of death the deceased belongs to the coroner of the county in which the death occurred. In forty-one of California's fifty-eight counties, the sheriff and the coroner are the same person. That is not to say the sheriff actually performs the autopsy, they simply carry out the duties assigned to the coroner by the Penal Code. But, running a morgue, having doctors trained in pathology on-staff, and handling all of the other complexities associated with death, and dead bodies, is extremely expensive. So, in these counties, the sheriff contracts with local physicians and mortuaries for medical examiner services.

In rural Del Norte County, where the sheriff functioned as the coroner, and with no county morgue, their bodies were taken to a mortuary in Crescent City. There, a local doctor, trained in pathology and on contract to the county, was called to perform the autopsy.

As he walked in the back door of the mortuary, the CHP sergeant had the feeling he'd been here before. Not in this particular mortuary he knew, but others just like it. The room was used to embalm bodies. The lighting in the room was sufficient, although not terribly bright. There were two steel tables with drain gutters to catch blood and body fluids next to a large sink, shelves cluttered with various size glass bottles marked with hard to pronounce names and warning labels, and an array of tools and cutting instruments neatly laid out. Rooms like this have an odor you never forget, he thought to himself. It was the smell of the formaldehyde in the embalming fluid, mixed with the antiseptic smell of the surgical soap used to clean the bodies.

Even though it was the sticks, and the doctor who conducted the examination had only done two previous gunshot wound death autopsies, she did a first-rate job. With the CHP shooting team sergeant and the Del Norte Sheriff's detective in attendance to take charge of the officers' uniforms and to observe the procedure, the doctor worked her way through the autopsy protocol, narrating as she went into a handheld tape recorder.

Unfortunately, in this case, there just wasn't much an autopsy would reveal. The obvious cause of death had been the gunshot wounds both officers suffered. By examining Jodie Castle's internal organs, the doctor was able to ascertain she had died almost instantaneously when the round fired into the back of her neck severed her spinal cord. Her husband, the doctor determined by the angle of the entry wounds to his face, had probably been sitting or lying on the ground when he was struck by the two rounds that killed him. The doctor added, that had he not been shot in the face after he was down, Dave Castle would have bled to death within minutes from the wound that disintegrated the femoral artery in his left leg.

As she matter-of-factly went through the autopsy procedure, the doctor talked to both investigators. Examining the bullet entry wounds, she gave the opinion both officers had been shot at very close range, judging by the amount of "tattooing" she found. Calling both investigators in close as she worked, she showed them the marks left by traces of black powder that had embedded itself into the officers' skin and uniforms. This, she explained, was residue gunpowder that had not been ignited when the round was fired. Both the cops knew what tattooing was, and how it was caused, but neither of them interrupted her. She went on to explain that although this residue gunpowder left the barrel at a high muzzle velocity, it only traveled a few feet. If it should encounter an object, the residue embedded itself, leaving distinct black splatter marks, like tattoo ink. She carefully removed the largest of the black gunpowder bits with a small pair of tweezers and wiped the residue onto a clean white cloth. She offered her best guess that, except for the one round that stuck

Dave Castle in the leg, all the other rounds had been fired from a range of less than three feet.

It was just opinion, she told the two officers, but from the angle of the entry wound on Jodie Castle's neck and path of travel the bullet had taken, there was a good chance the shooter was left-handed.

Whoever did this was one heartless son-of-a-bitch, the CHP shooting team sergeant thought to himself as he gathered up the white cloth with the gunpowder residue and packaged it in an evidence envelope.

The doctor could find no other signs of trauma to either officer, and a methodical examination didn't reveal any hair or fiber evidence that might have belonged to their murderer.

After removing the paper bags from the officers' hands, she scraped under their fingernails looking for skin or tissue that would tell her if one of the officers might have scratched their assailant. There was nothing. She then used a tongue depressor like wooden stick to scrape samples of the dried blood from the male officer's right hand into small clear cellophane envelopes and handed them to the sergeant.

He in turn secured the envelopes with an evidence label, marked the labels with information indicating where on the body the samples had been taken from, and initialed each envelope. They repeated this process three more times, taking scrapings from the left and right hand of each officer.

The CHP sergeant watched the autopsy intently, collecting hair and tissue samples from both officers, as well as a complete set of finger and palm prints to use for comparison and elimination of any prints that might be found on their vehicle. He also carefully examined and photographed the officers' uniforms, boots, and jackets before loosely folding, then sealing them in large brown paper bags. Paper bags, unlike the plastic type, would allow the uniforms to breathe and prevent the bloodstains from sticking to other portions of the uniforms.

His final task at the autopsy, after the doctor removed the spent bullets from the officers' bodies, was to lay each projectile on a piece of white paper, place a six inch ruler on the paper to provide perspective, and photograph each of them. The sergeant and the deputy then examined the bullets, each making their best educated guess as to caliber. Both concluded they were .38 hollow-points. He then etched his initials into each bullet to show chain of evidence and packaged each round individually in small cotton padded vials in preparation for sending to the crime lab in Eureka.

It took nearly four hours for the doctor to finish both autopsies. She'd done as good a job as any big city pathologist could have done. There just wasn't much to find and nothing much the autopsy was going to reveal. Determining the cause and manner of death when the bodies have numerous gunshot wounds, was not difficult.

Once she finished her work, and signed off on the death certificates, the deputy took charge of the bodies and released them to the director of the mortuary.

The CHP sergeant was the last one to leave the room. He didn't personally know Dave or Jodie Castle, but they were family nonetheless. Seeing two dead officers laid out on examination tables, gutted and sewn back together, with dried blood staining their bodies, wasn't the way anybody should go, he thought to himself. Yeah, it was always the risk you took every day, and you knew it might happen, but the odds were on your side it never would.

He was almost to the back door when he turned around and walked back to where the officers lay. He put one hand on Dave's left shoulder and took Jodie's right hand in the other, "California, the Castles are 10-10," he said out loud to the empty room, using the radio code for "end of shift".

—————

While Ray Silva and the officer from the shooting team were chipping away at the rock with the blood stain and the sergeant was watching the autopsy at the mortuary in Crescent City, Red Wolff and her chief were busy handling the dozens of other things that needed to be done.

One of the first tasks she had to accomplish was notification of the officers' families. Probably the only bright spot there was that the Castles had no children.

Red Wolff used her cell phone to call the CHP office.

"Highway Patrol," the civilian office manager answered on the third ring.

"Lisa, this is Erin, I need you to pull the personnel files on the Castles and give me the information on their 102 forms," she told the woman who functioned as clerk, secretary, office manager, and receptionist for the Crescent City CHP area.

Lisa Johnston had been the office manager in Crescent City for twenty-three years. While Lieutenant Wolff might have been the commander of the area, she was the one who kept it running. She'd seen five previous lieutenants come and go during her time. She really liked Erin Wolff, as she was proving to be easier to train than many of her predecessors.

Lisa had anticipated Red Wolff's call and had already pulled the Castles personnel files, knowing she would need the emergency contact information every CHP officer had on file for notification of next-of-kin.

In the course of their normal daily working relationship, Office Manager Lisa Johnston and Lieutenant Erin Wolff were on a first name basis, a pretty common practice around the Highway Patrol. Given the events of the day, however, Lisa Johnston shifted into formal mode, "Lieutenant, here is the emergency contact info you want, ready to copy?"

"Okay, got it," Red replied after jotting down the names, addresses and phone numbers of Dave and Jodie Castles parents. "Stand by one," she told Lisa Johnston.

Red Wolff thought about the information for a second. Dave Castle's parents lived in the foothills outside of Sacramento, Jodie's lived in Modesto. Two different CHP geographical divisions, she realized. "Lisa, can you give me the numbers for Valley Division and Central Division please?"

It took Lisa Johnston a few seconds to find the numbers and relay them to her lieutenant.

With the information she needed in hand, Red sought out her chief who was engaged in a conversation with Sheriff Jerome Williamson.

"Excuse me Boss, here is the contact information for the Castles," she said, handing him a piece of paper.

"Okay Red, thanks, I'll make a couple of calls."

Under normal circumstances, death notifications in California are made by the sheriff's department and are normally done in person. In most cases, if the next-of-kin lived in the same county, a deputy would be dispatched to make the notification face-to-face. If the next-of-kin lived in another county, sheriff's departments across the state had reciprocal agreements that they would make the notification as a courtesy. Since this was far from a normal situation, the Highway Patrol would make contact with the parents.

Over the next fifteen minutes, Vaughn O'Dell made calls to the CHP divisional headquarters closest to the homes of Dave and Jodie Castles parents. Within an hour, high ranking CHP management personnel would arrive at the homes of the officers' parents and inform them of the murders of their children.

While Vaughn O'Dell was making the calls that would set the notification process in motion, Red Wolff went back to supervising the scene at the vista point.

The open tailgate of her sergeant's SUV functioned as the command post, with maps spread out on easels, measuring tapes, cameras ready for use, and a radio mounted in the rear to facilitate communication.

"95-L, Humboldt, 95-L," the female voice of the day shift comm-op called from the communications center in Eureka.

"Humboldt, 95-L, go ahead," Red Wolff answered.

"95-L, the CHP King Air is ten minutes out from the Crescent City airport. The Critical Incident Response Team leader is requesting transportation," the comm-op advised her.

"10-4, contact the beat units nearest to McNamara Field and ask them to provide 11-48 to the office," Red Wolff told the comm-op, using the radio code for providing transportation.

She would need to get back to the office fairly soon, Red Wolff knew. There wasn't much more she could do at the vista point anyway. The shooting team's investigation would proceed without her and they would keep her in the loop as their work progressed. As commander, her focus would soon shift toward dealing with the psychological damage the murder of the Castles had already done, and would continue to do, to the other twenty-one cops and three civilians in her squad. Thank goodness for the help the team from Sacramento would provide, she thought to herself.

By 10:00 the rain and drizzle had subsided and from her position at the vista point command post, Red Wolff could see blue sky to the west out over the ocean. The wind had also freshened, and for the first time since leaving Tiburon at 4:00 that morning, she felt cold.

More people kept showing up at the vista point. Many were cops who came to see if they could help, civilians who just wanted to look, and a news crew from the television station in Eureka. The CHP officers and sheriff's deputies turned the majority of them away.

Red Wolff did a quick briefing with the news crew. Like news people everywhere, of course, they wanted access to everything, the officers' names, and detailed information about the investigation. Red wouldn't release the officers' names as she knew notifications had yet to be made, and there was very little she could tell them about what had happened. She knew it wouldn't take them long to find out who the officers were by talking to local people in town, so she cut a deal with the reporter and his cameraman giving them limited access to the scene in exchange for their promise not to release the names until their next-of-kin could be notified.

By 11:30 the scene at the vista point had pretty well cleared out. The bodies of the officers and their vehicle had been removed, and the shooting team had gathered as much physical evidence as they could find. There was nothing more they could do at that location.

Their next task was to drive north and south on Highway 101 looking for anything out of the ordinary that might have been discarded along the roadway by an assailant. They also stopped at every trash can and dumpster at other vista points, beach accesses, and businesses along the highway for five miles in both directions from the crime scene looking for items that might have been hastily thrown away as the murderer fled the scene. The shooting team's search came up empty.

Red Wolff watched as her sergeant, Dick Huddleston, closed up the backend of his SUV and drove away. He had been almost invisible since the ass-chewing she'd given him because of his failure to protect the crime scene. Red knew she would have to find a way to build his shattered self-confidence back up so he didn't mope around for weeks. She needed all of her supervisors to be strong and proactive in dealing with the other officers in the squad, especially over the next couple of days until after the funeral. She was still livid with him though. She'd let him stew for a few more days.

With nothing more to be done, the last of the sheriff's deputies and CHP officers left the vista point shortly thereafter.

Except for Red Wolff, Vaughn O'Dell, and Ray Silva, the vista point was empty.

"Red, unless you can think of anything else, I'm going to head back to the office," Ray Silva told his lieutenant, former graveyard partner, and career long friend.

"Yeah, me too," she replied, "Still a thousand things to do."

"I'm going to find a motel, check in, call division, and then I'll meet you at your office. I'll be here for at least another day," Vaughn O'Dell told her.

"Okay Boss, thanks for getting here so quickly and for all your help," Red Wolff told her chief.

Vaughn O'Dell just nodded, paused for a second, then spoke. "Red, you did a good job here this morning. From experience, I can tell you the really hard stuff is yet to come. You've got a squad of people who are going to be hurting, they'll wanna talk, and they'll want answers. They are going to need a strong leader to hold them together until they can make some sense out of this tragedy and move on. At the same time you have an area operation to keep running. Accidents won't stop happening, drunks will keep driving, and people will still need help out there on the road. So you'll need to be strong and keep focused on your job. To top it all off, you have the murder of two officers to solve. Once the shooting team finishes their initial investigation, I'll let them stay for a few days to run down any leads and to tie up any loose ends. They all have regular jobs and families to get back to. So you may find yourself having to work closely with that jerk-off sheriff. I'll be available by phone, and I'll drive over anytime you need me here. But mostly, everything that needs to be done is gonna fall on you."

"It's my command, my people, I'll handle whatever comes," Red Wolff replied, looking him directly in the eye.

"I know they're in good hands," he told her, his eyes locked on hers.

Vaughn O'Dell jumped into his car and started to drive away, then backed up to where Red Wolff was still standing staring out at the ocean. "Red, this kinda put a crimp in your honeymoon didn't it?" his tone of voice indicated his query was not so much a question as it was a statement acknowledging the unfortunate timing of the whole incident.

"It did, but it will have to wait. Mary Jean understands," she answered.

"Okay, see you in a bit," he said, driving off heading north on 101 toward Crescent City.

Standing alone now at the vista point, Red Wolff did a slow three hundred sixty degree turn, drinking in a last impression of the scene. It had clouded over in the last thirty minutes and was starting to rain again.

"Yeah, it put a crimp in my honeymoon, Ray Silva's also. It will also make it a lot harder to start studying for the captain's examination coming up in four months," she said out loud to the empty vista point. "But it put a really big crimp in the Castles."

Lieutenant Erin Wolff took one more look around, then slowly walked back to her car, sat in the driver's seat, and let her head sag down to her chest. She was tired, wet, and for the first time today, hungry.

Pulling her head up, she pressed it back against the soft headrest, closed her eyes, and put her mind in neutral. Her thoughts quickly drifted off and were soon doing a recap of the last couple of years. She'd been a lieutenant and the commander of the Crescent City CHP Area for almost two years. There were lots of great things about being the commander in a small rural county. She was her own boss, got to make lots of decisions regarding how to best utilize her personnel resources, and she had an opportunity to learn both the administrative and the political side of being a law enforcement manager. As the commander, she got to travel periodically to meetings which gave her experience interacting with other law enforcement agencies and other police administrators. The Highway Patrol gave her an unmarked car to drive, and the pay wasn't bad either. On the downside there were the personnel issues that went with the job, the need to discipline officers that screwed up, and the impossibly tight budgets she had to work with. And, there were the calls at 4:00 in the morning like she got today.

"Crap!" she yelled, the inside of her car reverberating the sharp loud sound in her ears. The one short loud yell made her feel better.

Her mind now focused, Red Wolff knew what she had to do. It was something she learned during her two years at the Air Force Academy, something her instructors had drummed into her about leadership during those twenty-mile physical conditioning hikes with a full rucksack, helmet, and rifle. Unknowingly, she broke out with one of her trademark half-smiles as she thought about those hikes in the woods and hills around Colorado Springs. At the time, she remembered thinking, this must be the only place in the world where you hike uphill going somewhere, and uphill going back.

She could still hear the instructor's voice as he yelled at the cadets, "If you're going to be the leader, then lead. If you can't lead, then follow. If you can't lead, and you don't want to follow, then get out of the way! It doesn't matter how tired you are, it doesn't matter how bad you're hurting. A leader's job is to ruck up, move out, and press on."

Ruck up, move out, and press on, she told herself.

CHAPTER SIX

Highway 101 was wet from the misty rain that continued to fall as a new storm front blew in from the west. Rivulets of water ran across the asphalt pavement in those locations where the roadway was banked against the curves in the road. Water soaked long boughs from the giant stands of redwood trees bordering the highway drooped over the road and dripped big splotches of water on the windshield of Red Wolff's vehicle as she headed north, back into Crescent City.

As she drove, her mind raced through a checklist of the things she had to do. Meet with the captain from the Critical Incident Response Team, check with the chaplain on the funeral arrangements, set up a meeting with the shooting team to get a preliminary report.

Then there were the people things she had to take care of. The whole Crescent City squad would be looking to her. That would mean a lot of one-on-one time with each member of her command. They would all handle the murder of the Castles a little different; some would become almost dysfunctional, while others would put up a brave front and soldier on. How she handled the next couple of days would be a test of her leadership ability, she knew.

Driving almost by rote as the highway twisted and curved northbound, her mind continued to reel off things yet to be done. As she reached the top of Crescent Hill and broke out of the redwood forest, the town of Crescent City lay below shrouded in a misty fog from the rain.

In the background she could hear the CHP radio as Humboldt Communications Center dispatched units on calls in Garberville and Eureka. For the most part she had been oblivious to the calls within the Crescent City area for the past several hours, figuring her sergeants would ensure units were covering everything.

"95-1, Humboldt, 95-1," the female communications operator's voice called.

Red Wolff drove and listened for the field unit assigned to the northernmost beat in the county that covered the unincorporated town of Smith River along Highway 101 to answer the call.

"95-1, Humboldt, 95-1," the comm-op called again.

After thirty seconds without a response from 95-1, she picked up the radio microphone in her vehicle. Pressing the red transmit button, she spoke into the mic, "Humboldt, 95-L."

"95-L, go ahead to Humboldt," came the reply.

"Humboldt, what call do you have for 95-1?" she inquired.

"95-L, an 11-82, two vehicles, blocking the roadway, southbound 101 at Ship Ashore," the comm-op related, her voice almost mechanical.

"10-4 Humboldt, 10-21 the office, contact S-1 and ascertain the status of 95-1," Red told her.

The comm-op acknowledged Red Wolff's instructions to call the CHP office via a landline phone, speak to the on-duty sergeant, and have the sergeant find out why the beat unit was not answering the radio.

She could visualize the call, a fender bender accident, with no injuries. Probably an out-of-towner traveling northbound who saw the unique looking restaurant and hotel next to the ocean built around the one hundred thirty-five foot long luxury yacht that had been towed onshore next to the highway in 1965 as a tourist attraction. More than likely the tourist decided at the last moment to make a left turn across the highway into the parking lot. The turn was probably made right in the path of a southbound vehicle. It happened all the time.

She also had a mental picture of why the patrol units weren't answering their radio calls. All the beat units were at the office, not out on the road. She'd seen it happen before. It was a natural reaction by the officers. One of their own, in this case, two of their own were dead. Dave and Jodie Castle had been their friends. They had shared danger together and worked together as partners. They felt a bond that was as strong as with any family member.

She'd been on the go since 4:00 in the morning, and she knew there was a long day ahead. Reaching the harbor and the city limits sign for Crescent City, she made a quick decision to grab a hamburger. The Burger King drive-thru at the split where the north and southbound lanes of 101 separated going through town, was the easiest. She ordered almost absentmindedly and was back on 101 within a couple of minutes. A Whopper Junior meal wasn't the greatest thing, but she ravenously devoured the burger and fries as she drove the last two miles to the office.

Pulling into the parking lot, she had to do a double take. There were at least twenty or thirty cars in the lot. People were carrying plates and covered dishes into the office front door and others were leaving. The whole office seemed abuzz with people. In the back lot of the CHP office, the area off-limits to the public, there were another twenty or so civilian cars, along with six black and white patrol cars.

She found a spot in the back lot to park and called Humboldt Communications Center to advise her location.

"Humboldt, 95-L is 10-19."

"95-L, Humboldt copies, at the office," the comm-op replied.

———

While Red Wolff was making her way from her vehicle to the back door of the CHP office, things were happening in Crescent City, around Del Norte County, and elsewhere in California, relating to the murders of Dave and Jodie Castle.

As horrifying, and tragic, as the crime was, the daily routine of most people went on as usual, unaffected. Parents picked their kids up from school, people kept their doctors appointments, went to work, or to buy groceries, and normal daily life for almost everyone went on without interruption.

Likewise, so did the routine police functions and duties of every law enforcement agency in the county. In the town of Crescent City, the two police department units on patrol answered calls, took crime reports, and wrote a few traffic citations. In the unincorporated portions of the county, sheriff's deputies did much the same as their police department counterparts. In the southern part of the county, the lone tribal police officer on patrol went about his normal routine, stopping to inspect the half-dozen salmon gill netted by a couple tribal members and talking about things happening along the Klamath River. Shifts changed, as they normally did at Pelican Bay State Prison, with several hundred correctional officers going on shift at 2:00, relieving those who started at 6:00 in the morning.

For a majority of the cops in Del Norte County, whether they were federal, state, or local, those cops who did the day-in and day-out police functions, the murder of the two Highway Patrol officers didn't change much in their daily routine. Yes, they'd be on the lookout for people, or vehicles, or events that didn't seem right, or that might relate to the murders. Each would each be a little more careful on their next vehicle stop, or when they responded to a call. A heightened sense of awareness always happened whenever one of their own was killed. That, of course, would fade away after a few weeks, and complacency would set back in, much the same way a driver would slow down for a couple miles after seeing an accident on the freeway, but go right back to driving too fast within a couple of minutes.

It wasn't, however, business as usual for everyone.

At his desk in the spacious corner office of the Del Norte County Sheriff's Department, Jerome Williamson sat staring out the large plate glass window toward the street below. The building's central heating system was pumping warm air into the office, and with his door closed, the smell of wet wool permeated the air from the drenching his expensive suit got while he was at the vista point. To top it off, his three hundred dollar Allen-Edmonds loafers were soaked, and they squished every time he took a step.

He was still fuming about being out maneuvered by that old CHP chief from Redding. His mind was racing on how he could put a positive spin for the media on not being the sole agency in the investigation. There was going to be nationwide press coverage on the murders of the two officers, and it was a chance for him to get the "face time" on television, and in the local paper, that would be invaluable if he had any prayer of being reelected.

Although the answer to his dilemma was there all the time, it took a while for him to figure it out. It suddenly flashed on him that he was thinking like he was still on LAPD, not in one of the most remote places in California. The Los Angeles Police Department was one of the largest police agencies in the nation. When a crime occurred that crossed jurisdictional boundaries or involved multiple agencies, LAPD was the proverbial six hundred pound gorilla. They just overwhelmed other agencies and assumed control. Here, however, he didn't have the resources or the personnel with the expertise to dominate the investigation. The solution was simple, "If you can't beat 'em, join 'em. They want a joint investigation, okay, I'll give them more than that," he said out loud while dialing the office intercom number for his undersheriff. There was a sly smile on his lips.

In less than five minutes he'd explained his plan to the undersheriff. "And I want them all here at 10:00 tomorrow for the news conference," he emphasized. Nodding that he understood, the undersheriff left to start calling all the newspapers and radio stations in the adjacent counties, and the two closest television stations, one in Medford, Oregon, the other in Eureka. Jerome Williamson's plan was in motion.

It's brilliant, even if I have to say so myself, Jerome Williamson thought. All he had to do now was contact the heads of the other law enforcement agencies and get them to buy into his plan. He knew, because all the public safety agencies were understaffed, a few agency heads would be reluctant to assign a person to the investigation for any length of time, but he also knew, none of them could refuse to participate because of the nature of the crime. Brilliant, he said to himself again as he picked up the phone to make his first call and leaned back in his chair.

Less than a half-mile from the Del Norte County Sheriff's Office, in the five by seven block downtown area of Crescent City that was the town's business district, U.S. Forest Service Senior Supervising Special Agent Andrew Dixon was in his office. His door was closed separating him from the main portion of the small office space leased by the Forest Service as their satellite office in Del Norte County. He was dressed casually, standard green Levi's, tan work shirt with Forest Service patches, and heavy lace up boots. He might have looked like any number of the other dozen or so Forest Service employees assigned to the Six Rivers National Forest had it not been for the .9 millimeter automatic in the holster on his hip and the badge clipped to his belt.

Unknowingly, he was straightening the items on his desk. His need for absolute order was almost a disease, as his hands moved things around. The phone directly aligned with the top right edge of the desk blotter, stapler and pencil holder precisely angled two inches from the phone, the pad of "post-it" notes placed even with the left corner of the top desk drawer, and his computer screen off-set from the key board six inches to the right. It was a ritual he went through almost every time he returned to the office before he could get down to work.

From outside his office, thanks to the paper thin walls, he could hear the voices of his two subordinate agents and the civilian secretary, as they talked loudly about the murders of the two Highway Patrol officers. He could also hear the irritating computer generated ring tone of the telephone as calls came in.

Andrew Dixon was not the world's most likable person. In fact, most of the people who worked for him disliked him immensely. He had a way of looking and talking to people that turned them off as soon as he met them.

Part of it was his attitude and mannerisms, his curt way of telling, rather than asking, his subordinates to do things. That way of working with people may have been well suited to law enforcement in his prior assignments at other national forests, but it was out of place and resented by the laid back type of people he was in charge of here. His subordinates found out quickly his management style left almost nothing open to discussion, and asking the question "why" would lead to a sharp rebuke, and the response, "Cause I'm the boss, that's why."

In his early forties, Andrew Dixon, other than having a shitty personality, could have been a poster boy to recruit people to a career with the Forest Service. He was tall, lean, and tan from years of hiking in the remote wilderness areas of the national forests where he worked. His sandy blond hair and piercing blue eyes gave him star quality good looks. He'd been a Forest Service cop for over twenty years, working his way up on the law enforcement side of the agency from clerk, to special agent, to supervising agent, to senior supervising agent. He wasn't really hot on the idea of transferring to Northern California, but the only opening for a newly promoted senior supervising agent was at the Six Rivers National Forest.

The position he promoted into eight months ago was newly created by the Forest Service. Normally each national forest had only a handful of special agents for an entire forest and maybe one supervising agent. For the most part national forest cops monitored the comings and goings in the forest, wrote a few citations for illegal campfires, and patrolled inside the boundaries of immense remote wilderness areas.

All that started to change last year when the first signs of large scale marijuana growing operations started to appear in the remote regions of the forest. The signs weren't hard to spot. The first tell-tale sign was a huge jump in sales of plastic pipe at local hardware stores. While marijuana was easy to grow, it was voracious in the amount of water it needed. PVC pipe, a doughboy pool, and a couple of battery operated pumps made it possible to irrigate huge hidden gardens in the remote hillsides of the wilderness area, far from the prying eyes of law enforcement, or a hiker who might unknowingly wander into a growing operation.

These weren't the little "mom and pop" operations run by '60s looking hippie escapees from Haight-Ashbury, but well financed, commercial farms, run by South American and Mexican drug cartels. Setting up growing operations in the Six Rivers National Forest was a natural expansion for the cartels. Law enforcement had tracked their movement northward from Mendocino and Humboldt counties over the last several years.

In the '80s and '90s these counties had been prime locations to grow Sinsemilla, the highly potent variety of marijuana with more psychoactive tetrahydracannabinal than the stems and seeds "shit" people smoked back during the "Summer of Love". At that time, most of the growing was done by small time operations run by a few local residents, or kids out to score a profit from four or five months work in the hills and forests. Law enforcement poured vast sums of money into eradication efforts, bringing in teams of officers to locate gardens, chop down the ten to fifteen foot tall plants, helicopters to hoist out the cuttings in slings, and then to burn the illegal crop.

It wasn't a game, but for the most part it wasn't deadly either. In the small time operations growers occasionally set traps to snare deer who found the tender buds to be a tasty treat, or set crude booby-traps to deter unwanted visitors from helping themselves. A few even armed themselves with pistols and rifles, but these were usually there to scare off campers and hikers who happened upon a garden.

Local growers knew when CAMP, the state Bureau of Narcotics Enforcement's, Campaign Against Marijuana Planting, was in town and simply stayed away from their gardens for a while. If they got raided, or "Camped on" as it was known in local jargon, it was the cost of doing business. There was always next year.

But, in the early part of the new century, marijuana growing took on a commercial and deadly bent. Drug cartels found it was easier, cheaper, and much more profitable, to cut out the cost and danger of trying to smuggle marijuana across the border from Mexico. They discovered the remote national forests of Northern California were ideal for their operations. For an investment of a few thousand dollars in equipment, by hiring illegals to tend the gardens, and by stationing a few trusted soldiers to guard their crop, they could reap enormous profits. It wasn't that easy, of course, some of their gardens still got raided by law enforcement and there was stiff competition from other cartel operations, but for the most part marijuana growing was producing huge payoffs.

The drug cartel operations might have gone on pretty much unimpeded by law enforcement had an overzealous soldier, guarding a remote four thousand plant garden the previous year, not opened fire on a trio of biologists who were conducting a survey of spawning trout in the Trinity National Forest. None of the unarmed biologists had been struck by the guard's rifle fire, but the damage had been done.

A joint federal, state, and local law enforcement task force swept into the area two days later. A federal Department of Alcohol, Tobacco, Firearms and Explosives special weapons and tactics team helicoptered in, and fast-lined down almost on top of the garden, while ground units set up a blocking formation to cut off the escape of the growers and guards as they ran. The operation netted five illegals from Mexico who had spent the last four months planting and tending the crop, living in tents, eating beans and deer meat. Three guards, one from Mexico and two from Columbia, were also arrested. Seven guns were confiscated, including two automatic weapons.

As a result of this incident, the Department of Agriculture made the decision to increase law enforcement presence in national forests both as a deterrent to marijuana growers and to protect its employees. It was this decision in Washington D.C. that brought newly promoted Andrew Dixon to the Six Rivers National Forest to be Senior Supervising Special Agent in charge of law enforcement eight months ago.

The sharp rapping sound on the flimsy hollow-core door to his office made him stop his compulsive straightening of the items on his desk, as the door opened.

"Excuse me sir, the district superintendent is on line one for you," his secretary said as she sheepishly stuck only her head through the door.

Looking up from the urgent task of rearranging his desk, he nodded, but didn't respond as she withdrew her head and closed the door.

One of Andrew Dixon's other slight character flaws was his dislike of women. It really didn't matter much to him whether they were pretty, or fat, dumb or smart. He disliked almost all of them.

This secretary he inherited was a classic. What a bimbo, he thought to himself. Asian-American, she was always dressed to the hilt, hair perfect, long painted nails, and a ton of rings on her fingers. She was okay at her job he guessed, but her demeanor was meek and she never said anything. He hated timid women.

But then, he hated strong women, also. His boss, the superintendent of the Six Rivers National Forest was such a woman, and now she was on the phone calling him.

He could picture her in her office eighty miles to the south in Eureka, at the headquarters for the entire national forest. She was a career U.S. Forest Service employee, a "tree-hugger", who started out as a wildlife biologist student intern while in college examining piles of bear shit in the forest to find out what they were eating. She'd parlayed her internship into a permanent civil service position with the Department of Agriculture and promoted her way up to become the superintendent for the entire million acre national forest.

Because the Six Rivers National Forest was so large and so remote, with parts of the forest in four different Northern California counties, there were satellite offices, like his, in each county. Each office was divided into two functions, forest operations and law enforcement. In the Del Norte County office, Andrew Dixon was in charge of law enforcement. His counterpart, in charge of forest operations, was another tree-hugger. Technically, his counterpart was in charge of all Forest Service operations in the county, and was, at least according to the organizational chart, his supervisor. But like most of the tree-huggers, he had less than a formidable personality. Just another career Forest Service employee, content to count fish and make sure there was toilet paper in the bathrooms. In practice, Andrew Dixon and his two subordinate agents, pretty much didn't answer to anyone and did their own thing.

Picking up the phone he answered the call, "Dixon," speaking curtly into the handset. He knew, of course, it was the superintendent, but his sense of maintaining the upper hand in his dealings with her meant he couldn't give her the courtesy of a greeting that acknowledged she was his boss.

"Andy, this is Joyce, what can you tell me about the two CHP officers who were killed up there, Washington is asking?" she queried.

"Well, superintendent, not much yet. Looks like it happened sometime early this morning. They don't have much to go on from what I can tell," he told her matter-of-factly.

"Any indication this may be drug related? Washington is concerned there may be a connection to marijuana growing in your area."

"We have some intelligence there are growers starting to show up in the area. Lots of plastic pipe being bought at the local hardware stores. They'll need to get their irrigation systems set up within the next month to be ready when the weather starts getting warmer in April to plant."

"Okay, offer whatever assistance you can spare to the locals, and keep me in the loop on the investigation. If this has anything to do with drugs I don't want Washington to find out about it from CNN," she told him, the tone in her voice letting him know, like it or not, she was still his boss.

Tree-huggers, he thought to himself, going back to straightening the items on his desk.

Another knock on the door and again his secretary's head appeared in the partially opened door. "Sir, Sheriff Williamson on line three," she said with that same sheepish tone in her voice.

"Afternoon, Jerry," he said picking up the receiver, his tone friendly and civil.

Their conversation only lasted a couple of minutes. "Sure, anything we can do to help, I'll be there at 10:00," he told the county sheriff as he ended the call.

It was almost 2:30, and he had things to do. Grabbing his green nylon windbreaker "callout" jacket with the words "Federal Officer" silk screened on the back and Forest Service patches silk screened on the sleeves, he shut down his computer, adjusted the screen one more time and left his office, closing the door behind him.

"I won't be back today," he told the secretary as he walked out, never glancing her way, or breaking stride.

"Yes sir," she replied in a voice so quiet she almost couldn't be heard.

Once he left the office, she got up from her desk and peered cautiously out the window to make sure he had driven away. Satisfied he was gone, she used her key to unlock his office.

She was far from a bimbo. In fact, she had a Master's Degree in sociology, an I.Q. over one-forty, and spoke fluent Japanese. Her husband was a psychologist at the prison, and they had moved to Del Norte County six years ago. With no kids at home, she took the job as a secretary with the Forest Service just for something to do. She'd come from a poor family and had grown up working on her dad's farm everyday planting seed, feeding chickens, and with dirt under her fingernails. The way she dressed, did her hair, and the jewelry she wore, were signs to herself that she had worked her way off the farm and out of poverty.

Without turning on the light, she made her way to his desk and started rearranging things, moving the computer screen a couple of inches to the left, putting the stapler next to his mouse pad, and folding up the feet on his computer keyboard.

"Pompous ass," she said out loud.

———

Sheriff Jerome Williamson's next call, after enlisting Andrew Dixon into his plan, was to the combined headquarters for the Redwood National and State Parks office located two blocks from the Forest Service office.

Before he made the call he had to get a refresher course from his undersheriff on how all these state and federal agencies interacted, and who had jurisdiction where. It was pretty confusing and he needed to have the undersheriff explain it to him a couple of times.

He ran it over in his mind one more time just to make sure he understood everything. There was the Forest Service, which was part of the U.S. Department of Agriculture. They had jurisdiction over the Six Rivers National Forest which encompassed over a million acres, most of it rugged mountainous areas. Then there was the National

Park Service, which was part of the federal Department of Interior. The park service ran the Redwood National Park, had their own administrative structure and their own cops. The really confusing part was that the Redwood National Park was almost entirely within the Jedediah Smith Redwoods California State Park. The state park had their own bureaucracy and state park rangers who were cops also.

Confident he had it clear, he dialed the number and asked to speak to Ranger Butler, the head cop for the National Park.

"Marv Butler here," came the upbeat voice over the receiver.

"Marrrvv," Jerome Williamson said, drawing out the name in much the same way patrons greeted Norm when he entered the bar on the old television comedy, *Cheers*.

"Jerry, you 'ole son-of-a-bitch, how are you?"

"Well, Marv, to tell you the truth, not so good. This deal with the two chippies getting killed is causing me some problems."

"How can I help?" Marvin Butler asked.

Marvin Butler and Jerome Williamson were drinking buddies. They'd met maybe six or seven months ago when Marvin Butler first moved to Del Norte County to take up his post as head law enforcement ranger at the Redwoods National Park. Since they were both single, they did a lot of eating out, especially at the Elk Valley Casino where food was less expensive than the many restaurants catering to the tourists along Highway 101.

Like in his conversation with Andrew Dixon, it only took a few minutes for the Sheriff of Del Norte County to enlist the support of his friend Marvin Butler and the resources of his agency into the plan.

"You can count on me," Marv Butler told his buddy, "I'm headed out of the office right now, but I'll be there in the morning. I'll make sure to tell my state parks counterpart to be there too."

If Andrew Dixon was the poster boy for the U.S. Forest Service and a big prick, Marvin Butler was the exact opposite.

Forty-five years old, he was just a little over five seven and had a middle-age paunch that hung over the top of his trousers. Easy going for the most part, he was well liked by all his subordinates and didn't get excited about much of anything. He had a round face and a pallor that was pale and washed out looking, causing him to burn, rather than tan, from all the time he spent outdoors. A curse of his Irish heritage he knew. He also had a nose that was beginning to exhibit permanent red lines caused by the blown out blood vessels on his face from his excessive drinking. Another gift from his ancestors.

His pack a day smoking habit, something he'd done since he was a kid, added to his ruddy complexion and gave his teeth a dull off-white color. He sported a neatly trimmed full beard, which he thought gave him a wise and trusted looking appearance, something, he believed, that completed his persona as an outdoorsman and head Law Enforcement Ranger. A lot of people in town thought he looked more like a Disney character without any fur.

Marvin Butler had been a National Park Service Ranger for about fifteen years. He'd gone to college on the east coast and actually started out as a police officer in a small town in Maryland. He had resigned after two years, telling the chief only that he was leaving for personal reasons. A year later, he took the federal civil service examination for National Park Ranger. His first assignment was to Yellowstone National Park in Montana. He'd spent a few years there, then inexplicably, he applied for, and was transferred to, the National Park at Mount Rainier in Washington State. His pattern was the same at this park, he did a good job, everyone liked him, but after a couple years he transferred again. His last assignment was to Yosemite in central California's Sierra Mountains where he stayed for nearly three years before promoting to become a Supervising Ranger at Redwoods National Park.

Being the head of law enforcement at the Redwood National Park, was a pretty easy gig. Similar to the Forest Service organizational structure, there was a superintendent who was in overall charge of the park and its two branches: Interpretation, and Law Enforcement. The Interpretation Rangers were the smiling fresh faces that greeted people as they entered the park, drove around in pickup trucks or SUVs making sure campers were safe, nobody was feeding the bears, and conducting wildlife tours. On Marv Butler's side of the operation he and one other Law Enforcement Ranger enforced rules, wrote citations inside the park, investigated whatever little crime there was, and made an occasional arrest.

Since it was only March and park operations were slow, he had time on his hands. The real influx of visitors wouldn't begin until the summer months, he knew. Marv Butler would be only too glad to help out the sheriff.

In the Century City District of Los Angles, near UCLA, in the western part of the city, Ross Glickner was having another of the hectic kind of days that were becoming normal. The bottom was falling out of the market for the fourth straight day. His big money clients were bailing by the dozens, taking millions of dollars in paper losses as they headed for anything that would stop the decimation of their portfolios. This was the worst he'd ever seen the financial markets. First, oil spikes at over a one hundred forty dollars a barrel, then four months later the mortgage crisis hits, the stock market goes into free-fall, and none of the rules of free market economics made sense anymore.

The wheels were coming off the investment company he'd founded nearly twenty years ago. Back then, everything he touched turned to gold. Well, paper gold anyway. He had more clients then he could handle. Hollywood stars, CEO's of companies, politicians, everyone wanted Ross Glickner to invest their money for them. Local trade journals and newspapers called him the "Broker to the Stars". Young and aggressive, Harvard educated, he was one of the new breed of money managers who took risks with their clients assets in order to make them big rewards. He'd made millions for all of them and a tidy sum for himself in the process.

The ride for the last twenty years had been heady, a house on the ocean in Malibu, a sixty foot yacht in Marina Del Rey, parties with the Hollywood elite, a vacation home in Bora Bora, new cars every year, and a beautiful wife.

She was gorgeous. Five years younger than him, she was slim, with shiny, auburn colored hair, and a smile so big, it somehow flashed not only her front teeth, but those halfway to the back of her mouth. And she was smart, witty, and just as hard working as he was.

Over the years, their marriage had survived its bumps and starts. Most of the time, any problems they had in their personal relationship, were directly related to fluctuations in the financial markets. But all-in-all, life was good. Then the financial crisis and recession of 2009 hit with a vengeance. Try as he might, Ross Glickner couldn't help but bring the job home with him. He was up late at night studying financial reports on the computer, watching CNBC to see how the international stock markets were performing, and then awake at 4:00 in the morning to get ready for the opening of the New York Stock Exchange at 6:30 west coast time.

It all started taking its toll on their relationship. Their fights weren't personal, but they were becoming more frequent. On Saturday she'd announced she was going to drive to Seattle to see her sister. Why not fly, he'd told her? No, she said, driving relaxes me, besides, her new BMW needed a good long drive.

She'd left Malibu early on Sunday morning, driving up the Pacific Coast Highway to Ventura, where she got on Highway 101 heading north. That night she called him from a hotel in the Napa

Valley, telling him she was fine, sipping on a very fine Merlot in her room. She would be heading out again the next morning, staying on 101 so she could see the redwoods, probably stopping in Grants Pass Monday night.

He hadn't heard from her on Monday night, and started to get a little worried. His calls to her cell phone all went to message. Then, by midday Tuesday, with still no contact, he was really concerned. Finding a map, he traced out her probable route up 101 from Napa. He started calling hospitals thinking she might have been in an accident. After three frustrating calls, his secretary stepped in. She made one call to the local Highway Patrol Communications Center.

Once his secretary explained the situation, the Highway Patrol operator began to check computer databases searching for the name Kim Glickner. Her first check was the CHP 144 database. Every person the CHP incarcerates, or who is hospitalized out of collision in Highway Patrol jurisdiction, has their name entered in this system. Since it's a statewide database, the operator in Los Angeles could view entries made from any location in the state. No, she told the secretary, nobody by that name was hospitalized out of a collision investigated by the CHP. The second system she checked contained information on any vehicle towed, stored, or impounded by any law enforcement agency in the state. Using the license plate number provided by the secretary, a statewide check did not show that Kim Glickner's vehicle had been stored or impounded. The entire call took less than three minutes.

It was only noon, Ross Glickner thought to himself. I know she hasn't been in an accident. Maybe her phone went dead, or she couldn't get a cell signal in remote Northern California. He decided to wait and see if she called tonight.

In the back of his mind, however, he had an uneasy feeling something had happened to her. He was tempted to call the police and report her missing, but he knew from watching cop programs on television, they wouldn't take a report until a person had been missing for seventy-two hours.

While Jerome Williamson kept personally phoning the heads of all the law enforcement agencies in the adjacent four counties, Red Wolff was making her way through the throng of people gathered at the Crescent City Highway Patrol Office. In the three plus years she had been assigned here, she had never seen the office this crowded. Besides the officers, sergeants and three civilians who worked in the command, there were more than a dozen officers' wives in the office, most sitting or standing in small groups, talking in hushed tones, or openly weeping.

At the front counter, ordinary citizens of the county were dropping by to express condolences, to make monetary contributions for a fund that had yet to be established, or to drop off food. Office Manager Lisa Johnston took the time to greet each person and thank them for coming by or for the food they brought. She also recorded every person's name and address with the intent of sending each a personal thank you letter from the area commander, Lieutenant Erin Wolff.

She made a big show of reverently taking each food item from the front counter to the back briefing room of the office, out of sight of the public. There, regardless of how good the items smelled, or how tempting they looked, the office janitor dumped them in the trash. Probably one hundred percent of the food being dropped off by the public was safe to eat, but cops are a suspicious lot, and eating food from an unknown source, even in a place like Crescent City, just wasn't done.

Except for the last three years, Red Wolff had spent most of her twenty year career in Los Angeles. Lots of cops had been killed in the line of duty while she worked there, but she'd never seen a response like this. It took her a second to put it in perspective. This wasn't Los Angeles, this was small town, rural California. The Castles weren't just cops to these people, they were family.

In one corner of the briefing room she saw Ray Silva standing with Julie and Mary Jean. Between the handshakes of condolence, the tears, the hugs from her officers and their wives, and the time she took to talk to each person, it took her nearly fifteen minutes to make it the twenty feet to where they stood.

Mary Jean's eyes were red from crying and streaks from the dried tears were visible on her cheeks.

"Hi Hon, how you holding up?" she asked, wrapping her arms around Red.

"Okay for now," she responded, her eyes surveying the crowd in the room. "Still have a crap-pot full of things to do. How was the drive up?"

"Long and rainy the whole way. What can Julie and I do to help?"

"For now I've got to talk with a bunch of people, can you stay a while and help out with all these folks? I'd like to start easing them out so we can get moving on other things."

"Sure, we'll stay as long as you need us," Mary Jean assured her.

Red made eye contact with Ray Silva and gave him a slight head nod indicating she wanted to talk to him alone.

As she turned to walk away Mary Jean called to her, "Erin, I love you."

"Thanks, I needed that," Erin Wolff smiled as she headed toward the sergeant's office.

Designed for two desks, a side table, and a couple of chairs, the sergeant's office felt crowded when it contained four people. Today there were ten in the small space.

Spotting Captain Steffani Taylor, leader of the Critical Incident Response Team, she slid her way past several people until they stood side-by-side.

"Thanks for coming, Steff," Red said to her friend.

Steffani Taylor had not seen Red come into the room, and when she realized who had spoken to her, she was a little startled. "Erin!" she exclaimed, while simultaneously wrapping her arms around her.

Captain Steffani Taylor had a couple more years on the job than Red Wolff. Her career track had taken her to the Bay Area after graduating from the academy. She had spent her entire time in and around San Francisco until she promoted to Captain and was assigned to headquarters in Sacramento. Although they had never worked together, they were fast friends. Like Erin Wolff, Steffani Taylor was gay.

Being a gay female on the Highway Patrol wasn't any big deal at the end of the first decade of the new century. Going back twenty-five years, however, it was a huge deal, especially when management turned a blind eye to the discrimination directed toward all female officers, and even more so against gay females.

Back in the late '80s, when there were still fewer than two hundred female officers out of a workforce of over sixty-five hundred, Steffani Taylor and Erin Wolff had been pioneers among the few gay females. With computers and e-mail still a couple years away, they, and a few other gay officers, established a communications network to keep each other in the loop regarding things going on around the state, who was getting a special assignment or a promotion, and events involving their gay counterparts.

Even though they worked in different parts of the state, they kept in constant contact via phone, and once e-mail became available to everybody, their network took on the ability to instantaneously notify everyone statewide of anything that involved a gay female officer.

"Red, I'm so sorry for the two officers. I'm sorry for you too, I know you were headed out on your honeymoon."

"Thanks Steff, I'll get by. How are things going with notifications, funeral arrangements, and counseling for my people?"

"Under control. Two of my other chaplains have contacted the parents, and they're being taken care of. I've got one of the best traumatic incident psychologists in California enroute. She'll be here tonight and will start working with your people tomorrow. How are you holding up?"

"I'll be better when we catch the bastard who did this. How are the funeral plans going?" Red asked.

"It's a little early yet on funeral arrangements. I was waiting for you to see if they have letters in their field files," Steffani Taylor told her friend.

"I've already had that checked. They've both got letters," Red responded.

The "letter" Erin Wolff and Steffani Taylor were discussing was something a lot of officers had done. It was kind of a combination short form will, funeral instructions, information on insurance policies, and anything else the officers wanted to convey to their spouses or families immediately after their unexpected line-of-duty death. Typically, such letters addressed things like burial or cremation, church service or not, the type of music they wanted. Having a letter was strictly optional, and it was kept in the officer's personnel file for ease of locating in the hours and days immediately following their death.

They made their way to Red's office where two white, letter-sized envelopes sat, unopened, in the middle of the desk. On both envelopes, handwritten, were the words "Personal – Open in case of my death".

At Pelican Bay State Prison, six miles north of Crescent City, Correctional Captain Nathan Steadman walked into the lobby of the warden's office. He was in a foul mood, and his mannerisms displayed his displeasure at being summoned to this place. The secretary told him to have a seat, the warden was in another meeting and would be with him directly. Being made to wait only added to his irritation.

Nathan Steadman was a big man. Over six feet six inches tall, he was almost all muscle, with huge arms and shoulders, and a narrow waist. His square shaped head was flat on the top, not egged shaped like many men, and he kept it shaved bald, adding to his ominous appearance. His light brown skin had a sheen that glistened constantly, and his deep set eyes gave him a look that said, "Don't fuck with me".

Nate Steadman wasn't a handsome black man. In fact, he was downright scary looking.

Being big, muscular, and scary looking was ideal for his job as a corrections captain, dealing with inmates day-in and day-out. They didn't try to run games on him, to double-talk him with jail house logic, or try to intimidate him with "stare-downs".

While being big, muscular, and scary looking was ideal for working in a prison, when you added *black* to that physical description, the dynamics changed considerably, especially when it came to white women. That fact had come home to him fifteen years ago while attending a conference in San Diego. On the first night of the two-day conference, he was riding the elevator down from his fourteenth story room, on his way to join several other officers for dinner, when the elevator stopped at the ninth floor. He was alone in the elevator car, and when the door automatically opened, there stood a young blond woman. She was in her early thirties, dressed in business attire, probably headed for dinner also. As the doors opened, she reflexively took a couple steps forward, then looked up to see the sole occupant of the elevator was an enormous black man. She froze in place after seeing him, paused for less than a second, then abruptly turned and walked rapidly away, down the hall and back toward her room.

The event had hurt him deeply then, and it continued to hurt him every time he saw an attractive, well-to-do looking, white woman. It wasn't the kind of thing you shook off easily. Cops weren't the only ones who did racial profiling.

Most people thought Nate Steadman was a nice guy. He was good at his job, kept mostly to himself, and didn't draw a lot of attention to his activities. You wouldn't have known it to look at him, but he possessed a Master's Degree in Public Administration, was a world class chess player, and loved Italian opera.

As an extremely shy person, he valued his privacy and had only a handful of people he called friend, none of them in Crescent City, or among the people he worked with at Pelican Bay State Prison. His idea of a great time was listening to Puccini's *Madama Butterfly* and sipping very expensive single malt scotch. He just didn't like doing those things in this God forsaken place.

Almost forty-five, Nate Steadman had nearly twenty years with the California Department of Corrections and Rehabilitation. He'd started out as a corrections officer a couple years after getting his Bachelor's Degree.

After college he had spent several years drifting from job-to-job, looking for something that interested him. He was twenty-five when he made his way to San Francisco, a couple hundred bucks in his pocket, and looking for a job. Entering the labor market in the early '90s, however, was a tough deal. California was in the throes of a mild recession. Good paying private sector jobs were hard to come by, Silicon Valley firms were laying off hundreds of people, and the bloom was coming off California's rose.

Not every industry though was suffering. California was in the midst of a massive campaign to build a dozen new prisons. With nearly a thousand corrections officers at each prison, there were plenty of job opportunities. He took the state civil service test for corrections officer, and after the training academy, found himself working inside San Quentin Prison.

On the north side of the Golden Gate Bridge, San Quentin was one of the oldest of California's thirty-three prisons. In addition to housing California's "Death Row", the inmate population was a mixture of medium and high risk prisoners making it an always dangerous place to work. The work wasn't all that hard, and he soon found it less than challenging. But, it was close to his home in Richmond, there was lots of stuff for a single guy to do off-duty, plenty of overtime, and he could work whatever shift he liked. It also gave him the ability to go back to college and earn his graduate degree.

After six years as a corrections officer, he began taking promotional tests working his way up through sergeant and lieutenant to his current rank of captain.

When California went on its prison building campaign in the late '80s and early '90s, it almost immediately hit a brick wall. The places the Department of Corrections wanted to build prisons, in the suburbs of metropolitan areas, close to the big population counties, with convenient transportation links, and medical services, didn't want them in their communities.

Conversely, small counties, mostly in rural Northern California, or the arid San Joaquin Valley, racked by high unemployment and a non-existent tax base, lobbied their legislators to have a prison constructed in their jurisdiction. Prisons meant construction industry jobs, hundreds of well-paid corrections officers, doctors, prison support staff, more lawyers for the court system, and state financing of new roads. There were downsides, of course, as lots of inmate spouses and their kids would move into the county so they could be close to their husbands. But all-in-all, prisons were a financial windfall for rural counties

Nate Steadman's first assignment as a new sergeant was to Pleasant Valley State Prison. The name was a misnomer. Located in the foothills of the California Coastal Mountain Range that separates the interior central valley from the coast, almost in the geographical north-south middle of the state, it was hot and dry, near the tiny farming community of Coalinga. Miles from anywhere, it was horrid duty.

He spent his time at Pleasant Valley and transferred back to San Quentin as soon as he had the seniority. Four years later he promoted again, and luckily, was able secure a lieutenant's position at that institution which meant he didn't have to move, again.

He wasn't as lucky when six years later he promoted to captain. Pelican Bay State Prison was about as far from anywhere and anything he liked to do, as you could get. Nate Steadman preferred the twenty-four hour a day lifestyle of the big city. There were clubs, world class entertainment events, sports, and fine restaurants. None of those things existed in Crescent City.

There was one other thing Del Norte County didn't have, it didn't have a lot of black people. It wasn't that he didn't like white people. Some of his best friends were white. He got along fine with just about all the white people he worked with and those in the community also. And, they seemed to like him, too. It was just that there were times when he longed for a jazz club in Oakland, or a good barbeque joint that served Kansas City style short ribs. But most of all, he missed the social interaction with what he thought of as his own kind of people.

In the late '80s, when construction began on Pelican Bay Prison, out of a population of nearly twenty thousand, there were exactly six black people in Del Norte County. Those numbers had, of course, changed over the past twenty years, mostly because there were a fair number of black corrections officers at the prison, and lots of black inmate's families had moved to the area. But even now the county's black population was still less than a thousand.

Even so, he was a captain, and as in any paramilitary organization, he couldn't socialize with officers, black, white, or Hispanic. He was management, and they were what the collective bargaining agreements called "rank and file". Pelican Bay was a lonely assignment for a single black man.

"Captain, the warden will see you now," the secretary told him.

He'd been in the warden's office nearly a hundred times during his assignment to Pelican Bay. As captain in charge of the reception and release centers at the prison, he had responsibility for the daily intake operations for new prisoners, and for those being released on parole. Anytime there were problems at the prison, he'd get called by the warden. He had no idea why he had been summoned to the warden's office today.

The warden's office was huge, intentionally so. With wood paneling that went from the floor to the ceiling, it had several large built-in bookcases all with neatly arranged volumes of legal books, California government codes, and Department of Correction's regulations. The massive wood desk sat in front of a plate glass window overlooking one of the inmate housing pods. It all combined to give the office, and its occupant, an intimidating aura. Behind the desk, studiously reading a document, sat the warden.

Of the four wardens Nate Steadman had served under while at Pelican Bay, he liked this one the least. As a Level IV prison, Pelican Bay housed some of the worst and most violent inmates in the entire California prison system. There had been on-going problems over the past three years, several race riots between black and Hispanic gangs, dozens of stabbings, and two inmates shot by tower guards. Each of these events saw a new warden appointed in an attempt to bring stability to the institution. The current warden had been appointed less than a year ago.

Wardens are Governor's appointees. While most come from within the Department of Corrections, not all have a corrections background. Some, like this one, had never been a corrections officer, never worked inside the walls, never had a cup full of inmate piss thrown in his face, or had a prisoner try to stick a five inch piece of sharpened metal from a bed frame in his back. This one had been a civilian administrator, starting off as an analyst at the Chino State Prison in Southern California, where he had been in charge of ordering supplies. Over the years, he'd worked his way up to manager of human resources at Mule Creek Prison in the Sierra foothills near Sacramento, and eventually to associate warden at Folsom. To Nate Steadman, he seemed an unlikely choice to be warden.

Somewhere north of forty years old, he was pretentious with subordinates, had thinning hair, a sallow complexion, and little black hairs growing from his nostrils. He was also a smoker. There were about a dozen state regulations, plus Department of Correction's policies, that prohibited smoking inside buildings owned by the State of California. He ignored them, his office reeking of stale smoke. White people, Nate Steadman thought to himself.

"Good afternoon captain," the warden spoke, looking at him over the top of his wire framed glasses. "I just got off the phone with the county sheriff. He is asking for our help with the investigation into the murder of the two CHP officers. Did we have any releases yesterday?"

Typical of his management style, he didn't ask Nate Steadman to have a seat.

"Five yesterday, warden. I'd have to check on exactly where they were paroled to," he responded.

"Do that, and let me know. Then, I want you to be at the sheriff's station tomorrow at 10:00. Lend him any support we can, and keep me advised of the status of the investigation. I'll be leaving shortly and won't be back today. You have my cell phone number. Call me when you find out about the ones released yesterday."

And just that quickly, his meeting with the warden was concluded. "White people," he mumbled as he left the office.

———————

"95-3, Humboldt," the radio called.

On patrol, although his heart wasn't in it, the officer assigned to the fifty mile long beat covering Highway 199 from the intersection with Highway 101 to the Oregon border, picked up the mic inside the patrol car. "Humboldt, 95-3, northbound at Patrick's Creek."

"95-3, assist Cal-Trans with a vehicle blocking the entrance to the maintenance station two miles south of Gasket," the far away voice dispatched him to a call.

Acknowledging the call, the officer looked for a place to turn around and began the twenty-five minute drive back south toward the small hamlet of Gasquet.

While the Highway Patrol's job was to enforce the law on state highways, the job of Cal-Trans, the state highway department, was to keep them repaired and open. Both agencies worked together and typical of a small town, everybody knew each other.

"Humboldt, 95-3, 10-97," the officer called as he arrived at the chain link fenced maintenance area where Cal-Trans had strategically placed bulldozers, skip loaders, and other heavy duty equipment used to move boulders and clear mudslides off the highway. It was one of three such stations along Highway 199.

Pulling into the short tree lined dirt driveway, the officer could see an orange, well-used, Cal-Trans pickup truck pulled as far to the right side of the road as possible, and a late model, silver-blue BMW parked blocking the entrance gate to the yard.

Dressed in blue jeans and an orange shirt, the officer recognized the sole Cal-Trans worker. Their kids had gone to school together for the last six years.

"Hi Darryl, you get tired of leaning on your shovel?" the officer chided him as he exited his patrol car.

"What took you so long? You have to stop to get another doughnut?" the highway worker shot back, a big grin on his face.

They shook hands and then the Cal-Trans employee got a deadly serious look, "I'm really sorry about your two officers. It was Dave and Jodie wasn't it?"

"Yeah, it was."

"Any clue on who did it?" the orange-shirted man asked.

"Nothing yet, we brought in a special team of investigators, they'll get whoever did it," the officer replied. "So what's up with this car?"

"Don't know. I came by to get a skip loader to move some rocks off the shoulder back near South Fork. The car was just sitting here. I looked around for the driver. At first I thought maybe somebody was taking a hike, or stopped to get a few pictures. But there's nobody around, and the car looks like it has been here a long time. The windows down, keys in the ignition," he told the officer.

Approaching the car, the officer saw the exterior was wet, and the open driver's window had allowed the rain to drench the seat. He also noticed the glove compartment was open, and a small pile of paper had fallen to the floorboard. Pretty odd the officer thought to himself, an expensive car like a "Beamer" abandoned in a remote place like this.

He did a walk-around of the car's exterior, but didn't see anything out of the ordinary. There were no signs the vehicle had been in an accident and the hood was cold to the touch indicating the engine hadn't run in hours.

Back in his patrol car, the officer sat behind the wheel and rotated the in-car laptop computer toward him. Punching up the screen for the Stolen Vehicle System, he typed in the BMW's license plate number. It took the system three seconds to respond and tell him the vehicle was not stolen.

Out of his patrol vehicle again, he had a brief conversation with his Cal-Trans friend then keyed the microphone clipped to the lapel of his uniform shirt that connected to the radio on his Sam Browne belt. "Humboldt, 95-3, 11-85 for storage," he said, his head cocked to the left to speak into the mic as he requested the comm-op to dispatch a tow truck to his location to store the abandoned vehicle.

Dutifully the comm-op checked the list of privately owned tow truck companies approved to do business with the Highway Patrol in the county and called the next one up on the rotation list.

"95-3, 10-39 to Smith River Garage, ETA twenty," the radio blared, the comm-op telling the officer a tow company had been contacted and would be there in twenty minutes.

With clipboard in hand, the officer returned to the BMW and began to complete the required form to document the specifics on the vehicle. He first did an inventory of the interior of the vehicle, then popped open the trunk. It took him a couple minutes to inventory the contents of the two fashionable suitcases, noting it was all expensive looking women's clothing and make-up. He then went back to his patrol car and again used the mobile digital computer terminal to do a registration check on the Beamer. Within a few seconds the registered owner information flashed on the screen, courtesy of the Department of Motor Vehicles database in Sacramento. Mechanically the officer recorded the information on the storage form.

A Malibu address, pretty ritzy location, the officer thought to himself, as he finished completing the form. Found where it was, with the driver's window down and the keys in the ignition, it was more than likely an unreported stolen that had been dumped at this location, the officer surmised.

The officer knew the comm-op would input his storage of the vehicle into the statewide and national databases. If it wasn't stolen, when the owner started looking for his vehicle, it would show up in the system as having been towed and stored by the CHP in Crescent City. If it did get reported stolen, the same computer system would show where, when, and by whom it was stored.

Twenty minutes later the flatbed tow truck arrived, the driver signed the officer's storage form and received the carbon copy.

"Humboldt, 95-3, vehicle removed, 10-98," the officer reported himself clear of the assignment.

It was almost 2:30 when he completed storing the vehicle, time to head back to the office for end of shift. He'd turn in the storage form with the rest of his daily paperwork. From there, within forty-eight hours, as required by law, Lisa Johnston, the office manager, would send a letter to the registered owner telling them their vehicle had been stored.

By 4:30 the flow of people dropping by the CHP office had all but stopped, and most of the wives and families had left, also. Still, about half the officers who were off-duty hung around, waiting for news, or trying to find some way to help. There wasn't much they could actually do, but being there at the office made them feel better than sitting at home. Most of these officers would head out soon anyway. It had been a long day for them, and some had to work that night or the next morning. At 5:00, Lisa Johnston locked the glass front door and closed the louvers on the mini-blinds.

In her small office, Red Wolff, Ray Silva, and Vaughn O'Dell sat listening to a debriefing from the shooting team investigators and the Del Norte County Sheriff's detective. They didn't have a lot to report. The sergeant gave them a short version of the autopsy, and one of the officers ran down a list of physical evidence they had collected at the scene. There wasn't much. Some partial tire tracks, a book of matches from the local casino, several soggy and crushed cigarette butts, all different brands, and the strands of hair found imbedded in the cliffside. As anticipated, the SUV patrol vehicle had not yielded any fingerprints. The officers' uniforms and the spent bullets removed from their bodies had been driven to the crime lab in Eureka for analysis. Normally it would take three or four days for the analysis to be completed, but Vaughn O'Dell had made a couple calls and the technicians would work on them that evening. Still, it would be late tomorrow afternoon before the results were ready. All-in-all, despite their best efforts, they didn't have much to go on.

Ray Silva joined the conversation telling the group he had contacted several of his local information sources to see what the buzz was on the street about the murders. He didn't call them "snitches" because they weren't. Most of them did have criminal records, and he had arrested a lot of them over the years, but just as often he'd let them go for minor offenses. They paid him back with little tidbits of information on who was doing what, or with other information regarding serious crime in the county. There was nothing being talked about on the street, he told the people in the office.

The conversation then turned to speculation about how two seasoned and safety conscious officers like the Castles could have been overpowered and basically executed.

"Davy was too good a "Highwayman" to let someone surprise him with a gun," Ray Silva began the conversation. "And Jodie was one tough lady. You could cut off both her arms, and she'd still try and kick you to death," he added.

"So why did Davy have to go for his hide-away piece instead of his service pistol? Remember, we didn't find his weapon," the shooting team lieutenant asked.

"Do you think they may have stopped or come upon a "Pipeline" car?" Vaughn O'Dell threw out to the group.

"What's pipeline?" the sheriff's detective asked, a quizzical look on his face at the unfamiliar term.

"We know a lot of meth gets cooked in the back country around here and Southern Oregon. Because everything is so remote, bad guys can rent a small house in the hills, bring in the chemicals they need, cook for three or four weeks, and manufacture a half-million dollars worth of Methamphetamine. Then they transport the stuff south to San Francisco or L.A. in cars. The highway is the pipeline," the shooting team lieutenant explained.

"Yeah, but all my people, including Davy and Jodie, were pipeline trained. They knew the things to look for, the indicators of a mule," Red stated.

"What indicators?" the detective asked, "This is all new to me."

"Pipeline is a nationwide drug interdiction program. Most state police and highway patrol officers are trained to recognize indicators of people running drugs. There are tell-tale signs of a mule carrying a load of drugs. Certain types of cars, with big doors, that have a lot of empty space in the door panels where you can hide packages of drugs. Then there are the people who don't fit the car they're driving. How often do you see a young person driving a big family sedan, or an out-of-state car with no suitcases? You add all these little indicators up and it gives you enough probable cause to check out the vehicle," the lieutenant explained.

"You mean profiling," the Del Norte detective stated.

"We like to think of it as good police work," Vaughn O'Dell told him.

"We've recently picked up some intelligence the drug runners are starting to operate in two or three vehicle caravans. A lead car to scout the way and look for cops on the highway, the mule vehicle in the middle, and a tail car a mile or so behind carrying guys with guns. As we get better at intercepting their drugs, they're becoming more violent and more prone to shoot cops who stop the mule car," the lieutenant finished his explanation.

"So what you're saying is the murders might be related to drug smuggling?" the detective questioned.

"Let's not lock ourselves into any one theory," the shooting team lieutenant interrupted. "This could be drug related, or maybe they stopped somebody who just committed another crime. They may have been trying to arrest somebody and a struggle ensued, somebody who didn't want to go back to jail."

"Well, we can speculate all night. For now, we need some good investigative work and a couple lucky breaks to solve this," Red Wolff said, closing the conversation.

"Right," Vaughn O'Dell added. "Let's keep digging, keep our minds and options open, and find the bastards who did this."

The meeting broke up with everyone heading off to accomplish other things. Vaughn O'Dell continued to talk with Red in her office.

There were still nearly two dozen people in the office. Coming from other parts of the closed office she could hear the voices of the shooting team officers as they discussed their investigation and Captain Steffani Taylor as she talked to somebody in Sacramento on the phone. She also picked up the sound of the private telephone line ringing and could see the flashing light on her desk phone.

Every Highway Patrol office has telephones lines which are published in phone directories for public use which are answered Monday through Friday, during normal 8 to 5 business hours. After hours, a recorded message tells callers to dial 9-1-1 for emergencies, or to call the nearest CHP Communications Center. For internal business and after-hours communications, every office also has an unpublished private phone number. That number is used by officers to call in and talk to a supervisor, by other police agencies to communicate with the Highway Patrol after-hours, and for spouses to contact each other.

"Excuse me lieutenant, Sheriff Williamson on the private line for you," Lisa Johnston, standing in the open door to the commander's office told Red Wolff.

"Thanks Leece," Red replied, using the short form of her office manager's name. As Lisa Johnston turned to go, Red called to her. "Lisa, it's getting late, nothing more you can do tonight, get yourself out of here."

"Okay lieutenant, I will," she replied, heading to her desk and going back to work on the mound of paperwork piled there.

"Evening sheriff," she spoke into the handset.

Vaughn O'Dell couldn't hear the conversation between the two, but he could tell by the expression on Red Wolff's face and the things she was saying, it wasn't good.

"Okay, let me discuss it with my chief, and I'll get back to you," Red said ending the conversation.

"So what's he up to now?" Vaughn asked.

"He's called a press conference for tomorrow at 10:00 to give a status report on the investigation and to announce he's forming a multi-agency task force to investigate the murders of our officers. He's already asked the heads of all the law enforcement agencies in the four county area to assist in the investigation and to be present tomorrow for the news conference," Red told him shaking her head.

"This guy's a real wingnut," Vaughn responded, also shaking his head. "But, I've pushed this joint investigation thing as far as I can. Ultimately it's still his jurisdiction and his investigation. Let's go with it for now and see what happens. I don't think having more people working on this will hurt."

"Okay Boss, but if I end up killing this guy, you'll know why."

"Red, it's after 6:30, time to take your own advice and go home. I'll stay and ramrod here for a couple more hours. If anything breaks, we'll call you."

Red Wolff wanted to argue with him. It didn't seem right to leave when the murder of her officers was unsolved, and other people were going to stay and keep working.

Vaughn O'Dell read her mind, he'd been in the same situation before and knew what she was thinking and feeling. "Look, you're the commander here, not a worker bee. You need to stay up on the bridge steering the ship, not down in the engine room tinkering with the motors. There are people to handle that. Go home! And take that old mossback, Ray Silva, with you."

———

It was just before 8:00 that night when Ray Silva walked in the front door of his home. The interior was comfortably warm, the woodstove radiating heat through the entire house.

The former Julie Bradley, now Julie Silva, his bride of less than three days, met him at the door with a kiss. At fifty-seven, and a successful businesswoman, she wasn't the type to play the "good little wifey" when her man came home. Tonight was an exception, and after the greeting at the door, she retreated to the kitchen to fix him a drink.

"Happy honeymoon," he told her, as he touched his bourbon and water to the glass of Chardonnay she held.

"Don't worry about it Ray, they'll be other times," she told him.

"Well, time is not on our side, and I owe Jodie Castle," he said somberly.

"We'll make the best of the time we have," she smiled, wrapping her arms around him.

A half-mile away Mary Jean Snider-Wolff was serving the dinner she'd prepared for her new spouse. From her time as a navy helicopter pilot, she knew the importance of hot food to people who worked long hours in stressful jobs. She'd done a combat tour aboard the nuclear aircraft carrier *U.S.S. Abraham Lincoln* and had been amazed at how ordinary eighteen and nineteen year old American kids performed hour-after-hour, day-after-day, during flight operations, in one of the most dangerous working environments in the world. Plenty of hot food had a lot to do with their performance, she knew. Thinking about it made her leg throb. It had been during that tour, she recalled, that her helicopter had been shot down over Kuwait during the first Gulf War while she was on a rescue mission. Her resulting injuries had forced to her medically retire from the navy.

"You went to way too much trouble," Red told her, as she ravenously dug into the chicken stir-fry with snow peas and white rice.

"Just eat, then head upstairs and take a hot shower," Mary Jean instructed.

Five minutes later Red was standing under a stream of nearly scalding water. The warmth began to ease the muscles in her back and shoulders. She'd not realized just how knotted up she was until the tension started flowing from her back.

While Red was in the shower, Mary Jean had quickly done the dishes, threw three more seasoned oak logs in the woodstove, and slipped upstairs. The light from a dozen or so scented candles bathed the bedroom in flickering soft lights, and the warmth from the stove overpowered the cold from outside.

She turned back the bed and slipped out of her clothes, pausing for a second to look at herself in the free-standing mirror in the corner of the bedroom. At forty-six, she still had a fairly good figure, and she'd been religious about working out to lose all the weight she had gained while pregnant with little Raymond. Her eye caught the ugly scar just above her right hip. It was a constant reminder of where a round from an M-16 had wounded her when she and Julie had been taken hostage two years ago during the terrorist's attempt to capture Crescent City. She'd survived the surgery okay, but somehow the scar from the through-and-through round embarrassed her.

Red came out of the shower wrapped in a damp towel and headed straight for the bed.

"Wow, this is really romantic. Not as romantic as I planned in Cabo for our honeymoon, but still," she said, leaving her thought unfinished.

"Lie down, I'll give you a neck massage," Mary Jean told her.

Stripping off the towel, Red gave it a heave back toward the bathroom and stood naked at the side of the bed for a moment.

Mary Jean looked up from her position in the middle of the bed, admiring her new spouse's figure. "Not bad for an old married woman," she said with a smile.

"The operable word being old," Red responded, climbing into bed and turning face down.

Mary Jean's fingers worked methodically, unlocking the tautly stretched tendons in Red's neck and upper shoulders. Minutes later she could hear the soft, rhythmic sounds of her breathing. She was fast asleep.

Internally, Mary Jean smiled to herself before slowly rolling out of bed to extinguish the candles.

Tired as she was and as much as her body craved sleep, Red Wolff's brain would not shut down. In a fitful half-sleep, she tossed and turned continually, images of the two dead officers flashing constantly in her mind.

CHAPTER SEVEN

Red Wolff was not the only one having a fitful night. Less than two miles away from the home of the Crescent City CHP commander, he was curled into the fetal position, wide awake, the crisp new sheets, and a heavy blanket pulled up to his neck against the cold.

He'd had a tough day. He couldn't remember if he'd slept the previous night, and he had a difficult time all day long staying focused at work. Each time the phone rang he jumped, and when someone knocked on the door to his office, he expected the police to rush in and arrest him. In between the conversations he was having with himself and the constant worked related interruptions, he was trying to piece together what happened the previous evening.

The streaming video in his mind wasn't playing what transpired at the vista point in sequential order. A brief snippet of the CHP vehicle stopping, panic, washing his car in the rain when he got home, the loud report of his pistol as he fired, a bright flash, hiding his bloody clothes, screaming, dumping the visquine wrapped body, everything was blurred. He willed himself to remember.

The first scenes to come clear in his mind were those when he returned home early that morning.

He wasn't quite sure how he had made his way back home, or how long it had taken before he had turned down the long driveway leading from the street to his garage. He remembered glancing at the digital display on his vehicle's clock radio, noting the time was just before 2:30, and that it was raining harder. The wind had picked up he recalled, causing the long branches of the redwood trees around his house to dance crazily in all directions. He had stopped his vehicle on the gravel driveway just in front of the garage door, killed the engine, turned off the lights, and got out. The video in his mind of the previous night was clearer now.

The first thing he did was take off his new cheap tennis shoes, then the new jeans and sweat shirt. He left them in a heap next to the driver's door.

With only whatever light the dark and overcast sky provided, naked and barefoot, he stumbled and felt his way to the side of the garage. He limped as he walked, his right foot throbbing with each step.

He found the garden hose coiled on the plastic holder mounted to the side of the garage and turned the spigot on about halfway. The wind and the rain were chilly enough, but now he felt the icy shock from the cold water as he sprayed himself off. Lying in bed he winced and shuttered as his mind recalled the frigid water from the previous evening.

The female officer's blood was caked on his hands and had splattered back onto his face and clothes. He worked methodically first rubbing his wet hands together to loosen the blood before rinsing it off with the hose. Once his hands were clean, he held the hose over his head with one hand and used the other to scrub his hair, face, and neck.

Satisfied he was as clean as he could get, given the lack of light, he returned to the pile of clothes. Shivering from the cold, his hands had difficulty fishing the house keys out of the blue jeans pocket. Once he located them, he carefully made his way to the side door of the garage.

He had not dared to open the roll-up entry door knowing it would activate the light on the automatic garage door opener. Even though it was the middle of the night and his house was not visible to his neighbors because of the trees and brush, opening the door would have sent out a bright beacon to anyone who might be up at that time of the morning bringing him unwanted attention.

Once in the garage, he closed the side door and flipped on the overhead fluorescent lights. Since the garage had no windows, he felt pretty secure. Grabbing a towel out of the rag bin, he dried himself off, then inspected it. A few pinkish smears were visible. He dropped the towel by the door so he would remember to pick it up later.

Looking around the garage, he spotted his old yellow rain pants and hooded jacket. Still naked, he put them on, then slipped on the rubber muck boots from the shelf where the rest of his work shoes were stored.

He was remembering now, and the events of last night were becoming more vivid in his mind.

He saw himself grabbing a black plastic trash bag and a couple of rags, then heading back outside. He was freezing as the wind cut through the openings of the rain jacket and up the legs of his pants. He was moving quickly now, a sense of urgency to his actions. Scooping up his wet and bloody clothes, he jammed them in the plastic bag. Next, he turned the hose on his car and began wiping down the exterior. He wasn't sure if the female officer's blood had sprayed onto his vehicle, like it had on him, but no sense taking any chances. It took him fifteen minutes to wash and wipe the entire car. He decided to leave it in the driveway, thinking the rain could only help wash away anything he may have missed in the darkness.

The video in his mind continued to stream, and he saw himself lying in bed the night before. Suddenly the video streamed to the vista point. He could recall everything that had happened now.

He'd only seen one or two other cars on the road during the entire ten mile drive from the south end of Crescent City to the vista point. Pulling his vehicle in facing south, parallel to the highway and about ten feet from the guardrail, he used the toggle switches on the driver's door armrest to open the front windows, killed the engine, and sat for a few seconds listening to the sounds of the night.

The physical layout of the vista point was perfect for his needs. It was about a hundred yards long, maybe twenty-five yards wide. It sat halfway up the grade that rose from sea level to nearly four hundred feet at the crest. Located on the southbound side of 101, it provided a stunning one hundred eighty degree panoramic view of the ocean. Several four story tall, rugged rocks stood just off the beach, like sentinels guarding the coastline. Not that he could see any of the pristine shoreline at night, or that he was there to admire the view. A wood and steel, three foot high guardrail at the edge of the paved parking area prevented sightseers from wandering too close to the edge. Two feet beyond the guardrail was a two hundred foot sheer drop to the water below.

The only bad thing about this location was curves in the highway on the north and southbound sides. There wasn't much sight distance in either direction, which meant a vehicle could appear on 101 at any moment, giving him very little time to react. Conversely, it was dead silent so he could hear an approaching vehicle, and the curves would allow him to see a vehicle's headlights on the pavement a few seconds before it actually came into sight.

He had to move fast. Satisfied there was nobody else around and with the quiet telling him there were no approaching vehicles, he was quickly out of his car and had the trunk open. Scooping up the visquine and raincoat wrapped woman's body in both arms, he lifted the corpse out of the trunk. As he had done on three other occasions since coming to Crescent City, he shifted the body so he could hold the weight on one arm and with his free hand, slammed the trunk closed.

Almost simultaneously with the trunk locking shut, he had seen the headlights of a vehicle approaching from the south, heading northbound. He only had a few seconds before it rounded the curve, completely exposing him, standing there with a dead woman in his arms.

The physical sense of panic, like a tingling electric wave, coursed over his entire body.

He had done the calculations and assessed his options in a nanosecond. He was six feet from the guardrail. He could make it there in three steps, one second after that he could launch the body over the side. Even if it were a police car approaching, and even if it stopped to see what he was doing, there was nothing illegal about being at the vista point at 2:00 in the morning. Strange, yes, illegal, no.

Shifting the woman's weight back to both arms, he was off-balance as he took his first step toward the guardrail. In his mind he could see himself stumbling, going down on his left knee, dropping the body next to the right side of his car.

More panic, sweating profusely now, he had recalculated his options. Opening the passenger's door with his left hand, in one motion he jerked the woman's lifeless body off the ground and sat her in the passenger's seat just as the approaching vehicle rounded the curve and came into sight.

His first thought on seeing the shape of the vehicle was relief, an SUV, not a big Ford passenger sedan, the type he knew the CHP and most of the other law enforcement agencies in the county used as patrol cars. Almost as quickly, his sense of relief evaporated when he saw the red and blue, roof mounted emergency light bar, then the white door with the gold CHP star.

It was the worst of all possible things that could have happened, he recalled thinking at the time.

The sound of the engine on the Highway Patrol vehicle throttling back told him it was slowing as it approached, and the beams from the headlights changing directions told him the officers were turning into the vista point. The big SUV had come to a stop fifteen feet directly behind his vehicle, and when the driver officer kicked the headlights onto high-beam, they illuminated the entire location.

In his bed, he began to toss violently from side-to-side, while the streaming video played on in his mind. It was almost like it was all happening again.

He could see himself standing adjacent to the closed passenger door of his vehicle. The head and shoulders of the dead woman wrapped in the black plastic raincoat clearly visible to the officers. As soon as he heard the driver put the vehicle into park, he had waved to the officers, then bent over, arms on the door sill, like he was talking to the passenger. When both officers got out of their unit, he reached in the open window, adjusted the rain hood on the woman's head, patted her shoulder in a comforting manner, then slowly walked toward the back of his car.

He recognized them both. They were the husband and wife team, his name was Dave, hers was Judy or Janie, something like that.

Even though it was almost 2:00 in the morning, with a misty rain falling, the breeze off the ocean freshening and the temperature in the high thirties, he was drenched in sweat. The rivulets of moisture running down the hollow of his spine created a tickling sensation he urgently wanted to wipe away.

"Hey guys," he greeted them as they met at the right rear bumper of his car.

"Que paso, jefe?" the male officer replied, using the Spanish question he knew cops often used for "what's going on?", and the Spanish word for boss to acknowledge his status. There had been a tone of friendly recognition and greeting in the officer's voice.

"Ah, you know, met this girl at the casino in town," he replied, gesturing back to his car. "We were headed to her place when she said she was sick. Too much to drink, I guess. Anyway, I pulled over here so she could get some air."

"You dog you," the male officer had chided him, while his partner stood off a little to the side, not amused.

"I know you're the head guy, but do they let you do this kind of personal business thing with your company car?" the male officer questioned.

"Well, I'm not supposed to. I only stopped at the casino to have dinner after I got off work, I didn't think I'd get lucky tonight. You know how it is," he answered the officer.

He remembered, as he talked to the officers, he had taken out a cigarette and fumbled with the matches before getting it lit.

As they stood there talking, headlights appeared from around the curve, heading southbound. Within seconds, a beat up old pickup truck rattled by at about thirty miles-per-hour, the driver glancing over, but never slowing. It was around the curve and out of sight, just as quickly as it appeared.

"She gonna be okay?" the male officer asked, already walking past him toward the passenger side door.

"Man, you're sweating like crazy, you alright?" the female officer questioned, a hint of suspicion in her voice.

He'd played the string out as far as it would go, he knew.

Dropping the matches he held in his hand, he reached back to his left hip and pulled the .38 out before the female officer could react. Sidestepping to her right, he clutched her body with an arm bar across her chest and jammed the five shot revolver into the side of her head. The male officer was just reaching the passenger's side door where the dead woman sat motionless, when his peripheral vision caught his moment. The officer turned to see him holding a pistol to his wife's temple and started to draw his weapon.

"Don't do it, I'll kill her!" he remembered yelling at the male officer, jamming the barrel harder into the female officer's head, causing her to flinch from the pain.

"What the fuck are you doing, what's going on here?" the male officer growled at him, anger and confusion in his voice.

The officer answered his own question a second later when he saw the dead woman's body in the car.

"Take your gun out and throw it over the side or I'll kill her," he told the male officer, gesturing with his head toward the cliff, as he shifted behind the female officer.

He remembered she had yelled "Don't do it, Dave, don't do it!" to her partner and husband. His reaction to her warning was to pull up on the arm bar until it was across her neck, causing her to gasp from being choked and rise up on the balls of her feet to relieve the pressure on her windpipe.

"Let her go man, we can work this out," the officer said, trying to buy some time.

"Throw your gun over the side or I'll kill her!"

The male officer stood motionless.

"I'll kill her right now if you don't do what I say," he remembered yelling at the officer again, almost pleading with him to give up his weapon.

"Shoot him Dave, damn it, shoot him, he's gonna kill us anyway!" she had implored her husband.

"Okay, easy, don't do anything stupid," the male officer said as he unsnapped the retaining strap on his holster and slowly pulled out his pistol, throwing it over the guardrail.

He recalled the officer's eyes staying locked with his the whole time.

Once the male officer had thrown his weapon away, he felt safe enough to release the chokehold he had on the female officer's neck and begin to move his right hand down to take her weapon. As he released the pressure on her neck, she moved her feet slightly, he assumed to regain her balance after being hiked up on her toes by his chokehold. He had howled in pain when she smashed the heel of her combat type boot down on the arch of his right foot.

She immediately tried to struggle free and draw her pistol at the same time. He reflexively pushed her away, and fired at the back of her head. The muzzle flash lit up the night, and the noise from the bullet being fired deafened him.

The high-velocity, half-jacketed, hollow-point round hit the female officer in the back of her neck, just above the top of her soft body armor. He didn't know it, but the round severed her spinal cord, killing her instantly.

As he continued to lie in bed, reliving the events at the vista point, the video stream shifted into slow motion.

He saw the female officer crumple face down to the asphalt and remembered the distinct feeling of warmth as her blood splattered back on his face and hands. He could also recall the screaming from her husband, and saw him bend over, pulling up on the left leg cuff of his uniform trousers.

It took him a second to realize the officer was going for his back-up weapon. He should have anticipated that many cops carried a second gun. Sometimes it was in a concealed shoulder holster rig under their jacket, or in an ankle holster like the male Highway Patrol officer was wearing. By the time it registered, the officer had drawn a six shot, .357 magnum revolver and was bringing it up to fire.

He remembered rushing forward three steps, firing two times at the officer. One round caught the officer in the right thigh, ripping apart his femoral artery, knocking him to the ground on his back, sending his snub-nosed "hide-away" revolver clattering to the pavement.

The streaming video went into frame-by-frame stop action mode as he saw himself walk up to the helpless Highway Patrol officer and, without hesitation, fire his last two remaining rounds into the officer's face. He recalled the officer's eyes defiantly staying locked with his the whole time.

And just that quick, it was quiet again, the only sound the low rumble of the CHP vehicle's engine as it sat idling.

He could see himself now in rapid non-stop motion. Quickly, he opened the passenger's door and lifted the dead woman's body out, leaving the black raincoat behind on the seat. Shifting her weight in his arms, he walked to the edge of the guardrail. Putting one foot atop the steel rail, he balanced the dead weight of her body on his knee and felt for the loose edge of the visquine. Once he had a good grip on the edge of the plastic with both hands, he simultaneously heaved the body away toward the abyss and pulled back on the plastic shroud, much like unrolling a carpet.

As the pliable plastic cocoon unraveled, the body spun horizontality flying clear of its wrappings, hitting hard on the very edge of the cliff, before disappearing into the darkness as it fell toward the water below. From over two hundred feet above, with the wind blowing, and his ears ringing from the gunshots, he couldn't hear the splash as the body hit the water twenty-five feet from the sheer rocky face of the cliff.

As soon as the body cleared the visquine covering, he'd balled the plastic up in his arms using a motion much like pulling a sheet off a bed, retreated to his car, grabbed the black raincoat and stuffed them both in another garbage bag which he threw on the floorboard of the back seat. As the video streamed on, he saw himself quickly scan the scene to ensure he left no tell-tale evidence of his presence.

Lastly, he grabbed the pair of disposable latex gloves he kept over the sun visor, slipped them on and ran back to the idling patrol vehicle. Opening the driver's door, he scanned the dashboard area where he saw what he was looking for mounted above the radio in the center of the dash. He had to stand on his toes and stretch across the driver's seat to reach the scratch pad. He slid the whole pad out of the holder. Written on the pad, in a column, were four license plate numbers. Three had been lined out. The bottom number was the plate number to his vehicle.

Stuffing the pad in the pocket of his sweatshirt he was back in his car within seconds, behind the wheel and moving. Slowly, he told himself, don't leave any acceleration skid marks or draw attention to yourself.

The video abruptly ended.

Lying there he could now recall having gone to bed the previous evening after washing his car, gathering up all his wet and bloodstained clothes, and taking a shower. He had awakened with a jolt around 7:00 that morning, groggy and disoriented.

He recalled being mad at himself. You have things to do yet, do you want to get caught, he had said to himself.

Everything was clearer now. He saw himself shaking the sleep away, picking up the phone on the nightstand, and calling in. He'd worked late last night, he had told his secretary, and would be in around 8:30. Because of the type of work he did, his hours were flexible, and because he was the boss, nobody questioned his comings and goings.

"Oh, did you hear?" the secretary added just before hanging up, "Two CHP officers were murdered last night."

He didn't need the streaming video to recall what he had done after calling in. He could recall everything that happened after hanging up the phone clearly. He remembered the rain had stopped and from his upstairs balcony he could see blue sky to the west, out over the ocean. With the wind picking up, the last of the heavy dark clouds would be blown inland, bringing rain to the lower elevations and snow near the Oregon border. It was just a brief respite, he thought at the time, as another storm and more rain, would probably arrive by the evening. He even remembered saying out loud, "What a God awful place this is to live."

He'd hurried to get everything done before leaving for work that morning. He was the boss, yes, and nobody questioned his comings and goings, but he couldn't vary his routine too much lest people begin to talk. The first order of business, before doing anything else, he knew, was to dispose of the several bags full of evidence that linked him to the woman.

He saw himself throwing on a pair of sweat pants, a sweat shirt, and hurrying downstairs. In the garage he found the old towel he'd used to dry off with last night, the two plastic bags containing the sheets from his bed, and the woman's clothes and purse. Outside he had gathered up his rain soaked blue jeans and tennis shoes. Doing a careful walk around of the garage, the driveway, and the interior of his car, he satisfied himself that he'd collected everything connecting him to the woman and to the CHP officers.

He remembered the sun had actually made an appearance by 7:30. Perfect, he'd said to himself at the time, it would help with what he had to do.

His actions after gathering up any incriminating evidence had been almost mechanical. Like many houses outside the city limits, his residence was on a large lot, almost two acres. Only about a third of that was home site, driveway, and surrounding area cleared of vegetation. The rest was trees, mostly redwoods, some oak, and lots of ferns and dense brush. Combined, they formed kind of a wall around his property, that couldn't be seen through from the street.

Like most of the other houses with trees and brush around them, the storm that had blown in the day before brought down lots of limbs, heavy branches full of redwood fronds, and giant ferns. The easiest way to dispose of all this debris was to burn it. Almost every house in the unincorporated portion of the county had a burn pit for just that purpose.

Gathering up several fallen limbs and loose brush, he piled it up in the pit, added a dozen pieces of seasoned oak firewood from his wood pile, and poured a half-gallon of gasoline on top.

The whole pile ignited with a loud whoosh when he threw the red highway emergency flare on top of the stack. The fireball erupted upward in a bright flash, maybe fifteen feet into the air, with a bilious grey cloud roiling outward from the burn pit. Because everything was wet from the almost twenty-four hour soaking of the previous day, the leaves, brush, and water logged redwood branches struggled to burn. In his mind's eye, he saw the large cloud of gray smoke that had drifted upward as the gasoline fed fire burned the moisture out of the vegetation and eventually ignited the seasoned oak firewood.

It had taken more than fifteen minutes that morning before the fire reached a point where it would sustain itself. Twice more he had to add gasoline to the smoldering pyre to coax the fire to keep burning. Once he was certain the fire would continue to burn without his attention, he tossed on the plastic contractor's bags containing all the evidence that could incriminate him.

The plastic contractor's bags and the visquine shroud he'd used to wrap the body, gave off a pungent odor and dense black smoke as it burned. Plastic products, he remembered, because they are oil-based, had a distinct smell while they burned. He threw more gas on the fire to generate more heat, and the flames began to consume the woman's clothes, the new blue jeans and sweat shirt he'd worn last night, and the blood stained tennis shoes.

Mesmerized by watching the flames, he'd let his mind momentarily drift off to thoughts of his mother. Lost in an almost hypnotic state as he watched the evidence burn that morning, the thought that he had killed three people within the last nine hours, never entered his mind.

It took another forty-five minutes for the fire to consume the pile. He stood next to the burn pit the whole time, stoking the fire with a long wooden pole to ensure everything burned. Satisfied with his work, he threw ten more pieces of oak firewood onto the pile to ensure it stayed burning for several more hours. When he got home tonight, he'd rake through the ashes and cull out anything the fire didn't consume.

Back in his house he quickly shaved, then jumped into the shower to wash off the smell of smoke.

He was dressed and on his way to work just before 8:30.

He'd gone through the motions of working today, answering phone calls, returning a few messages, and handling a little paperwork. In the early afternoon, he'd told his staff he had business to attend to and would not be back. As usual, nobody questioned his comings and goings.

He did have business to attend to. It just had nothing to do with his job.

His first stop was the local Chinese restaurant where he picked up some take-out food for dinner. He was back home by 3:00 and changed into some grubby clothes.

Despite the on-again, off-again rain that had fallen most of the day, the burn pit was still smoldering. He uncoiled the hose from the side of the garage and stretched it toward the burn pit. The whole pile sputtered and hissed as the water contacted the hot embers and still smoldering pieces of oak. A cloud of grayish smoke rose from the center of the pit as the water cooled and extinguished the fire still burning below the surface.

Once the smoke stopped rising and the pile resembled a batch of wet cement, he used a garden rake to carefully stroke the pile, sifting the mushy material back and forth, dredging up larger pieces of still glowing wood from the bottom of the pit, and examining closely for any items from the woman that might not have burned. Anything not completely incinerated was folded back into the pile.

His last act was to shovel the slushy debris into a wheelbarrow which he pushed deep into the heavy brush on the far edge of his property. Within a couple days, he knew, the vegetation would grow over any tracks from the burn pit into the brush. Dumping the load over the side of a hill, the rich bitch with the auburn hair was now just a memory.

The Chinese food he'd bought wasn't as good reheated in the microwave, but it was easy and he was tired.

As he lay in bed, content now he had everything sorted out in his mind, he was about to drift off to sleep when he remembered the press conference tomorrow at the sheriff's office. His mind went back into overdrive as he wondered what would come from that.

Chapter Eight

The alarm clock went off with an irritating buzz. In a much practiced reflex action, Red Wolff rolled toward the sound and her hand found the off button. It was still totally dark outside as she swung her feet to the carpeted floor and stood up. The upstairs bedroom was cool, but not necessarily cold. The extra logs Mary Jean had tossed into the woodstove the previous evening had kept the overnight chill away.

Slipping quietly into the bathroom, she brushed her teeth and pulled on her running gear. The clock next to the bed read 5:03 as she made her way downstairs and into the garage where her well worn running shoes sat next to the door. Lifting first her right leg and then her left, she stretched her calf muscles, did a couple shoulder rolls, and opened the side door to the outside.

The initial blast of cold outside air took her breath away and caused her to wonder if getting up four mornings a week to run was worth it. She wondered the same thing every morning, and every morning she went out into the cold.

It wasn't raining this morning so there were no clouds to trap whatever heat the earth had generated the day before. It was probably thirty-three or thirty-four degrees she guessed, and she could see the first signs of ice forming a crust on the windshield of her state car parked in the driveway. Long clouds of vapor appeared from her mouth and nose as she slowly drew in, then exhaled the cold air as she took her first couple of steps before breaking into a slow jog. Slowly heading up the driveway to the street, her nose picked up the smell of wood burning in a neighbor's woodstove.

It had been a crappy night. She'd slept almost seven hours, but it wasn't good sleep. Her mind constantly reeling off a lengthy list of questions, of things she had to do, and she kept seeing images of the bodies of Dave and Jodie Castle.

Running about half-speed, she was heading down the grade that would take her to level ground, the only sounds she heard were those of her running shoes hitting the pavement and her own breathing. It took a couple minutes to reach a reasonably level stretch of road. Once there she picked up her pace.

Running has always been one of her favorite pastimes, going back to when she was a teenager. She used the time to think, to work on solutions to problems, and to just plain relax. As she'd promoted up through the ranks on the Highway Patrol, she found it was a great way to relieve the stress of being the boss and stay in shape at the same time. Long ago she had made a vow to never let herself get in the horrible physical condition many high ranking CHP managers did. Nearly forty-five, she only weighed two pounds more now than she did twenty years ago.

She could feel the beads of sweat starting to form around her neck and run down her chest as she methodically put one foot in front of the other. The two lane county road was just wide enough for one car in each direction, with three foot deep, V-shaped drainage ditches on both sides, and a healthy growth of tall grass on the narrow dirt shoulder. Given the time of morning, there were hardly ever any vehicles to worry about.

It was still pitch black out, the sun not due to make an appearance for another ninety plus minutes. There was enough ambient light, however, that she could make out the shape about two hundred yards ahead. It was heading the same direction she was, but wasn't moving as fast.

She got one of her trademark half-smiles and picked up the pace slightly to close the distance.

Unlike Red Wolff, who was bundled in sweatpants, a hooded sweatshirt jacket, and gloves, Ray Silva always ran in shorts, his gloveless hands stuffed in the pockets of a lightweight nylon running jacket.

"Hey old man, aren't you cold?" she said coming abreast of him.

He didn't hear her as she glided up next to him, the ear pieces of his i-pod blocking out her voice. When he did sense her presence, he pulled the small plastic plug out of his left ear.

"Hey," he half-grunted.

"Aren't you kinda old to be out here trucking around in the dark?" she said, giving him a shot about his age.

"I can run your short little legs off, lieutenant, Ma'am," he shot back sarcastically, his stride never varying.

Running side-by-side now, Red laughed as she matched his steady mechanical pace.

"What're you listening to?" she asked.

"Oldies, '50s and '60s rock and roll, what else," he responded with a tone in his voice that said, you should have known that.

"An i-pod is pretty hi-tech stuff for an old married guy like you who can barely do e-mail," she continued to rib him about his age.

"It's absolutely way too hi-tech for me. I find the songs I want on-line, and Julie downloads them for me. I used to have a radio headset that picked up the oldies station in Medford. They played some great old stuff. Now, the stuff they call oldies is from the '80s and '90s. Stuff I've never even heard before, mostly heavy metal, lots of screaming, and words you can't understand. Now they call songs from the '50s and '60s, "music of your life". I'm getting old."

"How'd you sleep?" she asked.

"Like crap."

"Me too, my mind wouldn't shut down. Next thing I knew the alarm was going off."

"What's up for today?" Ray asked.

"I'm headed in early, need to see if the shooting team turned anything last night. Then the sheriff is calling a press conference at 10:00. The shrink will be at the office around noon to do a group debriefing for the squad and any spouses who want to attend. I'm having Mary Jean come. You should think about getting Julie to go."

"I'll mention it to her, but she seems to be doing okay," he replied.

They continued to run in silence for the next half-mile until they reached a natural turn around point and headed back.

"Ray, I could really use you to head up the investigation for me. The shooting team will only be around another couple of days. Once they go, you're the only one who has the investigative ability, the contacts, and the relationships with the other agencies to handle the job."

"Red, I'll do whatever you want. The Castles were my friends, and I owe Jodie a life."

She thought about his words, "I owe Jodie a life", for a second. Then it flashed on her. Jodie had killed a terrorist who had taken a bead on Ray a split second before he could pull the trigger. It was a matter of honor to Ray Silva that Jodie had saved his life, and he owed her one back.

"Done deal. Come with me to the sheriff's office at 10:00," she told him as they both picked up the pace for the last mile.

———————

Ray Silva walked slowly down his driveway and back to the street several times as part of a cool down routine after completing his run. Even with the morning temperature now hovering right at the freezing mark, his body would continue to pump out sweat for another ten or fifteen minutes before he stopped perspiring.

On his last trip up the driveway, he grabbed the newspaper lying on the gravel where his driveway met the road.

The local paper was only a few pages thick on most days. Typical of a small town newspaper, it covered local people and local happenings, who was getting married, fishing reports, and high school sports. Most of the world and national news it contained was over a day old and just skimmed the highlights of a story. For real news many locals read the *San Francisco Chronicle*. The only problem was *"The Chron"* didn't arrive in town until around six in the morning. Printed in the Bay Area around 9:00 the previous evening, bundles of the early edition were loaded on a Greyhound bus and dropped off in towns all along the 101 corridor north of San Francisco. A local distributer got the papers out to stores, markets, and gas stations in town by 7:00.

Quietly, Ray Silva opened the front door to his home and slipped inside, trying hard to minimize any noise in order not to wake Julie. He'd hit the coffeemaker's on button before he left to start his run, and the downstairs was filled with the aroma of fresh brewed coffee. Just as silently, he opened the door to the woodstove and tossed in a couple pieces of oak.

Pouring a cup of coffee for himself, he sat at the dining room table, hunted up his reading glasses, and opened the paper.

"God damn fucking rag," he bellowed.

Almost immediately he could hear the sound of Julie's footsteps above him. "Ray! What's wrong? You alright?" she called down.

"Yeah, fine Sweetie, sorry to wake you. You want some coffee?"

"Sure," she answered, her voice back to normal.

Ray poured her a cup and headed upstairs.

"What were you yelling about?" she asked again, now sitting up in bed, the lamp on the nightstand illuminating the room.

"Look at this," he replied, holding the front page of the local paper in front of her.

Julie scanned the tabloid's headline, then let her eyes shift down the page.

"That's it? Two CHP officers get murdered, and the front page story is about some Crescent City guy who has a parrot that can speak Spanish?" she said incredulously.

Ray turned the paper back toward himself and scanned the front page again noting the picture of a middle-aged man holding a large green African parrot and the accompanying three column story.

"There's a little story on page three that mentions the murders, that's it," Ray Silva said shaking his head.

"Is everyone on the local paper brain dead?" she asked, but her tone was more of a statement than a question.

"I don't know which I dislike more, journalists or lawyers?" he stated, getting up from the bed and heading for the shower.

"That would be a hard choice for most people," Julie quipped.

"Fucking rag," Ray said disappearing into the bathroom.

The office was already busy when Red pulled in just before 7:00. Inside, the shooting team investigators were huddled around one of the briefing room tables going over their notes and photos. Steffani Taylor was engaged in a heated conversation with the officer who was also her team's chaplain, and Ray Silva was working by himself at one of the office computer terminals.

Steffani Taylor broke off her conversation with the chaplain and walked toward Red.

"What was that all about?" Red queried, referring to the obvious disagreement between Steffani and her chaplain.

"He's really good at rendering onto God," she told Red, paraphrasing a passage from the Bible, "It's rendering onto Caesar, he has a problem with," she laughed.

"What're you talking about?" Red asked, more confused now.

"Well, Dave and Jodie's parents have agreed to a joint memorial church service and for them to be buried together here in Crescent City. My chaplain wants to be the one who officiates the service, but the parents want the Castles local pastor to conduct the ceremony. He wants me to override the parent's wishes."

"And are you going to do that?"

"Hell no!" Steffani stated adamantly, adding, "We'll do what the parents want, and that's what I just told him."

"So now his nose is outta joint?" Red laughed.

"Yeah, he's gonna sulk for a while and try to find a way to do an end run to get his way. FYI, he thinks all us gay people are sinners and doomed to burn in hell for eternity. Prays for our salvation every day."

"Damn. Burn in hell for eternity! I hate when that happens," Red laughed again, a half-smile on her face, heading toward her office. Vaughn O'Dell came in the back door from the parking lot just as she sat behind her desk.

"Red, let me get a cup of coffee, then let's talk," he told her.

He looked tired as he sat in the chair directly in front of Red Wolff's desk. He'd stayed at the office till nearly midnight working with the shooting team, handled a dozen calls from headquarters in Sacramento, and only managed a couple of hours sleep in a lumpy motel room bed.

"I got a call from the Commissioner last night wanting to know the status of the investigation," he began. "Didn't have much to tell him. He told me he'll be here for the funeral, and the Governor is coming, also. The association announced a twenty-five thousand dollar reward for any information that leads to an arrest and conviction of the murderers," he added.

The association Vaughn O'Dell was discussing with his lieutenant was the California Association of Highway Patrolman. It was the officers' union.

Long before collective bargaining became a right for California state employees, the association had been more of a fraternal organization. It sponsored group insurance for members and published a bi-monthly newsletter that announced retirements and promotions. It also held an annual convention, usually held in Las Vegas, or another resort location, euphemistically called a "Traffic Safety Conference" so that attendees could write the trip off on their taxes as a work related training expense. The only real benefit to traffic safety was that attendees didn't drive after consuming the unending flow of alcohol provided by insurance companies and other corporate sponsors of the conference.

Then, when government employees were allowed to organize and form unions in the early '80s, the California Association of Highway Patrolman became a union. Of the twenty-one unions representing state employees in California, it was one of the smallest in terms of membership. But, it was one of the most powerful. Every politician wanted the endorsement of the Highway Patrolman's Association. Consequently, the officers' union was always able to negotiate favorable labor contracts for their employees, and had a huge political action budget.

"I want you to make that announcement at the press conference our favorite sheriff is calling this morning," he told her.

She acknowledged his direction with a nod.

"Also, you know what to say about the investigation, right?" he asked. Not waiting for her to answer, he ran down a laundry list of politically correct buzz words and comments she should use at the press conference.

Concluding their discussion they headed to the rear of the office to meet with the shooting team.

About quarter of ten, with Red Wolff driving her unmarked state car, she, Vaughn O'Dell, and Ray Silva headed the three miles to the Del Norte County Sheriff's Office.

———————

Both sides of the street around the sheriff's office were lined with vehicles. Some were marked law enforcement cars, a couple of television news vans, in addition to an assortment of other personal passenger cars and pickup trucks.

Red steered her big metallic green Ford Crown Victoria sedan into the back parking lot. Her vehicle, a perk of being the boss, had complete police equipment, including an undercover handheld red spotlight, siren, and a CHP radio hidden in the center console.

The back lot was just as crowded as the street, mostly marked and unmarked law enforcement vehicles. She managed to find a spot in the far corner of the lot.

It was Ray Silva who noticed it first.

"Damn, it looks like a Crown Victoria convention with all these Fords here," he said to Red and Vaughn O'Dell as they walked toward the back entrance to the sheriff's facility.

"Yep, looks the government is doing their part to stimulate the automotive industry," Vaughn replied, glancing at the maybe eighteen or twenty big Fords in the lot. Only about half of the Crown Victorias in the back parking lot were marked. He could see door markings for the Oregon State Police, Humboldt County Sheriff's Office, National Park Service, Brookings Oregon Police Department, Grants Pass Department of Public Safety, the Yurok Tribal Police, and California Department of Corrections. And those were only the ones he could see. There were over a half-dozen unmarked Crown Vics also, all different colors.

"This is going to be a real dog and pony show," he remarked to his two subordinates as they reached the back door and rang the buzzer.

Ray Silva's comment about the number of Ford Crown Victorias at the sheriff's office was pretty much right on point. Nationwide, eighty-five percent of all law enforcement agencies used the Ford Crown Victoria as their marked patrol vehicle for uniformed officers and as their standard unmarked car for detectives and administrators. Because of the vehicle's rugged construction, rear-wheel drive, big V-8 engine, and interior roominess to carry police equipment, the "Crown Vic" was popular among cops. The Ford plant in Canada pumped out about a half-million vehicles a year for police work and another big chunk for taxis and limos.

The sheriff's roll call room was packed. Television cameras were set up in the aisle between the briefing tables, technicians in the back of the room holding flood lights, and reporters were flittering from one uniformed officer to another asking questions and sticking microphones in their faces.

At the front of the room, Sheriff Jerome Williamson was in heaven. He was shaking hands as fast as he could and taking time to have brief conversations with the law enforcement administrators from all over the four county area. At the same time, he was positioning each of them up against the wall and behind the podium. This will make a spectacular shot on television, he thought to himself smiling the whole while. Me, at the podium, with all these senior law enforcement administrators behind to show support. Me, announcing the formation of a two-state, four county, multi-agency task force to investigate the murders of the CHP officers, and me, heading up the whole thing. God is smiling on me today, he said to himself. For a fleeting second, his mind flashed on Nora Kendricks.

Walking into the room, Vaughn O'Dell stopped dead in his tracks when he saw the number of people crammed into the small space and the assortment of different law enforcement personnel.

"Who the hell are all these people?" he whispered to Red Wolff.

"Well, you know the sheriff," she began, noting he was attired today not in a natty suit, but in the uniform of the Del Norte County Sheriff's Office. "Starting from the left," she continued pointing to the cops in uniform lined up against the chalk board behind the podium, "The guy in the tan shirt and green trousers is the Sheriff of Humboldt County. Next to him is the Chief of Police for Brookings, Oregon, then the captain who is the commander of the Oregon State Police for the Southwestern Region, which includes all their posts that border on Del Norte County. The tall guy in the middle is from Grants Pass Department of Public Safety. On that department, their people are both cops and firemen. He's the fire chief and the police chief."

It took her another full minute to name all the players and their agencies. The Chief of Crescent City Police Department, the Public Safety Director of the Yurok Tribal Police, the head law enforcement ranger of the local National Park, the top cop from the Forest Service, the captain who was in charge of law enforcement for the California Redwood State Park, and dressed in his formal green dress uniform, the captain from Department of Corrections representing the warden of Pelican Bay State Prison.

Once Red Wolff took her place against the chalkboard, there were twelve of them standing behind Jerome Williamson as he approached the podium and began to speak.

His other shortcomings notwithstanding, Jerome Williamson was a glib and articulate speaker. He was in his element in front of the cameras and reporters. He began by expressing thanks to all his peers from the other law enforcement agencies who were standing behind him and his condolences to the families of the murdered officers. He then went on to say how, as Sheriff of Del Norte County, he was forming a multi-agency task force to bring all possible law enforcement resources to bear in the investigation in order to swiftly arrest and bring to justice those responsible for this heinous crime. He talked on for another five minutes about public safety and ensuring citizens were not endangered by the killer or killers among them, then gave a quick update on the status of the investigation.

"For whatever else he is, he's one smooth talking son-of-a-bitch," Vaughn O'Dell leaned over and spoke quietly into Ray Silva's ear as they both sat in the back of the room.

"Yeah, but he's still an arrogant jerk," Ray replied looking straight ahead.

Following his remarks, Sheriff Williamson introduced Red as the commander of the Crescent City Highway Patrol. She spoke for only a couple of minutes, ensuring she used all the right buzz words like interagency cooperation, joint investigative effort, and expressed her thanks on behalf of the CHP for Jerome Williamson's leadership in heading up the investigation.

"I think she's gonna puke," Ray whispered to Vaughn O'Dell with a chuckle in his voice as they watched her force the words out.

As he'd planned, Jerome Williamson let what should have been a brief fifteen minute announcement and update on the murder of the officers, turn into a media event, fielding questions from the press and talking about bringing those responsible swiftly to justice. It was only when he sensed restlessness from the heads of the other agencies standing behind him that he concluded his remarks and stopped taking questions.

After the press conference broke up, the heads of the various other law enforcement agencies, the Del Norte County sheriff's detective, the CHP lieutenant who commanded the shooting team, Red Wolff, Vaughn O'Dell and Ray Silva, all remained in the room while the T.V. technicians broke down their equipment. It took about ten minutes for the room to completely clear out.

All the players grabbed seats around the roll call tables, and Sheriff Jerome Williamson opened the conversation by giving everyone a more in-depth update on the investigation. He reiterated there still wasn't much to go on and they wouldn't have the results of the ballistics analysis until later that day.

His detective then took over the briefing and told the assembled group they had precious little to go on. All the cops in the county had been out grilling their confidential informants trying to develop leads, to get a name, and to find out what was being talked about on the street regarding the murders. Thus far, they had turned up nothing.

"Maybe that's significant," the Chief of Brookings P.D. spoke up. "If nobody on the street knows anything, we're probably dealing with someone from out of the area, or a local whose been flying under the radar."

That prompted a discussion between the heads of all the different agencies surrounding Crescent City about possible motives and suspects. It was the CHP lieutenant who brought the group back on point. He'd seen these multi-agency type meetings disintegrate before into long drawn out sessions where everyone gave their "who done it" opinion.

"Gentlemen, I would suggest we hold off on speculation and focus on what we know and what assistance each of your agencies can provide. For starters, can I get the name of a contact person within each department, somebody we can call if there is something we need from your agency. Second, if your resources allow, would each of you be willing to send a detective, or an investigator, to Crescent City tomorrow so we can compare notes and try to ascertain our next step?"

Everyone agreed to have a representative there for a meeting the following day, and the meeting broke up shortly thereafter.

———————

Following the meeting, the heads of each agency headed back to their respective departments. Some, the Sheriff of Humboldt County, the captain from the Oregon State Police Southwest Region Headquarters at Central Point, and the Sheriff of Josephine County, Oregon, had two hour drives ahead of them. Others, like the head ranger for the National Park Service, and the Director of the Yurok Department of Public Safety, whose headquarters were close, returned to their offices fairly quickly.

Dutifully, each convened a meeting with their staff and subordinates to fill them in on the press conference and to determine what assistance they could provide in the investigation.

At the joint Redwood State and National Park office, head ranger Marv Butler and his counterpart on the state level, held a meeting with all of their law enforcement personnel, gave them a rundown on the investigation, and picked their best person to join the multi-agency task force.

A couple blocks away, Andrew Dixon called the two Forest Service law enforcement agents into his office. Keeping them standing while he robotically rearranged the items on his desk, he filled them in on the status of the case and advised that since he had the most investigative experience, he would be joining the task force to represent the Forest Service. After concluding the meeting, still obsessed with the orderliness of his desk, he thought momentarily about calling the superintendent in Eureka to provide an update. Fuck her, he said to himself.

At Pelican Bay State Prison, Correctional Captain Nate Steadman made his way to the warden's office to give him a report on the meeting. Since he didn't have an appointment, he was forced to sit in the reception area and wait. Twenty-five minutes later, he was shown into the warden's office where he gave a quick and dirty summary of what had been discussed and the sheriff's request for assistance from all law enforcement agencies in the four county area.

"Very good, captain," the warden replied. "I want you to be the point person on this for Correction's and the prison. I can't help but think that a recent parolee may be involved. By the way, did you determine how many releases we had on the day the officers were murdered?"

"Five, warden," Nate Steadman replied, "All from the south state. I checked with the staff working that morning, and they personally saw all five get aboard the "Freedom Bus" heading south from Crescent City."

"Freedom Bus?" the warden asked, a quizzical look on his face.

"That's what parolee's call the Greyhound that takes them away from this place and to freedom," Nate Steadman told him. He wanted to add, if you knew anything about prisoners and what dealing with them is like, you would have known that.

"Yes, yes, of course, the Freedom Bus. Okay, help the local police in any way you can, and give me updates as the investigation proceeds," the warden told him, the tone in his voice telling Nate Steadman he was dismissed.

Fucking white people, Nate Steadman said to himself while closing the hand carved wooden door as he left the warden's office.

Ross Glickner had been up since 3:30. His wife had not called last night, and now he was really concerned something had happened to her. He would call the Los Angeles Sheriff's Department Malibu Station right after he checked the overseas markets on T.V. and did a little work on the computer.

At 6:30 local time, the stock market opened sharply lower in New York. Events in the Middle East were causing turmoil on the European markets, the dollar was down again against the Euro, and oil prices jumped six dollars a barrel. He got consumed trying to shore up his holdings and stop the hemorrhaging that was draining his client's portfolios.

He needed to contact the local sheriffs to report Kim missing, and he needed to get into his office to try and do some financial magic. In the end, he opted to try and do both. He headed to work, and since his office was within the city limits, he would call LAPD to make a missing persons report.

As he expected, the office was a madhouse when he got there just after 9:00. He quickly checked his voice mail hoping to find a message from Kim, but all that was there were a dozen calls from panicked clients. He had his secretary call LAPD.

It took almost two hours before the solo Los Angeles Police Department officer showed up in Ross Glickner's seventeenth floor office. He was an older officer, perhaps fifty, or even a little older.

About twenty pounds overweight, the officer looked tired and overworked. This was his eighth call of the morning, and he had three more backed up after handling this assignment. He liked working one of the several cars that only took crime reports all day long. It wasn't glamorous police work, and most of the time he had to deal with people who wanted action, usually the recovery of their stolen property, immediately. But the assignment did allow him to work alone, unlike most uniformed LAPD officers who worked doubled up doing much more dangerous patrol duty, responding to crimes in progress, and dealing with drunks, drug dealers and gang-bangers all day long. And, he got to work day shift, with weekends off. He'd have his thirty years in soon, then adios Los Angeles.

Ross Glickner spent a couple of minutes explaining the situation to the officer.

The LAPD officer's first instinct was to try and find a way not to have to take a report, or "kiss it off" in police jargon. Missing person's reports were complicated and required him to do a little extra work like driving back to the station to enter the missing person's information in the statewide database, and prepare a copy of his report to send to the Los Angeles Sheriff's Department.

He knew, however, that missing persons were a sensitive subject, and state law required any agency, regardless of jurisdiction, to take a report and file it within four hours. He also knew he then had twenty-four hours to send a copy to the sheriff's department, since the duty to investigate a missing person is the responsibility of the agency in which the missing person resides.

While Ross Glickner droned on, the officer's mind calculated the amount of hours all this would take and whether he would have enough time left on his shift to drop by the golf shop. He had been eying a new driver for the past month, and the owner of the shop loved cops. A fifty percent "police discount" on a three hundred seventy-five dollar club was too good a deal to pass up. He wanted to get that club and stop by the driving range on his way home to give it a rip.

Nodding as if concerned, when Ross Glickner finished talking, the officer removed the proper form from his clipboard storage box and went right into filling out the required information. It took him only three or four minutes to gather all the personal data on Kim Glickner, her vehicle information, and her last known whereabouts.

Telling the missing woman's husband he would file the report immediately, and someone would be in contact with him soon, they shook hands and the officer was gone.

Ross Glickner felt better. In his mind he could see the vast resources of the entire state swinging into action to locate his missing wife.

Back in his black and white patrol car, the officer looked at his watch, then headed for the golf shop.

By 11:45 Red Wolff, Vaughn O'Dell, and Ray Silva were all back at the CHP office. As on the previous day, there were an inordinate amount of civilian vehicles in both the front and back lots. Red remembered that the critical incident psychologist who specialized in dealing with the traumatic after effects of an officer being killed was at the office today. She would be talking to her officers and family members starting at noon.

JoAnne Mueller was one of the top three psychologists in California when it came to dealing with cops and traumatic incidents. In the '80s she'd been one of the early pioneers in the field, had written several books on critical incident counseling for cops and fireman, and was much sought after as a speaker at conferences across the nation. Although she had a private practice in San Bernardino, she was on contract to a dozen law enforcement agencies in Southern California and was utilized extensively by the Highway Patrol. She was an attractive looking woman in her early fifties, tall, thin, and suntanned.

Prior to the beginning of the group session, Captain Taylor suggested a quick closed door meeting that included Vaughn O'Dell. Once in Red's cramped office, Steffani spoke first. "Chief O'Dell, Red," she began slowly, looking for the right words, "JoAnne has talked to about a half-dozen of your officers so far one-on-one, and is set to do a group session in a few minutes that will include spouses and officers. She's sensing there may be a problem. I'll let her tell you about it."

JoAnne Mueller got right to the point. "I've done a lot of sessions with a lot of cops, and you get a feel for what works and what doesn't when it comes to doing counseling and debriefing. Your officers are as deep in depression and are hurting as bad as any group I've seen over the past twenty-five years. Normally, when I work with cops after one of their own has been killed, there is a suspect they can direct their anger at, or an incident, like a traffic accident, they can blame. What's happening here is unique because there are no suspects in custody, and so there's nobody for them to be mad at."

"So what do you propose?" Vaughn O'Dell inquired, his mind going back to the emotions he had when his son was murdered in the line of duty.

"Well, I've only done it a couple of times before, but I need to give them somebody to hate. In the absence of a suspect, they need to have a punching bag for their emotions. With your concurrence, I'm going to give them one." Not waiting for anyone to ask, JoAnne Mueller explained what she planned to do.

The briefing room was packed. Of the twenty-one officers, three sergeants, and three civilians assigned to the Crescent City Highway Patrol Area, only the two officers who were on patrol were not present. In addition, sixteen wives were seated around the four wooden tables.

Red Wolff, Vaughn O'Dell, and Steffani Taylor stood in the back of the room as JoAnne Mueller walked to the podium.

She had a relaxed way about her, her movement's fluid, as she adjusted a couple papers in her hand and looked at the audience.

She got right to it, no perfunctory introductions, and no soft words of condolence or expression of loss at the murder of two officers.

"So, I guess you are all pretty mad at Dave and Jodie for getting themselves killed?"

There was stunned silence in the room. It was exactly what everyone in the room didn't want to hear. It took maybe a full second and a half before one of the officers angrily shot back at her, "Mad at the Castles! You're making it sound like it was their fault!"

JoAnne Mueller didn't respond. The first officer had no more than stopped talking when another exploded. "Some bastard shot Jodie in the back and put two bullets in Davy's face while he was down on the ground! Does that sound like we should be mad at them?"

JoAnne Mueller was smiling to herself inside, the healing had started.

One after the other they lashed out at her. Loud angry voices, people yelling over each other, wives in tears. And on it went, almost non-stop for the next forty-five minutes. Another officer joined in, lambasting the psychologist for being insensitive, then a couple wives spoke, then another officer. They hated JoAnne Mueller, and they hated the unknown suspects who had taken their friends. They blamed the court system, politicians, the prisons, and anyone else they could think of.

Slowly, without those in attendance realizing, JoAnne Mueller, with a comment here and a question there, had shifted the focus of their hate and frustration toward an unknown person or persons who had murdered the Castles. The hostile nature of the officers' attacks on JoAnne Mueller subsided as they found a new target for their anger.

Then, just as skillfully, and just as subtlety, she changed the groups focus again by evoking memories of Dave and Jodie. Everyone chimed in. One officer recalled Davy's off-beat sense of humor and his former randy ways with women. Jodie's no nonsense method of doing the job, and how she had run over a terrorist with her patrol car, were contrasted with her volunteer work at the local elementary school. Everyone could visualize the Castles.

When she sensed the time was right, JoAnne Mueller brought the session to a close. She'd given them someone to hate, herself. And in doing so she brought them full circle, giving each of them the ability to heal.

———————

During the debriefing session with JoAnne Mueller, Vaughn O'Dell had told the office manager to put the public phone lines in the after-hours mode so they went to a recorded message and to lock the front door so everyone could attend the counseling session uninterrupted. Although the ring tone on those lines was muted, all during the session Red kept seeing the lights flash on the two public lines on the phone in the briefing room.

When the session ended, everyone resumed their normal duties, the phones were switched back to normal mode, and the front door unlocked.

News of the twenty-five thousand dollar reward being offered by the Association of Highway Patrolmen spread faster than a wild fire fanned by California's infamous Santa Ana winds. Even though the officers' association had set up an 800 number, dozens of calls were coming in on the regular business office lines.

Office manager, Lisa Johnston, had an exasperated look on her face as the phone rang again, and she dutifully answered with a pleasant, although forced, "Highway Patrol, how can I help you." Seated in the sergeant's office, two members of the shooting team were also fielding calls and writing notes.

"What the heck is going on?" Red asked when Lisa ended her call.

"The calls started an hour ago, something about a twenty-five thousand dollar reward. I've gotten calls from Crescent City, from Oregon, two from the Bay Area, and one from Kansas. They're all crazy," she said with a tone of obvious frustration. "Yesterday nobody knew anything, today, everyone knows who did it. Look at these messages," she continued, holding up a stack of papers. "Here's one from Oregon that says it was a group of Buddhist monks living in a commune near Roseburg. Another claims the Castles were murdered because they were involved in drug smuggling. The guys from the shooting team are getting the same kind of stuff."

"It's okay Lisa, just write down the info and we'll check 'em all out," Vaughn O'Dell told her.

It was nearly 6:30 when the officer from the shooting team returned to the CHP office. It had taken him almost four hours to make the eighty plus mile round trip from Crescent City to the crime lab in Eureka. As he pulled into the lot, he could see the business office was closed, but the entire interior of the building was lit up.

Inside, members of the shooting team were going over nearly fifty messages from callers who had information about the murders of Dave and Jodie Castle. They sorted them by those that had some shred of credibility and those that were outlandish. They then started making return calls to do phone interviews with the people who called with their tips earlier in the day. Anything that looked promising would be followed up on tomorrow with an in-person interview. It was going to be another long night.

The shooting team lieutenant was the first to review the written results of the ballistics tests conducted by the crime lab. He read it over twice.

"Are they sure about this?" he asked the officer who had picked up the report in Eureka.

"About ninety-nine percent. They're sending samples to the main Department of Justice lab in Sacramento to double check and confirm their analysis. That'll take a couple more days, but yeah, they think their results are accurate."

In addition to the four members of the shooting team and the Del Norte County Sheriff's detective, Red Wolff, Vaughn O'Dell and Ray Silva were still at the office, also. The shooting team lieutenant called a hasty meeting of all the players.

"Okay, here's the ballistics analysis and the results of powder residue samples we took from the officers' uniforms," he began. "The spent bullets removed from Dave and Jodie were .38s like we thought, half-jacketed hollow-points, made by the Winchester Ammunition Company in Illinois. The unique thing came from the powder residue. The techs at the crime lab did a second analysis when they first saw this, just to confirm their findings. The powder is a type that is used in a round called a "Plus-P-Plus". It's a little more refined than standard gunpowder so it produces more muzzle velocity than ordinary .38 rounds. Winchester puts trace markers in with every batch of gunpowder they make so they can tell lot numbers, what type ammunition, and manufacturing dates. As you know, the first "Plus" indicates it is a high-power round. The second "Plus" indicates this specific type of .38 round is only sold to law enforcement."

His statement caused an immediate outbreak of discussion between everyone present and some loud expressions of disbelief.

"Whoa, whoa everybody," Vaughn O'Dell said, trying to quiet down the group. "Explain what that means, sold to law enforcement only."

"Well, Winchester sold the stuff to any law enforcement agency in the country who wanted it, the feds, state cops, local agencies, whoever. The interesting thing is that they stopped making it in 2003," the lieutenant told the group.

"So, does that mean a cop killed Dave and Jodie?" Red asked, just as confused as everyone else.

"We shouldn't jump to that conclusion," he replied. "We all know how ammunition tends to grow legs and disappear at the firing range when cops are doing their qualification shoots. It's also possible that when Winchester stopping making this round, they may have sold off any remaining stock to gun dealers. We'll contact the Illinois State Patrol tomorrow and see if they can run down some info for us. We'll also do an internet search and check eBay, to see if anyone is selling the stuff online."

"Which is all great," Ray Silva spoke up, "But the possibility that a cop killed Dave and Jodie puts a whole different spin on this."

"A scary spin, considering when you count the nearly thousand corrections officers at the prison, there are probably close to eleven hundred cops in this county," Red stated.

"Not to mention all the retired cops," the Del Norte sheriff's detective added.

"Let's keep this information just between us for right now," Vaughn O'Dell said, looking at the entire group, but focusing on the Del Norte County detective. "First of all we don't want to jump to conclusions until we know more about the ammo and where it might have been sold to the public. Mostly though, we don't want people thinking there's a killer cop roaming around out there."

CHAPTER NINE

It had been a fairly easy day, a couple meetings, some return phone calls, the usual stuff. Leaving work early, as he usually did, because there was no one to tell him he couldn't, he had gone home and taken a nap. In the early evening he changed into some comfortable clothes and because he seldom cooked for himself, was on his way to dinner. He drove his work car as usual, flaunting the rules against personal use.

As he walked into the Elk Valley Casino, he noted it was a lot less crowded than normal for a Wednesday evening. There were a handful of people at the Blackjack tables, and only about sixty of the over three hundred slot machines had players feeding in coins. The recession the entire country was rapidly sinking into, might be the reason, he initially thought. No, he said to himself rethinking it, on most nights this place was busy, everyone hoping to hit it big at the tables, or win a jackpot on the slots. Eventually somebody would win the big one he knew, most would just continue to lose money that should have gone to pay the rent, buy groceries, or new shoes for their kids. In his mind gambling was a fool's errand, too much chance involved. He never took chances.

Located just over a mile from Highway 101, the casino was one of the bright economic spots in Del Norte County. Up until the late '80s, the Elk Valley Rancheria was just another of the nearly one hundred Indian reservations and rancherias in California, second in number only to Oklahoma. Scattered from the Mexican border to the Oregon state line, most were small, a couple hundred acres, and all were economically depressed. Then, when casino style gambling on Indian property was declared legal by the federal courts, things rapidly began to change. By the turn of the century, the Elk Valley Rancheria, like over forty other reservations and rancherias in California, had established casinos.

Many had started out small, erecting tents and Quonset huts to house their first casinos. The money rolled in as Californians flocked to the Indian run casinos often located within minutes, or a short drive from of their homes. It was cheaper than going to Reno or Las Vegas. As the money came in, many tribes reinvested to build sleek, modern, air conditioned casinos with fine dining, and a few even had hotels.

The four tribes that occupied the Elk Valley Rancheria not only built a first class casino, but they diversified their holdings to include a nearby golf course, an RV resort, and a bowling alley.

A creature of habit, he always ate dinner at the casino on Wednesdays. As he made his way toward the dining room, he passed by the bar area and said hi to a couple people he knew from work and to a few he knew by sight, but not by name.

The hostess saw him coming, as did two of the servers, who were less than busy tonight.

"Don't put him in my station," the older of the two female servers told the young high school girl who was hostess tonight. "He's a jerk, demands everything, and he's a lousy tipper," she added.

"Good evening, sir," the young girl greeted him at the hostess station, "Table for one?"

He nodded, but did not speak, his mannerisms stiff, his face stern and unsmiling.

The server who drew the short straw appeared with water and a menu moments after he sat down.

She was kind of like a lot of women in this town, he noted. Plain looking, not ugly, but not necessarily pretty, either. She didn't wear a lot of makeup, and her hair was kind of lifeless, no bounce or sheen to it. In the brief time he'd lived in Crescent City, he had not been able to put his finger on exactly what it was about the way women looked here. At first, he'd thought it was the climate, the temperatures that hovered in the forties and fifties most of the year, or the salt air. Or maybe it was the way they dressed, he thought. There weren't a lot of businesses in the county that required female employees to dress smartly in stylish dresses or businesses suits the way they did in more metropolitan areas. The standard work uniform for many females in this county, he had observed, was blue jeans, heavy sweaters, and often long-sleeved flannel shirts. He put it out of his mind as his cocktail arrived from the bar.

He knew the menu by heart. The food was good. Not a fine dining experience by any means, but well prepared, tasty, and reasonably priced. The King Salmon with Dijon Cream Sauce, he told the server. Not once in the brief conversations he had with the server did he use the words please or thank you.

"Very good, sir," she said, leaving to place the order. When she got ten paces from his table she muttered, "Jerk."

135

He sat looking around the dining room. There were four other couples having dinner and maybe two dozen empty tables. He glanced apathetically at the decorative shelves at the top of each wall adorned with California Native American artifacts, Yurok Indian woven baskets, fishing lures, and spears. A full-sized canoe occupied one entire wall. The soft lighting built into the shelves cast a warm glow over the entire room, and the single candle on his table flickered occasionally from an unseen draft. He had two candles exactly like it at home, he thought to himself.

Staring at the flame, his mind took him away from this place.

He could see his mother clearly as she opened the front door, exhausted as usual from her six day a week, twelve hour a day job as a domestic servant. Putting her purse and threadbare coat on the table in the entry hall of their small apartment, she smiled at him as she always did and rushed to give him a hug.

Even today he marveled how she could come home day-in and day-out, after putting in such long hours, and suffering the verbal abuse from the rich demanding people she worked for, and still have a smile on her face and a kind gentle manner with him.

Sitting alone in the dining room, a smile formed on his face as he remembered her. She was a saint.

It had been tough on her and him, when his father left them. It had come as a shock to her when she came home from work to find a note from him telling her he was leaving, nothing personal the note went on, she and the kid would be better off without him. He'd left her forty-seven dollars and instructions to file for divorce.

Easier said than done. She wasn't yet an American citizen, and her English, while understandable, still had a heavy German accent. That was 1969 when he was five years old.

His mother had told him the story many times how she'd met his father. It was 1963, she was seventeen, and just out of gymnasium, the German equivalent of high school, and he was a dashing young American G.I. stationed near her town. The build up for the Vietnam War was still two years away, and it had only been five years since Elvis had been stationed not too far away. American soldiers were still great catches for young German girls.

Her parents had not liked him, but she didn't care, she was in love. They were married five months later, and she left with him for the states when his year assignment in Germany was up. He was a career army man, a "lifer". He would go wherever the army sent him, do his twenty years, then retire with his pension and maybe buy a small farm, he told her.

When his parents left Germany, the army sent them to Fort Dix, New Jersey, about seventy-five miles south of New York City. He was born in the army hospital there in 1964. Try as he might, he had no real recollections of the two years his family spent at that post. Then, in 1966, his father had been transferred again, this time to Fort Ord, California, on the Monterey Peninsula, a hundred miles south of San Francisco.

Fort Ord and Monterey evoked mixed memories. He could recall living in base housing, all the streets clean, neatly mowed lawns, and a sense of orderliness that went with the structured lifestyle associated with living on a military base. He could also recall sandy beaches, mild weather, and his first school where he attended class with white, black, Hispanic and Asian kids. Life was good, his mother was happy, the sound of her laughter and singing German love songs filled their modest military home.

By 1967 the buildup for Vietnam was in full swing. The inevitable happened in the spring of that year. His father was a specialist in heavy weapons, a critical Military Occupational Specialty. He shipped out, actually he flew out, of Travis Air Force Base, forty miles east of San Francisco, in late March.

One of the bad things about having a spouse sent overseas, was the loss of military housing. He and his mother were forced to move into a small apartment in the neighboring town of Seaside. Not only was the apartment more expensive than their subsidized military house, it was smaller, and gone were his mother's flower beds which she had cultivated and tended everyday for the past two years.

He had only been three when his father left for Vietnam. Because he was too young for school and because his mother used her frugal, post-war, German upbringing to pinch pennies, they made out okay on his father's allotment check and whatever he could send home. It was a tough year, but she showered him with attention, and life wasn't too much different for a three year old.

His mother didn't share the contents of his father's few letters home. His tour was for twelve months, so he'd be back in March, 1968. Her ability to read English was pretty good, and she could sense the change in his mood and frustration in his words. Halfway through his yearlong tour, the letters stopped entirely.

He was four when his father came home. He was old enough to recognize the change. Confident and proud when he left, his father was now sullen and withdrawn, his eyes always had a distant look, and he was drinking heavily. They continued to live in the small apartment rather than move back into base housing. Their fights, mostly a result of his drinking, had been more frequent and often violent. He had distinct memories of seeing his mother beaten by his drunken father on several occasions and the local police arriving at their apartment to restore order.

His father's enlistment was up in 1969. He had ten years in, halfway to a twenty year retirement. Without a word, leaving only a letter and a few bucks, he chucked the army, his career, his family, and was gone. He never saw his father again.

No job, no income, no money other than a meager seven hundred sixty-three dollars in a savings account, might have been insurmountable obstacles to most people, but not to his mother. Applying her Germanic attitude and will to survive no matter what stood in her way, within two days she had a job as a motel maid.

The work wasn't all that hard, but neither did it pay that well. Between the cost of a baby sitter to watch her son, the rent on their small apartment, and essentials like food and clothing, there was almost nothing left every month. They got by, but just barely.

It was during their first months alone, in the evenings when she was home from work, that she started building up his belief in himself as a special person. She extolled his Nordic heritage, and his need to rely only on himself. At five years old, he didn't understand everything she was telling him, but he always said yes mama to the things she told him. She was a saint.

The motel job led within a year to much better paying employment as a domestic servant in the ultra-rich, gated community of Pebble Beach. Site of the annual Bing Crosby golf tournament, it was some of the most expensive real estate in the world. Huge mansions were tucked up in the groves of cypress trees on narrow winding roads. The entire community was secluded from view and was home to some of the richest people in the world.

Sitting at a table in the restaurant of the Elk Valley Casino, he could still see and still smell, even after forty years, the deep thick piles of fallen pine needles that carpeted the heavily forested community.

He picked at the salad the server had brought, while his memories continued to take him back to his childhood. He hadn't thought this much about his mother in a long time. Besides, the lettuce was kind of wilted. Normally, he would have sent it back in a heartbeat and chastised the server. Tonight he let it slide.

Working as a domestic servant, even though it paid better, had its drawbacks. For one, the hours were longer. Being nearly six at that time, he had started school. His mother got him up early, dressed and fed, and off to school before she headed for work. Even though she didn't get home until nearly 7:00, and as tired as she was, there was always a hot dinner, help with homework, and stories about his heritage.

Her one day a week off, Saturday, was their day together. He could still see and smell the beach, the pink cotton candy she bought him on Fisherman's Wharf, and feeding the ducks at El Estero Park. He pushed the salad away as he remembered.

Sundays, however, presented a problem. The sitter wasn't available that day so she took him to work with her. He had to be especially good she had told him, stay in the kitchen, no noise. Sitting at the table he didn't even notice the server removing his salad dish. So deeply was he involved in remembering he actually muttered, "Yes, mama."

The rich people his mother worked for weren't thrilled that she brought him along on Sundays. He was a retired army general. Typical of the times, since most women did not work outside the home, the woman's claim to fame was being the general's wife. Even though he spent a lot of time outside playing in the woods and was like a church mouse when he stayed out of sight in the kitchen, they just didn't like the idea of a kid around the house. But his mother was extremely good at what she did, catering to every whim of her employers and maintaining their home with German efficiency.

It was during these forced Sunday periods when he had to accompany his mother that two things began to happen which would imprint themselves in his mind and mold his personality.

The first involved the way his mother's employers treated her. For all the efficiency she brought to their home and extra things she did for the general and his wife, it was never enough. Typical of their class, they constantly nitpicked little things. Dust on the coffee table, too much salt in the potatoes, a broken dish. They were all little things. Being retired and with not much else to do, the elderly general constantly looked for things to complain about. His wife, aside from having other retired wives over to play bridge once a week, had little to occupy her time either. They were a classic example of post-World War II American affluence and an arrogant attitude toward foreigners.

Sometimes they double-teamed her. He complaining about some insignificant little thing she did, or forgot to do, always adding a comment about how America kicked Germany's ass in the war. His wife would add her two cents about how his mother should consider herself lucky to be living in the United States.

Even at seven years old he could see how deeply their comments wounded her and how often she had to fight back the tears after undergoing one of their verbal tongue lashings. He vowed that someday, somehow, he would take his mother away from this place and ensure she had servants of her own.

The second thing that happened, a direct off-shoot of the first, was the amount of time he began spending outdoors. He figured out by the time he was seven, the more time he spent playing in the backyard of the general's mansion, or roaming the heavily forested hillsides, the less he had to see his mother verbally abused. The late '60s were still a time when, at least in places like Pebble Beach, where a kid could roam and play without the fear of being abducted by a stranger, being gunned down in a drive-by shooting, or being arrested for trespassing.

The outdoors became the place where he commanded the birds and animals, and where, in his seven year old mind, he was in control. Soon he could name on sight, nearly every type of bird that inhabited the woods, he could read small animal tracks, and became adept at silently sneaking up on the raccoons, squirrels, rabbits, and deer that seemed to be everywhere. By reading books from the school library, he learned how to tie knots, to build a campfire, and trap animals. For him, the outdoors became a place where he could find solace. It was also the place where he would kill his first living thing.

Life went on year-after-year. Up early in the morning, off to school, his mother home by 7:00, dinner, homework, a bath, and off to bed. Five days a week. Saturdays were still their day together. Because of her work schedule, there was little time for doing the things other kids his age did, like Cub Scouts, Little League, and school activities. Even though he was going on thirteen, she still insisted he accompany her on Sundays.

As he grew taller and stronger, his mother grew older. Her hair was graying and deep creases had formed on her cheeks. By the time he was in the eighth grade, she looked old and tired. Her six day a week work schedule, the demands and abuse from her employers, and raising a son by herself, had all taken their toll. She was worn out by the time she was thirty-two. It pained him to see what was happening to her. He reaffirmed his vow to someday take her away from being a servant to other people and give her servants of her own. She was a saint.

The sound of the server's voice as she placed the salmon with Dijon sauce in front of him, snapped him rudely back to the present. For a brief moment he was unsure of where he was. Quickly regaining his bearings, he dismissed the server with a hand gesture and began to eat.

Looking around the dining room he saw three more tables were now occupied, and the noise was increasing from the gaming tables as the casino began to fill with a more typical Wednesday night crowd.

He and his mother still lived in the same small apartment in Seaside. During grammar school, he'd done extremely well. He was quicker than the other kids in his class picking up on things, and the extra time his mother spent with him every night on homework helped him excel in every academic subject. One area in which he was having difficulty was what the schools at that time called "working and playing well with others".

He didn't know it, and his mother didn't see it. Her doting on him when she got home from work, her stories about his Nordic heritage, her constant assertions to him that he was a special boy, and the need to only rely on himself, had shaped him into a spoiled and selfish child. He had few friends, and his lack of school or church related social activities meant he was never exposed to the whole spectrum of social skills needed to function effectively in life. None of these personality quirks improved over the years as he moved through junior high and on to high school.

Seaside High School was a fairly rough place. Actually located on the Fort Ord Military Post, it drew students from the town of Seaside, Fort Ord, and the city of Marina. About half the students were from military families, although with the army transitioning into a peace time mode and an all volunteer force, the base was shrinking in size and the number of military dependents shrank accordingly.

Seaside wasn't a typical military town, with lots of bars and wild soldiers roaming the streets. Instead, it was more of a bedroom community with small older homes for families that lived off base, military retirees, and the thousands of civilians who worked for the army. It had the largest black population between the Bay Area and Los Angeles. A good number of Filipino families had also immigrated to the Fort Ord area following the end of World War II.

By the time he started high school in 1980, he was still small for his age. At just over five-six and not quite one hundred thirty pounds, Seaside High School was not a good place to be small of stature, smart and aloof, and lacking in social skills. He got beat up his third day there by a much bigger black kid who took offense at something he said.

Getting beat up became a regular part of his high school life. His mother of course was furious and made several trips to talk to the school administration. They'd do what they could, but since he wouldn't tell the names of the kids who were beating him up, there was little they could do. He was smart enough to know that fingering the kids who beat him up would lead to an even worse beating.

It was the old general's declining health that saved him from a miserable three years at Seaside High School.

Now in his eighties, the general had a hard time making it up and down the stairs. His back no longer allowed him to do a lot of the outside chores like washing down the patio and raking up pine needles. His wife was still pretty spry, but bitchier than ever.

They offered his mother the opportunity for her and her son to move into the guest house and live there fulltime. The deal was predicated on his mother being able to provide the general with assistance more hours of the day, to assume responsibility for more household duties, doing the shopping, and driving the elderly couple to medical appointments.

She had jumped at the chance. The guest house was roomier than their small apartment, and even though the hours were longer, she didn't have to drive to and from work every day. It was also the opportunity to get her son away from that awful high school and enroll him in the private, prestigious, Robert Louis Stevenson School located within the gated boundaries of Pebble Beach.

For his mother, it was an expensive decision as the school's tuition wasn't cheap. But with the money she saved from not having to drive, the free rent at the general's house, pinching just the right pennies, and tuition assistance from the school, she made it happen. For him it was a new lease on life. Instead of a student body of over a thousand, there were less than three hundred kids at his new school. The classes were small, usually with a ten-to-one student to teacher ratio. Plus, nobody seemed to care about his lack of interpersonal skills or how he got along with the other students. An added bonus was he didn't get beat up all the time.

A majority of the students at the Stevenson School came from wealthy families. A few were from the Monterey area, but a larger number came from other affluent communities in California, other states, and even foreign countries. Some were the children of corporate executives, the parents of others were politicians, diplomats, or celebrities. A few slots were allocated to kids like himself from ordinary working class families. Most of the students lived at the school.

In the European style, as his mother had taught him, he held the knife in his left hand, the fork in the right while carefully slicing off a small portion of the salmon filet. Then, putting the knife down, he transferred the fork to his left hand. Being left-handed, he swirled the morsel in the cream sauce while he thought about school. He saw the girl clearly in his mind. It was the first time he'd thought about her in perhaps two or three years.

She was in three of his classes. She had shoulder length brown hair, wore large rimmed glasses that magnified her eyes, and had braces on her teeth. It was the first time he'd ever paid any attention to girls. She was probably not pretty by the standards of most boys his age, but she was beautiful in his eyes. In his mind, he could hear her laughter as she giggled with the other girls and could see her whispering and pointing as young girls do.

He was in love. Puppy love he knew, looking back on it now, but at the time it was the real thing. Now his lack of social skills and the traits that formed his personality were for the first time a hindrance to him. Too shy to approach her, he watched and worshipped from afar. Even if he had the courage to talk to her, he wouldn't know what to say.

He stopped eating now, his appetite gone. Half the salmon remained on his plate. He was close to hyperventilating.

It had taken him the better part of the school year to work up the courage to ask her to the prom. For months he'd practiced exactly how and when he would approach her, just the right words to say and the smile he would use.

The sting of her rejection still caused an almost physical nausea, even thirty years later.

He could see and remember every detail. It was a Friday, and the prom was a month away. He'd approached her just as he planned, right after lunch. She would be alone then, just as she always was before her next class, her girlfriends headed the opposite direction toward their own classes. As he sat at the table in the Elk Valley Casino dining room, his palms got sweaty, just as they had in the moments before he approached her that day.

"Go to the prom with you!" the tone in her voice was both mocking and incredulous at the same time. "I'd rather stay home and watch T.V. you weird little shit," she said loud enough that everyone else in the hallway could hear. With that, she bundled her books to her chest with both arms, as girls will do, and half-ran, half-skipped down the corridor to tell her girlfriends. Stopping her friends at the far end of the hallway, she gathered them in a small group, and the whispering and giggling started. Soon they were all looking and pointing his way, laughing.

Nothing in his upbringing had prepared him for the sting of rejection and the open humiliation in front of his classmates. His mother's stories of his Teutonic strength and how special he was, didn't apply to this situation. There was nowhere for him to retreat to, no pine forest where he could hide. All he could do was head to his next class. The mental anguish he felt was far worse than any physical pain he had received from the beatings at Seaside High School.

On Saturday the pine forest behind the general's house provided the solace he needed to deal with the pain of rejection and the laughter of the other students. Here he felt he could command the trees and the wind, and here the animals were his servants.

The rope snare he'd set earlier that morning held the jackrabbit tightly by the left rear leg. Pulling and struggling, the rabbit only made the rope tighter as it dug into its fur. He approached the trapped animal calmly. Stopping ten feet away, he sat on a pile of pine needles and watched as it alternately pulled violently against its restraint, then sat still, its eyes watching him warily, its nose twitching as it sniffed at the afternoon air.

For over an hour he sat quietly watching the jackrabbit. The afternoon fog was beginning to filter in among the cypress trees from the nearby ocean, and soon the damp mist would form a film of moisture on the trees and leaves.

He sat there alone that afternoon, the fog closing in, his mind wracked with the pain of rejection, watching the rabbit. After another twenty minutes, he slowly moved toward the trapped animal, and it began to struggle anew, its attempts to free itself even more violent as if sensing its fate.

He could see everything clearly now, the face of the girl laughing at him in the hallway at school, the general and his nag of a wife chastising his mother, and the kids who beat him up.

Strangely, once he pinned the rabbit to the ground, it ceased to struggle. Gently he eased the looped snare from its rear foot with one hand, while continuing to hold it pinned to the ground with the other.

Freed now from the rabbit's leg, the rope was just long enough to wrap around its neck. Pulling on both ends of the cord at the same time, the ligature cut into the rabbit's neck and began to squeeze the life out of its body. Suspended two feet off the ground the rabbit's hind legs kicked violently at the air while its entire body shuddered and shook trying to escape the inevitable.

As the rabbit went through its death throes, the pain in his mind went away. While he didn't realize it at the time, the pleasure he felt was almost like an orgasm.

"Was there something wrong with the salmon, sir?" his server asked, pointing to his half-full plate. She could see he had a faraway look on his face and perspiration on his forehead.

"No, take it, and bring me some coffee," he replied without making eye contact.

His three years at the Stevenson School seemed to drag by, as they tend to do for kids without a lot of friends and other activities. Fortunately, the girl who humiliated him didn't return the next year as her father had been transferred to Europe.

During his senior year at the school, the old general died. His mother stayed on to care for his wife and run the household. More duties fell on him like keeping the driveway swept of pine needles, washing down the patio, and little odds and ends things around the house. Typical of rich people, the general's wife didn't offer to pay him to do these things, assuming he was just another person to be ordered about and talked down to. But doing these things helped his mother out. She, after all, was the only woman that mattered.

Over the next two years, each time he had a problem at school, or when the general's wife bitched at his mother, or at him, he retreated to the forest, back to where he was the master of the trees and animals. Each time some small animal would feel his wrath. The neighbor's cat, he recalled, had made a high-pitched shrill sound as it went through its death dance while the rope tightened around its neck.

———————

The cup clattered against the saucer, and a small amount spilled out as the server set the coffee in front of him. Strange, he didn't seem to notice, she thought to herself. Normally an error like that would have elicited a sharp rebuke.

He noticed, but his thoughts were elsewhere.

She was really a saint, he thought to himself, as he recalled his mother. Through years of frugal penny saving and doing without for herself, she had amassed, what seemed at the time, to be a small fortune. It was enough, along with a partial scholarship, for college, she told him.

The only scholarship offer he got was from an east coast school. It meant leaving his mother, and he would have to live in the dorm and get a part-time job to make ends meet. It would be okay she had told him, she would be fine, and he could pursue his goal of a degree in business.

It was the first time he'd ever been away from home. Living on the east coast was a whole lot different than California, he recalled as he sipped his coffee. People always seemed to be in a hurry, they talked faster, and were quicker to be critical. It wasn't all bad, but it certainly wasn't the sheltered lifestyle he had grown up in. Plus, he missed his mother terribly.

Looking back on his college years, he realized he'd been a geek. Still pretty much a loner, he spent countless hours building computers in his dorm room and reading everything he could find on this newly emerging industry. By the late '80s, a few people, himself included, recognized that computers were the industry and the tool of the future. They also fit nicely with his business major.

For whatever else he was, or had become, he had filled out physically over the last several years. He had the sharply defined facial features of his mother and the lean body of his father. Nobody would describe him as handsome, but he had grown out of gawky adolescence into a young man. He still didn't know, however, that his interpersonal skills were lacking, and his mannerisms turned most people off. Not that, had he known, it would have bothered him much.

It was his third year at college when they met. He was working his part-time job as the 10:00 at night to closing at 3:00 in the morning cashier at a convenience store near the campus when she came in one evening.

A little on the plump side, she had brown hair and a shy personality. They hit it off immediately, probably because she was kinda geeky, just like he was.

Having a steady girlfriend and someone to talk with, opened a whole new world for him. It was also the first time he'd been with a woman. His mother had never, as mother's tended not to do back when he was growing up, given him the birds and bees talk. He was awkward at first, but since she was no more experienced than he was, they fumbled their way blissfully ignorant through their first sexual encounters.

"More coffee, sir?" the server appeared out of nowhere.

Nodding yes, he pushed the cup toward her, his concentration barely broken. Sitting in the dining room of the casino, he searched for a word to describe how his world had disintegrated twenty-five years ago. No single word popped into his head that was adequate to describe what had happened back then. After a moment, his mind seized on a phrase that seemed appropriate. In today's vernacular, what happened his final year of college would be called a "train wreck".

By their senior year they were making plans. They would move in together while they both finished college. Right after graduating they would get married. Meeting her parents was the first thing on their list.

She had told him her parents were wealthy and lived in a big house. In his mind he pictured a big home to be something like the general's house in Pebble Beach, and wealthy to mean they had enough money to live comfortably.

Looking back on it now he realized there was wealthy, and then there was wealthy. Nothing in his sheltered upbringing prepared him for where she lived. Pebble Beach was a gated community with guards at the entrance. She lived in a gated compound with its own security guards. Her parent's home was almost sixty acres, with a half-mile of river front, a small lake, twenty-seven rooms, and a columned portico entry.

Her father, an investment banker, had made a fortune in real estate during the post-World War II baby boom. Thinking back on it, he had liked her father immediately. Filthy rich, he still had a down-to- earth manner about him, wore blue jeans, and still did a lot of the chores around his estate. Her mother was a different story.

His first impression when he met her mother was that she could have been a younger version of the general's wife. From an old-moneyed eastern family, she was both snooty and condescending. She had a way of talking down to him that set off the same type of internal rage he felt when the general's wife berated his mother.

The weekend he spent at her parent's lavish home had been uncomfortable at best. Her mother made it clear by her attitude and comments, she didn't consider him good enough for her daughter on any level.

By then, however, it was too late, she was pregnant.

"Absolutely not," her mother had flatly told them both, marriage was out of the question.

She told her daughter if she insisted on this unsuitable marriage and having this baby, she would be cut off from the family's money and be on her own. She knew doctors who could terminate the pregnancy very discretely. She told her daughter she could move home, take a semester off from school, mother would fix everything. Besides, how could she face her society friends if they knew her daughter had become pregnant? Girls from her strata didn't do such things, and they certainly didn't marry his type.

She dumped him the week after they got back to school. It just wouldn't work out she told him. Yes, she thought she loved him, but

147

they didn't have a future together. She left school the next day and he never saw or heard from her again.

In the following weeks, alone and heartbroken in his dorm room, he tried to sort out his feelings and attempt to understand what had happened. In his mind, he came to the conclusion what had occurred was exactly like what had happened with the girl he'd asked to the prom, only on a larger scale.

It came to him like a revelation. He'd loved twice in his life. Both times the women he had chosen were from rich families, and both times they had hurt and humiliated him. In his mind he reasoned that they had rejected him because they were rich and thought themselves better than him. Yes, that was it, they were rich bitches.

His thoughts then reverted to Pebble Beach and how he had dealt with the rejection from the girl he'd worshiped and asked to the prom. The difference now was he didn't have the pine forests behind the general's house where he could flee to for solace, and there were no animals upon which he could take his vengeance.

Carefully examining the bill, he mentally checked the server's math in his head, calculated out a ten percent tip, and paid in cash.

Business in the casino and bar had picked up considerably while he had eaten, and there was a dull roar of background noise from all the people at the gaming tables mixed with the occasional loud ringing of bells when one of the slot machines paid off. As he made his way toward the entrance, he saw more than a few people he knew. He nodded or waved to those who saw him, but didn't break stride until he was out the door.

Standing just outside the entrance, he drank in the cold moist air before lighting up a cigarette. The rain continued to fall, almost like a mist, although driven as it was by the wind, it stung his face and hands as he crossed the parking lot to his work car. He continued to smoke the cigarette inside the vehicle even though policy forbade doing so.

Firing up the engine, he glanced at the digital clock on the dash. 8:42, it was early yet and the idea of going home to his empty house didn't appeal to him. The long, dark, wet, Crescent City nights were another of the things he disliked about this place. Making his way back into town, he headed down Ninth Street and pulled into the vista point parking lot at Brother Jonathan Park.

Situated on a small point where the coastline jutted out a few hundred yards into the ocean, it was a great place, during the day, to get a view of the town and the sea. As usual it was deserted tonight. He parked facing the ocean, killed the engine, and sat watching the occasional wave crash over the guardrail sending a geyser of white foamy water onto the hood of his car. He came here often. The rocky coastline, the trees, and the ocean reminded him of Pebble Beach and his mother. Soon he was mesmerized by the night, and his thoughts picked up from where they were while he ate dinner.

His last year of college was pretty much like his first. He spent most of it alone, with few friends, and even fewer outside activities. He went to class, did enough academic work to get by, worked his part-time job, and wrote home to his mother.

With lots of time by himself, he brooded about what he came to call "rich bitches" and the way they had treated him his entire life. The more he thought of them, the more his hatred grew.

Sitting in his car, the rain water running down the windshield, waves breaking over the guardrail, and the blowing wind causing the radio antenna to hum harmonically, he closed his eyes.

It had been close to twenty-five years ago, but he could still remember every detail of the first woman he killed. It was spring break of his senior year, less than three months to graduation. He already had a job lined up with the federal government and was making plans to move close to Washington D.C. when school was over.

As he had four nights a week for the last three years, he closed the convenience store where he worked to supplement his income, at 3:00 in the morning. The store was located a couple miles from campus, just off the main road through the small rural college town, and near the interstate. Business had been really slow, especially for a Saturday night. It was spring break, and most of the students had left campus on Friday afternoon, gone to wherever there was sun for the annual celebration signaling the end of winter. Since Mexico had yet to be discovered as a spring break destination, most had headed for Florida to drink anything with alcohol and fuck anything that walked. Still poor, surviving on his scholarship, whatever little his mother could send, and his minimum wage part-time job, things like spring break vacations were a luxury out of his financial reach.

He could see himself standing outside the darkened store, just locking the entry door when she pulled into the parking lot in her late model Corvette. The fancy yellow sports car skidded for fifteen feet and came to an abrupt halt when the front tires hit the bumper stop on the pavement directly in front of the door.

He could tell she was drunk as soon as she got out of her car. Using her right hand on the hood of the 'vette to catch her balance, she staggered toward him as he stood in the darkness in front of the door, the key still in his hand. Blond, slim, and pretty, she was wearing jeans and a heavy white knit sweater.

Sorry he told her, he couldn't open the store back up and sell her a bottle of rum. He'd like to, but state liquor laws forbade sales after 3:00.

He could remember her eyes, bloodshot and glassy as they were, as she used them to try to flirtatiously cajole him into reopening the store.

"Sorry," he told her again, starting to grow impatient.

"Please," she whined, grabbing his arm as she swayed unsteadily. "Come on, we'll party together. I'm the only one at the sorority house. I'm stuck here all alone because my grades are bad, and daddy wouldn't pay for my spring break trip."

"No, I can't. Besides, you don't need anything more to drink," he told her as he unlocked the chain that secured his bicycle to a lamp pole in the parking lot.

Her profanity laced tirade would have done a longshoreman proud.

"You asshole! Go ahead and ride away on your little bicycle, you cocksucker. Go back to your dorm and jack-off."

He was already a half-block from the convenience store when he heard the engine start on her car and the squealing of tires. With no shoulders or bike lane, he was riding as close to the shoulder of the dark and deserted road as he could. From behind he could hear the engine on the 'vette winding up, screaming in protest to be shifted into a higher gear. Within a second, the pavement around him illuminated from the headlights on the vehicle that was fast overtaking him.

Glancing quickly over his left shoulder, he could see the Corvette bearing down on him. She was driving on the right edge of the road, right at him, still accelerating. Leaping off the bike, he landed in the shallow ditch bordering the road, his bicycle landing on top of him as she swerved around him at the last second.

She honked as she went by, extending her hand out the window, flipping him off.

Wet and muddy from the three inches of water in the ditch, he crawled back onto the road. Except for the front tire which had come off the rim, his bike was okay. His left knee hurt, and he was a little shaken up, but was otherwise fine. Glancing around, there wasn't another car in sight. He started walking and pushing his bicycle. It would be a long and painful walk back to his dorm.

Just another of the indignities you have suffered from rich bitches, he said to himself as he walked, the metal rim of his bike making a scrapping sound on the pavement. Mentally he chastised himself, how much longer are you going to keep letting them torment you? What would your mother say? She'd be ashamed of you. She raised you better than this.

As he walked he mulled over what to do. His initial thought was to file a police report. No, he reasoned, look at the car she was driving, she's rich. She'll call her daddy. Her daddy will get her a lawyer, and she'll get off like nothing ever happened.

"I'll tell the police she was drunk, she tried to run me over," he said out loud to the empty night as he limped along pushing the bike. "No, that would do no good either, it would be your word against hers."

It took him nearly ninety minutes to walk back to his dorm. The pain in his knee and the tightness now settling into his back, made every step agonizing. He lay in bed for several hours but sleep didn't come, partially from the soreness he was now feeling all over, but mostly because he continued to berate him about rich bitches and how they treated him.

An unusually large wave broke over the guardrail, and the sound of water hitting the windshield as he sat parked at the vista point startled him. Foamy water drained down the glass as he peered into the darkness.

It was just this type of darkness that had helped him on that night so many years ago, he remembered.

Stiff, sore, and unable to sleep, he'd gotten up after tossing and turning in bed for several hours, taken a shower, and repaired the tire on his bike.

He had to work again today, but only from 4 till 10. Time enough to ride to the Howard Johnson's near the interstate for breakfast and to the library for a couple hours study time. Leaving the restaurant, he took the main road back toward campus then turned up the street where most of the fraternity and sorority houses were, a shortcut to the library.

The neat tree lined street was almost deserted. A couple of girls jogging, a middle-aged man walking a dog, Sunday papers still in the driveways of most houses and very few cars.

The Corvette was parked at an angle, half on the driveway, and half on the grass.

The pale green two story wooden house had a balcony on the second floor front and a porch built at the top of the three steps that led up to the entrance. He could see the Greek letters that announced the sorority's name mounted on a small wooden sign above the door. He slowed as he rode by, stopped on the street across from the house and watched for a few seconds. The house looked deserted.

Pedaling again, he continued slowly down the street, checking out other houses, making a mental picture of their colors, and then turned on another street which took him behind the row of houses. The back side of the entire row of houses was a forest of oak trees, bushes and vegetation. He walked his bike partially into the woods, left it leaning against a tree, and continued on foot.

Flanked by white painted houses on either side, the green house wasn't hard to spot from the back side. Another balcony on the rear, sturdy oak trees close to the house towered above the roof, a wood and glass back door led from the kitchen to the backyard.

Work that night was just as slow and boring as the previous evening. Spring break would last another week and without students in town, there weren't many customers. Most of the town's fulltime residents who were not students lived on the opposite side of campus, and the store was just far enough off the interstate that it didn't get a lot of business from travelers.

Tired from a lack of sleep the previous night, he headed straight to his dorm after work and crashed. He was asleep within minutes.

He snapped wide awake just before midnight, eyes open, staring at the ceiling.

It all started to play over in his mind. The girl and the prom, his recent breakup, the yellow corvette. He could see the rabbit, its legs kicking at the empty air, and his mother's face. His knee began to throb. The old general's wife was berating him again.

Unknowingly, as he relived that night some twenty-five years ago, his respiration rate increased, and the warmth of his breath began to fog the windows of his car.

Actually killing the girl, he found, had not been that difficult.

Dressed in dark clothing, he had ridden his bicycle to the woods behind the row of frat and sorority houses. Secreting his bike just inside the tree line, he made his way through the forest. The things he had learned from years of spending time in the pine forests of Pebble Beach guided his footsteps as he moved silently, careful to tread lightly on fallen branches and around patches of bare ground that would leave shoe prints. There were a couple of dim lights on in the other houses, night lights he surmised, as it was well past 2:00 in the morning. He froze for several minutes when a dog barked from a house down the street, then continued until he was directly behind the green house with the rear balcony.

He sat concealed behind a bush for nearly ten minutes, watching the house, listening to the night. The house was completely dark, although the street lights on the opposite side of the two story structure threw fingers of yellow light down the spaces between the homes on either side.

The flash of headlights from another car pulling into the vista point illuminated the interior of his car snapping him rudely back to the present. Just as quickly, it was dark again as the other car turned and parked well away from his before extinguishing its lights. He glanced momentarily in that direction studying the car. A couple of high school kids, he thought to himself before letting his mind take him back to that night.

Getting into the sorority house had proven easy. In small town rural America of the mid '80s, locking doors was not a big priority. The giant oak tree towered above the entire left side of the two-story structure, and its branches spread over the rear balcony. He could see himself climbing up the tree, stepping onto the top of the balcony's guardrail, and dropping silently to the deck. The unlocked door led into a hallway which in turn led to eight upstairs bedrooms. The whole house was quiet and dark, although there was enough light coming through the upstairs hall windows from the outside street lights for him to see.

Even finding her room was easy. She was the only one at the house, he remembered her saying the previous night. Only one room had light coming from the space between the bottom of the door and hardwood floor. Standing outside the door, he could see the light change every few seconds from bright to dark, then back to bright, back to dark. A television, he told himself. Slowly turning the door handle, the knob rotated. He cracked the door open just enough for the bolt to clear the frame and listened. The voices on the T.V. were louder now. Almost not breathing, he pushed against the door with his shoulder while holding pressure up on the door knob to take the weight off the hinges and prevent any squeaking.

With the door open enough now for him to peer inside, he saw her, face down, asleep on the room's only bed. The room was messy, clothes strewn on the chairs and in front of the closet, a half-empty rum bottle sat on the nightstand next to the bed. In the light from the television, which changed every time the camera switched to another character, or from scene-to-scene, he could see her clearly. Partially covered by a blanket, she was dressed in a lacy top that ended just below her waist, he thought it was called a "baby doll", and pink panties, one leg exposed, the other under the blanket. She was hard asleep, or more probably, drunk asleep.

He remembered he had been extremely calm and his actions unhurried. Looking around the room, he found her bra on the floor and a pair of pantyhose in the underwear drawer of her dresser.

In her intoxicated state, she didn't awaken until she felt her arms being pulled roughly behind her back and her face being pushed forcibly down into the pillow by an unseen hand on the back of her head. Even then her mind couldn't grasp what was happening. He sat straddling her back, his full weight forcing her down into the mattress. She struggled to breathe as he forced her teeth apart with the bra he had fashioned into a gag which he cinched tightly behind her head, before using the pantyhose to tie her hands behind her back. He remembered that wearing leather gloves had made it a little more difficult to tie the knots.

Sitting in his car over twenty-five years later, he could still recall the power he felt at that moment. Even though he had experienced that same feeling of power nearly three dozen times since that first night, nothing compared to the look of fear in the girl's eyes when he stepped away from the bed, and she recognized him.

Lying face down, her head turned to the side, looking at him, he remembered how her eyes bulged out as she struggled against the restraints. Her eyes, no longer flirtatious as they had been the night before, held the look of fear. He'd seen that look before in the eyes of the rabbit he had killed nearly seven years ago in the forests of Pebble Beach.

He pulled a small chair from the corner of the room and sat silently for perhaps twenty minutes a couple feet from the bed, watching her, much the same as he watched the rabbit years ago. As he watched, she alternately struggled against the pantyhose binding her wrists, or tried to talk to him through the gag that held her mouth open. She even used her eyes again, as she had done the night before at the convenience store, to send a message of a sweet reward if he let her go.

That was not to be. Ripping her panties off, he straddled her back. He could hear her sobbing as he used his left hand to pull her hair back roughly, causing her to arch her back in an attempt to escape the pain. As she did, he slipped the torn panties around her neck, then released her hair. He now held both ends of the silky garment in his hands behind her neck.

Her body bucked violently as he pulled tightly on the panties. She began to kick her legs and thrash side-to-side, the muffled sound of her screams lost in the pillow. Mentally he felt the physical rush of pleasure, and a sense of satisfaction washed over his body as she ceased moving.

In his mind, he fast forwarded to when he returned to his dorm room. It was almost dawn.

Lying in bed, with the first rays of the new days sun beginning to chase away the night, he felt at peace. Much like a person who shoots their first syringe of heroin and feels the warm glow of ecstasy from the drug coursing through their veins, he felt the thrill of power. He liked the feeling.

The sound of the engine starting on the car with the two high school kids caused him to lose his concentration. Glancing at the clock, he saw it was almost 10:00. Time to head home, he decided.

Driving along the dark and tree lined streets just outside the city limits of Crescent City, he continued to think about her.

He'd been sloppy and amateurish, he realized, in the days immediately following that night. He had taken too many chances and left too much evidence that law enforcement could follow-up on. The murder of the girl had been big news in the small college town. As good as their intentions were, the local police department was ill-equipped to handle a crime of that magnitude. By the time they called in the state police, much of the evidence he had inadvertently left at the scene, had been contaminated, and any trail that might lead investigators to him, had been lost.

Still, for the next several weeks, every time he saw a police car, or when a local cop came into the convenience store for a cup of coffee, his body shuddered, and a physical wave of fear swept over him from his toes to his scalp. He'd been lucky.

He'd always intended to move back to California to be near his mother when he graduated, but the job offer with the federal government was too good to pass up. Moving close to Washington D.C., he rented a small house in the country and began his working career.

In his first two years working around Washington, he killed three more women. He approached each with the meticulous Germanic efficiency his mother had instilled in him as a child. Each was a learning experience from which he refined his craft. Each time he felt that same psychological rush he had felt that first night.

He never, even in his thoughts, used the word murder. They were all rich bitches and they deserved what they got. They were the ones who looked down their noses at him and his mother, they were the ones who flaunted their wealth or position and who tormented him in his dreams. No, he told himself, he wasn't a murderer.

He came to realize, however, that he was a serial killer. Typical of the way he did everything, he began to read about serial killers, their victims, the way they killed, how they disposed of bodies, and how they had been caught. In a time before the internet, he would spend long hours at different public libraries pouring over books on serial killers. Always watching his own back, he never checked out a book on the subject. Someday, a sharp detective might check the libraries to see who was taking out books on serial killers. He didn't need his name showing up on such a list.

Through the knowledge he gained from books, he saw there were several mistakes he was making each time he killed a woman. The first dealt with trace evidence, the skin cells, hair follicles, and saliva that could be linked to a specific person through a new technology called DNA comparison. Another critical mistake, he realized, was not disposing of the clothes and shoes he wore after each time. Several serial killers, his reading had disclosed, were caught by the tread impression of the shoes they wore, or a single piece of hair from their victim that clung to the killer's clothes. Lastly, the biggest mistake most made was staying in one place for too long. No matter how careful they were, or how many precautions they took, eventually little pieces of evidence would add up, or a nosey neighbor would see something, or they would dump a body in the same place once too often. It didn't say so in the books he read, but the lesson was clear, simple mistakes will get you caught.

Halfway through his third year working at the same job, he decided it was time to transfer. A check of the Federal Jobs Register revealed thousands of opportunities in hundreds of different locations. They weren't all with the agency he now worked for, but at his pay grade he could easily transfer to a new department in a new location. Six weeks later he found himself in another state, working for a different federal agency.

Armed with the experience he had developed and the knowledge he gained from books, he found his new assignment to be a lucrative location for hunting women. Close to a vacation spot frequented by the wealthy, there were always dozens of rich single women, or married women without their husbands along, to choose from.

He was settling nicely into his new job and new surroundings. Always careful about when he looked for a new victim, he did little to draw attention to himself, and followed the number one rule of someone with a predatory and evil alter personality, blend in and look normal.

Although still a loner, blending in and looking normal, wasn't that hard to do. He dated occasionally, attended work related social functions, and gave the outward appearance of being just an average guy.

He also adhered to rule number two, don't get greedy. After killing two women within six months at his new work location, he went for over a year before the urge again began to build inside.

He might have stayed in this location for a couple more years had his mother not gotten sick. He rushed back to California on emergency leave to find her hospitalized and dying. A brain tumor the doctors had told him, fast growing, and inoperable. No, they couldn't tell him how long she had, two weeks, six months, they just couldn't say.

She still lived in the guest house at Pebble Beach, still working for the old general's wife who by this time was nearly ninety and suffering from Alzheimer's.

How to care for his dying mother was a dilemma. She was too sick and too frail to move back to where he worked, and since the army had shut down Fort Ord, there were no federal job openings in the Monterey area to which he could transfer. No matter. He quit his job, moved back to Monterey, rented a small house in the Carmel Valley and brought her there.

The end came in less than three months.

He had been devastated, he remembered, as he turned down the dark driveway to his house on the hillside just north of Crescent City. Pushing the automatic garage door opener, the roll up door retracted, the opener's built in light activated, and he drove inside. He sat there for a moment, thinking about that time.

He'd gone on a spree in the weeks after his mother's funeral, killing three women in less than two months. They all fit the usual profile of being young, pretty, and rich. Each of them had died a terrifying death as he took even more delight in prolonging their lives by choking them to the point of strangulation, before loosening the scarves he had begun to use as a tribute to his mother, allowing them to gasp for air. The terror he saw in their eyes each time he constricted the scarf gave him a sense of God like power.

After the third woman, the rage he felt at the death of his mother and the urges he had to satisfy his own need for power over women, was satiated. His grieving period was over; it was time to move on.

Reflecting on that period as he sat in his car in the garage that misty cold night, he had a number of options back then. He could apply for reinstatement to his old job, look for work in California, or simply do nothing for a while as his mother had left him a small inheritance, enough to not have to work for over a year.

In the end, he did all three. He liked working in the public sector, it was a place he could get lost in the crowd, the work was not hard, and nobody expected too much. He applied for reinstatement to his former position, but that had already been backfilled. There were openings in other places at the same pay grade he was told, although most were in less desirable locations. While he considered his options on going back to the federal government, he applied to several California police departments and for other non-law enforcement jobs with state and county governments. The process for getting any government job would take a while he knew, so he simply did nothing, frugally spending his inheritance, waiting for the right job offer to come along, one that met his specific needs.

CHAPTER TEN

Thursday had been a hectic, but unproductive day as far as the investigation into the murder of the Castles went, and tomorrow would be more of the same, Red thought as she lay in bed that night. Mary Jean was asleep, snuggled in close to her side, the heat from her naked body felt comforting as it warmed Red's side of the king-sized bed.

Turning her head slightly, she glanced out the slightly open sliding glass door into the darkness and listened to the night. It was dead silent, the on-shore breeze hardly strong enough to rustle the tree branches. Her mind was on automatic as it played out the events of the day she had.

The weather had changed six times during the day, from blue sky at sunrise to high overcast before she got to work, then dark heavy moisture laden clouds by noon which gave way to blue sky again. More rain pelted the town in the middle of the afternoon before a strong ocean breeze in the early evening blew out the remnants of the storm that had settled in over the North Coast for the past two days. It was like Ray Silva had told her when she first transferred here, if you don't like the weather in Crescent City, wait a couple hours. Tonight the sky was clear, and Red could see thousands of stars as she lay in bed. Hopefully the weather would hold for another day, she thought to herself, tomorrow was the Castles funeral.

Although the funeral and everything that went with it had occupied much of her day, she had done a dozen other things.

In the office before 7:00, she had whipped through her in-box, reviewing paperwork, signing requisitions, answering nearly two-dozen e-mails and doing the other things that went with being the commander. Even with the double homicide of her officers unsolved and a funeral the next day, the administrative part of the job wasn't going to go away, nor was it something she could put on hold.

The business office opened at 8:00, and the phones began ringing. Calls from reporters wanting to know the status of the investigation, other callers wanted information about the funeral arrangements, all on top of the normal everyday routine business.

Ray Silva showed up a little after 8:10 setting a large latte on her desk and dropping hard into one of the chairs in her office.

"Thought you could use this," he said gesturing to the latte.

"Yeah, thanks. What time did you get here this morning?"

"Around 6:00. Had a bunch of leads to follow-up on and people to talk to before they went to work."

"And?"

"Nada. Nobody's talking on the street, no rumors, no nothing," Ray replied, a hint of exasperation in his voice.

Red looked at him and nodded. She could hear the strain in his voice and a tiredness that was uncharacteristic of her career long friend.

"You okay?" she asked.

Ray Silva nodded, then spoke, "I've gotta be at the S.O. by 9:00 for the first task force meeting," he told her as he stood up.

"Damn, I forgot about that," Red replied, "Keep me in the loop, Ray. I've got a ton of things to do today."

Spending time with the parents of Dave and Jodie Castle took up a big portion of Red Wolff's day. It was one of those obligations that went with the job of being their commander, not to mention that Dave and Jodie were personal friends.

Both sets of parents had arrived in town by late morning and came directly to the CHP office. Twice in Red's small office, once with each set of parents, there were hugs of condolences, tears, angry questions about who and why, more tears, questions about the funeral. All of this occurring with the backdrop of normal daily operations, radio calls, telephones ringing, and walk-in traffic happening mere feet away in the business office.

It was one of the hardest things she'd ever done. In her twenty plus year career, Red Wolff had been shot at, nearly run down by drunks more times than she could count, seen her friends killed in the line of duty, been hospitalized twice as a result of traffic accidents, been in a dozen fights for her life where losing was not an option, and dealt with the seedier side of society on an almost daily basis.

None of that had been as hard as the several hours she spent with the parents that Thursday morning. As good a highway copper, lieutenant, and commander as she was, there was just no way to prepare for situations like this. Dealing with the relatives of officers killed in the line of duty wasn't something you could ever train for.

Captain Steffani Taylor had been her salvation. She had a relaxed and natural way of talking to the parents, of keeping them engaged by having them reminisce about their kids, having them relate funny stories, and recall happier times. She also got them involved in the planning of the funeral ceremony and helping to choose the music.

With Steffani attending to the parents, Red's time now began to be taken up with the large number of cops from outside the Crescent City area that were dropping by the office.

Police agencies from all over Northern California and Southern Oregon would be sending representatives to attend the funeral. For agencies within a three to four hour driving time, the representative could leave on Friday morning and make it for the service's 10:00 o'clock start time. For other agencies, and friends, who were a greater distance away, it meant arriving the day before.

Since Davy and Jodie had both spent a majority of their careers in Los Angeles, dozens of CHP officers who they had worked with over the years, began arriving by late Thursday afternoon. They had all come on their own dime, having taken vacation to make the fifteen hour drive. At four hundred fifty dollars a pop for the roundtrip, flying from Los Angeles was cost prohibitive. Almost all of Highway Patrol officers dropped by the CHP office to confirm where and when the service would be and to pay their respects. Many of the officers from L.A. had also worked with Red during her eighteen years in Los Angeles, and they dropped by the office to see her, also. From 3:00 in the afternoon until the office closed at 5:00, Red spent almost the entire time talking with people she had worked with up to a couple of years ago.

Talking all day, the constant coming and going of people, and the endless details that needed to be handled for the funeral, all took a toll. By 5:00 she was exhausted. A big portion of that exhaustion was mental brought on by the frustration she felt by the lack of anything substantial developing in regards to the investigation into the murder of her officers.

If Red Wolff's day had been bad, Ray Silva's wasn't much better.

He had gotten to the sheriff's office just before 9:00 for the first meeting of the multi-agency task force that Sheriff Jerome Williamson had orchestrated. There were nearly a dozen cops in the roll-call room when Ray walked in. Most were in civilian clothes, everything from coats and ties to jeans and flannel shirts. Many wore the favored light weight nylon windbreaker type jacket that had the initials of their agency or some reference to police officer silk screened on the back and a badge on the front. Doing a quick glance around the room, he could see several agencies represented by the names on the jackets, OSP, the Oregon State Police, and CDC, the California Department of Corrections. Others simply had the words SHERIFF, POLICE, FEDERAL AGENT stenciled on the back of their jackets. Ray recognized about half the people there as they milled about slipping coffee and talking in small groups, waiting for the meeting to start.

Andrew Dixon, from the Forest Service, gave Ray a courtesy nod, then resumed his conversation with another officer. Jovial National Park Service head ranger, Marv Butler, saw Ray and made a point to greet him with a handshake. Seated off by himself was Correctional Captain Nate Steadman.

Ray said a few more hellos then walked toward the back of the room and took a seat next to Vaughn O'Dell and the CHP shooting team lieutenant. Both looked tired.

"Hey Boss," he said to his chief.

"Morning Ray," he managed with a half-smile.

"Getting tired of sleeping in a motel bed, I'll bet."

"Yup. At my age, sleeping in your own bed is a big deal. Every little noise wakes me up, can't get comfortable, it's either too hot or too cold." Vaughn O'Dell paused for a second, before continuing. "What the hell am I telling you this for, you're just as old as I am," he said to Ray Silva with a humorous tone in his voice.

"How soon do you have to get back to Redding?" Ray asked.

"Assuming we don't have any more problems with Sheriff Wingnut, I'll leave tomorrow after the funeral. They want me back in division ASAP."

Both Ray and the shooting team lieutenant chuckled at Vaughn O'Dell's reference to Jerome Williamson as Sheriff Wingnut.

"Speaking of strange ducks," Ray said gesturing with his eyes as the sheriff walked into the room.

Wearing a dark gray suit today, Jerome Williamson looked impressive and very sheriff-like, as he called on everyone to take a seat.

"First of all, thanks to each of you and your respective agencies for your help with this investigation. I know we all want to catch the person or persons who murdered the officers. Let's get started with introductions."

Over the next several minutes everyone in the room introduced themselves and told what agency they represented.

As the introductions continued, Jerome Williamson leaned back against the wall and surveyed the scene before him. He was in heaven. He had all these cops at his disposal and an unsolved double homicide of two Highway Patrol officers that was front page news. Yesterday he'd done two television interviews with cable news network reporters that had been seen nationwide. His mind was racing on how he could capitalize on the press coverage to keep himself at the forefront of the investigation. After the introductions were completed, he took over again.

"Okay, thanks everyone. As some of you know, I was on LAPD for a lot of years, and I worked a few homicide investigations. This reminds me of a case I worked where we had an officer killed by a "gang-banger" in the East L.A. barrio," he began.

Enamored with hearing himself talk, Jerome Williamson missed the collective eye-rolling and looks that were exchanged between many of the cops in the room. With a typical big city cop mentality, within five minutes he had alienated almost everyone in the room by talking to them like they were poor country cousins. Yeah, they weren't big city detectives, but most of them had been cops for a long time, and all of them had worked and solved their share of cases. He kept talking.

"Jesus!" Ray Silva said, leaning to his right and whispering in Vaughn O'Dell's ear. "Hey chief, could you jab your pencil in my eye. It would hurt a lot less than listening to this fool ramble on."

Vaughn O'Dell choked down a laugh and managed to keep a straight face while listening to the Sheriff of Del Norte County as he continued to extol his experience and exploits on LAPD.

Politely, everyone in the room sat and listened. Only one person knew most of what he was saying was bullshit. That person was Jerome Williamson.

In the first ten years or so of his career, he had been to lots of homicide scenes. A few were domestic violence incidents where, fueled by alcohol, what had started as a family argument, spun out of control and ended with somebody dead. But mostly, they were drive-by shootings, where rival gang members killed each other, and a lot of innocent people, in order to uphold the honor of their gang. He'd also been the first supervisor on the scene for several officer involved shootings. As a patrolman, and as a sergeant, his duties had been limited to securing the scene, protecting evidence, and getting the names of witnesses. Detectives would arrive within an hour or so, and they would do the actual investigation.

The closest Jerry Williamson ever came to actually investigating a murder was while he was working for his Christian officers group sponsor as an administrative lieutenant developing policy out of police headquarters. His sponsor had arranged a sixty day temporary assignment to homicide bureau so Jerry Williamson could get his ticket punched for promotion. He didn't actually have anything to do with investigating a murder during this assignment, but being able to say he had done time in homicide looked good on his resume. He did learn how to talk detective during his assignment, plus he learned some interview techniques, and the procedural steps in conducting a comprehensive murder investigation.

Sensing perhaps that he had talked enough, Sheriff Jerome Williamson turned the floor over to his detective, and the CHP shooting team lieutenant, who gave the group a detailed rundown on everything they knew, shared pictures of the scene, and discussed the progress of the investigation up to this point, including forensic evidence and the ballistics reports.

"We did hear back from the Illinois State Police regarding the "Plus-P-Plus" ammo," the CHP shooting team lieutenant told them. "In the late '70s that round was the hottest thing you could get in a .38 bullet. Winchester manufactured millions of them and only sold to law enforcement agencies. Winchester is faxing us a list of all the agencies they sold to, but it looks like just about every department in the country that had .38s, used that type ammo. Then, in the late '80s, as more departments started going to semi-automatics, demand went way down. By the '90s, Winchester was only doing limited production runs, and in 2003, they stopped making it entirely. According to their records, they've never sold to anyone except law enforcement."

Everyone in the room squirmed a little in their chairs and several looked at each other. There it was again, that uncomfortable feeling that a cop had committed these heinous crimes.

"You know what it is you're saying?" the detective from the Brookings Oregon Police Department spoke up, verbalizing the thing that everyone in the room was thinking.

"Yeah, you could draw that as a first impression, but let's keep an open mind," the lieutenant replied. "Just because the ammo has a connection to law enforcement doesn't mean our shooter is a cop. We all know how ammo has a habit of walking away from shooting ranges. Maybe a cop had his weapon stolen, or it was issued to an ex-cop who never turned it in when they resigned. There could be dozens of other reasons."

"Pretty thin lieutenant," the Brookings detective responded, not trying to be argumentative, just stating the obvious.

"You're right. So we'll run that angle down by making a list of every agency in the two-state area that used .38 ammo during the years 1975 to 2003. Then we'll get lists of every officer who works, or worked for, those agencies during those time frames and cross check them against firearms registration databases."

What the CHP shooting team lieutenant just described was a massive, time consuming project. Everyone in the room was a veteran cop, and they each understood that good police work solved crimes, regardless of how long it took. None of them batted an eye.

"Okay, let's get started divvying up the things that need to be done and get to work."

Over the next thirty minutes they listed the things that had to be accomplished, and each of them took a task. The Oregon officers would check on stolen cars in their state, crimes committed the night the Castles were murdered, and each would get their feelers out for what the word was on the street. The officers from California would start checking on weapons permits, while the two federal cops would start checking on marijuana growing operations to see if there was any buzz that the murders were drug related. The corrections captain would have parole checks done on any parolees living in the two-state area.

The room was suddenly alive with action. Officers broke up into small groups or headed off to individually handle their assigned tasks. There was an almost perceptible excitement as they started their work.

Excellent, Jerome Williamson thought to himself as he watched the group break up, and the officers begin working on the investigation that would ensure his reelection.

By Thursday morning, Ross Glickner was a basket case. A cool, calculating genius when it came to financial matters, the stock market, and investing other people's money, he felt helpless dealing with the disappearance of his wife. He hadn't heard from her since Sunday evening. He'd filed a missing persons report on Wednesday, but here it was late Thursday morning, and he'd yet to hear from anyone as the LAPD officer who took the report told him he would.

Ross Glickner didn't know it, but he, his missing wife, and the report he filed, were caught up in jurisdictional and organizational bureaucracy.

Because he had filed the missing persons report on his wife from his work location within the city of Los Angeles, the initial paperwork was taken by an LAPD officer. But, as dictated by state law, the responsibility for doing the investigation fell on the agency where he resided. Since he lived in Malibu, that meant the Los

Angeles Sheriff's Department. The LAPD officer had forwarded his initial report to the sheriff's department just as he said he would.

Unknown to Ross Glickner, it was more complicated than that. For over a hundred years, Malibu, nestled along Highway 1, the Pacific Coast Highway, or PCH as it was known to the locals, was part of unincorporated Los Angeles County. Located just north of Santa Monica, Malibu wasn't so much a city as it was a place. People who lived there certainly didn't think of where they lived as a city, they used the cutesy word "colony" when referring to Malibu. Regardless of how it was thought of, the mere mention of the name Malibu conjured up images of long stretches of white sand beaches, the blue Pacific Ocean, surfers, trendy boutiques, ocean front houses, and the laid back Southern California life style.

As an unincorporated section of the county, the twelve thousand or so permanent residents and the hundreds of thousands of people who flocked to the area annually, received, at no cost, their criminal law enforcement services from the Los Angeles Sheriff's Department. Their traffic enforcement came from the Highway Patrol, also at no cost. That changed in 1991, when the residents voted to incorporate.

Incorporation meant Malibu residents would now have a lot more local control over their community. But it also meant paying for their own law enforcement services. The government of the newly incorporated city of Malibu had two choices when it came to law enforcement. They could start from scratch and build their own police department, or they could contract with the Los Angeles Sheriff's. The newly elected city council found, as the government leaders in forty of the eighty-eight cities in Los Angeles County had already discovered, that it was far more cost effective to contract with the sheriff's department.

It was a simple matter of economics. Rather than having to recruit, hire, and train new officers, buy police cars, build a police station and jail, develop a radio dispatch system, and go through the growing pains of establishing a new police department, it was cheaper to contract with the very agency that was already providing them law enforcement services. By contracting with LASD, the city of Malibu would receive complete police and traffic enforcement services. It was not, however, completely the same as having their own city police department.

Contracting with LASD meant the city got basic police services from deputies assigned to work exclusively in Malibu. The more deputies on patrol and the more police services Malibu wanted, the more it cost. On the plus side, contracting also meant Malibu got the services of the sheriff's radio and 9-1-1 telephone systems, jail services, the crime lab, forensic investigations, and the detective bureau. On the negative side, it did not mean, however, that those services were located in Malibu.

Ross Glickner's missing persons report did get processed by the Los Angeles city police officer late on Wednesday afternoon. By the time the report was reviewed and approved by an LAPD supervisor, it was late Wednesday evening. By that time of night, thanks to budget cuts, furlough days, and lay-offs, there were no civilian employee's on-duty to process the report. Thursday morning, during regular business hours, the report was processed and electronically transmitted to the Los Angeles Sheriff's Region One Headquarters in West Hollywood, about twenty miles from Malibu. Unfortunately for Ross Glickner, while there are some detectives assigned to West Hollywood, missing persons reports were handled by detectives from the Homicide Bureau located at the main LASD administrative building in Monterey Park, forty-five miles away, on the other side of the county.

By Thursday afternoon, the report made its way from West Hollywood to Monterey Park where it was logged into the computer, given a case number, and assigned to the Homicide Bureau. By 3:50 the report was on its way to the desk of sheriff's detective Benita Reynosa.

An eighteen year veteran, Benita Reynosa, Bennie to her friends, had spent the majority of her career working patrol out of the very tough Lennox sub-station in southern L.A. County. She was street tough and a hard worker, which had earned her a job as a detective and an assignment to the Homicide Bureau.

On LASD missing persons cases are investigated by homicide detectives. In the hierarchy of the Homicide Bureau the new kid got stuck working the less than glamorous missing person's cases. Even after eight months, Bennie Reynosa was still the new kid.

Missing persons cases, she had found, at least with missing adults, entailed lots of time spent doing leg work, driving to interview the reporting party, and time spent on the phone. That time was often for naught when the reported "missing person" showed up a few days later. In those cases, it was usually one-half of a relationship mad at the other half and running away from home for a few days. Other times an alcohol or drug induced bender, or a sexual tryst, could keep a person "missing" for several days.

Every detective had their own way of approaching a case. Bennie Reynosa started by opening a case file and running the names of the missing person and the person who made the report, through several databases. She started with California's Department of Motor

Vehicles system to obtain pictures and driving records on both Kim and Ross Glickner. Both had a couple of tickets in the past three years, nothing major. The two tickets on Kim Glickner's driving record were for speed, Detective Reynosa saw. Probably nothing, she thought to herself, but she made a note in the file.

Punching up another screen on her computer, she ran the Glickner's through NCIC, the National Crime Information Center, and CII, California's Criminal Identification and Information system. Within a few seconds she had a complete electronic criminal history on both. Again, there wasn't much there. Ross Glickner had been arrested once, nearly twenty-five years ago, for drunk in public. Using his date of birth, she calculated out the time frames in her head. He had been nineteen at the time, probably when he was in college. Kim Glickner's record was clean.

Lastly, Detective Bennie Reynosa ran the Glickner's and their Malibu address, through the Los Angeles Sheriff's Department's database called "Coplink". If there had ever been any contacts between the Glickner's and LASD, or if deputies had ever gone to their home, this system would show it. The computer made a couple of sputtering sounds after she hit the enter key as it searched several different databases. The screen flashed back a "Not in System" message within two seconds.

Okay, Bennie Reynosa said to herself, so they're pretty clean, no arrests, no domestic violence incidents, and no wild parties that brought the cops to their house. Picking up the phone, she dialed Ross Glickner's cell.

Their conversation lasted only a couple minutes. No, she didn't have any information on his wife, Detective Reynosa told him. Was he available so she could drop by his residence to talk with him and gather more information? It was a weekday, and the evening commute wouldn't end till about 6:30, she told him. She'd be at his house around 7:30, depending on traffic.

Hanging up the phone, Bennie Reynosa thought about their brief conversation for a few seconds. In her eight months working in homicide, she'd only worked a handful of cases where a missing person was actually missing. One case involved a wife who, after fifteen years of being used as a punching bag by her husband, had sought refuge in a battered women's shelter. The woman's neighbors had reported her missing when they hadn't seen her around for several days. It had taken Bennie Reynosa five days to run her down. In another case, a mother had reported her nineteen year old son missing when he failed to return from a weekend surfing trip to San Diego. Thanks to her proficiency in Spanish and several hours on the telephone, she was able to locate him and two of his friends, as guests of El Departmento de Policia, in Ensenada, Mexico. The case that stood out in her mind and the one that kept her focused on her work, involved a missing nine year old boy who had been abducted by a paroled sex-offender. The child's body had been found off of Interstate 15 near the Nevada state line. It took Bennie Reynosa four days to put that case together and track down the murderer.

There was something in Ross Glickner's voice on the phone that told her this wasn't just a run-away housewife, and there was substance to this report. He sounded genuinely concerned, almost panicked. There was no hesitation when she asked to meet him at his residence, in fact he sounded relieved that she was coming. She made a few notes in her file, shut her computer down, and headed for the parking lot.

Every detective in the Homicide Bureau had an unmarked vehicle they used in the course of their duties, to drive to crime scenes, to interview witnesses, and for court. Since they were always on-call and often had to respond from their residences, they were also allowed to drive their county cars to and from home. Like all detectives, Bennie Reynosa, had a Ford Crown Victoria.

It was close to 8:00 and completely dark when she pulled into the driveway of Ross Glickner's home. Located on a hillside on the inland side of PCH, had there been daylight she would have seen the home had an unrestricted view of the Pacific Ocean less than three-quarters of a mile away. The entire place exuded wealth. Everything was either polished imported hardwood or gleaming solid brass. Floor to ceiling windows led onto a large balcony, and flames burned at wood in the fireplace that served both the living room and the master bedroom. Pretty fancy digs, she thought to herself.

She also thought about her training, and the manual they called "Homicide Investigations for Dummies". It wasn't really a training manual as much as it was a compellation of one-liners and antidotes from her predecessors, things they learned either the hard way, or through good old fashion detective work. Rule Number One in the manual stated "Somebody the victim knew done it". Rule Number Two was designed to keep investigators on point. It simply said "Don't forget Rule Number One".

Bennie Reynosa started taking in things as soon as he answered the door. She had done her homework on Ross Glickner, and in her mind, she had pictured him to be an imposing and powerful

169

personality. He pretty much invalidated that image as soon as she saw him in person. Unshaven, his hair tousled, and wearing a baggy pair of jeans with a grey sweatshirt, he didn't look like the "Broker to the Stars" she had read about. He was tall, slightly built, and her first impression was that he looked a little dorky.

Things began to jump out at her as soon as she entered the home. First off, the interior of the house was very clean, and everything looked orderly. She noted the *Los Angeles Times* on the side table was the Thursday edition. There was a single pair of shoes by the couch and a medium-sized pizza box on the glass-topped coffee table. As she talked with him she casually lifted the lid to the box.

"Dinner?" she queried.

"Yeah, I picked it up on my way home. We don't cook much, even when Kim's here," he replied.

There were two slices still in the box she saw, and they looked fresh. The box was cold, as were the two slices of pizza, but the cheese hadn't coagulated, and the sauce still had a reddish color. She made a mental note of the restaurant name printed on the box and would drop by the establishment after the interview to verify Ross Glickner had picked up a pizza tonight.

"You have a housekeeper?"

As soon as she asked the question, Ross Glickner began to squirm. He hesitated, she could see his mind frantically searching for an answer.

"Well, ah, yeah, but ah, the thing is we had to let her go," he replied, unable to make eye contact with the detective.

Bennie Reynosa had seen that very same reaction to that very same question before. "Look, Mr. Glickner, I'm from homicide, not immigration. If you have an undocumented worker as your housekeeper, that's between you, Immigration, and the IRS."

Los Angeles County Sheriff's Deputy Benita Reynosa would have been the last one to say anything about an undocumented worker, or illegal alien, to use the politically incorrect term. Many times her mother had told her the story of how she and her father had trekked across the desert near the California border town of El Centro in 1968 entering the United States illegally. Her mother had been seven months pregnant at the time, carrying a baby who would grow up to be a detective.

"So let's try it again, do you have a housekeeper?" Detective Bennie Reynosa asked.

"Yes, comes five days a week, does a little cooking, cleans up, does the laundry, starts about 7:30. She's usually gone by the time I get home."

The questioning followed that track for several minutes while she gathered the specifics about the housekeeper.

The cleanliness of the house and the pizza were significant, Bennie Reynosa thought to herself.

All men were slobs she knew. But, even slobs were smart enough not to make a huge mess if they thought their wife might show up at any minute. The absence of discarded clothes strewn in the living room told her Ross Glickner wasn't leaving a mess everywhere. Since the only newspaper in the room had today's date, it probably meant the previous day's editions had been read, then moved to the trash. Another sign of someone being careful of how much mess they made. The pizza was the clincher. It was obviously tonight's dinner, and Ross Glickner was keeping the house clean lest his wife show up and chew his ass for leaving a mess all over the place. A woman after her own heart, Detective Bennie Reynosa smiled to herself.

According to the report he filed, Kim Glickner had left Sunday morning. It was now Thursday evening. From how little mess there was, you could make a reasonable deduction, she told herself, that if Ross Glickner didn't expect his wife back tonight or ever, the house would look a lot sloppier.

Bennie Reynosa spent about forty minutes interviewing Ross Glickner, getting little details asking questions, some subtle, some not subtle at all. Yeah, they were fighting, well not fighting fighting, arguing was more like it. The stress from his job was putting a strain on their relationship. And, yeah, it was unusual that she would just up and decide to drive twelve hundred miles to see her sister in Seattle. No, he told the detective, he didn't think she was seeing someone, and no again, he didn't have a girlfriend.

Satisfied she had all the information she needed, Bennie Reynosa asked him if she could look around the house. Of course, he told her, and stood back while she began looking around. She headed to the master bedroom first.

The room was huge, with a sliding glass door leading out to a large deck with a hot tub that could hold eight. There was one bathroom with two vanities, two sinks, two mirrors, and an oversized single shower with two shower heads. There were two closets.

"One for her and one for me," Ross Glickner told the detective.

Standing in the open closet doorway, Bennie Reynosa turned on the light and paused before walking in. The closet was maybe twelve feet long and twice that wide. Rows and rows of dresses, many with store tags still attached, hung neatly against the walls, and racks of shoes that would cause Imelda Marcos's head to turn were stacked three high on the floor.

From the doorway of Kim Glickner's closet, Detective Reynosa saw what she was looking for. Toward the back, on the top shelf, there were over a dozen suitcases. They were all different sizes, some small, some big, a few had wheels, others just shoulder straps. They were all different colors. Arranged in a row, sat a five piece Gucci soft-leather matched set. Cost about a month of my salary, Bennie Reynosa guessed.

"How many bags did your wife take?" she asked him as he stood outside the closet.

"One suitcase and her cosmetic bag," Ross Glickner replied, "I put them in the trunk for her."

The two-step plastic stool sat on the floor just below the location where there was an empty slot on the top shelf. The slot was just big enough for a rolling suitcase, the type you could carry on to an airplane, or for a quick get-away.

She mentally recalled that Kim Glickner was five-two. Taking another glance at her husband, she estimated him to be right at six feet tall. The shelf was about seven feet off the ground she guessed. Too high for her to reach without the step-stool, but reachable by him.

Looking in the drawers of the vanity, Bennie Reynosa could see spaces where various jars and bottles had been. In their place, imbedded in the wood, were small white rings left by whatever cream, ointment, or other cosmetic they held.

Bennie Reynosa took it all in, her face expressionless, giving away nothing, as she continued to look around. It was amazing, she thought to herself, how many homicides had been solved because the murderer, claiming their spouse had left on a trip, forgot to at least remove a suitcase, pack a few clothes, and toiletries to make it look like the victim had actually gone somewhere.

Back now in the living room, she queried him about his wife's car, credit cards, and cell phone number.

"Anything else you can tell me?" she asked as the interview was concluding.

Ross Glickner couldn't add anything.

As she'd learned to do in homicide investigators school, she saved one of her best questions until the end of the interview. By waiting until the reporting party had gotten comfortable, or when they sensed the interview was about over, a final zinger question usually caught them off guard.

In her best Colombo voice, making her question sound almost like an afterthought, she asked, "Why did you wait three days before you reported your wife missing?"

Ross Glickner got a funny look on his face, almost as if to say to the detective, don't you know, but responded without hesitation, "Well, you have to wait three days to report someone as a missing person."

"Where did you get that idea?" the detective asked shaking her head.

"That's what I always hear them say on T.V. cop shows. I thought that was the law."

"Not for several years, Mr. Glickner, you can report a person missing immediately."

Ross Glickner just looked at her.

So much for that question catching him off guard, she thought to herself. Had he fumbled for an answer, or given her some bullshit excuse, she might have put him high on her very short list of suspects. It was starting to look to her like Kim Glickner might really be missing.

After stopping by the pizza joint to verify Ross Glickner had picked up a pizza that evening and stopping at a twenty-four hour supermarket to pick up a salad for herself, it was close to 10:30 when Bennie Reynosa got back to her desk at the sheriff's administrative building in Monterey Park.

Her workday had started at 3:00 in the afternoon, and since detectives worked a four-ten plan, or four, ten hour days per week, she still had some time left on her shift.

Homicide Bureau was pretty much deserted, most of the partitioned cubicles were dark, as their occupants either worked a different shift, were out doing follow-up, or were off doing some no doubt important investigative work. The air conditioner hummed as filtered air, controlled to the precise temperature prescribed by Los Angeles County regulations, kept the large room tolerable to work in. Tolerable simply meant too cold in the winter, too hot in the summer. Bennie Reynosa didn't notice as she ate her salad while punching in the numbers to Kim Glickner's cell phone.

It took nearly ten seconds while the land line phone on her desk searched for Kim Glickner's cell phone. Once the two phones established a connection, Kim's phone rang six times before a recorded message came on the line, "the person you are trying to reach is unavailable or has travelled out of the coverage area".

It took her a couple minutes to determine who Kim Glickner's carrier was, find the number and contact the security supervisor at that company. Most were ex-cops and happy to help. Within a minute, an e-mail showed up on Bennie Reynosa's computer screen from the cell phone carrier with Kim Glickner's computerized phone records for the past six months attached.

She'd plow through the forty-two pages of numbers, dates, times, and length of call some other time, if she had to. Right now she was looking for calls made in the last week, more specifically since Sunday morning.

It was easy to follow Kim Glickner's trail once she left Malibu. She was a non-stop talker. Not that it mattered much, given the Glickner's net worth, but Bennie Reynosa hoped they had the "unlimited" minutes plan. Bennie followed Kim Glickner's drive north on Highway 101 as she left Los Angeles County, entered Ventura County, and continued north into Santa Barbara County. Kim Glickner made non-stop calls. Most were to 213 or 818 area codes, the greater Los Angeles basin. Each time she made a call, the print out listed the cellular antenna site that caught the call and sent it along to whomever Kim was calling.

It was like reading an annotated California road map, 9:37, call from Kim Glickner's cell phone to a number in Beverly Hills, lasted fifty-two minutes, made from Carpentaria. Next call 11:18, from Goleta, to Malibu, forty-one minutes. A gap of an hour and then another call, this one from south of Santa Maria. By noon Kim was between Paso Robles and Salinas, still on 101, still heading north, making good time, and still talking almost non-stop. Several calls lasted only a few seconds, ended, and then began again as a new call to the same number.

Bennie Reynosa let her mind drift off, and she could visualize the area where Kim Glickner was driving and using her cell phone. She knew the area fairly well, having made the drive numerous times as a kid when her parents traveled from L.A. to Castroville, near Monterey, to visit her mother's brother. In the last couple years, since her dad wasn't as great a driver as he used to be, she had taken over the duty of driving her parents up 101, through the Salinas Valley to visit her uncle. She knew the area well.

North of Paso Robles for about thirty-five miles, it was low rolling hills and hundreds of thousands of acres of cattle grazing land, almost no people and no towns. Highway 101 wound lazily through the hills and past the oil rigs sitting near the road. She could picture, going back to her childhood, what looked like big mechanical animals that slowly bowed and then reared up their heads all day long. She'd last driven that stretch of 101 six weeks ago. She remembered the cell service had been spotty at best. She also remembered the oil rigs were still dutifully pumping after all those years.

The computerized printout of times, places, and phone numbers corresponded to exactly what Ross Glickner had said. He'd gotten a call from Kim Sunday night. She was staying the night at a hotel in the Napa Valley, she'd told him. The print out confirmed Kim had made a call to her home phone from Napa around nine Sunday night.

So far Ross Glickner's story was holding water.

Bennie Reynosa followed the cell phone record through the next day. She didn't know much about California north of San Francisco, and she had to pull up a California map on the computer to match the locations where Kim Glickner's cell phone calls were made from to a reference point she could visualize geographically. Her direction kept heading north, still on Highway 101. The names were unfamiliar, Laytonville, Redway, Rio Dell, Trinidad, Orick. The last call on the printout came from Crescent City at 6:15 in the evening to a number in Washington. She would check on that call tomorrow, but her detective's instincts told her the number probably belonged to Kim's sister.

Bennie Reynosa stopped for a minute. Crescent City, why does that name ring a bell, she wondered to herself? Crescent City, her mind searched. Of course! It came like a revelation. Crescent City was where those two Chippies had been killed. When was that? Sometime early Tuesday morning the news stories had said. They had been overwhelmed by an as yet unknown assailant, their guns taken, and had then been executed the newspapers and computer news reports indicated.

An interesting coincidence Bennie Reynosa thought to herself. She traces a person from Los Angeles to Crescent City, and that person ends up missing around the same time as two Highway Patrol officers are murdered.

There was still enough time on her shift to do a couple more things. She dialed the number for the security department of the credit card company Ross and Kim Glickner used. They each had their own account. Unlike going through the 1-800 number as the general public did where there was a sometimes interminable wait, followed by speaking to someone in a foreign country whose English skills were marginal, Bennie Reynosa was connected immediately with a security supervisor. After explaining who she was, giving a special code number which identified her as belonging to LASD, she was connected to a supervisor.

It took less than ninety seconds for the supervisor to bring up all charges made on Kim Glickner's card from Sunday through Tuesday. He attached that report to an e-mail, pressed the transmit key, and one-point seven nine seconds later it was in Bennie Reynosa's in-box waiting to be opened.

"Anything else, detective?" the voice on the other end of the phone asked.

"Yes, can you put a trace on that card, and let me know anytime it gets used?" Detective Bennie Reynosa requested.

"Done," the peppy young voice told her.

There were seven charges on Kim Glickner's credit card during the time period Bennie Reynosa was interested in. Four were for fuel purchases, as she drove north. One for was the hotel in Napa on Sunday night, and two looked like they were for food.

The last charge had been made at a Shell gas station on Highway 101 in Crescent City early Monday evening. The card hadn't been used since.

While she didn't have anything to support it, she had a feeling about this one. Kim Glickner, or at least her cell phone and credit card, could be traced as far as Crescent City, over seven hundred miles from Los Angeles. While husbands are always suspects when a wife goes missing, it didn't fit in this case. The time frames and distances were too great for him to be directly involved. Indirectly, perhaps, but even that was a stretch from what she knew so far.

One more check before calling it a night. Punching up the Department of Motor Vehicles Registration screen on her computer, Bennie Reynosa typed in the license plate of Kim Glickner's car. The computer return was almost instantaneous. Late at night, when there weren't hundreds of users trying to input or retrieve vehicle information, the sometimes painfully slow DMV computer system was like lightning.

Just so she had a copy of the vehicle information in her case file, Bennie Reynosa hit the print key. As the computer formatted to print the screen, she scrolled down through the information. She mentally noted the vehicle info, 2009 BMW, sedan, and the plate number. The rest of the information, the date of purchase, vehicle weight, and the name of the legal owner, was mostly for DMV use in assessing annual registration fees. At the bottom of the page there was a section to list any official actions that involved the vehicle. Her eyes scanned the sole entry.

Action: Towed and Stored
ORI: CHP – Crescent City - 9150

Date: 03-24-10
Authority: 22651(b) CVC

She hadn't worked traffic in a while so it took her a moment to translate the shorthand entries on the DMV printout. The first three lines were easy. Kim Glickner's car had been towed by the CHP in Crescent City on March 24th.

She needed help translating the line that read "Authority" and the CVC, or California Vehicle Code section number.

Swiveling in her chair, she pulled a copy of the California Vehicle Code from the shelf behind her desk and thumbed through to the section number listed on the printout. Section 22651 gave the authority to peace officers to tow and store vehicles under certain conditions. Subsection (b) was the authority to remove a vehicle found abandoned on a state highway. Bennie Reynosa was familiar enough with the Vehicle Code and traffic law to know if Kim Glickner had been in an accident and was unable to care for her vehicle, the officer would have stored the vehicle and used subsection (g) as the authority. Likewise, had she been arrested, the CHP officer would have used subsection (h) to tow her vehicle away.

Bennie Reynosa read the computer printout again; subsection (b), "Abandoned on state highway". Weird shit, she thought to herself.

There was nothing more she could do tonight. Tomorrow she'd contact the Highway Patrol in Crescent City. Crescent City, another coincidence she pondered? It was late, and she was tired. Maybe this will make more sense tomorrow, Bennie Reynosa thought to herself.

It was almost one in the morning. She had just enough time to fill out her daily activity record. She made a few brief notations in Kim Glickner's case file and ended with "Investigation continuing, foul play possible".

———————

In Crescent City, at the Del Norte County Sheriff's Department, about the same time Detective Benita Reynosa was first opening a missing person's file on Kim Glickner, the multi-agency task force investigating the murder of CHP Officers Dave and Jodie Castle was wrapping up its first day of work.

Although they had never worked together before, and each of them had a little different way of doing business, they had meshed well and it had been a productive day. Database checks were in progress on .38 caliber pistols registered to cops in Del Norte and

Humboldt counties in California, and in Jackson, Curry, and Josephine Counties in Oregon. It would take a couple more days to come up with a list of names, as much of the information was older and had never been computerized. Those records had to be hand searched by task force members.

Captain Nate Steadman, from Pelican Bay State Prison, had quickly developed a list of prisoners who had been released over the past two weeks and had traced the whereabouts of all but a few through their respective parole agents.

He'd hit a snag determining the location of three recent parolees because their parole agents were off on involuntary furlough days ordered by the Governor in an attempt to address California's massive twenty-six million dollar budget shortfall. The three furlough days a month were not going over well with rank and file state employees. They were especially unpopular with members of the California Correctional Peace Officers Association. With over thirty thousand members, CCPOA, resented their officers being furloughed when CHP officers had been exempted. They would remember when it came time for the next gubernatorial election.

Nate Steadman would try to contact those agents tomorrow, but that would be an iffy thing as many parole agents tacked a sick or vacation day onto their furlough day to make it four days off.

Each of the investigators gave a short summary of their efforts, and then the CHP shooting team lieutenant spoke, "Okay, sounds like everyone made some progress today. The funeral is tomorrow, and some of us will be attending. It starts at 10:00. Can't say how long it will last. For those of you who can, let's meet back here at 1:30 tomorrow."

The day's work over, there was some subdued small talk as the group wrapped up their paperwork and headed for the parking lot. Some, at least those who had offices close by would head there, others had long drives ahead of them.

Ray Silva found himself walking out of the building next to Corrections Captain Nate Steadman.

"I don't think we've ever met," Ray Silva said, extending his hand.

"I don't believe so, Nate Steadman," the very large black man said with a smile, offering his hand to the almost as tall, but outweighed by forty pounds of mostly muscle, Ray Silva.

"Long-ass day," Ray Silva said.

"Very long and more to do," Nate Steadman responded.

"Me too," Ray replied, "My lieutenant will want a full briefing on what we found out today.

She's not going to rest until someone's in jail."

"I've got to get back to the prison and give my warden a complete update. He insists on knowing everything that's going on. Wants to make sure a released prisoner is not involved in this."

They shook hands again in the parking lot, Ray Silva heading for the marked black and white patrol car he was driving. Had there been a reason for him to be paying attention, Ray Silva would have seen Nate Steadman getting into a plain white Crown Victoria.

CHAPTER ELEVEN

Any time a cop is killed in the line of duty, their funeral involves a lot of "pomp and circumstance". In rural Del Norte County, where the two officers being laid to rest were popular and well known, the funeral took on all the dimensions of "a happening".

Having spent a majority of their careers in Southern California, the Castles had attended nearly a score of cops' funerals. About half had been for fellow Highway Patrol officers, the rest for police officers or sheriff's deputies, some they had worked with, others they attended just because they were cops. Not surprisingly, in their "Death Letters" they laid out their desire for a funeral patterned after those type services.

The Crescent City Lutheran church had seating in wooden pews for about a hundred forty people, maybe a hundred eighty if the church goers squeezed together. The parking lot could hold perhaps seventy-five cars, and on-street parking could accommodate another fifty or so within walking distance.

The service was scheduled to begin at 10:00, and by 9:00 the first police cars started to arrive. Many officers had spent the previous night in town, and nearly a hundred more had already descended on the small church. City police officers directed traffic and tried to keep the curb directly in front of the church reserved for the family and the many VIPs who were expected. By 9:30, streams of people, women in dark dresses and men in coats and ties, intermixed with cops in uniform, could be seen walking toward the church from far away parking spots.

As the civilians filed into the church, the officers, following some unwritten protocol, found their way to the grassy area on the side of the church and made themselves into a loose formation.

They were predominately CHP officers, in their tan pants, campaign hats, and formal green "Ike" jackets. Interspersed in the formation were green clad sheriff's deputies from Del Norte and Humboldt counties, and blue uniformed officers from the Eureka and Arcata police departments. Four grey uniform clad Yurok Tribal Police Officers and their director stood in formation, as did cops from the Redwood National Park and the Six Rivers National Forest. The Oregon State Police had sent five troopers in their silver blue uniforms and "Smokey the Bear" hats. Single officers were also there as representatives of police and sheriff's departments from throughout Northern California and Southern Oregon. Ukiah P.D., Santa Rosa P.D., Sonoma County Sheriff's Department, Brookings Oregon Police Department, and the Josephine County Oregon Sheriff's Office all had officers in the formation.

Two officers, one a trooper from the Pennsylvania State Police, the other from the Alabama Highway Patrol, were there to represent the National Trooper's Coalition. It was customary, they explained to the California cops standing around them, that the Trooper's Coalition always sent representatives whenever a state police or Highway Patrol officer was killed. By 10:00 there would be nearly three hundred fifty cops standing outside the church.

The interior of the church filled up quickly as local people who had known the Castles filed in. As they entered, uniformed officers directed them to one side of the church, keeping the other vacant for family and VIPs.

The CHP Commissioner and close to a dozen other high ranking brass, arrived about 9:45, flown to Crescent City on the Highway Patrol's Beechcraft King Air. Red Wolff had arranged for transportation for them from the airport. Immediately upon arrival, there was much handshaking, hugs for the family, and whispered condolences.

As police executives, the CHP brass routinely wore suits and ties on a daily basis, easier to travel to meetings and to conduct business before and after normal working hours. Most of them were older, late forties to nearly sixty. Today they were all in uniform. It wasn't a pretty sight.

Standing off to the side, Red Wolff, Mary Jean, Ray Silva, and Julie watched.

"Jeez," Ray Silva said to Red, half under his breath, using his head to gesture toward the Highway Patrol Commissioner, "The guy looks like a soup sandwich in uniform."

"Ray!" Julie elbowed him.

"Hell, look at him. That green jacket is stretched so tight, if the zipper breaks it will send shrapnel flying in all directions. We should get a paramedic down here on standby."

Red Wolff choked down a laugh. She had her own issues with the man. "Come on, time to get inside," she told the other three.

"No hurry, the Governors not here yet," Ray Silva replied.

"Yeah, you're right, they won't start till she gets here," Red agreed.

"Why in the world is the Governor coming?" Mary Jean asked.

"Election coming in the fall. Never hurts to use a cop's funeral to court the law and order vote and talk tough about crime," Ray chimed in.

"Or maybe she's coming to see you, Ray. After all, you two hit it off so well after the terrorist attack last year," Red deadpanned.

They all laughed recalling how Ray had gotten in the Governor's face when she wanted to flee Crescent City in the midst of the Islamic terrorist attack on the town the previous Fourth of July.

In her twenty plus years on the Highway Patrol, Red Wolff had been to her share of cops funerals. Regardless of how they were orchestrated, as final goodbyes, as fond remembrances, or, as some of the recent funerals she had attended were called, "celebrations of life", they were all sad affairs. There was no such thing, she knew, as a good funeral or a bad funeral. They were all bad as far as she was concerned. Nobody liked having their friends killed, and funerals just served to remind her how quickly things can change.

As Red and Mary Jean entered the church, one of her officers serving as an usher, handed them a folded paper program. It was made of coarse heavy stock paper with a color picture of a cross and a bright sunrise over the ocean on the front, superimposed with a short, meaningful to someone, verse meant to capture the somberness of the occasion. Inside were pictures of Dave and Jodie with an accompanying short bio of each. On the opposite page, an agenda of sorts, the names of speakers and songs that would be interspaced between each person who would talk. On the back, the program invited all attendees to the Crescent City Community Center for a reception, and an opportunity to share remembrances with the officers' families.

After they took their seats, Red glanced at the program. This had all the makings of a moon shot, she told herself. About half the funerals she'd been to were Catholic services, she recalled. That always involved a Mass for the Dead and all the ritual that entailed. Her experience had been that Catholic priests were pretty good at judging the tempo of a cop's funeral, and if the speakers ran long, or the crowd was growing restless, they could whip through a funeral mass in a big hurry, when necessary. A Lutheran service was a first, and she knew she was just along for the ride, no matter how long it took.

The small church had a raised dais in front with seven chairs, a podium on the left side, and an organ off to the right. Huge flower displays bordered each side of the dais, and two gleaming open redwood coffins sat in front. On-lookers could tell both officers were in full uniform. Large pictures of Davy and Jodie were on easels next to the coffins. Off to the side of each coffin, standing at attention, were two Highway Patrol officers dressed in formal uniform, with white silk ceremonial neck scarves and white gloves. They were Crescent City officers serving as the honor guard for Dave and Jodie. Every twenty minutes Sergeant Dick Huddleston would march two relief officers down the middle aisle and change the honor guard. How to conduct a funeral was all precisely laid out in Highway Patrol General Orders.

As the organist played *Rugged Old Cross*, the last people to enter the church were some of the three hundred plus officers who had been standing outside. While each pew might hold eight parishioners, they could barely accommodate six officers wearing their gun belts. Only about fifty five officers got seats, the rest would stand through the entire service, lining the walls on both sides from front to back. Another forty or fifty found themselves crammed into the double-door entry way. None-too-soon either, as if to signal it was time for the service to start, the sky, which had been darkening all morning, opened up with a drenching rain.

Unfortunately, the Governor had yet to arrive, and protocol demanded the service not begin until she got there.

The Lutheran Church in Crescent City had a forced-air heating system to combat the often very cold temperatures along the coast. Like most buildings in the county, it did not, however, have air conditioning. Nearly five hundred people, many of them cops wearing wool jackets, crammed into a space meant for two hundred, caused the temperature to soar in the church. Ushers and church elders rushed around opening windows, but the temperature remained uncomfortably high.

The Governor, twenty-five minutes late, was escorted to her seat near the podium. She lost a few votes among the mostly Democratic local people because of her tardiness. She didn't have very many votes to lose among the California cops, so all she managed to do by being late was reinforce their opinion of how little Democrats thought of law enforcement officers.

The service began with a computerized PowerPoint presentation on the large screen behind the dais. The program, flashing pictures of Dave and Jodie from early childhood, as teenagers, in uniform, and as a married couple, would run non-stop through the entire service. As soon as the organist finished playing *How Great Thou Art*, the Lutheran pastor welcomed everyone, directed some words of condolence to Dave and Jodie's parents, and related a few personal remembrances of the Castles. The honor guard changed. Next, the Highway Patrol chaplain spoke for almost twenty minutes. Soldiers of God, the Centurions of ancient Rome, blessed are the peacemakers, he droned on. When he finished, from an unseen CD player, Bette Midler sang *Wind Beneath My Wings*. Two more speakers, officers who had worked with the Castles in Los Angeles, told a few amusing anecdotes, and then another recorded song was played. The honor guard changed again.

From her seat, Red Wolff watched as the Governor began to squirm in her seat. The Highway Patrol chaplain spoke again, another recorded song. Then the Governor spoke. She did a lousy job, Red thought to herself, talking about how marvelous she thought the cops in Crescent City were and her hard line stance on crime. How about saying something about the two dead officers, she wanted to stand up and shout.

Another song, one of their favorites the audience was told, because it told the story of leaving the big city life to live in the country, Don McLean's *Castles in the Air,* played. The honor guard changed. Robotically, the PowerPoint moved from picture-to-picture. Around the church, people could be seen looking at their watches and moving about in their seats trying to stretch their legs and backs. The service had begun a half-hour late, and it was already past noon.

Ray Silva looked at the program and remarked sarcastically to Red in a hushed voice, "Is there going to be an intermission?"

"Ray!" Julie elbowed him.

Back at the podium, the Highway Patrol chaplain spoke again, "Bagpipes are the traditional law enforcement way of saluting a fallen comrade," he told the audience.

From the back of the church, two police officers from another agency, dressed in full regalia, tartan kilts, Tam o' Shanters, sashes, and knee socks, slowly paraded toward the front playing *Amazing Grace.*

"There's nothing traditional about bagpipes in California law enforcement," Ray Silva whispered to Red. "It's an east coast thing. And for the record, I hate bagpipes."

From the other side, Julie elbowed him again.

Seated on the dais, the Governor squirmed and stole a glance at her watch. The Highway Patrol chaplain was beaming as he watched the pipers come down the aisle. He rated this funeral one of his better productions.

Ray Silva wasn't the only one wondering how much longer the service would last.

Toward the back, innocuous, seated among the other service goers, he told himself, he had to be here. People would have noticed if you weren't, and somebody would have said something. When this is over, you make a short appearance at the reception, make sure you talk to some people, and then go.

He focused his attention on the podium and another in the endless stream of speakers.

It was almost 1:00 by the time the service ended, and the church cleared out. There was even a protocol for that. First, the officers solemnly filed out, reforming themselves into two columns on either side of the church's front door. Following them, came the civilians. After the civilians filed out, it was about five minutes before the two caskets were wheeled down the aisle to the front door.

What few people saw during that five minutes were the funeral directors, overseen by Captain Taylor, hurriedly removing the badges, name tags, shooting medals, and other decorations from the officers' uniforms before closing the coffins. The badges were state property, and they had to be returned to Sacramento along with any other state-issued equipment.

When the caskets finally exited the church, Sergeant Dick Huddleston called the assembled officers to attention and gave the command "Present Arms". Collectively every officer brought their right hand up in a salute which they held until both coffins were loaded in hearses.

"Order arms," Dick Huddleston commanded as the door to the last hearse closed. With that, the officers snapped their arms down, and the church service was over.

Standing in formation, Red Wolff made a note to herself to commend her sergeant on his performance today in handling the honor guard. She was still pissed off at him for how he botched the initial crime scene, but a positive comment from her would make him feel better, she knew.

The church service was over, but not the funeral. Officers now headed to their patrol cars and formed a procession behind the two hearses.

It was a little less than two miles on the streets of Crescent City from the church to the cemetery. The procession wound its way to

Highway 101 and turned north. It was like a giant snake with two black hearses at the head, and an undulating body of over a hundred patrol cars stretching behind, their headlights flashing and rotating emergency lights throwing out multi-colored beams reflecting off buildings and cars that had yielded to the curb as the procession passed.

With the rain continuing as a steady drizzle, only about a third of the people who had attended the church service made it to the gravesite. Both sets of parents and other relatives were shown to seats under a canopy, while the officers formed up in the rain. The pastor expedited his portion of the internment in deference to the rain and the cold wind that had come up over the last hour.

Not that it mattered much. There was a lot more ceremony to go.

First came the twenty-one gun salute. Seven officers positioned away from the gravesite fired three volleys from rifles into the air. Standing in the rain, about a hundred officers and a handful of civilians jumped each time a volley was fired. Then, choreographed to perfection, from a hillside in the distance, far removed from the gravesite, a lone bugler blew a mournful rendition of *Taps*.

The honor guard now carefully, with crisp, sharp, military precision, removed and folded the American flags from the caskets. Once folded, the flags were given to the Highway Patrol Commissioner who presented a flag to each set of parents. It was 2:24 when the graveside service ended.

Tired, her head splitting from a nagging stiff neck, Red Wolff let out a long sigh, then turned to talk with Ray, Julie and Mary Jean.

"Let's head to the reception, then call it quits. We're not gonna get any police work done today."

Silently, all four headed for their vehicles.

The Highway Patrol chaplain lingered with the parents by the gravesite as they said their last goodbyes, then escorted them back to the limousines that would take them to the community center for the reception.

Once they left, the chaplain stood by himself, the last one, other than the workers who were now lowering the caskets into the ground, at the cemetery. It had been a good funeral all-in-all, he thought to himself, just the right amount of religion, solemn remembrances of the two officers, and pageantry. Still, he was disappointed the families did not want the two dozen white doves to be released at the gravesite. It was always a nice touch. He was especially disappointed his captain would not push for a flyover of Highway Patrol aircraft in the "missing man" formation. That was always a crowd pleaser.

Eleven thousand dollars in fuel costs, landing fees at McNamara Field, and flight crew overtime to fly four airplanes to Crescent City for a twenty second flyover of the cemetery, didn't seem unreasonable to him.

———————

The first thing Detective Bennie Reynosa did when she got to work at 3:00 was call the Highway Patrol in Crescent City. She needed to find out more about the circumstances surrounding Kim Glickner's car being towed.

Making that call was a lot harder than she would have thought.

Funeral or no funeral, the Highway Patrol office needed to stay open to handle business, and officers had to be available to handle calls. To allow a maximum number of people to attend the funeral service, one officer was on patrol for the entire county, and one civilian stayed at the office to answer phone calls and handle walk-in traffic. Since there were two public phone lines into the office, one line was put on hold making it easier to handle one call at a time.

Bennie Reynosa was frustrated. Every time she dialed the number for the Highway Patrol in Crescent City, the line was busy. She tried four times in fifteen minutes and got a busy signal each time.

On her seventh try, the call rang through.

"Highway Patrol, Donna speaking," an exasperated, but friendly female voice answered.

"Hi, Detective Reynosa from Los Angeles Sheriff's Department, could I speak to the watch commander please."

The person Bennie Reynosa was speaking with was a civilian office assistant. She was really good at her job of filing reports, answering phones, and typing reports, but like it was to a lot of civilians, police nomenclature was confusing. Since the Highway Patrol didn't use the term "watch commander", she was a little perplexed with who this detective on the other end of the line wanted to speak to.

"Ah, who?"

"The watch commander, somebody who can give me some information on a car you towed."

Bennie Reynosa's tone had just a little edge on it, equally as perplexed that the person she was talking to didn't comprehend the term watch commander.

"Well, ah, there's nobody here right now except me."

Bennie Reynosa wanted to scream. Nobody there!

187

"Are you an officer?" she asked.

"No, ma'am, I'm an office assistant," came the reply.

There was a long silence on the phone.

It was one of those small agency things that big agency coppers, like Bennie Reynosa, didn't understand. In L.A. they had watch commanders, who were usually lieutenants, and sergeants working on every shift. Phones got answered promptly, regardless of the time of day or night, and there were always cops at the station to handle things. Rural small agency police work was different. Phones sometimes rang and rang because there was nobody to answer the call. It wasn't unusual at other times that there were no cops, only civilians at the offices and stations.

"Okay, I really need to speak to someone," Bennie Reynosa said, the impatience in her voice more pronounced.

"I can take a message for the sergeant," Office Assistant Donna Woten told Bennie Reynosa.

"Okay," the frustrated detective replied.

Dutifully, Donna Woten copied down the contact information on a three-by-five State of California message form. Following standard procedure, she put the message in Sergeant Dick Huddleston's in-box.

The interior of the Crescent City Community Center was brightly lit, a stark contrast to the dark sky outside as the drizzle turned to rain, and the brunt of a new storm blew in. With the central heat warming the building, it was comfortable, and the several hundred people gathered in small groups to talk, nibble on cookies, and sip juice or coffee.

Red had been to lots of these gatherings. Experience, however, didn't mean they were any easier. She never quite felt comfortable making small talk with the relatives, and it just didn't seem right to be drinking coffee and snacking after a funeral. But, it went with the job, and she made a point to spend time with the parents and other relatives of Davy and Jodie, talking and agreeing with everyone on what a fitting memorial service it had been.

Excusing herself after an appropriate amount of time, Red spotted Ray engaged in a conversation with some other people while Julie and Mary Jean had found a table.

She made her way to the table and sat. The bare metal of the folding chair seat felt cold against her backside through the wool uniform pants she wore that were damp from the rain.

Mary Jean wrinkled her nose as soon as Red sat down. "Oh, that smell of wet wool is terrible."

"Yeah, this pair is headed for the cleaners. I just put them on this morning, another six bucks shot," Red replied as she scanned the growing crowd in the room.

"Who's Ray talking to?" Julie asked, nodding in the direction of her new husband talking to a very large black man in a green uniform and another in a dark suit.

"The guy in uniform is a captain from the prison. Nate something, he's part of the group of people working on the case. The other guy in the suit is the warden from Pelican Bay," Red told them both.

"How do you know the warden, Sweetie?" Mary Jean inquired.

"He's a member of the Del Norte County Chief's Association, not that he has come to very many meetings," Red told them both.

"A lot of this police stuff is still new to me. Ray doesn't tell me much about his work, but since I'm moving up here, I'd like to know everything," Julie joined in.

"Almost every county in California has a "Chief's Association". It brings together the sheriff, the police chiefs from all the cities, the Highway Patrol commander, and any other law enforcement agency bosses. They get together and discuss police management issues, what's happening politically that affects law enforcement, new court rulings that impact operations, things like that," Red gave them a narrative overview. "Here in Del Norte, it's the sheriff, the Crescent City Police chief, the chief from the Tribal Police in Klamath, the head ranger and special agent from the national parks and the forest service, the commander of the Coast Guard cutter, and the warden from the prison. We get together once a month for a couple hours."

"Is the warden an officer, I mean like a cop?" Julie asked.

"Well, some wardens are, others aren't. Wardens are Governor's appointees. Some come up through the ranks from corrections officers, others were civilian administrators in the corrections system, and some have never worked around prisons, but get appointed. I'm not sure what this guy's background is."

"That's a screwy system," Mary Jean joined the conversation. "Do wardens carry guns?"

"Corrections Officers are peace officers by Penal Code definition, and even though most of them don't carry guns inside the prison, they almost all carry them off-duty. I know if I were a warden or a corrections officer, I'd carry one. You never know when you may run across some ex-con with an axe to grind," Red responded.

The conversation turned to other subjects as the three of them sat there.

"Erin, who is that strange looking older man over there?" Mary Jean asked Red Wolff, indicating with a slight hand gesture to a man sitting at a table by himself. "He's been staring our way for the last fifteen minutes."

Casually moving her head in that direction, Red looked at the man, made eye contact, and then turned back to Mary Jean.

"It's Indian Joe, pretty much a legend to cops in this county."

"Indian Joe? You've never mentioned him before," Mary Jean said with curiosity in her voice.

"He's lived here, like since, forever. Full-blooded Yurok, lives in a small shack near the mouth of the Klamath. He must be pushing seventy, works as a guide taking fisherman up river to catch salmon when he's not in jail. Been popped a half-dozen times for DUI, has a permanent revocation on his driver's license, not that it stops him from driving," Red chuckled as she recalled her numerous contacts with him.

"Why's he staring at us?" Julie asked.

"Let's ask him, he's pretty harmless," Red laughed, turning to Indian Joe and waving him over to their table.

At sixty-nine, Joe Dansby was in perfect health. Strong as a bull, he had only been to a doctor twice in his life. Once was when he was a kid to have his tonsils removed, back when they did that as a matter of routine. The other time was three years ago, to have a fish hook removed from his eye, an accident caused by one of the rich sport fisherman he guided up river. A little over five-eight, he had sunken cheeks, and the skin on his face was almost the consistency of finely cured leather. His long silver hair had wisps that had eluded the rubber band he used to fashion a pony-tail, giving him a slightly crazed look. He wore the only sport coat he had ever owned, bought thirty-five years ago, and by now well-worn and two sizes too big.

"Hi Joe," Red smiled as she stood and shook his hand. It was like grabbing a block of solid wood with a sheet of sandpaper wrapped around it.

"Hello Red," he replied with obvious courtesy and respect in his voice.

After Red made the introductions, and there was a bit of small talk, Joe leaned in toward Red's ear and spoke in hushed tones, "Red, can I talk to you, alone?"

Once off by themselves, Joe spoke quietly. "Red, I'm really sorry about Dave and Jodie, they were both good kids. Even when

Dave arrested me a couple years ago he was very polite about it, never made no drunken Indian comments or disrespected me."

"Thanks Joe. Yeah, they were both good officers. Hopefully we'll catch their killer real quick."

"That's what I wanted to talk to you about."

"You have some information?" Red asked with obvious interest in her voice.

"I'd gone to the casino, the one in town, on Monday night. Left about 1:30, headed back to Klamath. I'd had a couple pops, and you know I'm not supposed to drive."

Red nodded indicating Joe should continue.

"Anyway, I was driving my old pickup, and as I started down Last Chance Grade, by the vista point, you know where I'm talking about, I seen this Highway Patrol car, well actually it was one of those new SUV things you guys drive now. It was stopped behind a car. It looked to me like another cop car."

"Why did you think it was another cop car, Joe?"

"Didn't have no star or nothun on the door, it was all white, but it was the kind of car a lot of cops drive."

"Why didn't you get a hold of me the next day after you heard what happened?" Red asked, almost in disbelief.

"Red, I took a couple guys upriver that morning. No phones, no radio, just got back last night, that's when I first heard about Dave and Jodie."

Red paused, her mind racing, so many questions to ask. "Joe, what did you see? Was there somebody else there?"

"I seen Dave and Jodie, they were talking to some guy," Joe Dansby replied.

"Joe, what did the guy look like?" Red asked, a sense of urgency in her voice.

"I couldn't see his face."

"Joe," Red quickly replied, "Was he black, white, what?"

"Sorry," Joe said sadly, his eyes downcast, slowly shaking his head, "I only saw the whole thing for a couple seconds, it was dark, and I'd been drinking."

"Okay Joe, don't go away. Stay right here, I need to get Ray Silva," there was excitement in her voice.

Looking around the room, she spotted Ray still in conversation with the Nate whatever his name was and the warden. She headed in his direction.

"Excuse me guys," Red interrupted, "Ray, something's come up. I think we may have a witness."

All three men turned to her, instantly attentive.

"Who's the witness?" Ray Silva asked excitedly.

"It's Joe," she replied pointing to the old man in the ill-fitting clothes standing alone across the room.

"What did he tell you?" Ray pushed.

Red paused for a second and shook her head, "Not here, let's get a hold of as many people on the task force as we can and meet at the sheriff's office ASAP."

"Some of them are probably still there, and a bunch of them are here at the reception."

"Whatever, let's move on this, it's the first break we've had."

"Who is this Joe guy?" Nate Steadman asked.

"Local Indian fisherman and guide," Red responded, "Lives down on the Klamath."

Red and Ray said quick goodbyes to Mary Jean and Julie. Before they left, Mary Jean suggested getting together for dinner at their place around 7:00.

It was raining harder as Red and Ray, with Joe Dansby in tow, paused by the front entrance to the community center contemplating a run for her vehicle.

"You guys stay here, I'll get the car," he told her and was gone, jogging across the asphalt parking lot now covered with two inches of water as the drizzle had turned to a steady downpour.

As Red and Joe waited, Nate Steadman and his warden exited the building. She could hear little bits of the conversation between the two as the warden lit a cigarette and instructed Nate Steadman to keep him informed about the meeting.

About half the task force members, mostly those from Oregon, had left by the time Red and Ray arrived with Joe. You couldn't blame them, Red told herself, it was late Friday afternoon, and they had long rainy drives ahead of them. Still, they had all of the CHP shooting team present, as well as the detectives from Del Norte County and Crescent City Police. Also, there were Andrew Dixon from the Forest Service, Marv Butler from National Parks, and of course, Sheriff Jerome Williamson. Nate Steadman arrived a few minutes later.

Red started the meeting by explaining what Joe had related to her, and nine voices began asking questions.

"Whoa, one at a time. Yeah this is a good break, but we need to go easy. Remember Joe says he had been drinking, and it was dark. I suggest we have two people take Joe in another room, and see if they can jog his memory a little. If all nine of us start firing questions at him, any defense lawyer in the world will say we intimated him and planted information in his mind."

It was close to 5:00 when the Del Norte County Sheriff's detective and the CHP shooting team sergeant finished interviewing Joe Dansby.

The first thing they had done was take him outside in the rain to the Sheriff's Department parking lot where they asked him to point out a car like the one he thought he saw that night.

"I don't need to get wet," he told them, "It looked just like that!" Joe stated, pointing to an unmarked, light colored, Ford Crown Victoria.

Given the circumstances, the darkness, the brief amount of time Joe had actually seen anything, and the fact he had been drinking, they learned quite a bit more.

Joe couldn't swear it was a police car, but it looked like one. It was solid color, maybe white, but it could have been light colored also, and it had those small hub caps, the kind that only covered the lug nuts, not the entire wheel. Although he had not seen his face, the suspect, they gleaned from Joe was at least a head taller than Jodie Castle. Since she was five-eight, that would put him in the six foot to six-three range. No, he hadn't seen any other cars in the vista point, and he only saw the one person.

It was a lot more than they had a couple of hours ago.

They had gotten everything they could from Joe. They'd get back in touch with him next week to see if he remembered anything else. Okay Joe had told them, but Sunday he was headed about twenty miles upriver to check on his gill nets and wouldn't be back until Tuesday night.

Ray Silva made arrangements to get Joe home while Red stayed with the task force members.

"So where do we go from here?" she asked the group.

The CHP shooting team lieutenant spoke first, "Right off the bat we need to compile a list of every unmarked car used by any government agency in the Southern Oregon and Northern California counties. Cops aren't the only ones who drive unmarked cars. There are dozens of government agencies, federal, state, and county that use the Crown Vic."

"And we also need to do a Department of Motor Vehicles run in both states for privately owned Ford Crown Victorias and Mercury Grand Marquis's. Remember they are virtually the same car, only the Mercury has a little more chrome," Red Wolff added.

193

"But that will mean thousands of cars!" Jerome Williamson protested, "It will take days to go through the computer printouts."

"We'll limit the search criteria by zip code and only request information on privately owned vehicles in the three border counties in Southern Oregon, and in Del Norte and Humboldt counties in California," Red retorted, cutting off any further comment from Jerome Williamson.

While the discussion continued, Jerome Williamson glared at the female CHP lieutenant who was fast becoming his nemesis.

"Don't forget that a lot of old cop cars get repainted and sold second hand to the public," Ray Silva added, "We also need to find out what agencies have sold their old patrol cars."

"Okay, we've got a ton of things to do, it's Friday evening, and we need the help of a lot of other agencies and government departments to get the information we need. Unfortunately, that can't happen till Monday. Let's meet back here Monday morning," the Del Norte Sheriff's detective told everyone.

As the meeting broke up, a few people left right away. Red and Ray hung around talking with Andrew Dixon from the Forest Service and Nate Steadman from corrections.

"I'll be working on that list of unmarked cars over the weekend," the head Forest Service special agent told them. "Most of our vehicles are pickups and SUVs, and most of them are painted green and have door markings."

"We have a bunch of unmarked cars," Nate Steadman said, "Quite a few are unmarked Crown Vics, we use 'em for discreet prisoner transport and for our parole agents. I'll start on that tomorrow, but tonight I have to brief the warden."

"Thanks guys," Red told them as she and Ray headed for the door, "See ya Monday."

Seven hundred miles away, Los Angeles Sheriff's Department detective, Bennie Reynosa, had just returned to her office from doing some field follow-up on another missing person's case. She actually had six active cases she was handling, all assigned to her within the last week. One thing about working homicide bureau, there was never a lack of work.

The red message light on her phone was flashing, and the digital counter indicated five new calls. After getting settled in, she punched the flashing button to hear the messages.

"Son-of- a," she let the last word trail off silently, no return call from the Crescent City Highway Patrol . "Fucking Chippies," she said under her breath.

Unknown to Detective Bennie Reynosa, "Fucking Chippies" was probably an accurate comment.

It was well past 6:00 Friday night when Sergeant Dick Huddleston got back to the Highway Patrol office. The business office was closed, the lights were out, and the public phone lines switched to a recorded message. It had been a long and tiring day, and he was in no mood to return a phone call from some detective in Los Angeles, let alone the three other phone messages that had accumulated on his desk. He was already four hours past the end of his normal eight hour shift and looking forward to three days off. It didn't add to his mood that he was hungry and wet.

He hurried through his in-basket, quickly scanning over and signing off on a couple of reports, and filling out his daily time sheet, including an overtime form. Picking up the message slip one more time, he looked at it for a second and tossed it back in his in-basket.

"If it's important, they'll call back," he said out loud as he flipped off the light and headed for the locker room.

Usually Ray Silva was pretty subdued at dinner get togethers. Red, Mary Jean, and Julie had girl things to talk about that didn't involve him. Tonight, he was unusually quiet, even withdrawn.

Red and Mary Jean's house was cozy warm, bordering on hot. Ray grabbed his drink and headed out on the deck as the three girls gabbed away at the kitchen table.

The sharp change in temperature, from hot inside, to a brisk forty-six degrees outside, snapped Ray Silva's mind awake. Even though the rain had stopped, the air was heavy with moisture and everything around him had the perpetual wet look of things that were saturated with water. With all the deck furniture being soaked, Ray stood next to the guardrail, his drink sitting on the top rail, staring out over the valley below and the lights of Crescent City in the distance.

"What's the matter Ray?" Red Wolff asked as she took a position standing next to him along the guardrail.

Deep in thought, he had not heard her approach, and her words startled him a bit. "Oh, hey Red," he responded reflexively.

"What's on your mind, Silva?" she rephrased her query.

"Just contemplating life in general and how we planted Dave and Jodie today," irreverently referring to their funeral.

"Damn, planted is kind of a callous word, don't you think," Red replied.

"Dead is dead. In a couple weeks, a month at the outside, people will be going Davy who and Jodie what's her name, you watch. I guess it was the whole church service thing, the music, the people who showed up because it was expected, the rifle volley, the bugle, and those damn bagpipes."

"Hell, Ray, that's the way every cop's funeral is, you know that. Besides, that's what Dave and Jodie said they wanted in their letter."

In the course of a back and forth conversation, a reply by Ray Silva was in order. He stood silently for a long ten seconds, Red Wolff anticipating his response.

"Yeah, that's the way every cop's funeral is."

"You have a letter in your file, Ray?"

"Yeah, an old one, goes back to when my mom was still alive. Guess I need to update it to include Julie."

"You do that Silva, first thing Monday," Red told him.

The sky chose that moment to open up again. No light sprinkle turning into a steady rain, this was instant hard rain, the kind that obscured vision, with drops so big when they hit the wooden deck they made splashes that sent ten thousand little geysers of water two inches into the air.

As they retreated into the house, Ray mentioned to Red that he and Julie were making a quick trip to the Bay Area on Tuesday. They'd spend the night at Julie's house, take care of some business, and be back late Wednesday evening.

A few miles away, his home dark and chilly, moisture had coated the inside of the windows. The interior air was heavy and cold enough to cause vapor as he breathed.

In his mind, he was playing out the ramifications of the witness the Highway Patrol lieutenant had found. From what he knew, the witness had not seen his face, in fact, the old Indian couldn't even say if the man he saw was black or white.

The fact he had seen what he told investigators was an unmarked cop car, was a problem. On Monday the task force would start compiling lists of government agencies that used the Crown Victoria, and a similar list to identify civilian owners of that type car.

On the plus side for him, there were a couple of hundred unmarked police cars like his within eighty miles of here. Dozens of people drove them every day for their jobs. And, there are lots of Crown Victorias and Mercurys that are owned by civilians, too. On the negative side, he realized, while lots of people drive government cars during the day, only a select few take them home at night. It wouldn't take the cops long to narrow the list down.

Eventually he knew, given enough time, the task force's investigation would lead to his vehicle. The only way to prevent that from happening was to help the cops solve the murder of the two officers.

CHAPTER TWELVE

On the following Monday, with the funeral over, the multi-agency task force investigating the murders of Dave and Jodie Castle got down to serious police work. With the new information provided by Joe Dansby on a possible suspect vehicle, they split into two teams, one checking out police agencies that were still, or had in the past, used .38 revolvers in combination with Plus-P-Plus ammunition, the other concentrating on Ford Crown Victorias.

It was non-flashy, drudge police work, the kind people don't see on a sixty minute T.V. show. Nothing fancy, just hour upon hour of reviewing computer printouts, cross checking names and dates, making phone calls, doing field visits to interview people, and keeping detailed notes of everything they did.

The work went a lot slower as the four officers on the CHP Shooting Team, having completed their investigation of the actual shooting incident, left Crescent City right after the funeral and returned to their regular work locations. Ray Silva assumed the role of primary investigator for the Highway Patrol, although Red Wolff devoted every minute she could spare toward the investigation.

And they had actually made some progress. By Wednesday, the team doing the investigation on the ammunition had developed a short list of law enforcement agencies in the immediate two state area that used .38s and Plus-P-Plus ammo. Follow-up was already underway with those agencies to get the names of personnel who carried a .38 as their duty weapon and those who had privately owned .38s registered to them.

Conversely, the work of the team trying to run down what government agencies used Crown Victorias and also compile lists of private owners of that type vehicle, was mired in reams of paperwork and stacks of computerized vehicle registration printouts.

The biggest problem they faced was the Crown Victoria itself. In trying to develop criteria for doing computer searches on private ownership of the Crown Victoria and the Mercury Grand Marquis, they discovered the body style on both vehicles had not changed appreciably in ten years. Ford, it seemed, knew they had a winner in the 1998 Crown Vic, and over the next ten years they made only small changes to the vehicles exterior, adding an extra piece of chrome one year, a different front grill design the next. Basically, the 1998 model looked almost identical to every model year up to 2009. They also discovered Ford stopped selling the Crown Victoria to the public in 2008, and they only did fleet sales to taxi companies and governmental agencies after that.

It only took the Department of Motor Vehicles in Oregon and California a couple hours to extract the requested data using the criteria the task force developed. Still, the computers spit out the names and addresses of hundreds of owners who had vehicles in Northern California and Southern Oregon that met the criteria. Most were registered to individuals, while others were registered to businesses. The Crown Vic, and its sister, the Grand Marquis, it seemed, were popular cars.

Del Norte County had the fewest number of either type vehicle by simple virtue of there not being a Ford dealer in Crescent City. Dealership or not, there were nine Crown Vics and two Mercs registered in the county. Ray Silva and the Del Norte Sheriff's detective drew the job of contacting the owners. It didn't take long to eliminate them all as suspects.

Of the eleven vehicles, all of the owners could account for their whereabouts on the night the Castles were murdered. To a person, when asked where they were that night, each responded, with a slight irritation at the question, "in bed", as if to say, where else would I be?

That didn't automatically eliminate them as suspects, but it put them way far down on the list. The average age of the owners, Ray Silva and the Del Norte Sheriff's detective found, was about seventy-seven, and it didn't take a trained investigator to deduce they were probably not personally involved.

To the elderly owners, the two cops were learning, the Crown Victoria and Mercury Marquis were great cars. Big, heavy, four-door, rear-wheel drive, and American made. What else did someone who, as a kid, had lived through the great depression need to know when they went to buy a new car? The fact the car was actually made in Canada, was an inconvenient truth they simply ignored. For a half-century, they had been loyal Ford owners who couldn't conceive of owning anything else.

Just because the elderly owners weren't involved, it didn't mean their vehicles might not have been. As politely as possible, which given the crankiness of a couple of the owners, was a chore, they physically inspected each vehicle looking for any clues that might indicate the vehicle had been at the vista point the previous Monday night.

One vehicle, the investigators found, hadn't been driven in over two years. The owner, a widow, didn't know how to drive. Two other vehicles were located in closed and covered garages, with a heavy coating of dust and debris indicating they hadn't been moved in months. The remaining vehicles were also eliminated as being the wrong color or the owners were adamant that nobody but themselves ever drives their car.

The detectives working the Oregon side of the border would find ostensibly the same thing. Most of the privately owned vehicles that met their search criteria were owned by elderly people, and neither they nor their vehicle it seemed were in Crescent City the night the officers were murdered.

Unfortunately, work was going slower on running down information on governmental agencies that used Ford Crown Victorias. The problem was that just about every law enforcement agency and many non-law enforcement government agencies used the same type vehicle. Identifying the agencies had been fairly easy, but getting information on who had access to these vehicles would be a time consuming laborious process.

One by one the detectives on the task force began contacting each agency. It was pretty easy to develop lists of people who had cars assigned to them, the kind they used while doing their daily jobs and drove to and from work. It was harder, however, to track down the people who drove "pool cars", the ones that weren't assigned to a specific person, but were available to any employee while driving on official business. Most of these agencies, they found, didn't keep very good records on who drove the vehicle. They all had policies on signing out vehicles and a log that drivers were supposed to fill out, but the reality was almost nobody followed the policies or used the sign out logs as required.

Still, as slow going as it was, by Thursday, the task force had eliminated hundreds of private vehicle owners and had narrowed down the list of government owned unmarked Crown Victorias to less than a dozen agencies, with a total of about sixty-five cars to check out.

The list of vehicles in Oregon included four belonging to the state police, a couple used by the sheriff's department in Josephine County, and one from the Public Safety Director in Grants Pass. About a dozen other Crown Vics were used by various social service agencies, county officials, and federal agencies.

By far, the overwhelming number of Crown Victorias were used on the California side of the border by just about every government agency. The reason was simple, the State of California bought thousands of new cars every year. Many were for the Highway Patrol who replaced their vehicles when they reached eighty-five thousand miles. Hundreds more were bought for other non-law enforcement agencies. Because of the large number of vehicles they purchased every year, the state was able to negotiate fleet prices well below what an individual city or county, buying only a handful of cars each year, might pay for a similar vehicle from a local dealer. The state let individual cities and counties dovetail onto their vehicle contract which allowed them to realize considerable savings. As a result, almost every government agency in California had at least some Crown Victorias.

And that didn't include the federal agencies, of which there were four in Del Norte and Humboldt Counties that drove unmarked white Crown Victorias.

It was close to noon on Friday by the time they had their lists finalized and the names of every agency and person they needed to interview who either had access to an unmarked Crown Vic, or who had one assigned to them. Since a majority of the people and agencies were in California, they made the decision to begin that task the following week.

While the task force had been plowing their way through vehicle registrations all week in Crescent City, in Los Angeles, sheriff's detective Bennie Reynosa continued to work her caseload of missing persons.

By Tuesday, having not received a return call from anyone at the Crescent City Highway Patrol office, she did what cops do when they hit interagency roadblocks. She called a friend. This friend was actually her next door neighbor, a CHP sergeant assigned to the Highway Patrol's East Los Angeles Area. They had never crossed paths professionally, but their kids played together, and they had that loose social bond that went with being a cop which made it okay to call upon one another for favors.

"This is Ike," the husky male voice answered his cell phone on the second ring.

"Ike, Bennie Reynosa," the female detective responded, "I catch you at a bad time?"

"Hey Bennie! Nah, just getting ready for work. What's up?"

The Los Angeles Sheriff's Deputy spent the next couple of minutes explaining her problem.

There was a pause on the other end before Highway Patrol Sergeant Dwight "Ike" Murakami responded, "Crescent City. That's where the two officers were killed a couple weeks ago."

"Yeah, the vehicle I'm interested in was impounded by one of your people the same day," Bennie Reynosa replied.

"Jeez, you don't suppose there is any connection do you?" Ike inquired of his friend.

"How the hell do I know Ike, I can't get a call back from anyone up there to talk about it."

"I know the commander up there. She was my sergeant years ago. I'll give her a call, and see if she can hook you up."

"Thanks Ike, you're the best."

It took Ike Murakami a couple minutes to bring up the Highway Patrol website on his home computer and click his way to the page that listed the phone numbers for every CHP office in the state. Within two minutes he was talking to his friend, and former supervisor, Lieutenant Erin Wolff.

They talked, as old friends and professional colleagues do for a few minutes before Ike Murakami explained the purpose of his call. Ten minutes later, Red Wolff had the CHP Form 180, the storage report done by the officer who had impounded Kim Glickner's BMW, in her hand. She asked Office Assistant Donna Woten a couple questions and headed purposefully to the sergeant's office. Dick Huddleston was working that day, but was out in the field at the moment. Red Wolff picked up the stack of paperwork in his in-basket. She shuffled through a half-dozen reports and other paperwork before finding the phone message from the previous Friday.

She'd deal with him later.

"Missing persons, Detective Reynosa," the voice answered.

"Erin Wolff, CHP, Crescent City, I think we have a mutual friend."

"Lieutenant! Hey thanks for the call back. Yeah, Ike's a great guy."

The small talk went back and forth for a couple minutes.

"I really apologize for nobody getting back to you," Red told the LASD detective, "It's been hectic around here for the last couple weeks."

"Yeah, I understand. Any progress on your investigation?" Bennie Reynosa asked, a genuine sincerity in her voice.

"No suspects yet, but we're running down every lead, and we have a bunch of people working on it."

"Obviously if there is anything I can do from Los Angeles."

"Thanks for that, what is it you need to know about this "Beamer" we towed?" Red asked, directing the conversation back on track.

"Well, I'm working a missing person's case. When the husband hadn't heard from his wife in three days, he reported her missing. She was on a trip from L.A. to Seattle. A couple routine checks showed her credit card last used at a gas station in Crescent City, a week ago Monday, in the early evening. Then her car gets towed as abandoned the next day. I've checked all the hospitals and jails from Crescent City to Seattle, and she's not there. Her ATM and credit cards haven't been used since Monday, and there are no calls in or out on her cell phone. Can you tell anything from the paperwork about where her car was and what condition it was in?"

"I've got the impound report in front of me. I'll fax you a copy. Anyway, it says the vehicle was found blocking the entrance to a Cal-Trans maintenance station on Highway 199. Keys were in it, suitcases and clothes in the trunk. Nothing else on the report to indicate it was anything other than a routine vehicle storage," Red told the detective.

"I've never been north of the Bay Area, what kind of location is that?"

Red thought for a second about how to describe a two lane state highway going through the middle of a forest of redwood trees. "You ever see any of the *Star Wars* movies?"

"Only about four times each when I was in junior high and another dozen times or so with my own kids."

"Well, remember the Sky-Cycle chase scene through the trees? Luke Skywalker, the Storm Troopers, the Ewoks? How dense and thick the vegetation was? That was all filmed up here. The car was found just off the highway in a location exactly like that."

The phone was silent as Bennie Reynosa, city raised, big town cop, tried to visualize Luke Skywalker whizzing in between redwood trees.

"You said the keys were in the car, how 'bout a purse or wallet?" the detective inquired.

"Not listed on the report. If there had been valuables, my officer would have noted them on the inventory and booked them in as found property for safekeeping," Red replied.

The conversation continued for another five minutes as the detective asked more questions and tried to get a picture in her mind of the condition of Kim Glickner's vehicle when it was found.

"I assume the vehicle has been outside at an impound lot?" the detective stated, "Probably no use in trying to get prints from the outside after a week in the elements."

"Unless it was designated for special handling, it'll be outside in the rain."

"Okay lieutenant, I'm pretty convinced this is something more than a just a wife mad at her husband who doesn't want to be found. Everything points to a disappearance under suspicious circumstances. I'm gonna designate the vehicle as evidence in a crime. Can you do a favor for me?"

"I'm sure Ike told you my name is Erin, but everyone calls me Red."

"Red, got it. Could I ask you to have the vehicle sealed and have the tow yard move it inside a building for security until I can get a team up there to give it a going over?"

"I'll get it done today," Red Wolff replied, "Say, can you send me a Soundex of her license and any other pictures you have. I'll get them distributed to the local agencies."

"Sure, give me your e-mail and I'll shoot it right out to you. Red, I really appreciate your help on this. Ike said you knew how to take care of business."

Their conversation over, Detective Bennie Reynosa pulled up the computer files on the missing person's case of Kim Glickner. It took a couple seconds for the Soundex to load. When it did, the screen flashed to life with a full-sized, exact copy, of her driver's license. The smiling color photograph showed Kim Glickner's pearly white teeth and shiny auburn colored hair.

"I wonder where the hell you are?" Bennie Reynosa said out loud as she hit the enter key sending the information hundreds of miles to the other end of the state to a person she had never met.

Once her computer screen cleared, Bennie Reynosa brought up the investigative chronology, the narrative of everything she had done since being assigned this case. She sat for a moment organizing her thoughts, then typed in information about her phone call to CHP Lieutenant Erin Wolff and the results of their discussion.

Once she finished typing, she hit the enter key twice taking the cursor to a new line where she inserted today's date and made another narrative entry, "Foul play suspected".

While Bennie Reynosa was updating her report and sending Kim Glickner's photographs to Crescent City, Red Wolff sat at her desk, her fingers massaging her closed eyes.

It was only Tuesday, and she was exhausted. Up early in the morning to run, in the office by 7:00, she handled all her normal paperwork, e-mails and return phone calls by 9:30. By 10:00 she was at the sheriff's department helping the task force sift through the mountain of paperwork and follow-up on promising leads.

She was like a woman possessed, and it began to show. She'd unknowingly become increasingly irritable at work and curt with her staff. Now she just had another rock dropped in her rucksack by the detective from LASD.

The total amount of work involved in helping with the missing person's case was minimal. A couple phone calls, make a dozen copies of the person's photograph and get them distributed to other law enforcement agencies, and do a little follow-up. Most of it she could delegate to one of her officers to handle.

What she couldn't delegate was dealing with Sergeant Dick Huddleston.

With fifteen minutes worth of phone calls, Red was able to get Kim Glickner's BMW towed inside a building at the Smith River Garage and have the unit assigned to the north county beat go by the tow yard to put evidence seals on the doors, and wrap the entire car in evidence tape to ensure nobody entered the vehicle.

As she was finishing her last call, Red saw Dick Huddleston in the business office talking with Lisa Johnston. She called him into her office.

Red Wolff was a really good leader and an excellent commander. She didn't subscribe to any one particular management philosophy, but had developed a style of her own that took the best leadership and management techniques from the people she had worked for over her twenty plus year career. This was Sergeant Dick Huddleston's second major screw up in less than ten days, and it called for a major ass-chewing.

"Close the door, Dick," she said as he entered her office.

The expression on his face changed instantly. He'd worked for her a couple of years, but during that period, he could recall only a handful of instances when they talked behind closed doors. Almost every time, he recalled, he didn't like the topic, or the outcome.

"Up's what Boss?" Dick Huddleston said, his voice had a little tone of uncertainty.

Red didn't like it when he used the term boss. When most people used that word it had the connotation of respect and friendship. She always sensed the way he used it held a measure of contempt for her as his superior officer, her younger age, and women in general.

K.T. MINCE

"Dick, I just got off the phone with a detective from the Los Angeles Sheriff's. She left a message for you last Friday. Needed a return call. You remember that message?"

"I don't recall any message like that, Red," Dick Huddleston, not the quickest guy in the world, lied.

Red Wolff paused for a second, there was nothing that infuriated her more than the phrase "I don't recall". It was a cop's way of lying about something and still leaving themselves some wiggle room. It was an almost foolproof way of deflecting a question, especially in a courtroom. Few attorneys understood the meaning of the phrase, and they generally moved on to another question. What the phrase "I don't recall" really meant was "Yeah, I remember, but I'll get in trouble if I say I remember. So, unless you can prove it, I'll just say I don't recall. Then, if you can prove it, I'll say, oh, now I recall".

"Knock off the I don't recall shit, sergeant. This isn't a courtroom, and that crap won't fly here," she told him tersely, her eyes locked on his.

Red exhaled deeply. Now I've got two problems, she said to herself, first he blows off doing his job, then he lies about it.

One of the cardinal rules of being a good interrogator was to never ask a question you didn't already know the answer to. Red Wolff was a good interrogator.

Holding the phone message slip between her fingers, she held it up for him to see. "This help your memory, sergeant?"

"Well, um, I," Dick Huddleston stuttered, looking alternately at the paper message and the floor, searching for a way out of the box he put himself in. The fact that Red Wolff had changed from addressing him by his first name to using the title, sergeant, wasn't lost on him either.

The pleasant part of the conversation was over.

"Save it, sergeant!" Red Wolff snapped at him.

"But."

"I said save it. You screwed up, again. First you didn't protect the scene where the Castles were murdered. Then you just blow off this call from another agency. I did your job for you. Turns out they needed our help on a missing person, someone who is possibly in danger. And then, to top it all off, you lied about."

"Lieutenant I," Dick Huddleston tried to speak, a sheepish tone in his voice.

"Sergeant, we have two officers murdered, everyone here is doing as much as they can to help with the investigation, except you. The other sergeants and I are all trying to keep this command running and handle the things that come up every day. Everyone is pulling

206

their weight, except you. Your light-hearted and lackadaisical approach to being a supervisor is unacceptable," Red Wolff chastised him.

Dick Huddleston, in the middle of a mess of his own making and receiving the verbal reprimand he knew he deserved, was able to man up enough to look her in the eyes.

"That ends today! If my being a woman and your commander are somehow a source of irritation to you, I don't give a big rat's ass. You're going to start being a supervisor and doing things right as of this moment. I'm going to document both of these incidents, and they're going in your file. Screw up once more, shirk one responsibility, or lie to me again, and a year short of retirement or not, I'll see you fired."

Dick Huddleston didn't slink out of Red Wolff's office, but he didn't leave with his head up either. Lisa Johnston, Donna Woten, and another officer were in the business office when he came out. Even though Red had never raised her voice, they all knew he had just gotten a royal reaming out. As he walked by, they averted their eyes to let him retain a modicum of dignity.

After he left her office, Red Wolff rocked back in her swivel chair and put her boots up on the desk. She had a trademark, half-smile on her face. She was feeling better.

———

By Friday afternoon not everyone in Del Norte County was feeling better, however. Sitting in his office, the door closed, he stared blankly at the computer monitor on his desk. It was the end of a stressful work week, and he was deep in thought. It wasn't his job that was causing him stress though, it was watching and knowing the interagency task force was steadily narrowing down the list of people who owned Crown Victorias, or who drove them as part of their work, that gave him an uneasy feeling.

There was almost nothing he could do about the Crown Victoria he drove. Eventually the task force investigators would interview everybody who drove one. When that happened, he would be cooperative, even let them search his vehicle if they wanted. They'd find nothing. Unfortunately, that wouldn't stop the investigation. They'd keep looking, keep interviewing people, keep searching. That, he knew, might lead them back to him. In his mind, he continued to think of a way to derail the task force's investigation.

It came to him as he sat there, the gun. The task force, he knew, was also looking for a .38 revolver with special type ammunition. If they found that gun under the right circumstances, they'd consider the case closed. The investigation would be over, and they would stop looking for him.

He let his thoughts drift back over twenty years to how he acquired the gun. He could still see her in his mind. She was older, maybe late thirties, while he wasn't yet twenty-five.

His new job occupied most of his time for the first year after college. The incident with that rich bitch of a co-ed he had strangled in her dorm room, had scared him. Actually, it scared him a lot, and he lived every day for several years with the fear of getting caught, going to prison, and being executed.

Even though it frightened him every time he recalled strangling her, at the same time, it gave him a feeling of exhilaration and power. Consequently, over the course of those first years, as he learned and began to excel at his job, his mind was engaged in an endless struggle with the urges that battled for control of his will.

He was still shy and awkward around women and to a lesser degree men also, which gave him a limited social circle of friends. His interpersonal skills had improved somewhat, giving him a few professional acquaintances, but most of his co-workers gave him a wide berth. On the plus side, because he spent so much time working, it netted him a promotion with new responsibilities, more freedom, and the opportunity to travel on work related assignments.

It was on one of his first business trips that he began what would become over two decades of killing women.

It had been a full day. He was up and on the road early that morning, driving a couple hundred miles from his regular work location to get to an afternoon meeting with the local administrators. Following the meeting, he did a quick review of local written procedures and then a spot physical audit to verify compliance. By 5:30, his day was done. His normal procedure was to head out again, drive to the next location where he had a hotel room reserved and spend the night. That would put him in the right location for tomorrow morning where he would repeat the process, a meeting, a review of procedures, and a spot audit.

In the mid-afternoon, just as he was beginning his spot audit, a spring snowstorm blew in. It was late in the season for snow, and the state highway department had already moved most of their snow removal equipment from strategic locations along the interstates back to central depots for annual maintenance. The storm dumped four inches of snow in the first two hours closing most highways and stranding thousands of motorists.

Rooms at the nationwide chain hotel, the only one in town, and all of the motels near the interstate went quickly, as motorists scrambled to get a place to stay for the night. Weather reports told everyone to expect another five inches of snow overnight, and the state highway department reported roads wouldn't be opened until the next morning. He would have had to spend the night at the emergency shelter opened by the Red Cross at the high school gym if one of the local administrators had not been able to wangle him a room at the hotel.

For a chain hotel, it was more than adequate for his needs, clean rooms, bath towels that were soft and actually absorbed water, and a bed that, while maybe not comfortable, was good enough, and far better than a cot in the gym. Dinner at the hotel restaurant was actually pretty good, the server, a small middle-aged woman with a blank expressionless face, from some Central or South American country, probably an illegal, providing very attentive service.

The bar was crowded and noisy when he entered to get a nightcap. A thick cloud of cigarette smoke hung over the heads of the scores of patrons, who, stranded by the snowstorm, jammed into the establishment. He stood in the doorway surveying the scene, debating whether he really wanted a drink bad enough to venture in. He wasn't much of drinker, and the bar was just a distraction to keep from having to go back to his room.

Spying an empty stool at the near end of the bar, he made his way past several patrons standing behind the row of people already seated at the bar and pulled himself onto the stool. The solo bartender, a man in a white shirt, black bow tie, and green vest, acknowledged his presence with a nod before going back to drawing several draft beers.

Several minutes later, the overworked barman made his way over.

"Sorry, it's a madhouse tonight, what can I get you?"

"Vodka rocks," he said leaning partially across the bar to be heard over the din.

Almost as soon as the bartender headed off to mix his drink, he heard her voice. She was two stools away talking to a man whose back was turned toward him. The voice sent a prickly feeling up his spine.

Talking to a man was not an apt description. It was more like she was talking at him. Her voice had a combination of superiority and bitchiness that instantly reminded him of the mother of the girl he almost married in college. Just the thought of the mother caused his pulse to race, and he could actually feel his heart pounding faster. He had to do a subtle glance in her direction to convince himself it wasn't actually her.

And while it wasn't actually her, it might as well have been. As he listened to her talk, the man to whom she was speaking unable to get a word in, emotions he hadn't felt in several years came flooding back as she complained about everything, the snow, the quality of the hotel, the service, and the inconvenience the storm was causing to her trip. She even had that same southern twang to her voice that irritated him to no end.

Sipping his drink, he continued to hear her complaints over the considerable noise in the bar, each complaint grating at his mind and bringing back unwanted memories.

He sat there for nearly an hour, nursing the one drink, keeping his eyes mostly down or looking out over the crowd. All the while he listened as she continued bitching about things to the man seated next to her.

As the bartender placed a second drink in front of him, he casually picked up the book of hotel matches from the bar with his right hand, pulled off a single match with his left, and struck the blue painted head against the coarse striker pad on the back side of the match book. The match hissed to life with a bright orange burst, settling down in seconds to a short white flame. Puffing several times on the cigarette, the tip burned red, and acrid smoke curled up to join the cloud hanging above his head. It was the '80s, and smoking bans in bars and restaurants, especially in the east, were still a few years away.

The man, he could tell by now, had about all of her complaining he could stand, and realizing he wasn't going to get lucky tonight, made a quick exit. He could also tell she was getting close to being intoxicated. She wasn't drunk, or even close for that matter, but judging from her speech and movements as she tried to light a cigarette, she'd consumed enough not to be driving.

It was after 9:00, and the bar was beginning to empty out a little. It was a weeknight, and almost everyone at the hotel had places to go or business to do the next morning.

"Bartender, another," she told the still busy man behind the bar, pointing at her empty glass, "And close my tab, room 412."

It was one of those stupid things rich people sometimes do because they don't know any better. Or maybe if she did know better the alcohol numbed her senses enough that she didn't realize she did it. Either way, for anyone that wanted to know, she was in room 412.

Two dollars was a very good tip for a six dollar bar tab twenty plus years ago, he thought to himself, as he continued to recall the older woman, and the way he came into possession of the .38 revolver. A two dollar tip, funny the things you remember, he smiled to himself.

As he sat at the bar smoking and sipping at his second vodka, out of the corner of his eye, he gauged how much longer it would take for her to finish her drink. When he thought he had the timing calculated right, he left the two bucks under his glass and strolled casually out of the bar back into the main portion of the hotel. The festive mood of stranded travelers in the bar was in stark contrast to what had evolved into a lot of tired people occupying chairs in the lobby. Others, he saw, were using the banks of telephones, as cell phones were another ten years in the offing, desperately trying to find a room, any room, for the night.

Also in the future, at least at this chain hotel, in this mostly rural part of the southeast, were video security cameras on every floor, in the elevators, the parking lots, and stairwells. Of course, they had them in hotels in the big cities, and the company was putting them in when they built a new hotel or did a major remodel, but still, this was rural America in the late '80s.

It was one of those floor lay outs that lent itself to making victims out of hotel guests. The fourth floor was shaped like a "T", with the elevator at the base. The main corridor had twelve rooms, six on each side, and another corridor, with ten more rooms, crossed the top of the "T". Room 412 was the sixth room from the elevator, and the last room on the hallway before the cross corridor.

He heard the distinctive "ding" as the elevator stopped on the fourth floor, and moments later the sound of the double metal doors sliding open. With the hotel's heating system running, he couldn't actually hear her footsteps on the carpeted hallway floor, and he didn't dare make his move too soon. Standing out of sight in the cross corridor, he did a quick peek around the corner. It was her.

When he heard the sound of her key unlocking the door, he rounded the corner and strode her direction. Preoccupied with opening the door and extracting the key, her senses dulled by three drinks, she never saw him coming. For his part, he had less than three seconds from the time he came around the corner to ensure there were no other people in the hallway and make a decision. He already knew there was nobody in the corridor behind him, and a quick glance toward the elevator confirmed the hallway was clear. He was two steps away from her, moving fast, his footsteps silent on the carpet as she pushed on the door to her darkened room, then paused while feeling for the light switch.

The force of his shoulder into her back knocked the air out of her chest as she was pushed into the darkened room, stumbling and falling flat on her face. She tried to scream, but without any air in her lungs, all that came out were wispy gasps.

He was on her in a flash, using his knee to pin her to the ground while holding his hand over her mouth to prevent her from screaming. He easily picked her up with the one hand across her mouth and threw her face down onto the bed. Forcing her mouth and nose into the soft bedspread, she struggled to breathe while thrashing violently to escape his powerful grip.

He fought against her movements by keeping constant pressure on the back of her head while at the same time pulling back the bedspread enough to grab a pillow. Using his teeth and one hand, he pulled the pillowcase off, threw the pillow to the floor and fashioned a gag from the pillowcase. Her mouth now tightly gagged, he reached over and felt for the lamp on the nightstand, running his rubber gloved hand over the base and up under the shade until he came to the switch. Still holding her face down with one hand, he clicked on the lamp.

He remembered he had let out a curse when he saw the blood on his hand. Somehow, probably when he wrestled her from the floor to the bed, he had cut one of his fingers. It was no big deal, injury wise, but he could see a half-dozen places, on the floor, on her clothes, and now on the lamp, streaked with his blood. Nothing he could about it now, he realized, turning his attention back to the woman.

Roughly he twisted both arms behind her back and pulled the two foot long plastic cable tie he had taken from work out of his jacket pocket. Plastic-cuffs, as cops called them, he knew were originally invented for use in the aircraft industry to wrap bundles of wires. They had quickly found use in law enforcement as temporary restraints for prisoners, a sort of one time use handcuff. They were ideal for his purposes. Holding her wrists together with one hand he fed the pointed end of the plastic strip into the slot on the opposite end and jerked hard. The device made a sound like a zipper being pulled as the ratchet clicked against the serrations. Struggle as she might, there was no way the device would loosen, and the hard plastic edges began to cut into her wrists. Satisfied she was secure, he rolled her over on her back.

It was the second time he had seen the look. The first time was the co-ed years ago. She had the same look of terror on her face as the woman did tonight. Eyes bulging and darting side-to-side, short rapid breaths, skin instantly drained of color. He hadn't recognized the look for what it was years before. Tonight he did. Tonight he understood.

It was that look of absolute fear, of being bound and gagged, helpless and uncertain, and yet somehow resigned to what they had know was their impending death.

It was also the second time he had that feeling of power and control. It made up for all the inadequacies he had with women, for all the times they had hurt and embarrassed him, and the humiliations he had endured from rich women.

Pulling her pantyhose off and then using them to strangle her, had been a clever touch, he thought to himself.

The soft wrapping by his secretary at the office door, snapped him back to reality. "Good night sir, have a nice weekend," she said through the closed door.

Glancing at the clock mounted above the door, he saw it was nearly 6:00.

"Right," he responded, not wasting any words on normal pleasantries by returning her courtesy. Within seconds, his thoughts reverted to the woman.

He could see himself standing over her dead body beginning for the first, of what would be over three dozen times, the pattern he would follow. While it was a pattern in the sense that he did it every time, precisely in the same order, for him it actually took on the trappings of a ritual.

The first thing he did was not to panic and attempt to flee immediately after strangling the woman as he had with the co-ed. With Nordic precision, he took his time, ensuring he left no tell-tale obvious indicators of his identity. Patiently he used the rooms hand towels to blot up the blood stains from the cut on his finger, putting the towels in the plastic liner from one of the room's three trash cans. He'd take the towels with him when he left. The police, he knew, may still be able to recover usable evidence from the blood smears, but they were useless unless they had a sample of his blood to match them against.

Next, he looked for some small memento to take as a reminder of this woman. She had a few rings, but he couldn't get them off her fingers. Opening her single suitcase, he examined its contents. Travelling clothes, lingerie, toiletries, the usual stuff. Running his hand to the bottom, he felt a box.

Pulling the box out, he saw it was dark blue with the logo Smith and Wesson on top. Inside he found a brand new, five shot, .38 caliber, Chief's Special. Also in the box was a note from the woman's brother indicating he was giving her the pistol as a gift for protection when she travelled. She'd need to register the gun in her name, the note went on to say, and she would have to buy her own ammunition.

He stuffed the note and the pistol in his pocket.

It had been easy enough for him to run the weapon through several databases to ascertain it had never been registered. Over the next twenty years, as he moved and changed jobs, some involving law enforcement, others not, the .38 was a constant reminder of that night.

Now he had to devise a way of disposing of the weapon so that it diverted suspicion away from him.

CHAPTER THIRTEEN

"95-3, 95-1 bye," the CHP radio crackled in Highway Patrol Officer Oscar Zamora's unit.

"95-1, 95-3, southbound at Hiouchi, go ahead John," Oscar Zamora replied, using the car-to-car channel which transmitted on a different frequency so it did not interfere with radio traffic from the Humboldt Communications Center.

"You clear for a cup Oz?" Officer John Pederson inquired.

"Your pleasure," Oscar Zamora replied, the tone in his response indicating he was up for getting a cup of coffee, and his beat partner should choose the spot.

A brief silence followed until Officer John Pederson in unit 95-1 responded, "Northwood's."

"10-4, travel time," Oscar Zamora told him, meaning he would be there in the time it took to drive from his present location.

It was well after 8:00, and traffic was light, even for a Thursday evening. On duty since 3:00, a short timeout for a cup of coffee would break up the last three hours of his shift.

Oscar Zamora, who had been tagged in the academy years ago with a nickname derived from his initials, O and Z, had thirteen years on the Highway Patrol, the last eight months in Crescent City. A native of the Stockton area, just south of Sacramento, he'd done his first four years in Los Angeles, then started transferring north as his seniority increased in an effort to get closer to home. He had married an Anglo girl from Orange County, and they had three kids, two boys ages nine and eleven, and a daughter, the spitting image of her mother, aged seven. It had taken him nearly twelve years to get enough seniority to make it back to Stockton.

His hometown, however, had changed a lot in twelve years. Unemployment in California's Central Valley was pushing twenty-two percent, and the gang violence, especially among the Latino gangs, was out of control. Six months after buying a brand new home in Lodi, just north of Stockton, a drive-by shooting at his son's middle school had left two kids dead.

The next day, he put a transfer in for some place as far away from gangs as he could get. He'd never been to Crescent City before, but he knew anyplace would be better than trying to raise his family in the middle of a war zone.

For the most part, Crescent City was better. The rain was a downer, and his kids had to go out to play every day wearing sweatshirts against the cold, instead of the shorts and tee-shirts they wore in Lodi. But, on the positive side, he didn't have to worry about them getting gunned down in a drive-by, and he bought a great house with a small pasture and a couple horses. All-in-all life, was good.

His beat today was Highway 199, from the intersection with Highway 101 to the Oregon border. He had about fifty miles to cover, most it two lane, with the Smith River Gorge on one side and the steep sides of the mountains on the other. With not a lot of places where motorists could exceed the speed limit, most of his enforcement activity was directed at illegal passing, or motorists who drifted into the opposite lane of traffic. He'd only written one moving violation today and three "Del Norte Felonies" the euphemistic name CHP officers called mechanical violations, or "Fix-It" tickets, like a taillight out, or a missing rear view mirror.

While he didn't have a quota, which most motorists would argue he did, only one "mover" for the day was a little light on activity. One more for the day would keep the sergeant happy.

As he approached the end of Highway 199, he saw the big silver colored Chevrolet Caprice coming southbound on Highway 101. It was "cookin'", nearly eighty, he estimated. As the car passed in front of him at a right angle, he could clearly see the male driver. Locked in on his driving, he never saw the black and white CHP unit.

Traffic was clear as he punched his foot to the floorboard and accelerated after the rapidly disappearing Chevy. Highway 101 in this location is one of the few places in the county where there were two lanes in each direction. The four lane was only three miles in length and would end near the northern city limits of the town. It took him nearly a mile to match the Chevy's speed. A half-mile behind, he set his speedometer on eighty and held it steady. The Chevy was still pulling away.

"Close enough!" he said out loud and pushed accelerator to the floor again, the Crown Vic's big V-8 engine responding instantly increasing his speed to a hundred and five.

Just before the Crescent City limits, he was fifty yards off the Chevy's bumper and eased up on the gas enough to get a bumper pace for a quarter-mile. Matching his speed to the violator's car, he glanced at his speedometer. Eighty-six. Now the sergeant will be happy, he thought to himself, as he flicked on the revolving red and blue lights.

The big Caprice began to slow, first to sixty-five, then to thirty-five as it crossed under the Washington Boulevard overcrossing and into the city limits of the town. Slower now, the vehicle kept on going, but didn't pull to the curb. Using the hand operated white spotlight mounted on the outside of the driver's door, Oz flashed the powerful beam into the back window of the vehicle. Slowly the driver pulled to the side of the highway near the entrance to a gas station.

"Pull into the gas station," Officer Zamora instructed on the patrol vehicle's P.A. system. "Stop by the telephones," he told the driver.

As the violator's vehicle slowed and stopped, Oscar Zamora keyed his radio mic, "John, I'll be about ten late," he told Officer John Pedersen who was waiting for him to have coffee. It was probably just a routine stop, ten minutes to check out the driver and write a quick ticket. Not waiting for a response he was out of the car in an instant.

Holding his flashlight just above his left shoulder, much like you might hold a spear to throw it, he approached the left rear of the vehicle, his right hand resting loosely on the grips of his ten shot .40 caliber Smith and Wesson semi-automatic. He'd probably made twenty thousand vehicle stops in his career, and he treated them all the same, cautiously. He played the flashlight beam back and forth across the backseat of the Caprice ensuring nobody was lying there before taking another step toward the driver's door. The male driver he could see was watching him in the outside rear view mirror. Nothing unusual about that Oscar Zamora knew, but he nevertheless trained the flashlight beam on the mirror, the reflection causing the driver to avert his eyes.

Oscar Zamora could see the driver's left hand resting on the steering wheel, but not his right.

"Could you put both hands on the steering wheel please, sir," he said to the driver, in a tone meant to convey it was an order, not a request.

The driver, twisting in the seat, brought his right hand up and placed it on the wheel.

Satisfied now it was safe to do so, Oscar Zamora took two more steps forward and pivoted so he was in front of the driver's door looking into the passenger compartment. His eyes took in the driver's appearance and clothing, while his experienced, street-smart mind began processing the driver. Stay on guard, it told him.

"How you doin tonight, sir," Oz greeted the driver, the flashlight moving over the front seat and the floorboard. Not waiting for the driver to respond, he continued, "You're going a little fast, can I see your license and registration please."

The driver, a white male, who looked to be in his mid-forties, a couple days of scruffy beard, gaunt looking, kept his eyes averted as Oscar Zamora talked to him, reaching toward his back pocket. Reflexively, as the driver's hand went out of sight, Oz moved his right hand to the grips of his holstered pistol. When he produced a worn looking wallet, the officer's hand relaxed.

As the driver began to thumb through his wallet, he spoke for the first time, "Um, I, ah, must have left it at home," he said, unconvincingly.

"Right, how 'bout any kind of I.D," Oscar Zamora told him.

Thumbing through his wallet, the driver pulled out a well worn social security card and handed it to the officer.

"Stuart Green, that you?" Oscar Zamora asked the driver.

The driver nodded.

"Anything with a picture, Stu?"

While the driver went back to searching the contents of his wallet, Officer Oscar Zamora studied his face. Working in Los Angeles and then in the central valley, he'd seen a hundred or more who looked just like him. Whoever this guy was, he was a "Cranker", a methamphetamine user, the signs were all there. Several red ulcerated sores were visible on his forehead and the backs of his hands from the uncontrollable itching he did at the bugs he imagined were crawling under his skin. He was also missing several teeth. "Meth Mouth" had dried out the glands that supplied the natural saliva in his mouth to wash away bacteria and help keep his teeth clean. That, combined with the high sugar content soft drinks and junk food he constantly craved, had caused decay to set in and rotted his teeth away. Without the teeth for support, his cheeks had shrunk in, giving him the look of a toothless old man.

"Who's the car belong to?" Oscar Zamora asked.

"Ah, my buddy," Stuart Green said, again less than convincingly.

The officer and the increasingly nervous driver played the "what's your buddies name", "where does he live", "how come you're driving his car", "where were you headed" game for the next minute.

Checking the glove compartment, Stuart Green rummaged through a fist full of papers before handing the officer a crumbled registration card.

Oz examined the card confirming the vehicle he stopped was a 1996 Chevrolet. The name Stuart Green gave for the registered owner, wasn't the same as on the registration card.

"Says here the car belongs to somebody named MacAfee," the officer challenged the driver.

"Oh, yeah, that's right, Jimmy MacAfee," the driver tried to sound nonchalant.

Unseen by Oscar Zamora while he was questioning the driver who identified himself as Stuart Green, a vehicle, with its headlights extinguished, silently slid in behind the CHP patrol car and stopped. Exiting and quietly closing the door, the driver walked toward the officer.

"What you got Oz?" Crescent City P.D. Officer Doug Wilson asked when he reached the right rear of the light colored Chevrolet.

Officer Doug Wilson expected Oscar Zamora to acknowledge his presence by holding up four fingers, a signal everything was "Code 4". It was non-verbal cop talk to indicate everything was okay, and the situation was under control. Not this time.

"Hey Doug, not sure, can you stand by for a couple?" Oscar Zamora replied.

Officer Doug Wilson nodded and approached the vehicle on the right side, training his flashlight onto the rear floorboard and the front seat area.

Stopping to see what another officer was doing, regardless of which agency they worked for, especially at night, was routine in Crescent City, as it was in much of the north state, or any rural area for that matter. There were just too few cops, and sometimes help was a long way away. Crescent City Police Officer Doug Wilson would stand by with Highway Patrol Officer Oscar Zamora for a few minutes until it was determined everything was Code 4. He'd then probably stick around and "shoot the shit" for a few minutes with Oz, then head back to his regular patrol duties. It was the way rural police work was done.

Few cops could tell you exactly what it felt like, that feeling of something not quite right. It came with experience, the way somebody looked, or didn't look at you, their mannerisms, a hunch, instinct, or maybe curiosity. Whatever it was, whatever it felt like, or whatever caused it, Officer Oscar Zamora had that feeling.

"How about stepping out of the car, Stuart," he said to the driver while opening the door from the outside.

Stuart Green didn't object, in fact Oscar Zamora could actually see his body language change from being defensive to a kind of resignation at whatever was going to happen.

Because the driver was wearing a heavy wool coat with bulky pockets Oscar Zamora gave him a quick pat-down for weapons as soon as he was out of the car. Finding none, he directed him to the front of the CHP vehicle.

"Hey Stu," Crescent City Police Officer Doug Wilson said when he got a good look at the driver.

Stuart Green looked at the city police officer and shrugged in recognition.

"You know this guy?" Oz asked.

"Stu? Sure, I think every cop in the county has arrested him at least once."

"What's his story?"

"Long time petty thief, in and out of jail, does a little dealing in meth."

"Looks like a long time "Cranker" to me," Oscar Zamora said.

"Yeah, he uses as much as he sells," Doug Wilson responded.

"Doesn't look loaded tonight," Oscar Zamora said. "How about running him for me while I check out his car?" Oscar asked the city officer.

"Sure," Doug Wilson replied turning his attention to the driver. "What's your birth date Stuart?" the officer asked in preparation to running Stuart Green for warrants.

Stuart Green rattled off his date of birth, which caused Officer Oscar Zamora to remark, "Jesus, he's only thirty-two, he looks forty-five."

"Meth," Doug Wilson replied, shaking his head.

While the Crescent City Officer watched Stuart Green, CHP Officer Oscar Zamora was doing a search of his car. Without "Probable Cause" to do a full under the seats, inside closed containers, and check the trunk type search, the officer used his flashlight to survey the places he could see. In plain sight on the passenger's seat, he could see a plastic grocery bag full of junk food, Hostess Twinkies, a dozen candy bars, packs of doughnuts, two large bags of potato chips, and two six packs of twelve ounce cans of Coke. A full carton of cigarettes was on the front floorboard, and there were three empty, quart-sized plastic water bottles on the back seat.

Oscar Zamora had seen it all before.

Turning his attention to the driver's door, he shined his flashlight on the inside edge of the door, the portion where the back of the door met the center doorpost. Satisfied at what he saw, he walked back to where Doug Wilson stood with Stuart Green.

"What'd you find Oz?"

"Shiny screws," Officer Oscar Zamora told him with a sly grin on his face.

"Shiny what?" the officer asked, a perplexed look on his face.

"Shiny screws, on the door. I'll explain it to you in a second," Oscar Zamora told the Crescent City officer.

Turning his attention to Stuart Green, Oscar Zamora looked him in the eye. "You want to give me permission to search, or you want me to find it?" he queried the driver.

Stuart Green didn't answer, shifting his gaze toward the ground.

"Okay, whatever, we'll do it the hard way," Oscar Zamora said to the man. "You're under arrest for suspicion of transporting narcotics."

With that, he turned Stuart Green around and handcuffed his hands behind his back, followed by a more thorough search. After advising him of his Miranda Rights, something he did from memory, Oscar Zamora placed him in the right front of his patrol car, seat belting him in, and taking the keys out of the patrol vehicle's ignition. Nothing, he knew, was more embarrassing than to have a prisoner slip his cuffs to the front and drive off in your patrol car.

Once Stuart Green was secured in the patrol car, Doug Wilson asked, "What the hell's going on?"

What was going on was that CHP Officer Oscar Zamora, like every CHP officer since 1993, had been trained in "Operation Pipeline", and most city coppers, like Doug Wilson had not.

"Come on," Oscar Zamora told him, "I'll show you."

Over the next fifteen minutes Oz showed and explained to Doug Wilson about "Pipeline".

"In the early '90s the feds started a program to intercept drugs being transported in vehicles. At first it just involved cocaine and marijuana coming out of cities with seaports. The stuff came off cargo ships and got moved by vehicle on the interstate highways. It expanded after that to encompass meth. The feds realized there were lots of similarities in the things the transporters did. The driver's were all afraid of getting ripped off so they wouldn't leave their vehicles, even for a piss break, or to grab something to eat. So they carried a ton of junk food and empty jars or bottles to pee in."

When he finished explaining the indicators of someone who might be running drugs, Oscar Zamora began to remove the candy, potato chips and empty plastic bottles from Stuart Green's car.

"What's that got to do with shiny screws?" Doug Wilson asked.

"The transporters also liked big American cars, like this Chevy, the kind with space in the door panel to hide drugs," he told the city police officer.

Opening the driver's side door, Oz pointed to the three by five inch metal access panel on the backside of the door. The panel was held on with four small Philips screws. Everything on the entire back side of the door and the metal access panel, were all painted a uniform silver color. Everything that is, except the four screws.

"Look at the screw heads, what do you see?" he asked the Crescent City officer.

"I'll be damned! The screw heads are shiny, the paints gone. Somebody's taken the access panel off."

Using the screwdriver blade of the utility knife he carried on his Sam Browne belt, Oscar Zamora had the panel off in short order. Shining his flashlight in the opening, Oscar saw what he was looking for.

"Jackpot!" he exclaimed.

―――――

It was a jackpot. The three zip-lock plastic bags of powdered methamphetamine he pulled from inside the door panel weighed sixteen ounces each. About $250,000 street value, he estimated.

Oscar Zamora got that exhilarating feeling that comes from making a good arrest. The fun part was over, now came the follow-up and the paperwork. It was going to be a long night.

A bunch of things happened in the next hour.

Using his cell phone, Oscar Zamora called his wife telling her he might not be home for a while. His second call was to the "on-call" sergeant, Dick Huddleston, advising him of the seizure of a large quantity of narcotics.

Dick Huddleston was sound asleep when Officer Zamora called him. He grumbled at being woken up and considered going back to sleep. Then he thought better of it. The bite marks were still fresh on his butt from the ass-chewing his lieutenant had given him earlier in the week. Dick Huddleston got up and called Red Wolff, informing her of the arrest.

When he called, Red was still up, sitting in a big overstuffed chair by the woodstove in her pajamas and fuzzy slippers, going over the briefcase full of work she had brought home from the office. Maybe her counseling session earlier in the week had done some good, she thought after hanging up.

Red Wolff made one call, "Meet me at the office," is all she said to Ray Silva.

Within a half-hour, Red Wolff and Ray Silva were at the Crescent City CHP office talking with Officer Oscar Zamora.

"Good arrest, Oz," she told him after he related the circumstances of the traffic stop and observations that led to finding the drugs.

"Yeah, nice job, Oscar," Ray Silva told him, pausing a second or two before adding, "It's surprising though, Stu Green is a small-timer. Running a quarter mil worth of meth is way out of his league."

"What kind of a car did you say he was driving?" Red asked.

"A '96 Caprice, silver colored," Oz told her.

"Who's it registered to?" she queried.

"Kimberly MacAfee, local address. I ran that name through DMV. No hits."

Red Wolff pondered that information for a few seconds then spoke out loud to both officers, "You know, lots of police agencies used the Chevy Caprice as a patrol car in the '90s before everyone started getting Crown Vics."

"What's your point lieutenant?" Oscar Zamora asked.

"We've kept it pretty confidential that we have a witness who thinks an unmarked police car might be involved with the Castles," Red began. "He only got a look at it for maybe four or five seconds, it was dark and rainy, and he'd been drinking. It would be easy to confuse a Crown Vic for a Caprice."

"Madre de Dios!" he exclaimed in Spanish, "You think there's a chance this guy may be connected to the murder of the Castles?"

"It's possible Oz," Ray Silva chimed in, "One of the theories we're working on is the Castles may have stopped a car hauling drugs. You know enough about people who use meth to know they are capable of anything, even mutts like Stu Green."

Over the next five minutes, Oscar Zamora detailed the circumstances of the arrest to his commander and Ray Silva. Between the three of them they formulated a game plan on how they would interrogate Stuart Green. Since any more than two interrogators asking questions could be viewed as trying to intimidate an arrestee into making a confession, it was decided Ray Silva and Red Wolff would do the questioning. Fair enough Oz told them, he had an arrest report to write anyway.

"You want to be good cop or bad cop?" Red asked Ray, with a half-smile on her face.

"I've known this guy for years, let me start, you jump in when the time is right," he told her.

Stuart Green sat handcuffed to a bench bolted to the floor. He looked scared and pitiful, Red Wolff thought. She'd never had any personal contact with him, but his name was familiar and she knew he'd been "popped" several times before on various minor drug charges, possession of a few grams of meth, being under the influence of controlled substances, and a couple marijuana busts. This was different, she thought to herself. If what Ray Silva said was true, the amount he was transporting was way out of Stuart Green's league, and it was definitely way too much for the local market. The candy, Coca-Cola, and piss bottles in the car, indicated he was moving the meth somewhere a long way from Crescent City. Stuart Green was a "mule". Continuing to look at him, she had another thought. Who in their right mind, would use somebody like him to transport a quarter million dollars worth of drugs.

Carrying an unopened can of Coke, Ray Silva greeted Stuart Green with a friendly smile and un-handcuffed him.

"Grab a seat," Ray told him pointing to the small wooden table. "Want a Coke, Stu?"

Stuart Green eagerly popped open the can and took several large gulps, "Thanks, Ray," he said, "Can I have a smoke?"

"Not in a state office," Ray told him.

Stu Green shrugged his shoulders.

Ray Silva spoke first, "You got yourself in a shit-pot of trouble, Stuart. Let's see if we can fix this mess up," he told him. "I know Officer Zamora read you your rights, but let's do it again just so everything is on tape."

Stuart Green's face displayed no emotion.

Pressing the record button on the mini-cassette recorder, Ray began by reciting the date and time, location, the names of those present in the room, and the reason they were there. He then read Stuart Green his rights, asking him if he understood and wanted to answer any questions.

No, Stuart Green told him, he wanted a lawyer.

"You sure, Stu? You know lawyers will just muck this up, we'll find out what we want to know anyway, you'll get found guilty, and the amount of drugs you had will mean some serious jail time. Unless you help us, we can't go to bat for you with the D.A. and the judge."

"No way man, I'm a dead man if I snitch anyone off. These are some heavyweight dudes," Stuart replied, his voice both scared and whiney.

Rocking back in his chair so it was balanced on its back legs, Ray Silva interlaced his hands behind his head and thought for a moment while Stuart Green intently watched his every move.

Rocking forward, he pushed the stop button on the small tape recorder. The room was quiet for a few seconds before he spoke.

"Stu, I always liked you. Have I ever lied to you or done you wrong?" he asked.

Shaking his head, Stuart indicated no.

His voice remaining soft and steady, his eyes locked on Stuart Green's, Ray spoke again. "So here's the deal, Stu. The amount of shit you were carrying is worth twenty-five to life. No plea bargains, no probation, no time off for good behavior. This is what, your third fall for drugs? You've already done two lightweight stretches at minimum security prisons. But this makes you a "three-striker", so a conviction could mean prison from now till forever."

He paused and let that sink in. Red Wolff sat motionless.

"Man, I can't, they'll kill me," Stuart Green whined.

"Stuart, I'm Lieutenant Wolff," Red began, "It was my officer who arrested you."

"Yeah, I seen your picture in the paper for killing all those terrorists," he mumbled.

"Ray has told me you're not a bad guy. I'd hate to see you locked up for the rest of your life," she told him. "The really bad part is you're gonna do really hard time, it means a level three or level four prison. It's not like Vacaville or a minimum security joint, it means Folsom, or Cochran, or maybe even here at Pelican Bay. You ever been inside Pelican Bay, Stu?" Not waiting for an answer, she continued, "You're kinda scrawny, Stu, a young guy like you is gonna need protection. You'll end up being somebody's "Punk" in prison, waiting on them all day long, giving them blowjobs and getting fucked in the ass everyday for the rest of your life."

As she spoke, tears started welling up in Stuart Green's eyes, and soon tears were streaking down his cheeks. "Okay, okay, I'll tell you, but you gotta get me in witness protection or somethun," he said, using the back of his hand to wipe his eyes

Over the next hour, Stuart Green told his interrogators about the two ex-convicts and their girlfriends who were cooking methamphetamine in a deserted, dilapidated barn near the Oregon border. He'd met them through another local drug user, and they had hired him to make a run to the Bay Area. The car he had been driving belonged to the guy named Jimmy. He was a really bad dude, Stuart Green told them, just got out of Pelican Bay a month ago. Their operation was primitive, he continued, no electricity, no phone, water from a nearby stream. The nearest road was almost a mile away. They had set up shop a few weeks ago, hauling all the chemicals and glassware they needed in on foot, using propane stoves to cook the meth. And yeah, they did have guns, at least two rifles, a shotgun, and a couple pistols. They were bad dudes. Oh, and a couple nasty-ass dogs too.

Using maps of the county, Stuart Green had shown them the approximate location of the barn. It was really isolated, probably on federal land within the Six Rivers National Forest. It was close to 3:00 in the morning when they finished the interrogation. Oscar Zamora transported him to the Del Norte County jail and made arrangements to have him booked into a protective custody cellblock where he would be totally isolated from other prisoners.

It was too late to head home, just to have to turn around and be back in a couple of hours. To kill a couple hours, Red and Ray headed to Denny's, the only place in town open at that time of the morning for breakfast.

"This may or may not be related to the Castles," Red told her career long friend as they sat in the almost deserted restaurant, "But there are lots of coincidences here that are worth following up on."

"Yeah, but we'll need time to get a judge to sign a warrant and get enough people rounded up to do a search," he responded.

"Not if we involve corrections and have their parole agents do a probation search. One of the stipulations of being on probation is that parolees are subject to being searched any time without a warrant," she told him.

"So let's wake up that Nate guy, the captain from corrections on the task force, and have him arrange for some parole agents do a parole search. We'll tag along and see if anything connects the people running the meth lab to the murder of the Castles," Ray Silva said, his mind already thinking through the logistics of such an operation.

"Let's let him sleep another hour. I guess I'll have to notify the sheriff, too. It wouldn't bother me to wake him up though," she said with a half-smile.

Laughing, Ray shot back, "Damn, Red, you got a mean side I've never seen before. Where did you get that from, and where the hell did you pull that stuff from about being in prison?"

"I learned from the best, Silva, you!"

The preparation to do a search on the suspected meth lab took on the trappings of a military operation.

Ray Silva had called Nate Steadman around 6:00, advising him of the arrest of Stuart Green, the possibility of two parolees running a meth lab, and the need for parole agents to do a search. Because a search of this type was out of the ordinary, Nate Steadman in turn called his warden, something he would rather not have done.

Red made calls to Andrew Dixon from the Forest Service and Marv Butler, the honcho at the Redwoods National Park.

By 7:30, the briefing room at the sheriff's office was a busy place.

Since the Highway Patrol's only equivalent of a SWAT team was in Sacramento, in places like Crescent City, when special weapons were needed for high risk incidents like taking down a meth lab, the CHP called upon the local sheriff's department for assistance.

Several members of the Del Norte County Sheriff's Tactical Response Team were already there, dressed in their military style uniforms, carrying the special weapons and equipment they would need to lead the operation. Sitting in the back of the room, were two very large and burly looking parole agents from Department of Corrections.

Andrew Dixon and Marv Butler poured over maps with Ray Silva trying to determine the best route to take to reach the location of the suspected meth lab. Red Wolff peered over their shoulders as they traced roads with their fingers on the highly detailed Forest Service map.

"I know this area. It's about ten miles south of the Oregon border, off the Old Stage Road. It's near the State of Jefferson sign. No real roads, just some hiking trails and narrow logging roads. Really desolate," Andrew Dixon told them.

"I've never even heard of the Old Stage Road," Red interjected, "Where the heck is it?"

"It's the old road that used to connect Crescent City to Kirby, Oregon. It was an Indian trail at first. Then, when the gold rush started in 1850, they used it to haul supplies to the gold mining camps in Southern Oregon and Northern California. It was faster to send things through Crescent City than San Francisco back then. It kind of follows the same route as Highway 199. Most of it's not paved, and it mostly gets used by logging companies, hikers and tourists."

Ray Silva's knowledge of the county and its history, never ceased to amaze her.

"Pardon me Lieutenant Wolff," the ever polite Nate Steadman interrupted, "My guys have some information you might want to know."

Red left Ray Silva with the others at the maps and followed the corrections captain to a table in the back of the room where he introduced her to the two parole agents. They were both dressed in jeans, running shoes, and wore black nylon callout jackets with the words "Parole Agent" on the back in big white letters. Nate Steadman wore dark green coveralls, the kind most corrections officers wore inside the prison, and heavy combat type boots.

"Agent Carson ran the name Jimmy MacAfee through our database. His first name really is Jimmy, not James as you might suspect. He was released from Pelican Bay six weeks ago. He did twelve years for manslaughter," Captain Steadman told her.

"He really is a bad guy. Did a stretch at Folsom for second degree murder and another at Solano for manufacturing narcotics. We suspect one of the women your arrestee mentioned, is his wife. She moved up here a couple years ago. No idea who the other people might be," Parole Agent Carson told her.

Red started to ask a question when the sheriff's sergeant in charge of the Tactical Response Team called the assembly to order and directed everyone to take a seat.

He was about to start his briefing when Sheriff Jerome Williamson walked in the room accompanied by the warden of Pelican Bay Prison.

What the hell is he doing here, Nate Steadman wondered to himself?

Always the center of attention, Jerome Williamson took over the briefing telling everyone about the necessity for safety, the importance of tactical advantage, and the need to coordinate their movements. As usual, he couldn't help but throw in an antidote about his experiences on LAPD. Since this might be related to the murders of the two CHP officers, he added, he was going along, as was the warden of the prison since recent parolees were involved. Jokingly, he added, they would stay out of everyone's way. Nobody laughed.

Once the "Jerome Williamson Show" was over, the sergeant in charge of the Tactical Response Team started his briefing.

Red was impressed. Although this was the sticks and the sheriff's department Tactical Response Team, the equivalent of a SWAT team in other jurisdictions, didn't get activated very often, the sergeant in charge of the team was a pro. His briefing was meticulous. With just a couple hours to map it all out, he had devised a great tactical plan on how to take down the suspects.

His plan involved approaching the barn from four different sides, establishing an outer perimeter in case one of the suspects managed to flee, and minimizing radio communications.

It would take several hours to drive to a staging area two miles from the suspected lab and another hour for everyone to hike in and get in position, he told them. There were ten officers involved, twelve, counting the sheriff and the warden. No one was to take any action until everyone was in position. Everyone would work in pairs. The terrain was rugged and one person alone, could get hurt, or lost. Most importantly, if they needed help, they would have a partner.

The briefing broke up ninety minutes later, and small groups of officers headed off. The warden approached Nate Steadman and the two parole agents. He was dressed in blue jeans, hiking boots, and a plaid wool shirt. He also wore a black nylon callout jacket with the initials CDC, for California Department of Corrections, on the back, and a black baseball cap with a seven-pointed star.

"Captain, I thought it was important for me to go along on this "caper" with you," he said, using a word that had been out of police slang for twenty years. "It will also give me a chance to see you and your men in action."

"Do you have a weapon, sir?" Nate Steadman asked.

Instead of replying, the warden brushed back his jacket revealing a .9 millimeter automatic on his left hip.

As the warden walked away, Parole Agent Donnell Carson directed a question to Nate Steadman, "Is he authorized to carry a concealed weapon?"

"I don't know," Nate Steadman replied, "But, I'm not going to ask him if he is."

———

As Ray Silva drove out of the tunnel carved through the solid granite mountain just south of the state line, Red Wolff asked, "Where the hell are we going, Silva? We've been driving almost two hours."

"Oregon," Ray replied, one hand draped over the steering wheel of the black and white CHP vehicle. "It's quicker to drive to Kirby in Oregon and pick up the Old Stage Road there, then to come in from the California side."

Checking her rear view mirror, she could see a small caravan of vehicles following behind, two marked Del Norte Sheriff's units carrying the Tactical Response Team, another CHP vehicle with two of her officers, and an unmarked white Crown Victoria with Nate Steadman and the two parole agents. Bringing up the rear was another Crown Vic, this one silver blue, carrying the Del Norte County Sheriff and the warden of the Pelican Bay State Prison. Somewhere, either ahead or behind the caravan, were Andrew Dixon and Marv Butler in a Forest Service Crown Victoria.

Unseen, and lagging several miles behind, was a Forest Service Fire Truck, a precaution against fires that were always a potential with a lab due to all the volatile chemicals involved in manufacturing methamphetamine. Further behind, the Del Norte County Fire Department's Hazardous Materials response vehicle carrying two technicians equipped with the full body suits and breathing apparatus they would need to safely dismantle a lab.

The Old Stage Road was narrow and bumpy, the crushed rock and packed dirt surface rutted and slippery from all the recent rain. Towering redwood trees grew right at the edge of the roadway, and in many places the long boughs from trees on opposite sides had intertwined over the road to form a canopy.

About eight miles after crossing back into California, Red saw an old wooden sign on the edge of the road, its paint faded and letters hard to make out. As Ray passed the sign, she could make out the wording, *Welcome to the State of Jefferson.*

"What the heck is the State of Jefferson?" she asked Ray Silva.

"My dad used to tell me about it," Ray began, "Seems that in the early '40s the southern counties in Oregon and the northern counties in California tried to form a new state. Back then there were no highways, and they were so far removed from the rest of the two states they felt like they weren't getting any government services and no representation in congress for their interests. So they held a convention to push for an amendment to the U.S. Constitution to form what would have been the forty-ninth state, the State of Jefferson."

"We don't get much representation today. I can imagine what it was like seventy years ago. What happened?"

"They held their convention in Crescent City on December 3rd, 1941. Four days later, the Japanese bombed Pearl Harbor, and the whole thing just faded away."

Red shrugged, "It is really desolate out here. Hills and trees, and the underbrush is so thick you need to cut your way through. How much farther?"

"Couple miles."

"Okay," the Del Norte County Sheriff's sergeant told them as they all stood next to his patrol car, "Let's go over it one more time. My guys have done a reconnaissance of the area. The barn is about three-quarters of a mile in that direction. There's a small house we didn't know about near the barn. Smoke coming out of the chimney probably means the bad guys are living in the house and cooking in the barn. They saw one woman walking from the barn to the house.

She was carrying a shotgun. We need to improvise. We're gonna need two entry teams. One for the barn and one for the house. Two of my guys and one CHP officer will take the barn. Ray, you and your lieutenant are with me. We'll take the house. The rest of you will split up into twos and each take a different side of the perimeter."

With that he started issuing orders and splitting everyone up into pairs, "You two, the east side of the barn, you two circle around and come in from the west. You and you block the south side. Any questions?"

Nobody said anything.

"Everyone go to channel three on their radios, and let's do a radio check," he told them. It took a minute for everyone to synchronize their radios and ensure they all had communications.

"The entry teams will go first. It'll take about a half-hour for everyone to get in position. From now on, minimum radio communications. We'll do a radio confirmation that everyone is ready in twenty-five minutes," he told them.

"Game on," Red told Ray Silva as they started down a steep embankment and disappeared into the thick underbrush as the other groups headed off in their assigned directions.

The entire location was nothing but hills, gullies, redwood trees, and gigantic ferns. Everything was wet from the rain and footing was treacherous. It took nearly the full twenty-five minutes for all the teams to get in position where they had the house and barn encircled.

Situated on a small plateau, the house had no front door, and all the windows were broken out. Fifty yards away, the barn, half its roof caved in, and one of the doors off its hinges, had dozens of empty five gallon chemical cans and empty propane bottles strewn outside.

Exactly twenty-five minutes after they started, Red's radio crackled, "All teams report readiness," the hushed voice of the Del Norte Sheriff's sergeant called. One-by-one, everyone advised they were in position.

"Standby," he told them.

Jimmy MacAfee was a bad mother-fucker. At thirty-nine, he'd spent the better part of his adult life in prison. His latest stretch, at Pelican Bay, had been pretty tough time. About half of his twelve year sentence for manslaughter was spent in the Security Housing Unit, or "SHU" as the corrections officers called it, for fighting and various other violations of the prison's rules. In his mind, doing twelve years was a gift, considering he'd put a gun to the head of a guy in a bar in San Bernardino and blown his brains all over the pool table. It was the cost of doing business. Jimmy's business was manufacturing meth, and the guy had tried to rip him off for nearly a $100,000 in high-quality crank.

His attorney, a public defender, right out of law school, had plea bargained the first degree murder charge, which meant life without parole, down to manslaughter, which got him paroled after doing twelve years.

Gotta love those kids who believe the system is unfair to poor, misunderstood people like me, Jimmy MacAfee constantly laughed to himself. It was fair, he reasoned. After all, he'd never done a day for the other two people he murdered years before in another drug deal gone bad.

His wife had moved to Crescent City about two years ago. She'd done eight years at Valley State Prison for Women in Chowchilla, after she was arrested in connection with Jimmy's drug making activities. In Crescent City, she made a bunch of connections in the local drug scene, including a small time dealer named Stuart Green. The whole place was a bunch of small-timers she had told Jimmy. And, the whole area was a prime location to set up a lab. They could find some deserted place, cook several batches, and take off. Plus, she said, the local cops were a bunch of yokels, and there were so many desolate areas nobody would even know what they were doing.

But, they had a small problem. California law required that released prisoners had to be paroled back to the county from which they were sentenced. For Jimmy MacAfee this meant going back to San Bernardino.

Big fucking deal, he told his wife the day he walked out of the release portal at the prison. He had five days to report to his parole officer in Southern California. By the time they realized he hadn't reported, he'd be set up and cooking. A dozen batches and they'd get new identities and have enough money to live on for years.

Between himself, his wife, and with the help of another recently released ex-con and his old lady, it had taken them a week to find the deserted house and barn and pack everything they needed in on their backs. By having four of them, each buying small quantities of the chemicals and equipment they needed, some in Oregon, some in California, nobody would get alarmed and notify the cops. The Del Norte County Animal Shelter was only too glad to let him adopt the hard to place adult German shepherd and the Pit bull.

Their first batch hadn't turned out very good. It was okay, but not great. Luckily, Jimmy's wife knew how to get a hold of Stuart

Green, and Jimmy got him to sell the shit to his local clients. Then, they'd had one small explosion which put them out of business for a week until they could restock with the chemicals they needed. After a month, he had the recipe right, and he'd talked Stuart Green into making a run to the Bay Area with some primo stuff the previous day.

Today he had a splitting headache from breathing the fumes generated by the sulfuric acid in the drain cleaner and the acetone in the rubbing alcohol used to cook meth. The respirators his wife had bought were cheap, and they didn't do a very good job filtering the air. He'd worked all night tending the mixture as it cooked in the glass vials over the propane stove he'd lugged into this place.

Now, he was alone in the house, desperately in need of some sleep. His partner and the two women could do the cooking. He'd almost dozed off when the German shepherd started barking. He headed outside to kick the dog.

Any other time, Jimmy MacAfee would have grabbed a gun before he ventured out of the house. Today, his brain addled by the chemicals and not thinking clearly, it didn't cross his mind.

"Entry teams go, go, go," the supervisor of the Tactical Response Team shouted into his radio. From three sides, the officers from five different agencies descended on the house and barn.

The next forty-five seconds were a blur of cops running and shouting, weapons leveled at the people in the barn, screams from the two women, and barking by the Pit bull chained outside.

Tactically, it was a textbook operation. The entry team descended on the barn so quickly that the three people inside never knew what hit them. One minute they were tending the volatile concoction of chemicals, the next they were staring down the barrels of rifles held by cops in camouflaged uniforms, yelling and pushing them to the ground. They were handcuffed, and the barn was secured in less than a minute.

In the woods to the west side of the house, the two person team of Parole Agent Donnell Carson and his partner, who were assigned to cover the back door of the house, ran into a problem. When they started out of the trees toward the house, they encountered the German shepherd.

In using the dog to provide warning and ward off animals, Jimmy MacAfee had borrowed a technique used by marijuana growers. He had strung a lightweight metal cable ten feet off the ground between two trees about forty feet apart. He then attached a rope from the overhead cable to the dog's collar in such a manner that the rope slid freely on the cable. In that way, with the tether held up above the ground, the animal could run back and forth between ends of the cable, and the tether wouldn't get snagged on ferns and brush on the ground.

The shepherd came charging at the two person team, barking loudly.

The way the Del Norte County sheriff's sergeant had split them up into two-person teams, Donnell Carson had been assigned with someone who wasn't his regular partner. He and his normal partner did parole searches all the time, and they encountered barking dogs frequently. They were always cautious around such animals, but in three years of working together, they had never found it necessary to shoot one.

To his dismay, Parole Agent Donnell Carson saw the person he was assigned with today leveling his .9 millimeter at the eighty-five pound animal as it descended on them.

"Wait," he yelled at his partner, holding up his hand, preventing him from firing.

Donnell Carson was a dog person. He recognized the German shepherd's mannerisms, the way it ran toward them, the upright wagging tail, and the tone of its bark not to be signs of aggression.

As soon as it got near, almost like an overgrown puppy, the big shepherd flopped on his back, rolled around, then jumped up licking at Donnell Carson. It was almost like the animal was saying, get over here and pet me, I haven't seen anybody in days.

Alerted by the yelling of the entry team going into the barn, Jimmy MacAfee was out the back door of the falling apart house ten seconds before the Tactical Response Team supervisor, Ray Silva and Red Wolff came through the front door.

It only took the three of them seconds to make sure the one room house was empty. Ray Silva was out the back door a second later, catching sight of a male disappearing into the heavy underbrush.

"Out here," he yelled and started down the slight embankment toward the trees. Red Wolff and the Del Norte sheriff's sergeant were right on his heels.

Two pistol shots rang out, followed a second later by two more.

The vegetation was so thick it took Red Wolff and Ray Silva nearly a minute to work their way down the embankment and up the other side. Unlike the person they were chasing, they needed to move cautiously, weapons at the ready. They came out of the underbrush into a small clearing.

Jimmy MacAfee was lying face down, blood running from under his chest, soaking into the damp muddy ground. Four yards away Parole Agent Donnell Carson lay on his back, his eyes wide open, two bullet holes in his chest.

CHAPTER FOURTEEN

SHOOT OUT AT DRUG LAB, ONE COP DEAD, CHP MURDERER KILLED

Del Norte County Sheriff Jerome Williamson announced today that at a drug lab near the Oregon border the murderer of two CHP officers was killed in a shootout with officers who were conducting a raid. One officer from the Department of Corrections was also killed.

The front page headline in the local paper didn't contain a lot of details on what had happened, explaining that one man and two women had also been arrested, and the investigation was continuing.

Everything the paper printed the twenty-three year old "crime reporter" had gotten from the press conference Jerome Williamson held the day after the raid on the meth lab.

It was a tragedy that another law enforcement officer had been killed during this operation, Sheriff Williamson told the reporters from the broadcast and print media. Parole Agent Donnell Carson, was a dedicated officer who died in the line of duty. The suspect who murdered him was a hardened criminal who was also responsible for the murder of the two CHP officers two weeks ago. The case was broken thanks to the hard work of the interagency task force he had formed.

He also mentioned that as county sheriff, he had led the team that conducted the raid on the drug lab and had been actively involved in the arrest of the other suspects.

Red, Mary Jean, Ray and Julie went to dinner Saturday night. The seafood restaurant at the harbor was only about half-full, the tourist season and the influx of vacationers to the county, still a couple months away.

Red was unusually quiet, and even a glass of wine had not loosened her up.

"What's bothering you, Erin?" Julie asked, "You should be relieved the guy who killed Dave and Jodie is dead."

"Oh, nothing," she replied, not revealing that her thoughts were on everything that had happened over the last two weeks.

"That's a crock," Ray said, directing his remark right at her. "You're thinking about what happened up in the hills, aren't you?"

"Yeah, I am," she admitted, "It just doesn't make any sense."

"What doesn't?" Mary Jean asked.

"The whole thing!" she stated. "Ray, you interrogated the three people we arrested at the lab. Each of them swears Jimmie MacAfee hadn't left the location in nearly a month. If he hadn't left the lab in a month, then he wasn't the one who murdered the Castles two weeks ago."

"How do you know they're telling the truth Erin?" Julie questioned.

Mary Jean joined in, "Yeah, they're all drug addicts, aren't they?"

"That's exactly what the sheriff said. They're all drug addicts. Then he added they all had a reason to lie about whether Jimmie ever left the lab. He thinks they're lying so they don't get implicated in the murder of the Castles. So by saying Jimmie MacAfee never left, they figured they couldn't be connected to the murders."

"But they found the gun that killed the Castles. You said it was in that Jimmie guy's hand, and that he used it to kill the parole agent before he was shot by another officer," Mary Jean continued to probe.

"Ballistics tests confirmed the weapon we found in Jimmie MacAfee's hand was the same gun and same type ammo that killed the Castles. The problem is the same three drug addicts claim they didn't have a .38 revolver. Jimmie's wife said she bought four guns, two rifles, and two pistols from some "druggie" in Eureka. All four guns were stolen in a sporting goods store burglary in Santa Rosa a year ago," Ray jumped in, relating what they knew about the weapons found at the lab.

"And Jimmie's wife told us he didn't like revolvers because there aren't enough shots before you have to reload," Red Wolff added.

"Do you believe the wife's story Erin?" Julie asked, now feeling herself drawn into the whole conversation and the mystery that was being discussed.

"These aren't three brain surgeons we're dealing with. Jimmie's wife has done some hard time, and like any drug user, she's a skilled liar. The other guy we arrested seems to have been drawn into this whole cooking meth thing just for money. He never even met Jimmie

MacAfee until a month ago, and his girlfriend is just plain rock stupid. She's still wondering that the hell happened, and how soon she can go home. Hasn't got a clue how much trouble she's in," Red replied.

"What bothers me is Jimmie MacAfee," Ray told them. "There's no way anyone who looks like him could have taken down the Castles. Dave and Jodie were both good street coppers. One look at Jimmie MacAfee and every warning bell about officer safety would have gone off. Both of them would have been instantly on their guard. He looked like a bad guy, he had prison tattoos, shaved head, and he smelled bad."

"Did you discuss all this with the sheriff?" Julie queried.

"Well, discuss is the wrong word. We ended up in a shouting match. He has eyes on being reelected, and he needs this case to be solved so he can run on his record as a kick-ass crime fighter. He's disbanded the task force, and told me as far as he's concerned the investigation is closed," Red replied.

"What does your chief, that Vaughn O'Dell from Redding say?" Mary Jean asked.

"I laid all this out for him, and he's skeptical about Jimmie MacAfee, too. But he says Sacramento headquarters wants the case solved. Politically, the Commissioner is getting pressure from the Governor to close the file on the murder of the Castles and now the parole agent from corrections, too."

As their dinners came, Julie directed a final question at Red Wolff, "So are you going to close the case?"

"In the history of the Highway Patrol, there has never been an unsolved murder of an officer. This one's not solved as far as I'm concerned."

———

Had he heard Red Wolff's statement that the murder of the Castles wasn't solved, he would have been, or at the very least, should have been, afraid, very afraid.

Instead, four miles from where Red Wolff was having dinner, he was at home, his house brightly lit, a warm fire in the woodstove, while he sipped on a celebratory Vodka rocks.

It couldn't have worked out any better, he said to himself.

Staring into the glass door of the woodstove, he watched the flames lick up and around the two pieces of seasoned oak he had added to the fire. As the logs began to glow red on the edges, he relived the entire incident at the lab.

He had been struggling with how to derail the work of the task force by diverting the focus of their investigation in another direction. He knew that given enough time, the task force would eventually narrow their investigative efforts, and their investigation would shift his direction.

Then, everything just seemed to fall into place. A routine traffic stop for speeding turned into an arrest for narcotics. The car the drug runner was driving was similar enough in appearance to a Crown Victoria that the task force investigating the murder of the two CHP officers got involved. That led to the information about a meth lab being run by an ex-con on Forest Service land.

When he got the call early Friday morning about the arrest of the drug runner and the intent of the task force, with help from the Del Norte Sheriffs, to conduct a raid on the suspected lab, a plan almost instantaneously materialized in his mind. Given the fact that the lab was on federal land, that it was suspected parolees were involved in manufacturing narcotics, and there was a possibility the lab and the ex-convicts were connected to the murders of the two CHP officers, there was nothing unusual about him going along when the search was conducted.

With a rough plan in mind, he had secreted the .38, in its hide-away holster, inside the back waistband of his jeans and covered it with his shirt. On his hip, visible in its high-rise holster, he put a fourteen shot semi-automatic pistol. Lastly, he threw on a light weight callout jacket, not to hide the weapon, but to identify him as law enforcement.

As he sat though the briefing by the Del Norte County Sheriff's sergeant, he didn't know exactly how he was going to do it, but his plan was to plant the .38 he had used to kill the two CHP officers somewhere near the lab where it would be found. Once it was found, routine ballistics tests would be conducted that would connect the gun to the murder of the officers. The gun would be all the evidence anyone would need to come to the conclusion that the officers had been killed by someone connected to the meth lab.

In his mind, a logical scenario, one people would accept given the local desire to quickly solve the murders of the officers, would be that the CHP officers stopped the silver colored Chevrolet Caprice with one or more of the people involved in manufacturing methamphetamine in the car. The occupants of the car had overpowered and executed the officers. Anyone arrested when they raided the lab could protest all they wanted that the .38 pistol was not theirs. To a jury, they would all be seen as low-life scum, and nobody would believe them. One of them, or all of them, would take a fall for first-degree murder.

Another fortuitous break was when it was discovered there was a small house at the location in addition to the barn. That had forced the Del Norte Sheriff's sergeant to improvise, splitting the members of the raid team into several more two-person groups than he had originally planned. As a consequence, he was partnered with Parole Agent Donnell Carson.

In the course of his career, he had only been on a couple operations involving searches, and never before on one that involved a drug lab. He knew, however, that the first thirty seconds were when he had to plant the .38. It was during that time when weapons were being pointed, cops would be shouting, and people running, when confusion would be highest. Every officer would be focused on securing the suspects. Nobody would see him slip the weapon from his waistband and place it in a location where it was sure to be found. If everything worked out right, he'd help with the search after the suspects were secured, and he would be the one who "found" the gun.

He and the parole agent were in position, weapons drawn, fifty yards from the dilapidated house when the sheriff sergeant's "go" signal came over the radio. As they charged forward, coming out of the cover of the trees and brush, they could hear the shouts of officers and the screaming of the women as one of the other teams entered the barn.

The big German shepherd barking and running directly at them had scared the hell out of him. He had instinctively leveled his weapon at the dog and was preparing to shoot when Donnell Carson stopped him. Having been tethered and neglected for nearly a month, the animal's joy at seeing a human being caused it to jump and bounce between the two men, barking loudly, tail whipping rapidly side-to-side, making it difficult for them to continue their advance to the back door of the house.

By the time they got away from the dog and continued toward the house, he knew he'd lost that thirty second window when he could easily plant the .38 still secured inside the rear waistband of his jeans.

The loud sound of someone, or something, crashing through the underbrush, coming in their direction caused both of them to freeze. The shepherd, straining at its tether, continued to bark ten feet behind them.

A second later, Jimmie MacAfee came through a narrow opening between two giant ferns. They were less than six feet apart. Donnell Carson had yelled freeze, holding his .9 millimeter in a classic two- handed police combat stance. It was aimed directly at Jimmie MacAfee's chest.

It was one of those life or death decision moments for Jimmie MacAfee. He could almost see the ex-cons mind processing everything. Two cops, they have two guns, I don't have any. If I run or fight, they'll kill me. If I give up, it'll mean another long prison stretch. For whatever else he was, Jimmie MacAfee, was a smart guy. He processed his predicament in two seconds, then slowly starting raising his hands in surrender.

"Turn around, hands on your head," Donnell Carson had yelled in a commanding voice at Jimmie MacAfee. "Cover me," Agent Carson had said, as he holstered his weapon and moved forward to handcuff the surrendering Jimmie MacAfee.

He was standing to the right and about two feet behind Donnell Carson when he fired his semi-automatic. Both rounds caught Jimmie in the middle of his chest, or "center-mass", as cops call it. The force of the bullets caused Jimmie MacAfee to stagger backward then pitch forward face down.

"What the hell are you doing?" a shocked Donnell Carson had yelled at him.

The look of disbelief on Donnell Carson's face that he had shot Jimmie MacAfee just as the fleeing ex-con was raising his hands to surrender, turned to shock when the parole agent saw the .38 he held in his left hand.

"I'm killing the dirt-bag who killed you," he said calmly before firing two rounds from the .38 point-blank into Donnell Carson.

He'd worked fast after that, knowing the sound of the four pistol shots would bring the other members of the joint raid team to his location within seconds. Quickly he wiped down the .38 to remove any of his own fingerprints before starting to place it in Jimmie MacAfee's left hand. When the others got there they would see exactly what he wanted them to see, the ex-con who had shot and killed Donnell Carson, face down with a weapon in his hand. He was in the process of wrapping the dead man's fingers around the pistol's wooden grips when he heard people coming through the brush.

Taking a sip from his drink, he closed his eyes and laid his head back against the padded headrest of his overstuffed chair to better visualize what happened over the next thirty seconds.

He was still bent over the prostrate body of Jimmie MacAfee, trying to get the .38 placed properly in the dead man's left hand when the female CHP lieutenant and the older silver-haired officer appeared. Thinking quickly, he changed from trying to put the .38 in Jimmie's dead hand, to pulling it away.

As the Vodka warmed his insides, a slight smile came to his lips as he imagined how it looked to the two highway cops. They saw precisely what he wanted them to see, good officer safety tactics as he removed a weapon from the hand of a potentially still lethal suspect.

"He shot Agent Carson!" he had cried out, "I had to shoot him."

Not knowing whether the ex-con was alive or dead, the silver-haired CHP officer had handcuffed Jimmie MacAfee's hands behind his back, while the female lieutenant went to the aid of Donnell Carson.

"I had to shoot him," he had repeated to the CHP officers, a slight whine in his voice. "I've never shot anyone before," he continued his act, sitting down on a fallen log and putting his head between his legs.

Within a minute, several other members of the raid team were there. Everyone came to the same conclusion. Parole Agent Donnell Carson had been shot by ex-con Jimmie MacAfee as he was trying to escape. He in turn had acted to defend himself and had shot the man who killed his partner.

"Case closed," he said out loud, taking another drink.

———

Just like Sheriff Jerome Williamson, the Del Norte District Attorney had an election coming up. Since getting reelected meant running on his record, he opted not to pursue murder charges against Jimmie MacAfee's wife and the other two defendants who were arrested at the drug lab. The sheriff's detective had built a "slam dunk" case on the meth lab. Catching the three of them actually manufacturing illegal drugs made that part pretty easy. They'd all get long sentences anyway, and he could run as being tough on drugs.

On the other hand, the case against the same three for the murder of Dave and Jodie Castle was shaky at best. That charge was based largely on circumstantial evidence, namely the .38 taken from Jimmie MacAfee's hand.

In deciding not to file murder charges, the D.A. reasoned that proving Jimmie MacAfee's .38 had killed the officers was easy. Trying to connect the three arrested at the drug lab with the actual murder would be almost impossible. Druggies or not, he didn't believe he could get a conviction for first degree murder. His opponents would use losing a capital punishment case against him during the election campaign. Better to prosecute for just the drug lab, where he had solid evidence and was sure to get a conviction, than to risk his record on a "not guilty" verdict when it came to the murder charge.

———

The question of Jimmie MacAfee being the real murderer of Dave and Jodie Castle remained a bone of contention between Red Wolff and Jerome Williamson.

One of their classic, and now becoming more frequent, knock down drag out arguments about the entire investigation into the murder of the Castles, concerned the gun.

"Jimmie MacAfee's wife was adamant they didn't have a .38, and she said Jimmie never left the lab once they started cooking," she had pointedly told him.

"Of course she would say that lieutenant," he had told her in a condescending tone, "It's the whole drug culture thing. They're all liars. You Highway Patrol people don't understand these types of investigations."

"I understand enough to know you just want this case closed, regardless if the real murderer has been caught!" she fired back.

"This case is closed as far as my agency is concerned!" he roared at her. "I'm shutting down the task force and pulling my detective off the case. You can investigate it all you want!"

Standing behind the closed doors in Jerome Williamson's office, Red Wolff steeled her emotions, spread her feet apart, and put her hands on her hips, staring directly into his eyes. "You bet I will! When I find the real murderer, I'm gonna come back to this office and shove it up your ass!"

CHAPTER FIFTEEN

Once the Del Norte County District Attorney declined to prosecute the murder case against Jimmie MacAfee's wife and the two others arrested at the lab, all the evidence related to the murder of the Castles was released by the sheriff's department to the Crescent City CHP. Under normal circumstances, that evidence would have been shipped to Sacramento and destroyed. This wasn't a normal case in Red Wolff's eyes.

Her office at the Crescent City CHP command was only slightly larger than a partitioned cubicle found in many businesses across the country. Aside from the luxury of a small window and a door, they weren't the greatest of digs.

In spite of its small size, Red jammed every bit of evidence into this limited space. On the floor were five cardboard boxes crammed full of paperwork, records of interviews, stacks of photographs, autopsy reports, physical evidence recovered at the vista point, and reams of computer printouts on Crown Victorias and their owners.

Red Wolff stared at the boxes of evidence on the floor, considering her next move. She knew she was contemplating taking on something entirely new in her career. In her twenty plus years she had investigated over a thousand vehicle collisions, written nearly that many arrest reports for everything from drunk in public to armed robbery. Twice she had apprehended suspects wanted for murder.

Almost all of these arrests had come about, however, as a result of something related to a traffic stop or her regular patrol duties. A routine stop for a traffic violation might have led her to see a gun under the seat. Checking out the gun and the driver, led to a warrant check, which might lead to the person being wanted in connection with a more serious crime. Or, as happened several dozen times, she might be on patrol when a "BOLO", or "Be on the lookout" was broadcast by the communications operator giving the description of a vehicle wanted for a just occurred crime. And, as luck would have it, that very vehicle, out of the thousands of vehicles on a busy street or crowded freeway, would be right in front of her. Good police work, sometimes, was just a matter of being in the right place, at the right time.

Likewise, as a sergeant, and now as a lieutenant, she had conducted numerous what cops call "internal investigations". A majority of these were personnel complaints where a citizen complained about the actions of an officer. Things like, "The officer was rude", "The handcuffs were too tight", or "The officer illegally towed my car", were fairly common. Since it was CHP policy that every one of these citizen's complaints was investigated and documented, regardless of how ludicrous it seemed, she had gotten good at interviewing complainants and closing investigations.

More serious complaints, those involving allegations of excessive use of force, sexual harassment or racial discrimination weren't as prevalent, but she had investigated her share of these incidents, also. They were more complicated to conduct and required a greater and more in-depth investigation as they often resulted in the officer getting punitive days off without pay if the allegation was a serious violation of departmental policy. She had also investigated several cases that involved criminal conduct on the part of an officer. Occasionally, these type investigations were related to the officer's on-duty conduct, things like soliciting sexual activity with a violator, using excessive force, or stealing money from an arrestee. Incidents of that nature were uncommon, but they happened, and generally resulted in the officer being fired. Four times in her career she had investigated the off-duty criminal activity of officers that sent them to prison. It always amazed her that cops sometimes thought they were immune from things like child molestation, shoplifting, or felony drunk-driving.

The thought of not embarking on her own investigation and simply accepting the idea that Dave and Jodie Castle had been murdered by Jimmie MacAfee, never entered her mind. Call it intuition, an educated hunch, or being stubborn, the whole thing, trying to connect the murder of her officers to the ex-con just didn't pass the smell test.

What did enter her mind was that she still had a command to run. Anything she took on would have to be in addition to her regular duties. As commander, she was still responsible for everything Highway Patrol related in the county. Required reports still had to be completed on time, personnel items had to be dealt with, officer work schedules and beat assignments had to done every month, meetings attended, and emergencies handled.

In addition, Red knew if she was going to be competitive in the statewide captain's examination coming up in a few months, she would need to put in a lot of time studying to get up to speed on the political, governmental and internal issues facing the department.

Simply being a good commander and a hard worker, wouldn't get her on the promotional list. There were lots of good lieutenants around the state, and about sixty of them would be vying for the twenty or so captain's vacancies that would occur in the next two years. If she wanted to be one of the twenty, it would mean hours and hours of studying for the make or break, thirty minute oral interview that would determine who would get promoted.

Shifting her gaze, Red Wolff looked at the computer monitor on her desk. As a conditioned reflex she opened, read, and deleted the two new e-mails. Nothing important, her mind told her. Then, out of curiosity, she typed in the address for the official California Highway Patrol website. The high speed line connected in seconds, and she browsed the home page for a few moments before scrolling down to the link that took her to the page entitled "Badges of Honor".

This page, actually, eight pages, listed the names, and displayed the pictures, of every CHP officer killed in the line of duty. It began in 1929, the year the Highway Patrol came into existence, and continued to the present. Red hit the link that took her to 2010. Whoever it was in headquarters that was responsible for keeping the website up to date was doing their job. Red bit her lip when she saw the pictures of David and Jodie Castle and read the short narrative that told the circumstances of their deaths.

Idly, Red scrolled back to 1929 and began to count the number of officers who had been killed in the eighty-one year history of the Highway Patrol and the causes of their deaths. During that period, twenty thousand people had worn the CHP badge. For most it was a calling, a life-long career. Others had stayed for only a brief time before deciding that being a "Highway Cop" wasn't for them. It had been all men up until 1974.

Just over two hundred men and two women, who had worn the badge, had died in the line of duty. Nearly forty percent had been killed in motorcycle accidents. A vast majority of those accidents occurred prior to the '60s when the primary patrol vehicle all over the state was a motorcycle. Being a former motorcycle officer, Red knew just how dangerous two-wheel traffic law enforcement could be. Her experience as a motorcycle officer was mostly on freeways where everyone was going the same direction. Many of the officers who had been killed prior to her even being born, had died when a driver violated their right-of-way at an intersection. Some of the really old-timers she had worked with early in her career had called these the "soft-hat" days, a period before motorcycle helmets became standard equipment, and the only head protection officers wore was their "bus-driver" type cloth hat.

Over a hundred officers had died as a result of something directly related to vehicle collisions. Some were hit by drunk drivers, while others died as a result of a crash while pursuing a violator.

Forty officers had died from gunshots. The shooting incidents ranged from an officer gunned down while eating lunch at a coffee shop, to several killed as soon as they approached a vehicle they stopped for a traffic violation. Two had been killed with their own guns after struggling with wanted felons. The most infamous CHP involved shooting was in 1970, when, on a spring night, just north of Los Angeles, four Highway Patrol officers died in a ninety second gun battle with two heavily armed ex-convicts. The "Newhall Incident", as it came to be known, was considered the catalyst that changed officer safety tactics nationwide when it came to dealing with drivers suspected of having weapons in their vehicle.

Red clicked the web page closed.

Bending over, she picked up and opened a large manila envelope from the top of the first box. Within a couple minutes the entire wall on the opposite side of her desk was covered with photographs of the crime scene, the dead officers, and their vehicle. It had begun.

———

She was careful to make sure her regular duties came first. Every report went out on time, she monitored everyone's overtime and kept a tight rein on her budget. With one eye, she was constantly looking over Sergeant Dick Huddleston's shoulder making sure he was doing his job as a supervisor. She, also, attended every meeting her position as Area Commander required. As always, she took time to interact with her subordinates on a daily basis. For all intents and purposes, it looked to almost everyone that things at the Crescent City CHP office were back to normal.

But it was far from normal.

Over the course of the next two months, Red Wolff's quest to find the real killer had become an obsession. Every spare minute she had was spent going over reports and running computerized record checks on people and vehicles through NCIC and CII. Red was in the office every day by 7:00 in the morning reviewing records of interviews. She spent her lunch periods cross checking and finishing the work of the interagency task force put together by Sheriff Jerome Williamson. Quitting time at 5:00, when the business office closed, didn't mean time to go home, it just meant fewer interruptions while she combed over the boxes of evidence.

"What the hell are you still doing here?" Ray Silva barked at her as he stood in the open doorway of her office in civilian clothes. It was nearly 8:00 at night.

"Let's keep a civil tone when we address our commander, shall we Officer Silva," Red replied, trying to sound like a hard-ass.

"Oh yes ma'am, Lieutenant Wolff, ma'am," Ray replied mockingly.

Red laughed.

"So what are you doing here?" Ray asked.

"More stuff to go over. Still trying to make some sense of all this. The more things I learn, the more confused the whole thing gets," Red told him.

"Like what?"

"Well, the gun for instance. I have a friend that works for the feds. He's with Alcohol, Tobacco and Firearms. He owed me a favor so I asked him to run a records search on the .38 that killed Dave and Jodie and ended up killing that parole agent, Donnell, ah, what's his name?"

"Donnell Carson," Ray finished her thought for her.

"Right, Donnell Carson," Red replied, her speech rapid, her normally fluid arm gestures jerky.

He'd known her for twenty plus years. She was his friend. They'd spent years working together as partners on the freeways of Los Angeles. Together they'd laughed and cried over the things they encountered and the people they'd dealt with during that time. They had also shared the life threatening danger nearly two years ago when Islamic terrorists had attacked Crescent City. Whatever you called that bond that comes from complete trust and putting your life in someone else's hands, Ray Silva felt that bond with Red Wolff.

Which was why he was worried about her. He'd never seen her like this before.

Red continued talking, "Anyway my friend with ATF traced the gun back to a robbery and homicide in some podunk little town in Southern Virginia twenty years ago. I called the chief at that department, and he told me the case is in a cardboard box in a storeroom. It took some persuasion, but he dug it out and e-mailed me a summary. Seems they think the victim had returned to her hotel room and interrupted a burglary in progress. The hotel had been full of people who were forced to find accommodations due to an unseasonable snowstorm. The murder wasn't discovered until late the next day when a maid entered the room. By that time, the guests had all left, scattered throughout the Middle Atlantic States and points beyond. The town only had eight cops back then, one who acted as detective. It took them nearly three months to run down and interview over seventy-five hotel guests and twenty employees. They didn't come up with any leads, and they didn't have the resources to actively pursue the investigation. After six months, they packed the case in a box, marked it unsolved, and stuck it in a storeroom."

Ray Silva was processing everything Red had just told him as fast as he could. He also knew she needed to quit work for the night. "Red, let's go get a drink. You can explain this whole thing to me again. I'll buy."

Ten minutes later they were at a table in the bar attached to one of the more popular restaurants in town.

"What the heck are you doing out this time of night anyway, Silva?" she asked as their beers came.

"Just got back in town. Julie and I were in the Bay Area for a couple days," Ray replied taking a big swallow from the long-necked beer bottle.

"Another trip to the Bay Area," Red said, her mind calculating that he and Julie had just made the same eight hour plus trip two weeks prior. "You're not thinking of transferring down there are you, Silva?"

"Nah, come on Red. I've only got six months before I turn sixty and have to retire. Besides, it's like when we first worked together in Los Angeles, I can't turn you loose on the people of California without me around," he laughed.

They each drank two beers while continuing to talk about the status of her investigation.

"So the gun gets stolen in a robbery that ends up being a murder," Ray said. "Guns get stolen all the time. And, our esteemed local sheriff was right that drug users trade them for cash or for more drugs. They also steal them from each other."

"All that's true, but once a gun gets stolen, it usually turns up somewhere being used in another crime. Some druggie gets popped, and the gun is found in their car, or cops find it when they do a search warrant. This gun gets stolen on the East Coast, drops out of sight for over twenty years, then shows up at a drug lab in the mountains of Del Norte County. How did that happen?"

"Don't have a good answer for you on that one, Red. What about DNA? Did the police back east find any semen or blood?" Ray inquired.

"Well, according to the chief of police I spoke to, the woman wasn't raped, so no semen. They did find blood stains from the suspect in the room. But they never had the blood analyzed, and he's not sure what shape it's in today."

"Never analyzed," Ray said shaking his head.

"It's understandable. Remember back twenty years ago DNA was almost seen as witchcraft. Most big departments were just getting into how to collect and preserve bodily fluids back then. There were only a dozen or so labs in the whole country that could do the analysis, and it took months to get the results. Plus, it was really expensive, and a good defense attorney could shoot so many holes in the theory of DNA that they confused the hell out of juries," Red told him.

"Oh, you mean like that football player guy who killed his wife in Los Angeles when we worked down there," Ray deadpanned. "BJ or something like that."

"OJ, and quit jerking my chain, Silva," she laughed.

Ray Silva flashed a smile then got serious again, "So what are you going to do?"

"I'm trying to get the chief of police to send me some of their blood evidence so I can get it DNA analyzed and run it through the national database to see if we get any hits. The chief there won't release anything without the permission of his district attorney, who won't release anything without a court order and a search warrant from California. So, the whole thing is stuck in the bureaucracy of a small town somewhere near the Virginia and North Carolina border."

"Jesus, it's amazing that the entire justice system of this country doesn't have a permanent limp from shooting itself in the foot so often," Ray observed shaking his head.

"Want another beer?" he asked.

"Nah, two's my limit, you go ahead though," she told him.

"'I'll pass too, but we need to talk," he told her, a deadly serious tone to his voice. He didn't wait for her to reply.

"Red, you're killing yourself with this Castle thing. It's taking over your life. You're spending every spare hour you have working on this. You're neglecting Mary Jean and little Ray. You haven't taken a real day off in months. You spend every weekday working on this murder and all weekend studying for captain. You've stopped running in the mornings so you can get to work earlier. You're not sleeping right, and you look like shit!"

You have to really care about someone and be secure in your relationship with that person, to be so brutally frank, Ray Silva knew, as he spoke those stinging words to his career long friend.

Red Wolff's facial expression didn't change, her body didn't cringe, and her eyes didn't blink as Ray's words cascaded out and dowsed her verbally with something she had been beginning to recognize in herself.

"Crap, Ray! Don't hold back, tell me what you're really thinking," she said, a half-grin on her face.

Ray Silva laughed. It was the type of laugh only those who had shared the kind of experiences he and Red had shared could muster, or understand.

She laughed back.

"It's that obvious?" she asked.

"I guess you haven't noticed people around the office scatter when you're there. Your secretary is walking on pins and needles, afraid to disturb you. Dick Huddleston even put in to work night shift to get away from you. Christ, Dick hasn't work nights in fifteen years. His night vision is so bad he'll probably kill himself out there driving in the dark."

"I saw that he signed up to work nights, but I thought it was because I've been on his ass about other things," Red chuckled. "Okay, I get it. I need to back off a little."

"No, Red, you need to back off a lot. I'm with you, the real killer of Dave and Jodie is still out there. The gun is the one piece of evidence that ties everything together. Let it rest a while. You get back to being yourself and doing the things you are good at. Leave being a homicide detective alone for now. You have a family to worry about and a captain's test to study for. Something will happen that will pop this whole thing wide open, and we'll find the killer."

———————

Because it ran along the north side of the Smith River, locals called State Highway 197, North Bank Road. It was a shortcut that let traffic on Highway 101, mostly from the Oregon coast, connect with Highway 199 by not having to drive all the way into Crescent City.

Like many of the secondary state highways in this part of California, the road surface was crowned in the middle to allow rainwater to runoff on both sides. As you drove, you could actually see how the middle of the road was significantly higher than the edges. In some places there were narrow grassy shoulders, the three or four foot width not suitable for stopping. Other stretches had wider dirt covered locations which were often used by fisherman during the day, who found them handy spots to park, open their trunk, grab their fishing pole, and toss a line in the Smith River.

At almost the same time Red Wolff and Ray Silva were finishing their beers, he was eastbound on this very dark and very deserted road.

It had been two months since the raid on the drug lab, nearly three, since the night he murdered the two CHP officers. During this entire period, he had opted to maintain a low profile until the furor died down, until the papers stopped printing stories about the murders of the CHP officers and the parole agent, and until he felt the time was right.

It began to feel right the prior week. The local paper was back to printing its usual junk, and there was less talk about the murders as people accepted, because they wanted to accept, the idea that an ex-con had perpetrated these crimes. Mostly, however, it was because law enforcement in the county had new crimes to deal with.

The urges had returned, also. Slowly at first, then over the last three days, it was almost all he could think about. He knew it was time. He had to make a business trip to Eureka that week and had stopped by the Bayshore Mall after his meetings were finished. There were a couple of women's apparel stores in this mall where he'd shopped for scarves in the past.

Tonight he had ventured the less than twenty miles from Crescent City to Brookings, Oregon, for dinner. There was a seafood restaurant near the harbor he really liked that did a Dungeness crab in a white wine sauce that was superb. It was just past 8:30 when he finished and headed back toward California.

Driving south through Brookings, he patted his pockets for a cigarette. He had meant to pick up a couple packs earlier that day, but the time slipped away, and now he found himself rummaging with one hand through the glove compartment and center console as he drove. His hand recognized the feel of the cellophane on the pack in the glove box and sent a signal to his brain that he would soon have a cigarette lit.

Still driving, his eyes only leaving the road for quick glances, he pulled the last cigarette from the pack before crumpling it in his hand and tossing it on the passenger side floorboard. In the same motion he pushed in the lighter on the dashboard and put the cigarette between his lips. Twenty seconds later the lighter popped out, and he held the red glowing recessed end to the cigarette. Puffing as he inhaled, the cigarette ignited. After replacing the lighter, he inhaled deeply. The end glowed red, but instead of the nicotine laced smoke his body craved, he drew mostly air.

"Shit!" he exclaimed as he held the cigarette at arm's length where he could see the place the white paper holding the tobacco had separated from the tan colored filter.

No big deal, he told himself, there was a mini-mart at the south end of Brookings where he could grab a pack.

There were a couple other vehicles in the parking lot as he pulled in, a beat up '70s model Ford pickup, a newer model Nissan SUV, both with Oregon plates, and a very shiny Toyota Camry registered in Washington. As he entered the store, he held the door for the middle-aged woman who politely said thank you before getting into the Nissan and driving away.

Besides the male clerk, she was the only other person in the mini-mart. Shapely, blond hair, maybe late twenties, early thirties, she was dressed in blue jeans and a heavy knit pullover, white sweater. He had to do a double-take. She could have been the girl's twin sister.

It all came back in an instant. He was the geeky clerk at a store, working his way through college, and she was the spoiled co-ed who had tried to run him over as he rode his bicycle because he wouldn't sell her a bottle of rum.

The sight of her brought back a flood of emotions. Fear, the feeling of power, and the smell of the ditch he had fallen into. He even felt pain in his knee, just like the pain he felt that night as he pushed his wrecked bicycle back to the dorm, limping the entire way. But mostly it brought the pent up urges he had been feeling, instantly to the surface. The whole thing disoriented him and he left the store without buying a pack of cigarettes.

She came out a couple of minutes later and jumped in her Camry. With Washington plates, he expected she'd turn left out of the parking lot and head north. If she did, he knew it would be far too dangerous if he attempted to stop her in Oregon. He had home court advantage in California, he said to himself, not in Oregon. When she turned right, south toward California, his breathing began to get shallow, and the urges that had been building for the last week overwhelmed his will to contain them.

By the time he got his car started and headed back south on 101, the Camry was nowhere to be seen. The highway was only one lane in each direction, and all he could see ahead were the red taillights of half-dozen cars and pickup trucks, and the box shape of a big-rig truck pulling a semi-trailer.

"Damn, damn," he yelled as he open palm smacked the steering wheel of his Crown Victoria with both hands. He'd lost her. He was almost hyperventilating, his breathing short and clipped, and his pulse racing.

Traffic picked up speed as it left the south city limits of Brookings. But with only one lane in each direction, and the steady flow of traffic coming north out of California, it was impossible to cross into the opposing lanes to pass.

"Damn, damn," he yelled again.

Less than a mile south of the Oregon border, motorists on Highway 101 encounter several large green signs advising them they are approaching a California Agricultural Checkpoint. Located at every major highway "port of entry" into California, these 24/7 checkpoints were called "bug-stations" by local residents.

The fear of insects and pests that could destroy California's agricultural industry meant every vehicle crossing the border into the state is stopped, and the driver asked if they have any fruits or vegetables. Backyard grown, or commercially grown uncertified produce is confiscated.

They had always reminded him of toll booths at the bridges around the Bay Area. The entry to the agricultural checkpoint was about eighty feet wide, with cones and barriers funneling traffic down into lanes that ended at a stop sign near the inspection booth.

The Smith River Ag-Station checkpoint had three lanes. Two lanes had small tollbooth type covered structures just big enough for the inspector, a telephone, and a small electric heater. It got damn cold sitting in that booth all night. The third lane, which was wider and not covered, was for trucks, motor homes, and over-width vehicles.

At night, because traffic is light, there is generally only one lane open, with one inspector on duty. Traffic slowed as it approached the checkpoint and funneled into the single lane. From what he could tell, as the big-rig blocked his view, he was the third vehicle in the queue.

The flashing yellow turn signal from the semi-trailer caught his attention as the big truck moved out of the line of vehicles and edged to the right toward the lane designated for trucks. Once it was clear, he eased forward to close the forty-five foot gap left by the truck. Directly in front of his vehicle was the Camry.

The actual inspection process takes only seconds as the inspector asks where a motorist is coming from and if they have any fruit or vegetables. It's an honor system. Answer no to the question about carrying any produce, and you are on your way in a matter of moments.

Ag-inspectors always note the license plate on a car as it approaches the checkpoint. They know for the most part, cars with California plates are local Del Norte County residents heading home from shopping in Oregon where there is no sales tax. Inspectors also recognize the same cars being driven by the same people.

"How you doing tonight, Boss?" the inspector said to him as he stopped directly adjacent to the inspection booth door.

"Good. Just had dinner at the harbor in Brookings," he replied, trying to be polite while keeping his eyes on the Camry as it pulled rapidly away.

Seeing nobody directly behind him, the inspector began to engage in small talk. "You're driving your work car tonight I see."

"Yeah, I was out this way anyway," he replied, a hint of impatience in his tone.

"They don't let us do that with our cars," the inspector told him, not picking up on the change in tone.

The Camry was out of sight by now.

"Nothing to declare, right?" the inspector asked and answered his own question as two cars were approaching the queue.

"Right, see ya," he said, accelerating rapidly away.

It took him nearly four miles to catch up to the Camry. Traffic was light on 101 and almost nonexistent when she turned onto North Bank Road.

As he drove, he prepared. From the back seat he retrieved his callout jacket and baseball hat with his agency's logo on the front. It was a little tricky letting go of the steering wheel at sixty-five miles-per-hour to pull his arms through the sleeves on the jacket, but he managed by holding the wheel steady with his knees. From under the front seat he pulled the red spot light, plugging it into the cigarette lighter receptacle. Lastly, from the center console he removed his .9 millimeter pistol, securing it to his left hip.

Holding the illuminated red spot light steady, he flashed his headlights on and off high beams several times to get the driver's attention. Typically, the first thing that happened was the driver would hit the brakes momentarily, then, after slowing, the vehicle would continue on until the driver found a wide area to stop.

Perfect, he said to himself, after she stopped well off the road. Exiting his vehicle, he held the flashlight in his right hand and slowly walked up to the driver's side window.

Willingly, she already had her window down and was looking through her purse which was now on her lap, for her license.

The whole thing, he knew, counted on her not getting a good look at how he was dressed. The callout jacket, which he wore, zipped closed, with its stenciled on shoulder patches and badge, and baseball hat with embroidered logo, would maintain the illusion for a while.

A couple things played in his favor. For one, television and movies had for years planted the idea with people that cops dressed anyway they wanted on patrol. Blue jeans, flannel shirts, t-shirts, leather jackets, and especially callout jackets. As long as what they wore had some type of official looking patch or badge people willingly accepted that the person wearing them was a cop. The average person never looked twice or gave a second thought to how a cop was uniformed.

The second thing was that in a lot of locations, cops dressed exactly that way.

Only once, in over twenty times he had used a red light to stop a woman, had she questioned his appearance and been suspicious of his identity. His flashlight had ended that problem.

As the woman retrieved her license, his rage grew exponentially. Up close she looked even more like the co-ed who had been his first victim. She didn't have a lot of indicators that she was a rich bitch, no oversized diamond rings or gaudy gold jewelry. Even her mannerisms and speech were polite. None of that mattered tonight. Rich or not, she was his.

He was slightly bent over now, half looking in her window, pretending to examine her driver's license. He held her license in his left hand, the flashlight in his right. He needed only to maneuver a little closer with the flashlight.

The flashlight had cost a little over a hundred-fifty dollars. You couldn't buy them in California, as they were illegal to possess, even for cops. But they were easily purchased in neighboring states, or from the internet. His was nearly fourteen inches long, powered by three, nine volt batteries. With a halogen bulb, it threw out a powerful beam that could be blinding when shined directly into someone's eyes. Its most unique feature, however, was the built in electrical stun gun. The two quarter-inch long electrodes, located on opposite sides of the flashlight's three inch diameter head, looked like little more than rounded protrusions.

When the electrodes were touched to a person's skin, and the special switch located near the regular on-off button was activated, it sent a jolt of 400,000 volts of electricity through the victim rendering them helpless for up to thirty seconds. More than enough time to subdue them, apply handcuffs, and move them to the trunk of his car.

———

It had been one long day for Trooper Tony Dutton. The court case he had to appear on in Medford was a holdover from when he was assigned to the Oregon State Police Post in Central Point. He'd transferred to Gold Beach three months ago, and this was the fifth time he'd had to make the nearly three hundred mile round trip to testify.

He had left the Gold Beach Post around 5:30 that morning driving a gold and dark blue painted state police Crown Victoria. There was no easy way to get from Gold Beach to Medford. The quickest way was south on 101 along the Oregon coast for fifty miles into California, where he could take the cut-off at Highway 197, and then go north on Highway 199, winding up the Smith River Canyon for seventy miles until he got to Grants Pass. There, he could pick up I-5, south for thirty miles to Medford. It was a pain in the ass drive.

He had spent all day hanging around the court, not getting on the stand until nearly 4:00. By the time he finished testifying, it was after 5:00. He'd driven back to Grants Pass where he stopped and had dinner with a trooper he used to work with.

He was dog tired, and his eyes hurt from the glare of the headlights of the oncoming vehicles he had encountered for the last two hours while driving south on the mostly two lane Highway 199.

It was after 9:00 and Highway 197 was deserted. As he rounded a long sweeping curve in the road, heading west, he could see the headlights of two cars, one behind the other, stopped on the eastbound right shoulder.

He figured it was a traffic stop even though he didn't see any emergency lights flashing. CHP officers, he knew, seldom left their red and blue lights on after they made a stop, a precaution against having a drunk home in on the flashing lights and ram into the back of the patrol vehicle.

Tony Dutton was tired and wanted to get home. He still had over an hour drive ahead of him. But, tired as he was, he knew the right thing to do was stop and at least make sure the officer was okay. Slowing, he nosed his Crown Vic onto the right shoulder directly across from the officer he saw standing by the driver's door of a shiny Toyota Camry with a cute blond woman behind the wheel.

The officer, he saw, wasn't dressed in uniform, although he was wearing one of those nylon jackets with lettering on the back, stenciled patches on the sleeves, and a ball cap with a logo on the front. He could, also, see the officer was driving an unmarked, not quite white colored, Crown Victoria.

It looked to the trooper that the situation was under control. A second later when the officer turned his way, Tony Dutton, still seated behind the wheel of his vehicle, held up four fingers.

The unknown California officer flashed four fingers back, giving the "Code 4, I'm okay" signal. Good enough, Trooper Dutton said to himself as he waved and glided off the shoulder continuing westbound.

He was beside himself with rage as he drove toward home.

He had returned the woman's license almost immediately after the trooper pulled away and gave her some bullshit story about stopping her for weaving across the centerline. As soon as she drove away, he made a U-turn and headed the other way, wanting to ensure nobody else saw her Camry and his vehicle in the same vicinity.

The appearance of the Oregon State Police Trooper had interrupted what, up to that point, had been a perfect situation. The woman had come within ten seconds of having the electrodes contact her neck. After that, in less than a half-hour, she would have been naked, tied hand and foot to his bed. Sometime later that night, he would have strangled her with the new scarf he had purchased in Eureka and her body disposed of.

She would never know how close she came to dying.

Letting the woman go, however, was a no-brainer. The trooper had seen his face and his car. Better to let this one go, he reasoned, as he turned off Highway 101 near Elk Valley Road.

Somewhere she'd taken a wrong turn. Her computer generated map showed the route to Crescent City was directly south from the Oregon border on Highway 101. What she hadn't counted on was the stretch of freeway just north of the town.

In California, bicyclists, pedestrians, and motor scooters, are prohibited from travelling on freeways. The thinking behind this law is simple, traffic is traveling at high speed and riding a bike, or walking on a freeway, is just too dangerous.

What confused the computer map programs and lots of pedestrians and bicyclists also, was that highways like 101, change back and forth from being regular highways to being freeways. In locations where there are stop signs, traffic lights, cross traffic, and intersections, the road is classified as a highway, open to any type of vehicle and pedestrians. In other locations, where there are no cross-streets, intersections, or signals, the highway is classified as a freeway, where pedestrians and bicycles are prohibited.

Having dutifully gotten off of Highway 101 when she saw the sign that prohibited bicyclists, she was now at the intersection of Elk Valley Road and Highway 199. Unfortunately for her, while there was a sign that told her she couldn't use the freeway to get to Crescent City, there wasn't one telling her which road to take that would get her to the town.

With redwood trees bordering the road and no street lights, it was rural dark. To Aimee Lawrence, who was cold, tired, hungry, and lost, it was frighteningly dark.

Twenty-six years old, she'd taken a semester off from the University of British Columbia where she was completing her doctorate in Native American cultures. While she was not technically working on her degree, the semester long sabbatical would give her the chance to take a break from the academic world, and the opportunity to first hand visit many sites along the Pacific Coast where Native American villages had once thrived.

Her parents had been adamantly against the idea of her travelling alone by bicycle. Not that their protests did much good. Aimee Lawrence was a strong-willed, independent woman. The previous summer she had hiked deep into the Canadian woods, alone, excavating an ancient Okanagan Indian village. Protest as they might, the best her parents could do was to elicit a promise she would provide them an itinerary listing where she planned to be, the motels and other places where she would sleep, and a promise she would call every night.

The big car slowed as it came around the corner, the driver switching on his high-beams which caused her to look away and shield her eyes from the intense light.

The man who approached her seemed to be wearing some type of uniform jacket with a badge and a baseball hat with a police logo. Carrying a flashlight, he had greeted her and asked if she needed any help. The man was helpful, but he appeared to her to be upset about something. She wrote it off as her own nervousness.

She didn't pay much attention when he shifted the flashlight from one hand to the other as he pointed out directions on her map.

When the two electrodes touched her neck, she let out a loud cry as the voltage coursed through her body, temporarily paralyzing her central nervous system. She crumpled to the shoulder of the road, her bicycle falling into the drainage ditch.

CHAPTER SIXTEEN

"95-3, Humboldt, 95-3."

"Humboldt, 95-3, clearing a stop, at Kings Valley," Officer Oscar Zamora responded.

"95-3, meet the citizen regarding possible found property, Elk Valley Road near 199," the monotone voice from eighty miles away directed him to another call.

It was nearly 9:30, and this was Oscar Zamora's sixth call of the morning. Oh well, he said to himself, it's always busier on day shift, especially on a day like today when it had been raining steadily. Besides, nobody twisted his arm to sign up for the morning shift. He'd worked nine straight months of afternoon shifts, then a three month stint of graveyards and needed a change. The nice thing about it was he was home by 4:00, and it gave him a chance to coach his son's Little League team.

There would be no practice today, he realized, this late season rain storm was forecast to linger for another day. Turning onto Elk Valley Road, he could see an older model pickup truck on the shoulder, the driver seated behind the wheel.

Oscar disliked wearing the rubberized yellow rain pants and jacket. They were great protection against the rain, but they made driving uncomfortable, and even though they were nearly thirteen years old, they still had that same smell many rubberized products have. Not necessarily foul, just funky.

Shifting positions, the rubberized pants clinging to the seat, he exited his patrol car, readjusted his gun belt, and met the driver of the pickup, who was already out of his vehicle, on the shoulder.

"How's it goin," Oscar Zamora greeted the man.

"Oh, fine officer, just fine," the elderly man replied.

He looked about seventy-five to Oscar Zamora, bald on top with wispy snow white hair on the sides. He had a friendly smile and was a little hunched over from arthritis, Oz surmised.

"How can I help you?" the officer asked.

"I was headed into town, needed to pick up some feed for my chickens, when I saw this bicycle down there," he said, pointing to the three foot deep ditch on the shoulder. "I thought it was maybe an accident, so I stopped. Looked all around and didn't see no one. It looks like there's a backpack and some other things with the bike. I'm too old to be climbing around down there so I called the Highway Patrol."

Oscar Zamora thought about it for a second. This was one of those jurisdictional things. Technically, if it was an accident, which this didn't appear to be, as he could see no damage to the bicycle, the call belonged to the Highway Patrol. On the other hand, if this was just an abandoned bicycle, or it was stolen, it belonged to the sheriff's department.

He had worked with plenty of officers in his career who would have taken one look at the bike, scanned up and down the shoulder for a rider, and then, seeing no one, would inform the citizen to call the sheriff, jump back in their patrol car and drive away.

These were the same officers Oscar Zamora knew who clamored for pay raises every year because they had such dangerous and stressful jobs.

"Okay sir, let me get some information from you, and I'll take it from here," he told the elderly man as he opened his report writing folder. Five minutes later, the man was on his way with a wave and a big thanks from Oscar Zamora.

It took him a few minutes to muscle the bike out of the ditch and back up onto the shoulder. There he did a quick visual check for damage, then opened the front and rear saddle bags looking for some identification or information as to the bicycle's owner. Finding only clothes, toiletries, several books on Oregon and Northern California Indian tribes, and some handwritten notebooks, he hoisted the lightweight bicycle into the trunk of his Crown Victoria patrol car.

"Humboldt, 95-3, 10-98, enroute 10-19 for follow-up," he called on the radio advising the comm-op he had completed the assignment she had dispatched him to and was headed back to the office.

———

Vaughn O'Dell sat in Red Wolff's office talking. It was one of his semi-monthly visits. As an assistant chief, he spent about half his time every month on the road, visiting the nine CHP commands that were his responsibility. Generally he stayed a half day with the local commander, talking about issues, conducting informal inspections of various management functions, and checking on routine operations.

Today, Vaughn O'Dell had a special purpose for his two hundred-fifty mile trip from Redding to Crescent City.

"Your command looks like it's getting back to normal Red," he told her as they both drank coffee.

"Pretty much, Boss," she replied. "It's been three months since the Castles were killed. We got two new transfers in last month to replace them, and life goes on."

"For everyone but you, I hear," he said, his tone indicating he was aware of her on-going investigation into the Castles murder.

Red Wolff took another sip of coffee, but didn't reply.

"So how's your one woman quest going?" he inquired.

"Still trying to get information on the gun that killed the Castles and the parole agent, still trying to sift through the stuff the task force did, and still trying to make some sense of the whole thing," she told him.

"And you're still convinced that ex-con wasn't the guy who killed Dave and Jodie?"

Red Wolff nodded.

"Okay, you stay at it as long as you want so long as your operation here doesn't suffer," he cautioned her.

After a short, purposely interjected pause to let his words sink in, he continued.

"Red, this is my last trip here. I'm retiring at the end of next month, and I wanted to see everyone in Crescent City one last time."

"I'm gonna miss you, chief, you've been a great boss and a strong mentor," she told him. "I've learned a lot from you."

"Which is the other reason I came. The captain's test is in a month. I was in Sacramento last week and picked up some scuttlebutt on the issues that are hot items with the department right now and the types of questions that might be asked at your oral interview."

It was just like him, Red thought. He was weeks away from retiring yet he made it a point to drive all the way over here to help her prepare for her interview.

Over the next hour, while Red Wolff took notes, Vaughn O'Dell related the issues that he thought would be covered on her captain's test interview. He gave her an in-depth primer on fiscal restraint, California's budget woes, personnel management, collective bargaining, and political relations. Very little of what they talked about had to do with actual law enforcement. Each issue, however, was part of the reality of being a police manager and was something she had to be conversant in to get promoted.

By 11:00, Vaughn O'Dell was talked out, and Red's mind was spinning.

"Let's grab some lunch," he suggested. "Where's that old mossback, Ray Silva?"

"In the Bay Area for a couple days with his wife. He's been going down there a lot," Red answered matter-of-factly.

As they headed out the back door of the office to the parking lot, Vaughn O'Dell and Red Wolff encountered Officer Oscar Zamora as he wheeled the bicycle into the covered parking garage.

"Hey Oz, whatcha got?" she asked as they both walked his direction.

"Not sure lieutenant," he replied, "Maybe an accident, maybe stolen. A citizen found it in a ditch."

"That's a pretty expensive bike," Vaughn O'Dell observed as he bent over and examined the frame. "It's an Americano, top of the line in touring bicycles, probably three grand or better."

"For a bicycle!" Oscar Zamora exclaimed.

"Yeah, it's the kind people use on long road trips. See the saddlebags on the front and rear, they're called panniers. Whoever was riding this was on a long trip," he added.

"What are you going to do with it?" Red queried.

"I'll check accident logs for the last couple of days and contact the sheriff and P.D. to see if anyone has reported it lost or stolen. I'm gonna go through the saddlebags, ah, panniers, to see if there is any info on the owner, and run any frame numbers I find through the system. If no one claims it, I'll mark it as found property, and the truck from Sacramento can pick it up in six months and take it back for auction," Oz told them both.

"Ooh, what happened to your neck, sir?" his secretary asked, obvious concern in her voice over the deep red gash on his neck that ran from just below his ear almost to his collarbone.

"It's nothing," he told her curtly, not even breaking stride as he walked purposefully toward his office. "Tripped in the dark outside while getting some firewood and fell against the wood pile."

"Are you okay, sir?" she asked.

He didn't answer, closing the door to his office.

"No, I'm not okay you dumb bitch. It hurts like hell, and it won't stop oozing," he said out loud as he looked at his face in the mirror of the private bathroom in his office. The gash had that red hue common with new wounds and scratches.

Twice before he had women fight back before he got them tied down securely. The effects of the flashlight stun gun were almost always incapacitating for the time it took to strip off their clothes and tie their hands and feet to the four posts on his bed. In the two prior instances, he had punched them both in the face knocking them unconscious.

263

The bicyclist, although she was only five-six, was deceptively strong, and she had fought violently for her life. She had somehow slipped her hand out of one of wrist restraints, punching and scratching at him.

The whole thing had unnerved him, and in his rage, he had immediately strangled her to death with a new scarf. That had occurred within thirty minutes of getting her to his home. He actually spent the next nearly two hours meticulously going through the cleanup procedures and preparing to dispose of her body.

It hadn't unnerved him so much, however, that he didn't take time to collect a memento of this encounter. Her black hair was cut short and had a feel to it like it had not been washed in a few days. Nonetheless, he snipped off a six inch strand, putting it in the plastic sandwich bag along with the inexpensive ring he took off her right hand.

Dumping her body at the vista point was not practical. It was a Thursday, and there were more cops working tonight, plus, the tide chart indicated the next outgoing tide wouldn't be until around sunrise. Even though there wouldn't be a great deal of traffic at that time of the morning, people would be travelling on Highway 101 heading to and from Crescent City right past the vista point.

Around midnight, he had headed north on Highway 199 until he came the hamlet of Gasquet. Three stores, a restaurant, small motel, and a post office, it was where the Old Stage Road started. Once it was a place where travelers in covered wagons stopped for the night before paying to use the toll road built by Horace Gasquet. Today, it was one of those places where you knew it existed only because the speed limit changed from sixty-five to thirty-five for a quarter-mile.

Turning onto the Old Stage Road, he drove slowly over the rough unpaved surface for about five miles before coming to a place where a deep ravine, with the Smith River directly below, bordered the road. This far from anything, the night was a deep black, the only light from the thousands of stars visible only in locations like this.

The drop from the road to the river below was a good eighty feet. He couldn't see them in the dark, but he knew there were large jagged granite boulders all along both banks of the river. With any luck, her body would hit the river and be swept by the current under a rock where it would decompose. If it washed up on the river bank, the bears, mountain lions, or coyotes would take care of it for him.

Running his finger gingerly over the gash on his neck, it reminded him that the three, nine volt batteries in his stun gun flashlight were probably low, and that's why it hadn't completely incapacitated the bicyclist. Yes, he thought to himself, the stun gun consumed a lot of power each time he used it. He made a mental note to change the batteries.

—————————

Aimee Lawrence's parents were worried. Actually they were worried sick. Aimee hadn't missed a day calling in since leaving on her bicycle trip over three weeks ago. Today, Sunday, was the third day without any contact from her. They called her cell phone constantly, only to have the recorded voice tell them the party they were trying to reach was unavailable.

Using the itinerary she provided, her father had been able to confirm she had stayed at, and checked out of, the motel in Port Orford, Oregon. That was Thursday morning. According to her schedule, her next stop was supposed to be Crescent City, California, seventy miles south on Highway 101. Calling the motel where she had a reservation for Thursday night, he learned she never checked in.

He spent almost all day Sunday calling every police department, sheriff's office, and hospital between Port Orford and Crescent City.

Dealing with hospitals was pretty easy as they all had systems that could confirm if an Aimee Lawrence was, or had been a patient. Getting information from law enforcement, depending on the agency, was either a lot more difficult, or totally impossible. It was a Sunday and most agencies just didn't have systems to do much more than provide information on incarcerated persons, or accident victims. The answer he got most often was to call back on Monday.

—————————

After the task force investigating the murder of Dave and Jodie Castle had been disbanded, Ray Silva went back to working patrol. It was actually the thing he liked most about being a California Highway Patrol Officer. Even after thirty-two years on the job, he saw everyday as an adventure, and he never got tired of dealing with people, investigating accidents, helping disabled motorists, and responding to calls. He would miss it when he turned sixty at the end of the year and would have to mandatorily retire.

One of the "bennies" of being the oldest guy in the Crescent City squad was that he didn't have to work graveyard shift. Not all of the over one hundred CHP commands around the state did it, but in Crescent City, it had been a long standing policy that officers over fifty years old were exempt from working graveyard shift.

In the old days, especially when he worked in Los Angeles, Ray Silva lived on graveyard shift. He loved the freedom of driving fast on wide open freeways, arresting drunks, working the kind of hellacious crashes, and quirky incidents that seemed to only happen on that shift. Now, however, he found his reflexes weren't as fast, especially when dealing with combative drunks, that the glare from headlights played havoc with his eyes, and the cold damp night air of Crescent City didn't agree with his old bones. Mostly though, not working graveyards meant being able to cuddle up with Julie every night.

That Sunday morning he and Oscar Zamora were the only two officers working. It was 6:05, the sun having just come up, as they sat in the deserted CHP office. Ray idly thumbed through the briefing book on the sergeant's podium, reading and signing off on roll call items, while Oscar Zamora worked on a report.

"What're you workin on Oz?" Ray asked, more out of courtesy than curiosity.

Oscar Zamora gave Ray the *Reader's Digest* version of his investigation into the bicycle.

"Ray, come outside into the carport and have a look at these numbers on the bicycle. I've run them every way I can think of, but they always come back with no match," Oscar told Ray Silva.

A minute later Ray Silva and Oscar Zamora were examining a nine digit number, followed by the letters CA, etched into the neck of the bike just below where the handle bars met the frame.

"I thought it was a social security number, but when I run it though the system, it doesn't match anything. With the letters CA I thought it might be a California Driver's License number, but all California DL's start with a letter, then the numbers. I'm at a loss. Got any ideas?" Oz asked.

Ray Silva got a shit-eating grin on his face. "I'll deny this if you ever tell anyone," he said to Oscar Zamora. "I had a girlfriend once, from Canada, met her in Mexico, she could do things to you that are illegal in most states," he laughed.

"Ah, come on Ray, not another story about the old days," Oz kidded him, with a sly smile of his own.

"Okay, young officer," Ray's changed tone back to the voice he used when he trained new officers right out of the academy. Then, laughing at himself, said, "That's a Canadian Social Insurance number. Kind of equivalent to our social security number."

Five minutes later, Oscar Zamora slammed the phone down.

"God damn bureaucratic son-of-a-bitch, fucking Canucks!" he yelled to the empty, except for Ray Silva, briefing room.

"Problems, young officer?" Ray asked, maintaining the "old veteran" tone in his voice.

"I called the Canadian embassy in San Francisco. They won't give me any information about Canadian citizens over the phone. They say the information is confidential. They want an inquiry request on official departmental letterhead. The guy I talked to says I'll have a response in about six weeks."

"Life's a bitch, ay," Ray Silva said, doing a really lousy job of mocking the Canadian national habit of adding the term "ay" to the end of every sentence.

Oscar Zamora gave Ray Silva a fuck you look.

Ray Silva walked into the men's locker room, returning a few minutes later with a tattered notebook he'd retrieved from his locker.

"Before you go home and throw away all your Gordon Lightfoot CDs, lemme see if we can expedite the process," he told Oz.

"Gordon, who?" the younger officer said, having no idea who Ray Silva was referring to.

Using his personal cell phone, Ray punched in a number from his notebook.

Oscar Zamora could only hear Ray Silva's portion of the conversation, but his mind filled in the details.

"I'm fine, Jack, how about you?" Ray said, then pausing while listening to the other person talking.

"Yeah, I know what time it is. Do you know how to spell Canada?" Ray laughed, again pausing while the person on the other end of the line responded.

"Jack, can you help me run down someone from their Canadian Social Insurance number?"

Oscar Zamora watched and listened for the next five minutes as Ray Silva talked to someone named Jack, giving that person the number from the bicycle frame.

"Oh yeah, Julie's fine, we got married a few months ago. How are Adrian and all the assorted little Jacksons?"

A minute later, after several more exchanged pleasantries, Ray Silva ended the conversation.

"He'll have the information for us by noon tomorrow," Ray told Oscar.

"Who the hell was that?" Oz asked in amazement.

"Buddy of mine. Royal Canadian Mounted Police. He and his whole family came through Crescent City on vacation a few years ago driving a motor home. Got broadsided by some kid in a pickup truck. Wrecked the crap out of the RV. Anyway, I worked the crash.

It took almost a week to get the parts and fix his vehicle, so I had all of them stay at my house. They had a great time, Julie and I took them all around and did the tourist thing. We stay in touch."

"What was that about spelling Canada?" Oz asked.

"It's a joke. You spell Canada, C, ay, N, ay, D, ay," Ray laughed

Oscar Zamora just shook his head.

"95-1, Humboldt, 95-1, 11-79, Lake Earl Drive at Fort Dick," the radio speaker mounted on the wall of the briefing room called.

"Time to go to work," Ray said, grabbing his notebook and heading to his patrol car. "Nothing like an accident with injuries to start off a Sunday morning."

On Monday, within a half hour of each other, two things happened, both related to Aimee Lawrence.

Around 10:15 that morning Ray Silva's friend from the RCMP called back with information that linked the Canadian Social Insurance number to a PhD candidate at the University of British Columbia. Being thorough, he also provided her address and phone number in Vancouver, B.C.

Since Oscar Zamora had the next two days off, Ray Silva took over the investigation. His phone call with Aimee Lawrence's parents took about fifteen minutes. For her parents, hearing from an officer of the California Highway Patrol, was a double-edged sword. They were relieved to at least know she had made it to Crescent City, but now they were frantic knowing her bicycle was found, but she was missing.

To help local authorities with the investigation, Aimee's father e-mailed several recent photos of his daughter to the Highway Patrol office.

Ray Silva handled the conversation as gently as he could. Experience told him something was wrong. Based on what he knew up to this point, he could sense this investigation wouldn't have a pleasant ending.

Victor Worthington lived to fish. It was Steelhead Trout season, and hardly a day went by when he couldn't be found somewhere on the Smith River.

But because of the rain Friday and Saturday, the river had been flowing too fast, and the water level was too high for Steelhead fishing. The rain stopped late Saturday night, and the water level started to recede on Sunday.

Today, Monday, he was at one of his favorite spots, just below Gasquet, at the location where the north and south forks of the river joined together to begin their thirty mile journey to the ocean. It was a rugged spot to get to. Parking on the shoulder of Highway 199, he had to traverse several narrow trails and climb over a dozen fallen trees to get down the sixty or so feet to the river bank.

There would be no fishing today.

The naked body of a woman was partially submerged, and he actually had to climb out on a large rock to confirm what he saw was a body. The climb back up the ravine was a lot harder than the trip down. Since he didn't own a cell phone, he had to drive back to the market in Gasquet to call the sheriff's office.

Because he used a landline to call 9-1-1, the call was routed directly to the Public Safety Answering Point for calls originating over regular phone lines, in this case, the Del Norte County Sheriff's Department.

The sheriff's 9-1-1 operator, who was also the sheriff's radio dispatcher, took the information and broadcast the call via radio to the sheriff's unit working that part of the county. In his patrol car, the CHP officer working that beat monitored the call on his scanner and responded to assist.

It took the sheriff's search and rescue team a good portion of the day to mobilize, drive to the location, deploy their equipment, and affect the recovery of the naked woman's body.

Since they had no idea who the woman was, she became a Jane Doe for the time being. Her body was taken to the funeral home under contract to the sheriff's department, where the contract pathologist would conduct an autopsy later that afternoon.

When the officer working the Smith River Canyon returned at the end of his shift, Ray Silva talked to him about the dead woman. He had a bad feeling.

No, he told Ray, he didn't get a good look at her. She was white, maybe thirty, short black hair. No, she didn't have any identification. The sheriffs didn't know who she was.

Ray Silva knew.

A minute later he was knocking on Red Wolff's office door, and five minutes after that they were on their way to the funeral home. Entering through the back door, they saw the same doctor who had

269

performed the autopsy on the Castles and the same Del Norte County Sheriff's Detective who headed the investigation into their murders.

The body, completely covered with a sheet, lay on the same steel table that held Davy Castle three months prior.

"You're getting more than your share of homicides to investigate," Red said to the young detective.

"What makes you think this is a homicide, lieutenant?" he responded, a questioning tone in his voice.

As the doctor organized her tools and started the paperwork, Ray explained how the CHP had recovered a bicycle and had been able to trace it back to a woman from Canada who was three days overdue in arriving in Crescent City.

Ray Silva had an eight by eleven manila envelope in his hand. "Her father e-mailed me her picture," he said as he opened the envelope and withdrew a black and white, copy machine reproduction of the photograph.

Handing the picture to the detective, Ray gently pulled back the sheet from her head.

"Aimee Lawrence," he said.

There was silence as the three cops and doctor looked at the bruised face.

"She was pretty once," Red Wolff said.

Nobody responded.

"You want to use that name, Aimee Lawrence?" the doctor asked the sheriff's detective as she sat finishing her preliminary paperwork.

The young detective nodded affirmative.

The doctor was every bit as meticulous with the autopsy on Aimee Lawrence as she had been on Dave and Jodie Castle. She narrated her way through the external examination, making reference to the ligature marks on her neck, voicing an opinion she had been strangled.

She also called everyone's attention to some residual material around Aimee Lawrence's breasts. Scraping some of the material off, she rubbed it between her gloved fingers and said, "Looks and feels like wax. Candle wax."

"What are those two little dark marks on her neck?" Red Wolff asked.

Turning the dead woman's head to the side, the doctor put on her magnifying glasses and bent close to the marks, using a small flashlight to brightly illuminate the area.

"They look like electrical burns, the flesh is black around the edges," she said, standing up and pulling off the glasses.

"Any idea what caused them?" Red pressed.

"I've seen electrical burns caused by high voltage wires before, but these look different, almost like it was done intentionally, like with a cattle pod," she offered.

"Or a stun gun?" Ray Silva queried.

"Yeah, I guess that's possible, a stun gun."

Ray and Red looked at each other in silence.

As she continued her examination, the pathologist noted two torn fingernails on Aimee Lawrence's left hand.

"Got some residue under these torn nails," she showed everyone as she held the lifeless hand up, before carefully using a pick like probe to scrape little bits of flesh from under the jaggedly torn nails.

When she got to Aimee's head, she ran her fingers through her scalp, pulling the wet and matted hair apart.

"This is interesting," the female pathologist said. "Look here, she's missing a big strand of hair. Like someone cut it off."

"Is it possible that's the way she wore her hair?" the Del Norte detective asked.

Both the female doctor and Red Wolff gave him a big "you dumb shit" look that said, women don't wear their hair with big chunks missing.

"Look at the ends," the doctor said, shining her light on Aimee Lawrence's hair. "She hasn't had a haircut in a while. See how the individual hairs are split just about everywhere on her head, except in this one little spot right here, where it was cut recently."

When the autopsy was over, the two Highway Patrol officers and the sheriff's deputy, met outside the mortuary.

Red watched as the deputy casually pulled out a cigarette and matches. She'd never been a smoker and took a couple steps back as the deputy cupped his hands around the match to protect the flame from the stiff wind that had come up.

"Now what?" the deputy asked.

"This looks like it's all yours," Red told him. "You're the homicide detective, but it looks to me like she was kidnapped, maybe where the bicycle was found, or maybe somewhere else, and the bike was dumped by the road. She wasn't sexually assaulted according to the doc, she gets strangled, but not before clawing her attacker, and her body gets dumped in the river."

The deputy just stared at Red Wolff, taking another drag off his cigarette. That's pretty much how I see it, he told himself.

"Anyway, come over to the office, and we'll give you the bicycle as evidence and the contact information on her parents," Red

271

continued. "Oh yeah, one more thing, how about giving me one of those samples of flesh from under her fingernails."

"You're still working on Dave and Jodie, aren't you?"

Red nodded.

"Okay, I think it's a waste of time and money, but I'll get a sample to you."

As Red lay on her back, Mary Jean was face down, partially on top of her, one leg hooked over Red's leg. The warmth of her body felt good. Mary Jean was dead asleep, tired from another trying day with little Ray, who was becoming a precocious and non-stop, on the go, two year old.

Red was asleep, but her mind was in that place that it often was the last three months, too many things to keep sorted out, too much information to process. After the autopsy, she'd gotten home around 6:00, had dinner, played with Ray, then spent two hours studying the things Vaughn O'Dell had briefed her on for the captain's test. Studying was difficult tonight, and she couldn't stay focused on the material she was reading as her mind kept flashing back on the autopsy. Something about it kept revolving around in her mind, but she couldn't pin it down.

She'd finally given up trying to study and gone to bed about 11:30. Her body fell asleep right away, but her mind was in high gear. Departmental budgets, grievance procedures, fleet operations, emergency incident preparedness, interspaced themselves with images of Aimee Lawrence's badly distorted face, the ugly black marks on her neck, and the torn fingernails.

When it finally clicked, she sat upright so fast it sent Mary Jean halfway across the bed.

"What is it Erin? Is little Ray crying?" Mary Jean asked, her mind still in sleep mode.

"It's nothing Babe, go back to sleep," Red Wolff told her spouse, as she swung her legs out of bed, opened up the nightstand drawer, pulling out a notepad and pen.

She wrote one word on the pad. Hair.

The phone picked up after three rings, "Missing persons, Detective Reynosa."

"Detective, Erin Wolff, Highway Patrol, Crescent City," Red said, using her first name rather than her rank to identify herself. She always thought that using lieutenant was a little pompous.

"Oh, hey Red, how are you," Bennie Reynosa greeted her, the instant bond of having worked together on a prior occasion kicking in for both of them.

Red Wolff's call to the Los Angeles County Sheriff's Detective was a direct result of her nocturnal epiphany about hair.

The next day she had gotten to the office early and worked her way through the boxes of evidence from the Castle case that were still stacked in her office. In the third box down, she found the sealed manila evidence envelope she was looking for. Following procedure, she initialed the chain of evidence log on the front of the envelope and broke the seal.

Inside the envelope were six photographs and, in a plastic zip-lock bag, the fifteen or so strands of auburn colored hair that had been found at the vista point where Dave and Jodie were murdered. The hair was still shiny, and the photographs depicted where it was found.

In the course of their investigation, nobody had been able to make any connection between the hair and the murders. The shooting team investigators had found the hair with bits of scalp imbedded in a granite rock at the edge of the vista point, right at the spot where the cliff ended in a two hundred foot drop to the ocean below. At the time, since everything at the scene was evidence, they had gathered the hair as part of their investigation. It had been looked at and discussed several times by the investigators, but nobody had a logical explanation how it got there or if it had anything to do with the murder of the officers.

After a few more seconds of informal banter, Red Wolff got to the point of her call.

"So did you ever find that missing woman, the one whose car we found abandoned up here?" Red inquired.

"No. Strange case. We had a forensics guy go over the car, he came up empty. Her credit cards and cell phone were never used again. It's like she just disappeared. I eliminated her husband as a suspect. I've checked him out backward and forward. No girlfriends, or boyfriends for that matter. Seems like a straight shooter, and he loved her. I wonder where you find guys like that today," the divorced detective added a personal editorial comment.

On the other end of the line, Red Wolff chuckled silently. I wonder what she'd think if she knew I was gay, she thought to herself.

"Anyway, it's a back-burner case now, still open, but not being actively worked. We just don't have anything to follow-up on," Bennie Reynosa continued.

She then added, "Why are you asking?"

Red related the raid on the drug lab, Jimmie MacAfee, the murder investigation being closed by the Del Norte County Sheriff, and now the murder of a female bicyclist.

"The hair being clipped from the bicyclist got me thinking about the hair we found at the vista point where my officers were killed," Red related.

"What color is the hair you found?" the detective asked, her interest now peaked.

"Auburn."

"Red, Kim Glickner's hair was auburn. I took samples from a hairbrush at her home. I've kept them to do a DNA match if her body shows up someday."

"I'm not all that familiar with how DNA works. Can you get a match from a strand of hair?" Red asked.

"Depends, is it just hair or do you have the root?" Bennie replied.

"About fifteen strands of hair, the root, and what we think is flesh from the scalp. Nobody here could connect the hair to the murder of my officers, so we just hung on to it. In a few months I'll have to ship it to Sacramento where the usual procedure is to destroy it."

"Christ, Red, don't let them destroy anything. Look, it's a long shot, but send me a half-dozen strands of hair. I'll have DNA tests done on the hair I took from her home and the hair you send me. Should get results in a couple weeks." There was excitement in Bennie Reynosa's voice.

As much as he knew about birds, plants, trees, and the animals of the forest, he'd made a serious mistake, he realized, when he dumped the bicyclist's body.

How stupid of you, he chastised himself, to dump the body in the river when it was swollen and running fast. You had to know when the rains stopped the water level would drop, and the flow would slow.

From what he had learned in law enforcement circles, the body had been found partially lodged under a rock on the east bank of the river, near Gasquet, just where there was a slight bend in the river.

He could visualize what had happened. After he dumped the woman's body, the fast flowing river had sucked it under and carried it downstream. The churning water had bounced the body against the boulders and battered her face. Then, in the location where the river curved, the water flow got slower near the banks, but continued at its regular flow near the center. In the slower moving water near the river bank, the weight of her body caused it to sink and lodge under a rock. Then, when the rain stopped and the water level dropped, it exposed her body. Just my luck he chastised himself again.

The stinging from the cut on his neck caused him to have another thought. While the task force investigating the murder of the CHP officers was active, he had steady access to information on the status of the investigation, leads they were following, and suspects. Now, even with his contacts, he still hadn't been able to get any information on the autopsy. The local paper had released her name and carried a brief story about the murder, but it was nothing he didn't already know. Finding out if the autopsy had revealed any evidence about the attacker was proving more difficult.

It didn't worry him too much, however, as he remembered after he strangled her he had wiped the woman's hands down to remove any traces of his skin after she had dug her nails into his neck. He thought he got everything.

Things started happening quickly over the next two weeks.

Unexpectedly, a large package arrived from the small town near the Virginia and North Carolina border. It didn't come in an official looking envelope, and there was no return address on the shipping label. Inside was the police report on the unsolved murder of the woman in the hotel twenty years ago. In addition to the report, there were photographs, several hair fibers, and dried blood samples they had never been able to trace back to a suspect in the horrible crime.

In the package there was a note.

Dear Lieutenant Wolff,

I hope this helps with your investigation. Twenty years ago I was a rookie officer when this crime occurred. It has always weighed heavily on my family that we were never able to find the killer. Maybe, if you find the murderer of your officers, I'll find the person who killed my sister. The gun was a present I gave her for protection since she travelled all the time.

275

As we discussed over the phone, I didn't give her any ammunition.

By the way, I sent this evidence without permission of the District Attorney. I'm sure he would have gotten around to sending this to you eventually. Things move slower here and I'm just hurrying the process along. If you need to talk to me, call me at home.

John Hubbard
Chief of Police

Ray Silva was with Red as she opened the package and read the note.

"Holy crap, Ray, the murdered woman was his sister! He's now the chief of police in the town where his sister was murdered, and he gave her the gun," she said handing him the note.

"And the guy has a set of cajones, too. Not afraid of repercussions to his career for sending this stuff to us," Ray observed.

In less than an hour, Ray Silva was driving toward the state crime lab in Eureka with evidence from two different crimes. In one package he had twenty year old hair and blood samples taken from a crime scene three thousand miles away. In the other package were two small bits of flesh taken from under Aimee Lawrence's fingernails four days ago.

The California Department of Justice supervisor told Ray the same thing he told Red Wolff when she called earlier that day, "Even if we put a rush on it, the best we can do is three days. It takes time to run the tests, time for the computer to do its thing, and time to analyze the results."

For the next few days, while she waited for the report from the crime lab, Red threw herself into reviewing, for the third time, the written reports prepared on the murder of her two officers and spent a great deal of time reexamining the evidence collected at the scene.

It was one of those things she had read several times before. Buried as it was in the autopsy report, it had not registered like it did this time. In her report, the female doctor and contract coroner for the county, had offered an opinion that, from the angle of the bullet which struck Jodie Castle in the back of the neck and the amount of unburned gunpowder clinging to her clothes and skin, the shooter had been left-handed.

By itself that comment would probably not have meant anything had Red not absentmindedly picked up the clear plastic bag containing a book of matches from the local casino recovered at the murder scene. At the same time her mind flashed on standing outside the mortuary the previous day talking with the Del Norte Sheriff's detective and watching him light a cigarette.

Opening the bag, she pulled out the matchbook and flipped up the cover. The book was about three-quarters full, the shredded stumps where six or seven matches had been torn out clearly visible.

Red stared at the match book and then tried to imitate lighting a cigarette several times. The ritual of how to light a cigarette was lost on her. The closest experience she had was smoking a cigar once, but that had only lasted for three puffs before the smell made her sick.

"What the heck are you doing?" Ray Silva laughed when he got to her open office door and saw her going through the motion of striking a match.

"You were a smoker once weren't you?" she asked Ray.

"Everyone was a smoker when I was kid," Ray replied. "Smoked till I was about twenty-five."

"'I've watched a million people light cigarettes before. There's a fluid motion to it that I can't do. You want to try?" she asked Ray.

"I've got a better idea," he said, motioning for her to follow.

Sergeant Dick Huddleston, now working afternoon shift, a place where he sought refuge from his commander who had been on his ass for the last two months, started his shift at 2:45. Normally she left when the business office closed at 5:00, meaning he could enjoy three-quarters of his shift without her looking over his shoulder.

He looked nervous when she followed Ray Silva into his office.

"Hey Dick," she greeted him with a smile.

Dick Huddleston gave a mumbled greeting in reply, his eyes looking nervously at Red, then shifting to Ray.

"Dick, I need a favor," she told him, "You're a smoker, aren't you?"

Dick Huddleston had no idea what was going on, but his pulse was racing, and he could feel himself begin to sweat.

Red Wolff could see the instant change in him, "Relax, Dick, I just need some help. Grab your smokes, and let's head out to the carport."

A minute later, a thoroughly confused Sergeant Dick Huddleston was standing in the back parking lot, lighting a cigarette.

"You're right-handed, aren't you Dick?" Red asked.

"Yeah," he replied in a more relaxed manner, blowing out a long stream of grayish blue smoke. Whatever the hell was going on, the cigarette calmed his nerves.

"Okay, one more time. Start over. Light another cigarette," Red told him.

She and Ray watched as he extinguished the cigarette he was already smoking and pulled a new one from the pack in his uniform shirt pocket. Fishing first on the left side and then the right, he pulled a book of matches from his trousers. Holding the book in his left hand, he opened the cover and tore off a match from the book. Striking the match, he ignited the cigarette.

"Stop," Red told him, "Lemme have the matches."

Taking the matches, she opened the cover. The book was about half empty.

"Can I keep these?" she asked an even more confused Dick Huddleston.

Two minutes later Ray Silva was in Red's office.

"What the hell was that all about?" he asked.

"Look at these matches Dick used," she said, handing the book to him.

Ray opened the book, turned it over several times, looking for something that she saw and he didn't.

"What?" he said, handing the matches back.

"Now, look at these matches from the vista point," she told him.

Ray looked at the second book of matches, then picked up the book Dick Huddleston used.

"I'll be dammed," he said, shaking his head. "Dick's right-handed, he held the book of matches in his left hand and tore out a match closest to the edge of the book with his right hand."

"Correct" she said, "And the matches from the vista point all had stumps on the left side of the book, meaning the person who used them was more than likely left-handed. Which jibs with the coroner's opinion that based on the angle of the bullet, the person who killed Jodie held the gun in his left hand."

Had she been a trained homicide detective, Red Wolff might have determined from the evidence she had at that very moment, who had savagely killed her officers. Unfortunately, as good a copper, and as good an investigator as she was, it didn't click. Events over the next few days would further confound her efforts to identify the murderer.

Which was unfortunate, as it meant three more people were going to die.

CHAPTER SEVENTEEN

Bennie Reynosa had several friends who worked for the Los Angeles County Sheriff's Scientific Services Bureau. As she walked into the building at 11:15, she carried two white paper bags and a large manila envelope.

It had been two days since she talked with the Highway Patrol lieutenant in Crescent City. The strands of auburn hair and photographs had arrived overnight, and she spent the morning digging out the hair samples she had taken from Kim Glickner's hair brush at her Malibu home over three months ago.

This was the first real lead she had since being assigned this investigation as a missing person's case. She was excited and wanted to hand walk the hair strands through the process to ensure the techs got a sense of how important the case was. The evidence technicians, she knew, thought every case was important. But sometimes, with a little tweaking of the system, it was possible to get a little extra and faster service.

As she got on the elevator with five other sheriffs employees headed up to the third floor, the smell coming from the two white bags she carried turned several heads. A detective in a sports coat, with a ghastly looking purple tie, laughed and remarked loudly, "Only one thing smells like that! Somebody's having Tommy's for lunch."

That set off a chorus of laughter, and a discussion broke out instantly on each person's favorite Tommy's selection. Unanimously, everyone concurred it was the double cheeseburger.

Tommy's was an L.A. institution. Started by a Greek immigrant, it had grown from a single wood framed walk up, to over fifteen locations in the L.A. basin. The burgers were good, no question, but it was the chili that came on everything, that made them great. Tommy's had a clientele who would drive for miles for a Tommy's burger.

It only took Bennie Reynosa, with the help of the Tommy's burgers, a minute to convince the crime lab supervisor and his assistant, how important her case was. Wiping the chili off their chins as they devoured the burgers and fries, they agreed it might be possible to expedite their analysis.

Had she seen the method the Los Angeles Sheriff's Detective used to get the hair evidence analyzed quickly, Red Wolff would have laughed. The first Tommy's location was on Rampart Boulevard, just off the Hollywood Freeway. It would have taken a calculator to add up the number of times she and Ray Silva had eaten there at 4:00 in the morning when they worked in Los Angeles.

———————

For next three days Red handled her regular duties as commander and spent every spare minute at work reviewing the case file on the Castles. In the evening, she put in three hours every night studying for the captain's exam, framing answers to questions, and verbally practicing responses to the questions she anticipated the oral interview board would ask.

She'd taken a break from studying on Saturday when she and Mary Jean drove to Medford to pick out some new interview clothes at the mall. The pants suit she chose, actually, the one Mary Jean, with her better eye for fashion, chose, was very stylish. Dark blue pleated slacks and a matching jacket, she set it off with a high-collared snow white blouse and a red scarf, to accent her strawberry blond hair.

"Excellent!" Mary Jean said, as Red came out of the dressing room. "You'll make captain just on style points. Now some shoes."

"Let's not get crazy on shoes, Sweetie," she told Mary Jean. "You know heels aren't my thing."

"No problem, let's do this. We'll buy a pair of heels that go with the suit. You wear some flat shoes so you're comfortable until you get to the interview location, keep the heels in your purse. Once you get there, switch shoes just before the interview."

They were home late Saturday afternoon, and Red went back to studying.

On Monday morning the sky was a brilliant cloudless blue. Summer was starting on the North Coast. The whole county felt busier as scores of motor homes clogged the highways, and cars with license plates from Washington, Oregon, Canada, and Idaho were a common sight. License plate frames on cars with California tags revealed they were from every part of the state.

Around 10:00 that morning, as Red sat in her office, with the door open, doing her commander thing, she had pretty much tuned out the sounds of routine business going on a few feet away, the phone ringing, and people coming and going at the front counter. Office Manager Lisa Johnston appeared in the doorway.

"Excuse me, Erin, a Detective Reynosa, from Los Angeles on line one for you," Lisa told her commander and went back to her desk.

Red Wolff took a deep breath before picking up the phone.

"Erin Wolff," she said, the anticipation in her voice obvious.

"Red, Bennie Reynosa here. It's a match!" the detective seven hundred miles away blurted out, unable to control her excitement.

For the next five minutes, they discussed the significance of having found the hair strands at the scene where the two CHP officers were murdered.

"That's great news, Bennie, but how did hair from a missing woman end up twenty-five miles from where we found her car?" Red asked the detective.

"Good question. But I'm betting it means Kim Glickner is dead. My gut tells me she was probably abducted near where your people found her car, and her body was dumped off the cliff at that vista point. From the look of the photographs you sent, her head probably hit the ground when she was dumped over the side, and the hair imbedded itself in the rock. Any chance we can do a search of the water, or the beach in that area?"

"Not likely. The water is always rough in that location, and it's been nearly three months. A corpse would have washed up on shore by now. Since nothing's turned up, it's a good bet the tide and currents have sucked the body out to sea," Red replied.

"Okay, I'm gonna reclassify this as a homicide. I'll start contacting all of the agencies in your area to see if they have info that can help me."

"We have a county law enforcement chiefs meeting tomorrow, I'll bring this up," Red told her.

"Great, anything they have will help." As an afterthought the Los Angeles detective asked, "Say, did you turn a suspect in the murder of the bicyclist?"

When Red told her no, Bennie Reynosa paused for a second, then added, "You're right on the state border there aren't you? You have several county sheriff's offices and local police departments. Have any of them reported any missing persons, kidnappings, or unsolved homicides lately?"

"None that I know of, but it's worth checking. I've got just the guy to handle it," Red replied as the conversation ended.

———

Ray Silva was driving along the coast, just outside the city limits. It was a spectacular scenic location as the road was right on the ocean. He had just passed the Brother Jonathan scenic outlook, headed toward Washington Boulevard, when the radio called.

"95-1, Humboldt, 10-19, see 95-L."

Ten minutes later he was in Red Wolff's office.

Red quickly conveyed the information about the hair found at the scene where the Castles had been murdered, matching that of a wealthy missing woman from Malibu.

"Do you still have contact with the people from the other agencies who were on the task force?"

Ray nodded yes, not sure where this was going.

"Here's what I need you to do," Red told him, explaining her suspicions.

"Might take a couple days," he told her.

Of all the law enforcement agencies in the county, only the sheriff's department had a conference room suitable for the monthly meeting of the Del Norte County Chief's Association. They generally ran for a couple hours, and then, those that could, went to lunch as a group at a local restaurant.

The chief's association was a loose confederation of law enforcement executives. Some agencies paid the seventy-five dollar annual membership fee for their chief, while others had to pay it out of their own pocket. Andrew Dixon, from the Forest Service, was president this year. The meetings did exchange some information, but they were more social, than substantive.

It was one of the first meetings in a long time when the heads of all eight law enforcement agencies in the county were present. Even the warden from Pelican Bay Prison was there, a very unusual occurrence, as he normally sent Captain Nate Steadman in his place. Today both were present. Everyone socialized a little before the meeting started, breaking up into their usual cliques to swap lies and whisper about this person or that.

Jerome Williamson, the warden, and the Crescent City Chief of Police stood together near the coffee, while Marv Butler from National Parks, laughed with the Director of the Yurok Tribal Police in another part of the room. Andrew Dixon was off by himself on his cell phone.

A couple people had already grabbed a seat, as Red Wolff and Nate Steadman stood together, just observing the others.

Leaning into Nate Steadman, Red said, "I see the "badge bonding" is going well," gesturing with her eyes toward the small groups around the room.

Nate Steadman laughed, "It looks more like the monthly pecker measuring contest. Who's the most powerful, and whose gonna support Williamson for sheriff in the fall."

Dead on point, Red thought to herself as everyone started heading for their seats.

The big topic at today's meeting was the murder of the bicyclist from Canada. Jerome Williamson had his detective attend the meeting to give each of the agency heads a briefing on the status of the investigation.

No, he told them, no suspects at this time. The bicycle recovered by the Highway Patrol had been checked for fingerprints with nothing being found other than those of the woman and some belonging to the officer who pulled the bike out of the ditch.

On the positive side, small bits of skin and flesh, they assumed from the attacker, had been found under the dead woman's torn fingernails.

"It looks like she scratched the shit out of him," the detective told the group. "We sent the skin the coroner scraped from under her fingernails to the crime lab for analysis, and the results will be run through the national data bank to see if the suspect is in the system."

"Anything you want to add, Lieutenant Wolff?" Andrew Dixon asked looking at Red.

She had never liked him. Crescent City was a small town, and she'd heard the stories about how he treated his employees, especially women, since transferring in to become the supervising special agent less than a year ago. Mostly, however, she disliked his management style of making enemies on purpose. It was something he did with regularity.

"No, nothing about the bicyclist, Andy," she replied, knowing the use his first name would piss him off. "But, I just got some info that may link the murder of my officers to a missing person's case from Los Angeles."

Continuing on, Red explained her conversations with Bennie Reynosa and the hair found at the vista point where Dave and Jodie Castle were murdered. The LASO detective was asking for any information local agencies might have, she told the group.

"Well, that seems to be a coincidence to me," Jerome Williamson interrupted. "Besides, I solved the murder of your officers, the suspect is dead, and that case is closed," he told the other chiefs, an officious tone to his voice.

The feud between Red Wolff and Sheriff Jerome Williamson regarding the investigation into the murder of her officers was no secret to the other members of the chief's association, and they waited for her response, anticipating some hostility.

"Be that as it may, sheriff, the detective in L.A. would appreciate any information local agencies have."

An almost visible letdown by the other people in the room could be seen, disappointed no verbal fireworks occurred between the two.

For one person seated around the conference table, the information about the missing woman from Los Angles and the hair found at the vista point sent a shudder through his body. His thoughts shifted to that rainy night three months ago. He could see the naked woman's body as he launched it out of the plastic Visquine wrapping and over the guardrail. In his mind's eye, he saw her head striking the rock an instant before it fell over the precipice and out of sight into the blackness toward the churning water two hundred feet below.

Fuck, he said to himself, shifting uncomfortably in his chair.

Five of the chiefs, six counting Red, met for lunch at a local restaurant. Although the atmosphere was cordial, Red was never comfortable when she was around Jerome Williamson. The lunch time conversation was fairly light and focused on sports, political issues, and the ramifications of some recent court rulings on police operations.

After lunch, Red was seated in her car in the parking lot retrieving voice mail messages from her cell phone as the other chiefs stood outside the restaurant talking. As she listened to her messages, she idly watched the five other chiefs across the lot as they talked and laughed. Unconsciously her brain registered that two of them were smoking.

One of the voice mail messages Red had was from the Department of Justice Crime Lab in Eureka. She punched a couple buttons on the keypad, and the phone automatically called the number.

After a few courtesies with the crime lab supervisor, their conversation got to the point.

"Well, the skin and flesh samples from your bicyclist were usable. We got enough sample to run DNA," he began. "The stuff from the homicide in Virginia was really contaminated. Nobody's fault really. Back then when they preserved bodily fluids as evidence, nobody knew about DNA. It's done a lot different now days."

"So the two samples don't match?" Red replied.

"No, they match. The problem is, it will never hold up in court. The sample from twenty years ago was so degraded, and there was so much contamination, that it would never get admitted as evidence in court. Any good defense attorney would rip the results to sheds. I doubt a judge would even let it be presented to a jury."

"But the two samples match, right?" Red asked, the tone in her voice not arguing the admissibility of the DNA. She had long ago given up on the things the judicial system did and the rulings of judges.

"Sure. They match," the criminalist confirmed.

Ray Silva was at the CHP office when Red returned from her chief's meeting.

Ignoring several paper messages on her desk, she called him into her office where she related the information she had just learned from the crime lab.

"So where does that leave us?" Ray asked.

"How are your inquiries with all the other agencies going on missing persons and unsolved homicides?" she asked.

"Done."

Over the next thirty minutes, Ray Silva gave Red a detailed account of his investigation.

"I talked to the task force people from the Oregon State Police, Grants Pass Department of Public Safety, the Brookings Police Department, and the sheriff's departments in Josephine, Jackson, and Curry Counties. They did computer runs on kidnappings, homicides, unsolved deaths, and missing persons. In the past two years, they have had their share of murders and missing persons. Only two are still open cases. Both involve well to do women who just disappeared. One was near Grants Pass. Her car was found abandoned on the shoulder of Highway 199 at a location where the Rogue River is close to the road. The speculation is she committed suicide, although her body has never been found. The other woman disappeared in a regional park just outside Brookings at a place where hiking is popular. Her purse and money were in the front seat of the car. It's still an open missing person's case. They think she might have fallen off the hiking trail, and her body just hasn't been found yet. Both of these women disappeared within the last eight months."

"Hang on, Ray," Red told him, digging into her desk drawers until she found a map of Northern California and Southern Oregon. Using a blue marking pen, Ray circled the two locations on the map. "Where was Kim Glickner's car found?" she asked.

Ray traced his finger along a yellow line on the map representing Highway 199 and circled a spot saying, "About here."

"What did you find out about Humboldt County?" Red pressed Ray Silva, while her mind rapidly processed everything.

"All this area south of Del Norte County is Humboldt County," Ray began, using his hand to sweep a large area on the map. "Anyway, people tend to disappear in Humboldt County a lot. Mostly it's because of the marijuana business. People move into the area from all over the country looking to make a huge profit growing pot. Some do, others grow enough to last them a while then move on, and some end up dead. In all of Humboldt County there have been six murders in the last two years, all drug related. The police and sheriffs know who the killers are, they just can't prove it."

"Any missing persons?"

"One. A woman from Nevada. She was northbound on 101, driving a Cadillac. Got a flat tire north of Orick," Ray said, pausing to point out the location on the map. "Anyway, she used that "On-Star" emergency thing to call Triple A. When the tow truck arrived, the Caddie was there, but she was gone. The tow truck driver called CHP. Humboldt Dispatch rolled a Highway Patrol unit from Eureka to check it out. When the officer couldn't find anyone, he called the Humboldt sheriffs, and they took it as a missing person's case. That was five months ago. Nothing new on it since."

"Awful lot of woman just disappearing," Red remarked. "Show me where the bicyclist's body was found and where Oz found her bike."

After he marked the two additional locations on the map Red Wolff sat back in her chair, not saying anything, the metal hinges squeaking as the back rest reclined slightly. Ten seconds later she opened the top drawer of her desk and pulled out a well worn wooden ruler. Carefully, using a different color marking pen, she began to draw lines on the map from all the circled locations marked by Ray Silva.

When she was done, the six dark lines she had drawn on the map resembled a star, with the lines heading outward in all different directions. The center of the star, where all the lines met, was Crescent City.

"So what do you think, Red?" he asked after she finished marking the locations on the map.

"You really want to know?"

She spent nearly a half-hour on the phone with her boss, Vaughn O'Dell, discussing her suspicions.

"There's no other way?" she asked when he told her she had to turn the investigation over to the sheriff's department.

No, he had told her, this was clearly out of the Highway Patrol's jurisdiction. There would be a huge outcry from the California State Sheriff's Association if the Highway Patrol investigated a crime like she was describing, instead of turning it over to the local authorities. The sheriff's association, representing all fifty-eight county sheriffs in California, would go to the Governor and complain. It was an election year, and the sheriff's association was extremely powerful politically, he continued. The Governor needed the support of their organization, something she surely would not get if she allowed the Highway Patrol to investigate this case.

"But I'm not sure this guy isn't a suspect," Red had implored. "Can't we get the Department of Justice to handle the investigation?"

She already knew the answer to that question.

"Red, the captain's test is next week. The last thing you need to do right now is cause a shit-storm," he told her before they ended their conversation.

"What can I do for you lieutenant," Jerome Williamson said, not even trying to hide the condescending tone in his voice after she had taken a seat in his office.

As hard as it was, Red stayed completely professional as she explained the purpose of the meeting and laid out the results of her investigation.

"A serial killer!" he roared. His volume meant to be intimidating and his tone mocking Red Wolff's investigation. "That's the most ridiculous thing I've ever heard. You take information on three missing women scattered over a hundred miles apart in two different states, add it to the bicyclist being murdered, and come up with a theory there's a serial killer in Del Norte County. You're a highway cop lieutenant. You have no training or background in this sort of thing."

287

"I'm only here today because I was ordered to turn over my investigation to you," Red told him, her voice outwardly calm, although she was seething on the inside.

"Let's face it lieutenant, you have never been satisfied that I found the person who killed your officers. You simply won't accept the fact they were killed by some low life ex-con. It's all pretty clear to me what happened. Your officers stopped Jimmie MacAfee when he was running a load of drugs. He killed them both with a .38 revolver. The same .38 he used to kill that parole agent when we raided the lab. Christ, he had it in his hand when he was killed. For the last time, that case is closed! There is no serial killer running loose in my county. Stick to writing tickets and calling tow trucks for little old ladies."

"As I've told you several times, sheriff, there is no way Jimmie MacAfee is the person who killed my officers. First of all, there is no indication he ever left the lab in the mountains. Secondly, there is no way he could have taken down two veteran cops like Dave and Jodie Castle. Plus, how do you explain the hair of a wealthy woman from Malibu being found imbedded in a rock at the vista point where my officers were murdered, when her car was found abandoned nearly thirty miles away?" Red countered.

"Purely a coincidence, lieutenant. Perhaps she committed suicide by jumping off the cliff. Then some local kid finds her car and takes it for a joyride before abandoning it. Or maybe this woman from Malibu was despondent. Maybe your officers encountered her parked at the vista point in the middle of the night. Your officers might have been killed by her, and then she jumped over the side," Jerome Williamson retorted.

"Bullshit!" Red shot back.

"I don't buy any part of your investigation or your theory about a serial killer, Lieutenant Wolff," he said arrogantly. "But, since you seem to have this case solved, would you mind telling me who the supposed serial killer is?"

"It's a cop!" Red told him forcibly.

"A cop!" he replied incredulously. "What do you base that outlandish claim on?"

"The statement of Joe Dansby, the only eyewitness we have."

Jerome Williamson slammed the palms of his hands down on his desk. "You're basing this whole idea of a serial killer and the murder of your officers, on what some old drunken Indian says he saw for maybe three seconds? This conversation is over, Lieutenant Wolff."

"So what did you expect, Red?" Ray Silva said to her when she returned to the Highway Patrol office late that afternoon.

Red didn't say anything.

"The guy is up for election in four months. You couldn't possibly think he would announce to the world that there's a serial killer, let alone a serial killer who is a cop, loose in the county. He would have to admit that Jimmie MacAfee didn't kill Dave and Jodie. All that would expose him as the boob he really is. The papers would crucify him. That cable news person, the one who does the investigative stuff, Nancy Grace, would be up here doing live programs for her cable news program. You can almost see the T.V. screen with big letters talking about the incompetent sheriff. She'd have interviews with the missing women's families and cops in New York and Chicago, who have never even heard of Del Norte County, providing "expert" analysis on the story."

"Maybe I should call her?" Red said with a half-smile.

"Maybe you should just solve it yourself," Ray responded. There was no mistaking that he was deadly serious.

"How do you suggest I do that, Silva?" Red answered, "I was told to turn the case over to the sheriff."

"And you did just that. Were you told you couldn't help the sheriff with his investigation?" Ray asked slyly.

"That's kind of a fine line in following orders don't you think?"

"I think this may be a Catholic investigation, Red."

"What the heck is a Catholic investigation?" she asked, never in their twenty plus year friendship ever hearing that term from him.

"It's an investigation where you don't ask permission, you go ahead and do it. Then, if you get caught, you beg forgiveness," Ray Silva told her, stone-faced.

Red let out a laugh that came from her belly as she spoke, "You're gonna get me fired, Silva."

Ray Silva's expression never changed.

"Let's get started," she said.

For the next three hours, behind the closed doors of her office, Red Wolff and Ray Silva listed the things they knew about the disappearances of the four women in Northern California and Southern Oregon. They also made lists regarding the meth lab, Jimmie MacAfee, Indian Joe, Kim Glickner's hair at the vista point, the flesh taken from Aimee Lawrence's fingernails, and the .38 caliber pistol.

Using large sheets of easel paper which they taped to the walls, they began to lay out a chronology of every event beginning with the murder of the woman in the hotel in Virginia.

"So, twenty years ago there is a murder, and a .38 caliber pistol is stolen from the victim. That gun, loaded with ammunition sold only to law enforcement, is used to murder Dave and Jodie," Ray verbally began, ready to use a magic marker to record the event.

"Correct, but for the sake of the chronology, the only thing we know is that the gun is stolen, not about the ammunition." Red corrected him. "That part will come later. Remember, the chief of police said when he gave the gun to his sister as a present, he didn't give her any ammo."

"Got it," Ray acknowledged, "What's next?"

"Twenty years go by. Then, over the last eight to ten months, women start to disappear in and around Del Norte County," Red told him.

Ray crossed checked the notes he had taken from his conversations with surrounding police agencies on the missing women, then recorded each disappearance in order on the paper taped to the wall.

"Make a note on the side that when those first three women disappeared, Jimmie MacAfee was still in prison. He didn't get out until just before the woman from Malibu disappeared."

"Okay. Then a couple things happened at the same time," Ray spoke out. "Sometime in the early evening of a rainy night nearly four months ago, Kim Glickner disappears on Highway 199. We know she was in Crescent City by her credit card receipts, and we know she was supposed to stop for the night in Southern Oregon, but she never checked into her motel."

Red followed up, "Right, and the same night, well actually early the next morning, the Castles are murdered at the vista point on Last Chance Grade. But before they are, Joe Dansby goes by in his old pickup and sees what he believes is an unmarked police car, a Crown Victoria, the male driver was talking to the Castles."

Ray Silva printed out the information on the paper, then stepped back to take in everything they had written up to that point.

"So now the investigation at the vista point starts. The shooting team uses the dispatch tapes to determine it was forty minutes from when the Castles left the deputy at the bus incident, until the time when Humboldt Communications Center called them to respond to the DMV office's silent alarm. That would mean whoever Indian Joe saw the Castles with that night, was the killer. And the killer was driving a car that looked like an unmarked cop car," Ray added, writing furiously on their makeshift blackboard.

Both of them paused for nearly a minute just processing the information they had posted on the walls. Ray ripped off a clean sheet of paper and taped it up.

"The shooting team does their thing, taking pictures and collecting evidence. They find almost nothing, a partially used book of matches, that may or may not be connected to the murders, a cigarette ground up and soaked by the rain, and some strands of hair that turn out to be from Kim Glickner," Red offered.

"And don't forget, Davy's pistol was missing," Ray added as he wrote.

"The autopsy showed that both Davy and Jodie were killed at close range with a .38 that fired hollow-point ammunition sold only to law enforcement," Red said, motioning for Ray to add that information to the list. "Oh, I almost forgot, the scratch pad was missing from their vehicle," she added.

"Which tells us the killer knew something about police procedures. Another thing that points to a cop being the killer," Ray stated.

"One more point about the autopsy," Red interjected, "The coroner said she thought from the angle of the entry wounds that the shooter was probably left-handed."

"Then two months go by, we find no suspects, no hits on Crown Victorias, no cops with .38s that match. It's like whoever did this knows what we know, and he keeps his head down," Ray said thinking out loud.

"Oscar Zamora makes a routine speed stop and turns up a local guy transporting three pounds of meth. That leads us to a lab in the mountains and Jimmie MacAfee. In the course of trying to flee, Jimmie shoots a parole agent with the same gun that killed Davy and Jodie, before he's shot and killed," Red Wolff narrated. "Everyone jumps on the idea that MacAfee killed our officers, even though his wife swears he hadn't left the lab since he started cooking, and she says they never had a .38."

"Everyone thinks the murders are solved, and the killer, in this case a serial killer, thinks the heat is off and finds another victim, Aimee Lawrence. She scratches the guy, and he strangles her to death. The killer dumps the body in the Smith River, but not before he cuts a lock of her hair as a souvenir. The body gets recovered, and they find bits of what we assume to be the killer's flesh under her fingernails. That leads us back to an unsolved, twenty year old homicide from Virginia, the same one where the gun was stolen," Ray finished the story.

"Don't forget that waxy residue the coroner found on her chest," Red added.

The private telephone number for the CHP office rang on Red's phone. Ray could only hear her side of the conversation.

"Sorry Babe, I lost track of time. Ray and I are working on something," Red explained, then paused while the caller talked. "Sure, I'll ask, hang on."

Taking the phone from her ear, she spoke to Ray Silva, "Ray, it's Mary Jean, she wants to know if you and Julie want to come over for dinner."

"I'm up for it. I'll have to call Julie and set it up."

Time had gotten away from them. It was approaching 6:30, and although the summer sun was still high in the sky, long shadows from the numerous trees around the Highway Patrol office were starting to creep across the parking lot.

———————

By 7:15, Ray and Julie were at Red and Mary Jean's house. Even though it was nearly mid-summer, Mary Jean kept the woodstove fired up to chase away the always present dampness that was part of living in Crescent City and to keep the house warm enough for little Ray.

Dinner wasn't one of Mary Jean's gourmet specials, but the chicken with mushroom sauce, rice and a three bean salad hit the spot. A couple glasses of wine made it perfect.

After a quick cleanup, Red and Mary Jean shuffled a protesting little Ray off to bed. A half-hour later they rejoined Ray and Julie in the living room.

"How's the studying going for the captain's test?" Julie inquired.

"I'm as ready as I can get," Red replied, "Been studying every night, my head is stuffed full of facts, figures, and useless information."

"Plus, I put her through interview questions and make her verbalize her responses out loud," Mary Jean added.

"When is your interview?" Ray asked.

"Next Tuesday, 11:15 in the morning. Mary Jean and I are going to drive down to Sacramento the day before and get a motel. That way I'll be fresh for the interview. We'll head back as soon as it's over," Red told him.

Ray nodded, and the four way conversation paused while Mary Jean refilled everyone's wine glasses.

"So what were you two working on so late tonight?" Julie asked.

"Oh, more on Dave and Jodie and the bicyclist from Canada," Red told her.

For the next hour, as the twilight lingered over the ocean to the west, the sunless sky changing from fiery orange to pale blue to ink black, Red Wolff and Ray Silva recapped the results of their afternoon's efforts to make some sense of the investigation. Julie and Mary Jean listened intently. Occasionally Julie, with her corporate management background, would ask a question to clarify something. Mary Jean, thinking like the naval officer she had been, added her thoughts also.

Had a big city detective like Benita Reynosa, or a former LAPD commander, now sheriff, like Jerome Williamson, seen the interaction between the four, they would have been appalled. Discussing active cases with spouses was something they just didn't do. For them there was a distinct separation between their work and private lives. For them, it was okay to discuss business off-duty with another cop, but never with non-cops, even family.

It was different in rural locations and between tight knit friends. For them, this was "family business", and it impacted Julie and Mary Jean, just as much as it did Red and Ray.

"So we have four women who disappear in the last year. Well, actually the last ten months," Red stated. "We also have a bicyclist who was kidnapped and murdered. What common denominators do we have?"

"They were all driving expensive cars. Even the bicycle was expensive. They were all attractive, and they were all rich," Ray replied.

"Okay, what else?" Red asked the other three.

"Erin, didn't you say all of their vehicles were found near major highways?" Julie inquired.

"Yes!" Red answered enthusiastically, "That's a common link between them. What else?"

"I don't know if this is important, but you said in the last ten months," Mary Jean said, thinking out loud. "If all these women disappearing is related and there were no disappearances before that, doesn't that point to someone who just moved here?"

Red and Ray paused, contemplating what Mary Jean had said.

"I hadn't thought of that. It's certainly something to consider. Could be someone new to the area, or someone who has been here for a while that has gone back into business," Ray said.

"Or maybe someone who has been in prison, like that Jimmie person," Julie added.

"True, but Jimmie MacAfee was in prison when the first three women disappeared," Red reminded them.

"Let's get back to the four women disappearing. They're all rich, good looking, and driving expensive cars," Red Wolff told the other three, already knowing the answer to the question she was about to ask them.

"How could someone pick and choose those four specific women, get them to stop their cars on the highway, and then abduct them without anyone noticing?"

"Damn!" Ray Silva said loudly. "People did notice, but they didn't pay any attention. The guy used a red light to pull the women over. They stopped and people going by thought it was just a traffic stop."

The only sound in the room was the occasional crackle of the logs in the woodstove as everyone considered what Ray Silva had said.

"Oh, Ray, that's so frightening. To think someone is masquerading as a policeman, using a red light to stop, kidnap, and then murder women drivers," Julie replied, an obvious tone of fear in her voice.

"But what if it's not someone masquerading as a cop. What if it's a real cop, driving a real cop car?" Red told the trio as they sat staring at her.

"Which is why Indian Joe said he saw an unmarked police car at the vista point the night the Castles were murdered," Ray dovetailed onto Red's statement.

"And it would explain how somebody was able to take down Dave and Jodie. They either stopped, or encountered, someone driving an unmarked police car, someone they knew, and someone they wouldn't suspect of being a murderer," Red verbalized her thoughts.

Another uncomfortable silence filled the living room as all four of them processed the frightening picture they were collectively painting.

"Christ, it would be so easy. Use a police car with a red light to stop a woman, kidnap, probably sexually assault, and then murder her. Dump the body in the ocean. Nobody suspects anything because it's a cop car. Even Dave and Jodie would have let their guard down if they were dealing with a cop they knew."

"Even if someone, cop or no cop, tried to kidnap me, I'd fight back," Mary Jean said defiantly.

"Me too," agreed Julie.

"Most women probably would," Ray told them, pausing for a second before adding, "But if they were incapacitated and couldn't fight back?"

"How do you incapacitate someone by the side of a highway?" Julie asked, "By knocking them out with your club, spraying them with Mace?"

"With a stun gun," Red interrupted. "Remember the burn marks on Aimee Lawrence's neck? The coroner thought they looked like electrical burns."

"The shock from a stun gun would give whoever is doing this plenty of time to subdue the woman, get her in his car, and be gone in a matter of seconds," Ray added.

"Ray, you're scaring me," Julie told him.

"It's just a theory guys," Red told Mary Jean and Julie, conscious that the conversation had elicited fears in both women.

———————

The next day, Friday, was Red's last work day before heading to Sacramento on Monday for her captain's test interview. As usual she was in the office handling paperwork, reviewing reports and doing the things other CHP area commanders were doing all over the state. Once she had her regular duties out of the way, she turned her attention to the investigation Sheriff Jerome Williamson had declined to take on.

After lunch, Red spent nearly two hours going over the wall charts she and Ray had worked on the previous afternoon and another hour writing down the things that were discussed at dinner with Ray, Julie and Mary Jean.

Something Mary Jean had said kept popping back into her head. It was her comment about the disappearances all happening over the last ten months. She couldn't get the thought out of her mind.

Getting up from her desk, she closed the door to her office to block out the noise and sat back down. Picking up a pen she began to doodle on a notepad. She scribbled little one or two word notes, drew arrows from key words to other connecting items, and circled important points.

She'd lived in Del Norte County for over three years. The population of around twenty-five thousand had stayed pretty constant, a few people came, and others moved away, as they did everywhere. There were no big industries in the county that enticed people to move here, and people who had jobs hung on to them. Fishing and lumber employed a couple hundred people, and the tourist industry accounted for a couple hundred more. Between the feds, the state, the county, and the city, government was probably the biggest employer in the area, she concluded. Of that group, the state prison employed nearly fifteen hundred people, over a thousand of them being correctional officers, and therefore, technically cops by Penal Code definition.

Government was a different story when it came to stability of the workforce, she realized. Not all government, she corrected herself, but the federal and state governments.

At the city and county government levels, most of the employees were locals. Maybe they weren't all locals in the sense they were born in the county, but locals in the sense that most of them had lived and worked here, for a long time. Many had grown up in the area. They went to school here, they had parents who lived just down the street, their friends were here, and their kids were born here.

When they began working for the city of Crescent City, or the County of Del Norte, they had started at the bottom and worked their way up. The chief of police had started out as a patrolman. Twenty years later, he was the chief. The manager of the county water department began by reading meters and had been promoted over the years to become the department head. Red could think of dozens of other examples of people who were career civil servants in the city and county governments who had lived here their whole lives. The thing they had in common was that they didn't have to transfer in and out to promote within their organizations.

Conversely, as she thought about state and federal employees, she saw a different picture. At the worker bee level, those who did the actual work of filling potholes in the highways with hot asphalt, working behind the counter at the Department of Motor Vehicles, the clerks who answered phones, the mechanics who repaired the vehicles, and the janitors who cleaned the offices, it was generally the same as with the city and county workers. People who held these jobs were, by-and-large, locals. They were people from the community. Many were lifetime residents of the area. Most had no desire to promote, if promoting meant leaving the area, and they were in the positions from which they would retire.

At the management level, it was a different story, she realized. For those who wanted to promote, it meant either moving to, or moving away from the area. Most people who fit into that category had no ties to the North Coast, Del Norte County, or Crescent City. Some who moved to the area would find the county to their liking and jump off the promotional merry-go-round. For others, Del Norte County was a brief stopover, a couple years working in the boonies to get their tickets punched, as they continued up the promotion ladder with their organizations.

Sitting back in the chair, Red looked at her notes.

Ten months
Government employee
Knows police procedures
Crown Victoria
Maybe Left-handed

The knock on the door brought Red out of her deep concentration. A second later Lisa Johnston opened the door and struck her heard in.

"I'm going home Erin," she told Red Wolff. "You have a nice weekend, and good luck on your interview Tuesday."

It took Red a second to realize it was after 5:00, and the office was closed for the weekend.

"Thanks Leece. I'm available by cell, and I'll call in on Monday. You have a great weekend, also. See you Wednesday."

With the front door locked, the office was dark, quiet and deserted. Everyone working that afternoon, including Sergeant Dick Huddleston, was out on patrol. Alone in the office, the only sound Red could hear was the occasional radio call from the speaker on the wall in the business office.

Ripping the page of handwritten notes off the pad, she started on a new page. Picking up her pen she wrote down the names of people who met her criteria. There were four names on her list.

Jerome Williamson – Sheriff
Andrew Dixon – Forest Service
Marvin Butler – National Parks
Nate Steadman – Corrections

Putting her pen down, she stared at the names. Except for knowing whether or not they were left-handed, they each met the profile she had developed. They were all newcomers to the area over the last year. All were more-or-less transient, as their government jobs had brought them here, and their government jobs would transfer them out. They all knew police procedures, and they all drove Crown Victorias supplied by their agencies.

As an afterthought, she added the name of the warden of Pelican Bay Prison.

As commander, Saturday and Sunday were Red's regular days off. That meant chores, grocery shopping, restocking the wood pile by the side of the house, and maybe washing her personal car, if the weather permitted.

For Ray Silva, back on dayshift, Saturday was a workday as he had Sunday and Monday off this month.

Red headed into town around 10:00 that morning and gave Ray a call on his cell.

"What's up, Red?"

"Hey, got time for a cup?"

"You bet, how 'bout the Captain's Table in the harbor. Seems fitting," he quipped.

"Screw you, Silva."

The Captain's Table had maybe five wooden booths. Not quite on the water's edge, it had a great view of the boat repair yard and dry dock. Inside it had the expected nautical décor on the walls and marine maps varnished into the table tops. The biscuits and gravy were the best in town. The coffee was so-so.

"So what are you doing out and about today?" Ray asked.

"Honey-do's and chores."

"All set to leave Monday?"

"Yeah, but I need you to do something for me while I'm gone."

"Name it," Ray told her without hesitation.

"Jimmie MacAfee's wife and the other two are still in jail here, right?" she asked.

"Yup, their trial isn't set until next month," Ray replied.

"I need you to talk to her for me."

"No problem Red, what do you want to know?"

After the waitress refilled their coffee, she explained the information she needed from Jimmie's wife.

"I'm off the next couple of days, is Tuesday okay?"

"Sure, I'll be heading back from Sacto that afternoon, give me a call," Red told him.

CHAPTER EIGHTEEN

It's not much of an exaggeration to say that Sacramento, like almost the entire Central Valley of California, has two seasons, fog and heat. Low-lying, wet, chill-you-to-the-bone Tule fog often settled on the valley floor and hung around for weeks at a time in the winter, blocking out the sun, giving the area a gray dismal look, and a perpetually wet feel. Then suddenly, sometime in June, it's a hundred and six humidity-filled degrees.

In their Sacramento motel room, May Jean had the air conditioner cranked up to "max cold" after Red came out of the shower. Her interview was in ninety minutes, and they had it planned out to the second.

Because policy prohibited anyone other than a state employee from operating Red's Crown Vic, they had driven Mary Jean's car from Crescent City in order to split the driving time. Mary Jean would drive Red to the interview location and drop her off right at the front door of the building. She would be out of the air conditioned car, into the air conditioned building in seconds. All she had to do then was find the interview room and change into the heels she carried in her purse. After that it was a simple matter of dazzling the interview panel.

Highway Patrol interview panels consist of three people, two are uniformed, and one a civilian. The uniformed officers are always two ranks above the position being interviewed for. So as a lieutenant, trying to promote to captain, Red Wolff found herself being interviewed by two deputy chiefs and a pleasant looking Hispanic woman who was the chairperson of the interview panel.

She knew one of the deputy chiefs on the panel, having worked for him early in her career when she was an officer, and he was a lieutenant. Having somebody you knew, and who knew you, on the interview panel was always a plus. If that person liked you, they could help you out with answers to questions during the interview, or if you screwed up an answer, they could downplay your response after you left the interview room when the three-person panel deliberated your score. She'd never met the other chief on the panel, although she knew him by reputation.

During the interview, the chief she knew smiled, giving her encouragement with head nods and positive feedback to her answers. The other chief betrayed nothing, remaining stone-faced through the entire interview.

Forty-five minutes later, Red was sitting in the front seat of Mary Jean's car.

"Well?" Mary Jean asked.

"I don't know. I think I answered all their questions okay. They didn't ask me anything I wasn't ready for. Got lots of encouragement from one of the chiefs. The other guy's expression didn't change during the whole interview."

"Sounds like it went good. When will the results be out?"

"They have two more days of interviews. Then they have to finalize the scores. So maybe Thursday or Friday," Red told Mary Jean.

"Wow, two more days of interviews. How many people are taking the test?" Mary Jean asked.

"Statewide, about sixty-five lieutenants competing for about twenty or twenty-five jobs. The list is good for two years. Depends on how many current captains retire, or get promoted to assistant chief during that time," Red related.

"So you have about a three to one chance of getting promoted."

"Not that good. Remember a bunch of the lieutenants who took the test are in headquarters or division staff jobs. They all have high-ranking sponsors who want to see them promoted. If you have the right person pulling strings for you, it's possible you could mumble your way through the interview, not answer any questions correctly, not have the experience, and still get promoted," Red related.

"Doesn't seem too fair to me," Mary Jean said, a disgusted look on her face.

"Like I've told you before, the words fair and Highway Patrol, shouldn't be used in the same sentence," Red said, a half-smile on her face and a chuckle in her voice.

"And if you make the list, where will they send us?" Mary Jean asked, her curiosity peaked, and using the word us to indicate where you go, I go.

"Anywhere they want. More than likely back to Los Angeles."

"That wouldn't be the worst thing," Mary Jean said as she maneuvered through traffic back to the freeway. "I got a late checkout from the motel. Let's go back there, you can change, and we'll head home. Traffic's pretty light so we should be back in Crescent City by 9:00."

Shortly after 1:00, with Red in her jeans and a tee-shirt, little Ray in the back, strapped into his car seat, and Mary Jean driving, they left the motel.

"Which way do you want to go?" Mary Jean queried.

"Well, we came over the top to get here, let's try the coast," Red replied.

"It will take a bit longer, all those motor homes on 101," Mary Jean threw out.

"Yeah, but it's prettier, a lot cooler, and we're in no hurry."

Mary Jean effortlessly made her way out of the motel parking lot, through a couple Sacramento city street intersections, and took the on-ramp for westbound Interstate 80.

There are two ways to get to Crescent City from Sacramento. A little faster, although farther in miles, was the route that went from Sacramento, straight up I-5 for three hundred miles, into Oregon. At Grants Pass you pickup Highway 199 for the ninety mile drive down the Smith River Canyon to Crescent City. It was an easy drive, two lanes in each direction most of the way, but it was boring, and the outside temperatures hovered near the century mark.

Shorter, but with a longer driving time, was the route west from Sacramento on I-80 to Vallejo. Then, twenty miles across Highway 37, skirting the north side of the San Francisco Bay, to Petaluma. There you pick up Highway 101 for the three hundred mile drive north to Crescent City. Better than half of those three hundred miles are two lanes in each direction, pretty wide open, and traffic is generally light. The negative to taking this route are the stretches with only one lane each way where lumbering motor homes bring speeds down to a crawl. There are also places where summer time highway maintenance projects sometimes shut down the highway for thirty minutes to an hour. But it's a scenic drive, and the temperatures are much cooler.

Mary Jean would have preferred taking the route up I-5, through Oregon. That's the route they'd travelled on Monday to get to Sacramento, and it was an easier drive. But, it was Red's call, the trip was for her, she thought to herself, as she accelerated up to speed and smoothly merged into the four westbound lanes of I-80.

———————

Mary Jean and Red weren't the only ones driving that day.

Ray Silva, after two days off, was back on patrol Tuesday morning. His shift would be over at 3:00. Halfway through his workday, he'd stopped at the Del Norte County jail and met with Jimmie MacAfee's wife as Red Wolff had requested.

As he expected, she was less than thrilled to talk to him. She was a hard woman who'd run on the ragged edge of being in-and-out of trouble and in-and-out of jail her whole life. As a consequence, her opinion of cops, and her desire to help them with anything, was on the same level.

It took Ray almost twenty minutes of coaxing and listening to her complain about her treatment at the jail and how her husband had been gunned down, before he got the answer to the question he came there to ask.

After he left the jail, Ray thought about giving Red a call and providing her with the information he'd learned about Jimmie MacAfee. Glancing at his watch, he saw it was early yet, not quite noon. Red would still be in her interview. He'd call her later.

He hated flying in the little turbo-prop commuter aircraft United Express used to serve the North Coast. They were noisy, they got bounced around terribly by the turbulence from flying low over the mountains, and the seats were really crammed together. Plus, they were expensive. This trip cost the taxpayers over four hundred dollars just for the flight. He could fly to Hawaii for less, he thought to himself. Add in per diem for meals and lodging, plus a rental car, and the cost for this one day meeting in Sacramento was pushing seven hundred dollars.

It would have cost even more had he opted to fly out of Crescent City instead of driving the seventy miles south to the Arcata Airport and leaving from there. The flight schedule was better from Arcata, even though it would make for a long day when you added in the driving time from the airport back to Crescent City.

These quarterly meetings were a pain in the ass as far as he was concerned. He and his peers from all over the state had endured a long day of discussions about budget cuts, labor problems with the unions, and potential layoffs. The fiscal picture was ugly, and the projections were, it wasn't going to get much better in the next year.

His brain was fried and he was tired by the time he settled into his seat on the small plane shortly before 9:00 that night. It was three across seating, one seat on one side of the aisle, two on the other. The Embraer 120 could carry thirty people, but tonight's flight was less than half-full.

Not that it made much difference as in the two seats in the row ahead of him were two women who talked throughout the hour long flight. It was just his luck, he said to himself, that the acoustics on the aircraft made it possible for him to hear every word they said as the two women raised their volume to be heard over the noise of the engines.

It was a combination of the long day, the travel, the meeting, and now these two women talking so loud they were obnoxious, that fueled his rage. Most of the time it grew slowly, taking days or even weeks to reach a crescendo that sent him hunting for a new victim. But tonight, it seemed to come upon him like a sudden squall at sea. By the time the pilot turned onto final approach, it was all he could do to not reach across the aisle, over the seat, and throttle both of them.

His rage didn't subside as he made his way across the small parking lot to his work car. Three minutes later, he was northbound on Highway 101. It was nearly 11:00, the sky, a cloudless, star-filled black.

Highway 101 was deserted, not a car as far as he could see. He'd be home in ninety minutes, he visualized, pushing the accelerator down, the Crown Victoria's engine responding. A little over seventy was a safe speed with a wide open road, he told himself. The chances of encountering a CHP unit this time of night were about zero.

"Son-of-a-bitch," he yelled as the yellow "Low Fuel" light illuminated on the instrument panel. As soon as it came on, he remembered he'd been low on fuel when he got to Arcata the day before. But he was running late that day and didn't have time to fill up before his flight to Sacramento.

What had been a low simmering anger now exploded into a full blown rage. It wasn't like he could just take the next exit off 101 and find a gas station. First of all, you didn't find gas stations at every exit in this part of the state. Secondly, even if there was a station, there was a good chance it would be closed this time of night. Unlike metropolitan areas, much of the North Coast wasn't open twenty-four hours a day.

There were some stations about ten miles ahead, he knew, but if they were closed, there was nothing for the rest of the way to Crescent City. Reluctantly, his rage building with every mile, he took the next exit, turned around, and headed back the direction he came.

He didn't hit an exit with an open gas station until the junction with Highway 299, just south of where he started from. Here he found three stations, a couple twenty-four hour fast food joints, and an all-night mini-market.

Driving back from Sacramento had turned into an adventure in patience for Red and Mary Jean.

They'd done fine until they got just south of Santa Rosa on Highway 101, where an overturned gas tanker truck had closed the highway. It took them almost an hour of sitting in stop-and-go traffic to travel three miles to the next exit where they were detoured around the tanker and finally back onto 101.

They made pretty good time for the next two hours until little Ray woke up fussy and needing his diaper changed. Additional stops followed along the way for food, gas, and bathroom breaks. Mary Jean's projected get home by 9:00 time was close to three hours behind schedule.

Around 8:30 her phone rang. Ray Silva, the caller I.D. number told her.

"What's up old man?"

"You're gonna miss me when I'm gone," Ray told her sarcastically.

He was right about that, she didn't tell him, he was definitely right about that. Ray would "sixty out" in less than five months and be forced to retire.

"Maybe I can find some other old "Portagee" guy to be my buddy," she said with a laugh.

"How'd the interview go?"

"I've been thinking about it for the last six hours. I think I did okay. We'll find out in a couple of days."

"Where are you?" Ray asked.

"We're almost to Garberville. Had a few delays and a couple of baby stops along the way. We'll be back in town around midnight."

"Julie's coming back tonight, too. She's been in the Bay Area for a couple days, had to finish up some business with her old company. I talked to her about an hour ago, she was in Rio Dell, about thirty miles north of you guys." Ray told her, making conversation.

"10-4. Say, did you talk to MacAfee's wife?" Red inquired.

"Sure did, and you owe me big-time. That is one hard-ass woman. Had to promise her a carton of cigarettes before she would talk to me."

"And?"

"Jimmie MacAfee was right-handed, just like you thought," Ray confirmed.

"See, that's another of those things that points to him not being the guy who murdered Dave and Jodie. The coroner said the person who killed the Castles was probably left-handed," Red reiterated.

As he'd grown more powerful within his organization, he had become less tolerant of people and the little things they did that didn't agree with his well ordered, structured ideas of how the world should run. A legacy of his sainted mother and his Germanic upbringing, he supposed. At any rate, he was quick to criticize things people did that he didn't like, and he never hesitated to use his position to chastise them when it suited his purpose.

In his mind, he also reserved to himself the power to punish those who were outside his sphere of influence in the work environment, particularly women who flaunted their wealth, or thought they were superior to him.

It seemed like the whole day had been a conspiracy against him. The meeting, the bumpy flight, the two women talking loudly on the plane, and then having to turn around to get gas, had all been little irritants that added up to bring his rage to the surface.

Now, as he stood in the cold after 11:00 at night fueling his car, this middle-aged rich bitch, in her big black Lexus SUV, pulls up to the pump in front of him making it impossible for him to drive straight out. He'd have to back-up. It was the last straw.

Pulling out of the station, he parked on the street and waited. After she pumped her own gas, the woman circled out of the station, onto the street. He was standing on the sidewalk smoking a cigarette as she passed his vehicle.

With overhead street lights providing just enough illumination, he could make out the license plate frame when she stopped at the cross street just before the on-ramp. Normally, frames had the name or location of the dealer, which in turn would tell him if this was a rich bitch. As her vehicle passed by, he saw the dealer frame had been removed, replaced by one with the letters and numbers KA 4993. He'd seen those same numbers and letters on other license plate frames before. He wasn't sure what it stood for. Probably something to do with religion he surmised, like a Jesus Fish symbol, or the Greek word IXOYE. No matter, the Lexus was the top of the line, custom wheels, deep black paint job, and was brand new. Rich bitch he told himself, as he took another drag before flipping the cigarette away, opening the back door of his car and putting on his callout jacket and baseball hat.

Red stopped for gas and a chance to stretch their legs in Fortuna. It was nearly 9:30. Little Ray was fast asleep. Mary Jean took over driving, and they were back on the road in less than fifteen minutes.

"Couple hours yet, Babe," Mary Jean said to Red. "Why don't you grab some sleep?"

"Nah, I'm fine. You have any gum?"

"In the glove box."

As Red rummaged through the glove compartment, she came across a book of matches.

"You been smokin' again?" Red asked in a jovial tone, waving the matches in her hand.

"Busted," Mary Jean, who had never smoked in her life, laughed. "They're for the BBQ when we do picnics at the beach. Remember the time last year we got down there, put in the coals, and then didn't have a match? I put them there for emergencies."

Red gave her a courtesy laugh, but her mind was examining the matches. About half of the individual matches in the book were gone.

She and Mary Jean were both right-handed. All of the missing matches were from the right side of the book. Sitting in the passenger's seat, the steady hum of the tires on the pavement, it all started to come into focus.

Her mind flashed on watching Dick Huddleston light a cigarette using matches. It was a smooth fluid motion, he didn't even seem to look at the book. He was right-handed, and he ripped out the individual matches the same way each time, from the right side of the book.

Then in her mind she saw the book of matches found at the vista point the shooting team had collected as evidence. There was no way anyone could say definitively that the matches were connected to the murders, but they were bagged and tagged nonetheless. She could see them clearly in her mind. The book had seven or eight matches torn out. All from the left side.

Red sat motionless in the seat, her eyes fixed on the book of matches in her hand.

Closing her eyes, she saw herself in the parking lot outside the restaurant, after they finished lunch. She had gone to her car and was retrieving messages from her cell phone. Five of the members of the Del Norte County Chief's Association were standing together. Two were smoking. Only one had lit his cigarette with his left hand.

Then it hit her, the raid on the lab. Jimmie MacAfee was right-handed. When Ray and I came out of the bushes, he was taking the gun out of the ex-con's left hand. No, she corrected herself as she continued to visualize the scene. Parole Agent Donnell Carson had already been shot and was on his back, dead. He was bent over the body of Jimmie MacAfee, but he wasn't taking the gun out of his hand, he was trying to put it in his hand!

"It's him!" Red said.

"It's who, what are you talking about?"

As Mary Jean continued driving, eating up the dark miles on the almost deserted Highway 101, Red explained who she thought the killer was.

"Don't you see, it all fits. Dave and Jodie were good cops, especially when it came to officer safety tactics. The deputy told us after they took care of the situation on the bus, Dave said they were headed back toward town to look for drunk drivers. That means they probably encountered him at the vista point and stopped to see if he needed help. When they saw who it was, they would have been less than on their guard because they were dealing with someone in law enforcement, driving an unmarked police car."

"Why was he at the vista point anyway?" Mary Jean asked.

"To dump the body of Kim Glickner. The vista point is a perfect place. There is no beach in the vicinity for the body to wash up on, the waters deep, and the currents would carry her away. When he threw the body over, her head hit the rocks at the edge of the cliff leaving those strands of hair. Anyway, sometime before or after he dumps Kim, the Castles show up. They recognize who he is. He lights a cigarette, he's left-handed, pulls the match from the left side of the match book. Indian Joe drives by. He panics, drops the match book, pulls a gun on them, there's a struggle, and he kills Dave and Jodie."

"Slow down, Babe, it's hard to follow all this," Mary Jean said.

Red Wolff was on a roll, everything was falling into place in her mind.

"So, because he's in law enforcement, he knows everything the task force is doing. The task force starts to focus on the type of ammunition used to kill the Castles, the kind only sold to police agencies. He knows that will eventually lead to him so he needs to have the gun found in such a way that it stops the investigation and closes the case on the Castles. You following all this?"

Mary Jean nodded.

"And the raid on the meth lab gives him the perfect way to do that," Red said shaking her head. "We were all split into two-person teams. He was probably going to plant the gun after everything was secure. We'd find the gun when we searched the place, and the druggies at the lab would take the fall for murdering the Castles. Only Jimmie MacAfee runs when the raid starts. He runs straight into him and the parole agent. Now he can't plant the gun, so he shoots Donnell Carson with the .38 and the same ammo that killed the Castles, then he shoots Jimmie with his duty weapon. He knows we're looking for a left-handed shooter, so he tries to plant the gun in Jimmie's left hand. But Ray and I come along before he can get it in his hand, so he makes it look like he's taking the gun away."

"Then everyone jumps on the fact that the same gun used to kill the Castles was found in that Jimmie guy's hand and case closed," Mary Jean wrapped up Red's narrative.

"Right, except Jimmie's wife said they didn't have a .38, and Jimmie wasn't left-handed," Red concluded.

"But a person can shoot a gun with either hand," Mary Jean said, questioning Red's conclusions.

"Sure they can, Sweetie, but people are either right or left hand dominate. They'd carry a gun and shoot using their strong hand. For Jimmie MacAfee, that was his right hand."

"What are you going to do now, arrest him?" Mary Jean asked, slowing down as they entered the Eureka city limits.

"It's not that easy. It all makes sense, and all the pieces fit, but it's all circumstantial at this point. I'll need to talk to my boss, and see if he has any ideas on which way to go. I can't just accuse a high ranking law enforcement executive of killing two Highway Patrol officers and of being a serial killer, just because he's left-handed. I want to make captain, not be an unemployed lieutenant."

"Couldn't you get his DNA and maybe check on his history. I mean if he really is a serial killer, wouldn't there be missing women and unsolved murders, at other places he worked before coming to Crescent City," Mary Jean asked.

"You would have made a good detective Sweetie," Red said with a half-smile.

CHAPTER NINETEEN

It was close to 11:00 as they drove into Eureka. Like Crescent City, Highway 101 ran through the town, not around it, and for much of the way the two northbound and two southbound lanes were separated by several city blocks. The streets were deserted, a few cars here and there, but most of the thirty thousand population was long since at home by that time of night. Catching all the traffic signals green, they were out of Eureka and back up to freeway speed in less than six minutes.

"Don't you think you should call Ray?" Mary Jean asked.

"It's late, and there's nothing he can do tonight," Red replied. "Want me to drive?"

"Would you, my eyes are killing me," Mary Jean told her, the sound of relief in her voice.

The next twenty miles were two lanes in each direction of wide open freeway, and Red had the speedometer set at eighty. After that, Highway 101 changed back and forth from open multi-lane freeway to narrow winding two lane road, then back to freeway.

By the time they got to Klamath, it was nearly midnight. Only about twenty-five miles to go, Red thought, as she smoothly glided through the curves on the dark two lane road. Mary Jean, she could see, was in that half-asleep, half-awake zone, her head jerking occasionally, as she rolled side-to-side in a futile effort to get comfortable.

With no on-coming traffic, Red had her high beams on to illuminate as far ahead as she could. Deer were always a problem at night. She'd seen several already standing right at the edge of the road nibbling on vegetation. A hundred fifty pound deer could smash the heck out of the front end and windshield of a small car like Mary Jean's Honda Accord. It could also ruin the deer's whole night.

The Trees of Mystery tourist attraction, on the north side of Klamath, closed at 7:00 in the evening. An area of giant redwood trees, hiking trails, and a gondola ride, it was a favorite stop for visitors over the last fifty years. Created out of a grove of giant, two thousand year old trees, for tourists from all over the world it was a chance to walk among, and touch, some of the oldest living things on earth. It was hard to miss, with a wooden forty-nine foot tall carved figure of Paul Bunyan, standing next to his thirty-five foot tall blue ox, Babe.

It was also a spot where local high school kids would occasionally try to paint Babe's balls their school colors. The parking lot, Red knew, should be deserted, and out of reflex she glanced to the right as she drove by.

The lot wasn't deserted tonight, her high beam lights catching the reflection of shiny paint on a vehicle parked near the front of the lot next to the highway. There was something familiar about the car, she'd seen it somewhere before. Slowing, she gently pressed the brakes, then made a U-turn. Something didn't look right.

Normally, had she been in her state Crown Victoria, she would have used the radio to call the beat unit to check it out. Tonight, in Mary Jean's car, she opted to give it a quick check by herself. If something was amiss, she could use her cell phone to call 9-1-1.

Getting involved off-duty, with no radio communications, was something she had only rarely done in her twenty year career. Sure, she'd stopped at accident scenes over the years to help, just like any other citizen. Twice, however, she'd been forced to get involved in situations where she had to draw a weapon. Once, it was to protect two little old ladies who were being robbed by gang-bangers at a gas station in Los Angeles. The other time she'd run down a purse-snatcher at a mall. It was dangerous, and the department frowned on officers who got involved in off-duty incidents unless they had no choice. Tonight, she didn't feel she had any choice, but with Mary Jean and their son in the car, she needed to be especially cautious.

Except for the shiny black Lexus SUV, the lot was deserted.

"Are we home?" a sleepy Mary Jean inquired, yawning and stretching her arms.

"Give me my gun from the glove compartment," Red told Mary Jean, her eyes scanning all around.

"Erin, what is it?" Mary Jean asked, now suddenly wide awake, the sound of apprehension in her voice.

Taking the .40 caliber pistol from Mary Jean, Red slipped the holster's retaining clip into her waistband and drew the weapon.

"That's Julie's car," Red stated.

"Julie's car! How do you know?" Mary Jean said, even more apprehension in her voice.

"There aren't many black Lexus SUVs in the county and none with a KA 4993 license plate frame, except hers."

When Red Wolff said the vehicle had a KA 4993 license plate frame, Mary Jean knew instantly it was Julie's vehicle.

Years ago Red had explained to her that KA 4993 was the Federal Communication Commission's identification call sign for the California Highway Patrol radio system. Officers, Mary Jean knew, bought the frames at the academy PX and put them on their cars, or their wives cars, to identify themselves to other officers. It's a way of saying "I'm Highway Patrol" that only another CHP officer would understand, Red had told her.

"Be careful," Mary Jean cautioned as Red opened the door, her service pistol in her right hand, a small flashlight she retrieved from the door panel in her left.

Holding the flashlight at shoulder height, her arm extended away from her body, Red approached the left side of the Lexus. A quick check of the cargo area and back seat revealed they were empty. Shuffling forward, she scanned the driver's compartment. Empty. Pulling on the handle, the door opened.

Using the flashlight to add illumination to the vehicle's interior light, Red quickly took in everything. The glove box was open, papers were scattered on the floor and on the passenger's seat. The keys were still in the ignition. As she played the light beam around the interior, she caught the reflection on the steering wheel. It was blood.

She could tell from the consistency it was fresh as it was still a dark red and had yet to coagulate. Taking an extra second, she walked toward the front of the Lexus, putting her hand on the hood. It was still warm, and there was no damage to the front end. Quickly slamming the door closed, she ran back to Mary Jean's Honda.

Without saying a word, she grabbed her cell phone and hit a speed dial number. Holding the phone to her ear she waited and listened for the cell to connect. After ten seconds she disconnected and checked the visual display.

"Son-of-a-bitch!" she exclaimed. "It's the trees. They're blocking the cell signal."

Jumping back in the car, Red shifted into reverse and punched the accelerator. The Accord leapt backward, tires screeching in protest as she spun the wheel violently to the left. The small car responded as the weight shifted from side-to-side, leaving black tire marks as it slid to a stop just before she slammed the transmission into drive and pushed the pedal to the floorboard.

Mary Jean and Red Wolff had been with each other for over fifteen years. She knew Red would tell her what was happening when she could. For now she remained silent letting her life partner focus on whatever was going on.

311

The Honda hit the edge of the parking lot where it joined the highway, and Red jammed the wheel to the right heading north, the speedometer climbing rapidly past seventy.

"There's blood in the car, and the phone is in a dead spot. We need to get out of these trees," Red finally spoke.

"Oh my god, Julie," Mary Jean said, her voice controlled. She might not have been a cop, but she had been in plenty of dangerous spots as a former navy helicopter pilot to know that panicking and getting hysterical, wouldn't help anything.

"Try Ray's number again. Number two on the speed dial," Red told her as she started up Last Chance Grade.

Grabbing Red's phone, Mary Jean looked at the digital display. "Still no signal," she said.

It took another minute until they reached the top of the grade.

"Try it now."

Mary Jean could see three signal strength bars on the display and punched the number for Ray Silva.

"It's ringing," she said handing the phone to Red.

Three rings later, a sleepy Ray Silva answered.

"Red, what's up?"

"Ray, listen, is Julie with you?"

"What, no, she's not home yet, why are you calling?"

Quickly she explained finding Julie's Lexus in the deserted parking lot with blood on the steering wheel.

"If she'd been in an accident someone would have called me," Ray replied.

"Ray, there was no damage to the car."

Seldom in his thirty-plus year career had Ray Silva ever been at a loss for what to do or say. The phone was silent.

It was Red Wolff who spoke.

"Ray, I think he's got her."

Even though her hands were cuffed behind her back, she was still fighting him.

After pulling his Crown Victoria inside the two-car garage at his house and closing the door, he popped open the trunk. As soon as the lid opened, she sent a vicious kick with her left foot at his face. The heel of her shoe caught him squarely on the chin, sending him staggering rearward, the back of his head slamming in to the metal garage door.

It sent him into a blind rage, and he pummeled her with three full force blows to her face. Even then, she still struggled against the handcuffs which held her arms behind her back, and he could hear the force she was exerting through the scarf gag that held her mouth agape.

Only by shocking her again with the stun gun flashlight, was he able to subdue her enough to physically lift her out of the trunk. He'd never before had to apply a second shock to anyone, and he'd never had anyone fight as hard as this woman had. Then it hit him, the batteries! He had meant to change them after the bicyclist. Low batteries resulted in less than a full jolt from the stun gun. That's why she was able to fight back, he told himself.

She was older than his normal victims, maybe mid-fifties, though still a good-looker. As he picked her up, he could feel the tightness of her skin and the hardness of her body.

Maybe this wasn't such a good idea, he thought as he carried her upstairs to his bedroom. Maybe he should just kill her right now and dump the body. He had a bad feeling about this one.

Then it dawned on him. It was the coldness of the house that made this one feel different. He'd been gone for almost two days on his trip to Sacramento, and without at least a low burning fire to keep the chill away, the house felt cold. Nothing to worry about, a fire would solve that, and then he could deal with this rich bitch.

Flopping her limp body on the bed, he began to remove her clothes while he mentally flashed back on stopping her. He'd followed her for almost fifty miles since leaving the gas station at Highway 299. She kept a steady speed between sixty-five and seventy, and he had hung back a couple hundred yards, sometimes losing sight of her taillights around curves or in places where the highway undulated up and down. Traffic was so light that many times he saw no other cars on the road for miles as both vehicles drove north. Only two other cars had passed him during the hour long drive. Both were long gone by the time they reached Klamath.

Just after crossing the bridge over the Klamath River, he accelerated and closed to within three car lengths of the Lexus. He had the red light ready. The Lexus slowed as soon as he flipped the switch on the light, and she pulled over into the deserted parking lot of the Trees of Mystery.

It went wrong almost from the start. He approached the woman's car on the left, giving her a smile and a greeting. She looked a little confused when he told her she had been stopped for doing sixty-five in a forty-five zone. She got her registration out for him and was about to give him her license, when he saw the signs in her eyes.

"Who are you?" she asked, her eyes surveying the strange uniform he wore, her voice stern and demanding. At the same time, she started to move as far to the right as she could in the bucket seat, but restrained by the seat belt, she didn't have the ability to slide to the passenger's side.

He was committed. She'd seen his face, heard his voice, and seen the hat and callout jacket he was wearing which identified his agency. She'd also be able to identify his car if he tried to drive away. Reaching quickly into the car, he cupped his right hand behind her neck in a vise like grip and violently pulled her toward him, smashing her face down twice into the steering wheel. Momentarily stunned by the force of the blows, as blood streamed from her broken nose, she ceased resisting. It was enough time for him to touch the twin electrodes of his flashlight stun gun to her neck. She cried out in agony and then went limp.

He had her handcuffed and in the trunk of his car in a matter of seconds. The night was still and quiet again. Not a single vehicle had gone by.

After stripping her, he tied her hands and feet to the posts at each corner of his bed. She was still unconscious, dried blood covered her face, and fresh blood was flowing from the corner of her mouth where he had hit her while she was in the trunk. Although she was going to die, he didn't want her to die yet. With dried blood blocking her nose, he decided to remove the scarf gag from her mouth so she could breathe. He would need the scarf for other purposes anyway.

He slapped her several times across her cheeks to see if she was conscious. Getting no response, he headed downstairs to start a fire and retrieve his weapon from his car.

"Ray, I know who he is!" Red spoke into the cell phone while negotiating the curves through the tall stands of redwood trees that bordered both sides of the highway.

"Who is he?" Ray shouted to his cell phone that was now on speaker as he pulled on a pair of blue jeans.

As she continued to race north, the four cylinder engine on the Honda pouring out all the power it could, Red Wolff told her lifelong friend who she suspected had kidnapped his wife.

"That bastard!" Ray exclaimed, his voice sounding tinny over the cell phone's speaker. "I know where he lives, I'm going there now."

"Ray, he's probably had Julie for about thirty minutes. How do you know where he is now?" Red replied.

After tying his running shoes, Ray Silva switched off the speaker, bringing the tiny phone up to his ear.

"I don't know where he is, but his house is a place to start."

"Ray, wait for back-up. I'll call the comm center," she told him. There was no reply.

"Ray, Ray?"

The connection was gone.

"Highway Patrol, what is your emergency?" the gravelly male voice answered after two rings.

"Smitty, Erin Wolff, listen, don't talk," Red Wolff told Leonard Schmitt.

For the next twenty seconds Red told the veteran communications operator the situation with Julie Silva being kidnapped and Ray enroute to the suspect's house.

"Contact our graveyard unit and have them respond to the house for backup. Call the S.O. and have their deputy's respond, also. I'm less than ten minutes away from there now. I'll stay on the line."

"10-4, copy. 10-23 one," Smitty acknowledged what he needed to do and told her to standby.

Over the phone, Red could hear the "Beep-Beep-Beep" of the signal tone used to alert field units of an emergency call, then a slight pause until she heard his voice broadcasting over the radio.

"Attention all Crescent City units, 11-99, Officer Needs Help," Smitty called, while at the same time punching up the direct connect phone line to the Del Norte County Sheriff's Office dispatcher.

Between the sound of the engine whining and the background noise, Red couldn't hear the response from the CHP field unit, or Smitty's conversation with the sheriff's dispatcher. A few seconds later, he was back on the phone to Red.

"Lieutenant, we only have one unit working tonight. They're at the tunnel on 199 working a crash. They're enroute, but they're fifty miles away! The Sheriff's have two units tonight, one's in Smith River, ETA ten minutes, the other's booking a prisoner; he's clearing the jail now. His ETA is also ten."

"Okay Smitty, I'm closest. I'll be there in less than five. Keep the help coming, and roll an ambulance."

The house was starting to warm up, and he felt more relaxed as he walked casually back up stairs to his bedroom. She was conscious now and staring at him. He could see that her lips were pursed in contempt, and there was no fear in her eyes. He was going to enjoy this one.

Except for a small amount of light from the two pine scented candles, one on each nightstand in short glass vase holders, the kind used on tables in restaurants, the bedroom was dark. The smell reminded him of the cypress forests of Pebble Beach and of his mother. The flickering flames danced crazily in their vessels, casting shadows that moved and gyrated on the ceiling.

Moving toward the bed, he set his pistol on the nightstand and reached down to stroke her hair.

"Don't touch me you sick son-of-a-bitch!" she screamed as she twisted against the restraints binding her arms and legs.

The sound of the back of his hand slapping her across the face echoed off the walls.

"For an old bitch who's going to die soon, you're pretty feisty," he grinned down at her as he started taking off his clothes.

Once he was naked, he pulled a black sleep mask from the nightstand and began to slip it over her head. She twisted her head violently side-to-side to no avail, as he slid the mask down over her eyes and positioned the strap across the back of her head.

The uncertainty of not knowing, or not being able to see what was going to happen next, he had learned, only heightened the anxiety of the women he had killed before and infinitely increased the pleasure he derived. Almost instantaneously her respirations increased, and her chest began to heave up and down more rapidly. He visualized the rabbit he had caught in the leg snare behind the old general's house. He could see its eyes darting and its nose twitching.

Picking up one of the candles from the nightstand, he poured a small amount of the molten wax on to her chest.

The pain, although momentary, was excruciating, as the hot liquid splattered across her breasts and almost instantly hardened against her skin.

"Like that, rich bitch?" he laughed as she screamed in pain.

Ray Silva didn't have a plan, he was running on instinct. Not just instinct, but an instinct rooted in over thirty years experience of dealing with life or death situations, of dealing with people at their worst, and with the unexpected.

In a normal situation, one where he was responding to a call, he would have reacted like a cop and driven up the hill with his lights out, parked fifty feet away on the street, and walked cautiously down the gravel driveway to the house.

This wasn't a normal situation, this was personal.

Ray had the presence of mind to approach the house slowly, his duty pistol at the ready, flashlight in his other hand. He knew he only had one chance at this, and anything he did had to be done fast in order to save Julie.

The house was dark, although he could see a faint flickering light source coming from the upstairs bedroom. Silently he tried the double front doors. Locked. They were solid core oak, the type he couldn't just bust open with a shoulder like in the movies.

Headlights appeared at the top of the driveway, and Ray saw a small car approaching. He recognized Mary Jean's Honda.

Red Wolff was by his side in an instant.

"Ray, back-up will be here in five minutes, wait."

"Julie's in there. I know it." he replied, moving toward the side of the house.

"You can't be sure of that, we have no warrant, and no probable cause to break down the door," she told him, while trying at the same time to physically hold him back.

She might as well have saved her breath and her strength.

"Like I give a shit!" he said in a low guttural growl.

Using his flashlight for only a few seconds at a time to light his way, Ray navigated around to the side garage door. Locked also. Picking his way silently to the rear of the house, he located the wooden steps that led up to the downstairs deck. Red Wolff was right on his heels, weapon drawn.

As he made his way across the deck, his footsteps making no noise, he came to the slider that led into the living room. It was locked, too.

The scream from upstairs was unmistakably Julie.

"Now we have exigent circumstances," Ray yelled as he fired two rounds into the five foot wide sliding glass door.

The flames from the barrel of his pistol lit up the night, and the sound reverberated across the valley. The safety glass was still falling, having formed itself into thousands of little glass beads, hitting the wooden deck and the carpeted living room floor as Ray Silva rushed inside.

He was on his guard, weapon pointed, flashlight playing over the large living room, looking for any threats. When he saw the staircase, he broke into a run.

"Ray, wait!" Red yelled as she started after him.

It was switch back staircase. Seven steps in one direction up to a landing, then eight steps in the opposite direction to the bedroom door. Ray was taking them two at a time. Red was a full second behind him.

The sound of the shots being fired caused him to drop the candle. The rest of the hot wax splashed half on the bed, half on blindfolded Julie's left side. She let out another scream as the liquid burned her skin.

Picking up his .9 millimeter, fourteen shot pistol from the nightstand, he took three steps toward the bedroom door and pointed his weapon at the figure he could see charging up the second portion of the staircase in the almost total darkness.

They fired almost simultaneously, his one shot catching Ray Silva in the upper right chest. Normally, a shot like that would have been enough to incapacitate an average man and send him reeling backward.

Ray Silva was far from average. Running on adrenalin and with a full head of steam, the round barely stopped his forward motion. It didn't affect his aim at all. Ray did a "double tap", firing two rounds in rapid succession, as Highway Patrol officers are trained to do.

Both of Ray Silva's shots caught him just to the left of his heart. The entrance wounds were less than an inch and a half apart. The controlled expansion, .40 caliber ammunition cut its way into his chest cavity, the soft core of the bullets mushrooming as they went. One round severed his aorta, the other tore a four inch hole in his left lung. The force of the impact threw him back into the bedroom. He was dead before his body crumpled to the ground.

Ray Silva took three more steps up the stairs before falling, face down.

Red Wolff didn't pause, stepping over Ray, and continuing into the bedroom, weapon pointed.

In the dim light from the remaining candle, she could see his body. He was flat on his back, arms outstretched, his weapon on the carpet, six feet from his hand.

He looked dead to her. Even so, had she had her handcuffs she would have secured his hands behind his back. Without cuffs, the best she could do was retrieve his weapon and slide it into her waistband.

Once she had his weapon, she shined her flashlight on his face. Looking up at her, his lifeless eyes fixed on the ceiling, was the dead face of the warden of Pelican Bay State Prison.

Moving to the bed, she shifted her attention to Julie.

"It's okay Julie, you're safe now," Red whispered softly, removing the blindfold.

Flashes of red and blue emergency lights that came through the windows from outside the house were bouncing off the interior walls of the darkened room. Noise from downstairs told her help had arrived.

Once the first Del Norte deputies got there they covered Julie with a sheet and untied her arms and legs.

Red moved out of the way and looked around. "Ray!" she shouted out loud.

He had rolled over on his back and propped himself up against the wall at the top of the stairs by the time Red got to him.

It was bad. Bright red, frothy blood, coming from the mouth was never a good sign, she knew. And there was a lot of it. Ray was alternately gasping, then coughing, with each breath.

"11-41 will be here soon," she told him, indicating an ambulance was on the way.

Ray Silva's eyes were fixed on hers. He had a slight smile on his face, not the big toothy grin he was known for, the one she had first seen twenty years ago in Los Angeles, but a kind of, "I know something you don't know" smile.

"Julie okay?" he asked between coughs, blood spraying from his lips.

"Yeah, she'll be fine, don't talk," Red told him, holding his hand.

"Did I kill the guy, who killed me?" he questioned.

Red Wolff squeezed the hand of her career long friend. They both knew.

"Yes."

CHAPTER TWENTY

The Highway Patrol shooting team returned to Crescent City for the second time in less than four months. This investigation was pretty straight forward. There was no question of jurisdiction, and strangely, no problems with the county sheriff.

The official investigation indicated that CHP Officer Ray Silva and Lieutenant Erin Wolff had responded on a kidnap in progress. During their response, they heard the screams of the female victim and had forcibly entered the suspect's house. A gunfight ensued in which the suspect and Officer Silva exchanged fire. The suspect was killed instantly. Officer Silva succumbed to his wounds shortly thereafter.

The Del Norte County Sheriff's Office took the lead in following up on the suspect who had been killed and conducting the investigation into his past.

In cooperation with the California Department of Corrections, the FBI, and numerous other law enforcement agencies in California and Virginia, it was determined that the suspect had been responsible for the murders of at least twenty-seven women. The actual number, authorities believed, was closer to forty, but they did not have sufficient evidence to link some of the crimes to the suspect.

In a small town near the Virginia border with North Carolina, thanks to a positive match on DNA, the police department was able to close the twenty year old case of a woman murdered in a hotel room.

Their investigation revealed the suspect had once been a low level employee with the Federal Bureau of Prisons. His job had been to conduct field inspections on equipment purchases and inventory procedures. In this position, he travelled extensively to federal correctional facilities in the Mid-Atlantic States. It was surmised that in this position he had access to and had stolen, the .38 caliber ammunition sold only to law enforcement.

He had resigned from that position to return to California to care for his ailing mother and had subsequently been hired by the California Department of Corrections as a civilian employee in much the same capacity. By tracing his work history with corrections, it was determined there were several disappearances of young wealthy women and several unsolved homicides in every prior location he had worked.

Investigators also learned he had progressively promoted within the organization, working his way up through the system to become a non-peace officer business manager within the Department of Corrections. That led to a promotion to assistant warden at another correctional facility, before finally receiving a Governor's appointment as warden at Pelican Bay.

It was also revealed that while he wasn't a peace officer, he was intimately familiar with law enforcement procedures and weapons. The investigation was critical of the executive management of the Department of Corrections for failure to have a system in place to identify his flagrant and continual violations of policy. Specifically, the investigation revealed that he constantly carried a weapon, which he was not authorized to do, and that he utilized his state vehicle for personal business. Both these facts were well known to both his superiors and subordinates, but neither took any action to correct these violations of policy.

The FBI had done a psychological profile on him in an attempt to determine how he had gone undetected for so many years, and what factors contributed to his behavior.

In regards to behavior, a profiler delved into his upbringing and early childhood, ascertaining that his actions were typical of other serial killers. An alcoholic father, a doting mother, and uncorrected anti-social tendencies as an adolescent, had all contributed to a deep seated hatred for women. Especially they determined, women who had status and wealth.

They also found he had an extremely high I.Q. which they attributed to his ability to stay undetected for nearly twenty years. Interviews with co-workers, subordinates, and his superiors, revealed he had the ability to charm those who could promote his career. Conversely, he could be vindictive and ruthless in dealing with those who crossed him. These traits, however, the investigation revealed, he was masterful in concealing from his superiors.

Bottom line, although the State of California's final report did not say so directly, the system failed.

What didn't fail, were the dozens of civil law suits for "wrongful death" being filed against the State of California by the families of his victims. It would be years, and tens of millions of dollars, before they were all settled.

The day after the incident, Red Wolff returned to her office for the first time. On her desk, Office Manager Lisa Johnston had put Ray Silva's personnel file. Opening the folder, she saw Ray's personal information page with his date of birth, height, weight, blood type, and next-of-kin. There was also a two by three inch color photo. Red stared at the picture. His hair was shorter, almost completely grey, and his face had deep creases around his eyes. He still had his toothy grin. The date on the photograph indicated it was three years old.

Since personnel file pictures were replaced every five years, Red flipped to the back of the folder and pulled out an envelope that held all of the prior pictures of Ray Silva.

My God, she said to herself, as she slowly shuffled through the six photographs taken over Ray's thirty plus year career. The first three photos were in black and white, the oldest being his graduation picture from the academy. It was dated 1975, when he had jet black hair. It was the first time she'd ever seen him without a moustache.

A half-smile came to her face when she looked at the third picture. Still in black and white, it showed a face more lined by age, some grey streaks among the still full head of hair, a salt and pepper moustache, and the always present grin. She didn't need to look at the date on the back to know it was taken right around the time they first met. He, the veteran with twelve years on the job, she, the rookie, right out of the academy.

With tears welling in her eyes, Red put the photos away, she couldn't look anymore.

Flipping to the opposite side of Ray's file, she found the envelope she was looking for. It was a simple plain white envelope, the flap sealed shut. On the front she recognized his printing. *"Funeral Instructions"*.

Using her knife to slit the top of the flap, she pulled out the single page of unlined paper and read.

"Silva, you old mossback," she said out loud to nobody but herself, laughing.

Later that same day, she visited Julie Silva at Sutter Coast Hospital. The room was full of flowers, bright metallic balloons, and several stuffed animals. It all seemed out of place for someone who had just lost her husband.

Julie's face was swollen and discolored, her lips still puffy from the savage beating she had taken, and a large bandage covered her nose.

Even so, Julie managed a slight smile.

"Julie, I know it's tough, but we need to plan for Ray's service," Red began. In her hand she held Ray's letter.

Julie nodded.

"These are Ray's funeral instructions. Do you know what he wants?" she asked.

"Yes, we worked on them together. We wrote them just after the Castles were murdered." Pausing to catch her breath and clear her throat, she continued. "Erin, there's something you need to know," Julie struggled to form the words through her swollen lips. "Ray had pancreatic cancer. We found out last fall. It was inoperable. The doctor's gave him a year. It was the reason we got married. He wanted to make sure I was taken care of."

"He never said anything!" Red replied, a look of disbelief on her face.

"You know how he was," Julie mumbled. "Even after seven years together he was still a mystery in so many ways."

"Why didn't he just retire when he found out? You guys could have had some time together."

"He was going to. He was going to tell you when we were in Mexico. Then the Castles happened. He always told me he owed Jodie a life for saving him when the terrorists attacked two years. He said he couldn't retire until you guys got the person who killed them," Julie struggled to get the words out.

"And that's why there were so many trips to the Bay Area, wasn't it?" Red queried.

"Yes, he had a great doc at the University of San Francisco Cancer Center. The drugs slowed it down. He knew it was just a short reprieve."

Red sat silently, tears again filling her eyes.

"So," Red said after a few moments, holding up Ray's letter, "Is this what you want?"

"You want him coming back and haunting us both if we don't?" Julie coughed as she laughed.

"I've never been to a CHP funeral on a Saturday afternoon," Assistant Chief Vaughn O'Dell told Red Wolff as he sat in her office. "And I've never heard of one where nobody wore a uniform."

"It's what he wanted. No uniforms, no service, no sad speeches, no Governor, and especially no bagpipes," Red told him.

"Okay, time to head over there, you want to ride with me?" he asked.

"Nah, I have a stop to make first, I'll meet you there," Red told him.

"By the way, congratulations on the captain's test. Number seven out of sixty candidates is quite an accomplishment."

"I owe it all to you, Boss. Without your help, I would have never been ready for the interview."

"You should get promoted in a few months. Any preference on where you want to go?"

"I'll take what comes, L.A. or the Bay Area would be best," Red told him.

The Del Norte County Sheriff's Office was deserted. It was Saturday, and all of the employees who did the routine Monday through Friday business were off. Red Wolff had set up the meeting specifically to ensure there were very few people around.

Sheriff Jerome Williamson was seated behind his desk when she walked into his office. He didn't have that smug look on his face today.

"Red, come in please, have a seat," he smiled.

Spare me that phony ass smile, Red said to herself as she closed the door.

"What can I do for you?" he said, gesturing again for her to take a chair.

Red stood in front of his desk, both hands on her hips.

"It's time to answer for Ray Silva," she began. "He's dead because you're an arrogant asshole. I sat right here in your office two weeks ago and begged you to take over the investigation. I told you Jimmie MacAfee didn't kill the Castles, and I gave you all the evidence you needed to investigate a serial killer loose in the county. You let your hatred for the Highway Patrol and for me because I'm gay, cloud your judgment. You let your political ambitions and the need to get reelected, get in the way of doing your job. Now Ray Silva is dead. He's dead because of you! On Monday I'm going to the Department of Justice and have them do an investigation. I'm going to the newspapers, too. I'll tell them the whole story. I'll tell them you refused to take over the investigation because you knew it would cost you the election if it came out there was a serial killer and cop murderer, operating in the county that you couldn't catch. When all that comes out, the state sheriff's association won't support you, even your own local deputies will vote against you. The district attorney will do an investigation, and he'll probably file criminal charges against you for malfeasance. At the very least, the Del Norte County Council will vote to remove you from office."

With that she turned and was gone.

—————

The parking lot of the community center was jammed. Hundreds of cars, pickups, and several dozen motor homes were crowded into the lot. There wasn't a police car in sight.

Red had to park at the far end of the lot. As she walked toward the entrance, she could hear the loud sounds of the bass guitar lick from The Iron Butterfly's, *In-A-Gadda-Da-Vida*. Red got a half-smile on her face. It was before her time, but it was one of Ray's favorites.

The building was filled almost to capacity. Every table was full of people, ordinary people from Crescent City, Highway Patrol officers from around the state, and dozens of cops from other agencies. There wasn't a uniform in the room. There were a few people in coats and ties, probably from out-of-town, Red figured. The majority, however, were in casual clothes. Blue jeans seemed to be the preferred dress.

The noise was almost deafening, people laughing, helped along by the three kegs of beer strategically placed around the room.

The Beach Boys were singing *God Only Knows* by the time Red found Mary Jean and Julie sitting at a table in the middle of the room.

Seated with them was Ray's nephew, Ralph. He was a week away from graduating from the CHP academy.

"Ralph!" Red exclaimed, giving him a big hug. "Thanks for being here. I know how much Ray wanted to be at your graduation to pin on your badge."

"Thank you, ma'am," Ralph replied, his academy training not letting him refer to her by her first name.

"Knock off the ma'am crap, Silva," she snapped at him, a smile on her face.

"Yes, ma'am," he replied.

Red punched him on the arm, and they both laughed.

"Did you get your assignment yet?" she asked, inquiring where he was going to be sent for his first duty location after graduation.

"Marin," he replied, then added, "Would you do me the honor of pinning on my badge at graduation next week? Uncle Ray would have liked that."

"Of course," is all Red could manage, emotions welling up inside.

"Pardon me, ma'am," a voice said from behind, as a hand touched her lightly on the shoulder. The voice had a distinctively southern drawl to it.

Turning, Red found she was face-to-face with a middle-aged, white guy dressed in jeans, with a leather belt, and big shiny cowboy buckle. His eyes were a little red and the half-full plastic cup of beer he held swayed back and forth.

"Ma'am, Trooper Austin LeMont, Texas Highway Patrol. Ma'am, condolences from the National Trooper's Coalition on the death of your officer. I have a flag for you to present to your officer's widow. And may I say, ma'am, I thought we had some pretty good beer in Texas, but yawl's California beer is mighty tasty," he said, holding the cup up in a toast.

"Thank you Trooper LeMont. Ray would have wanted you to enjoy yourself," Red told him.

As he walked away, Julie whispered to Mary Jean, "I wonder what he would say if he knew it was Pacifico, Ray's favorite Mexican beer."

The celebration of Ray Silva's life really got going around 4:30. The potluck table was over fifteen feet long, with food down both sides. The music volume got louder as the evening progressed.

"They say we're young and we don't know," Sonny and Cher sang the words from *I Got You Babe*, the music almost drowned out by the crowd.

"Erin, is anyone going to say anything?" Mary Jean asked.

Red shook her head to indicate no.

"It's not what Ray wanted," she told her, barely audible over the music and people laughing. "Heck, I'm not sure he won't be pissed off about the one picture of him we put up there," she continued, referring to Ray like he was there.

"He'd love it. He'd growl about it, but he'd love it," Julie added, managing a laugh while pointing to the two-by-three foot photograph sitting on the small table in the center of the stage next to the deep blue colored ceramic urn that contained his ashes.

"Ray's instructions were to keep it light and upbeat. No sob stories, no feeling sorry. I didn't dare cross him in life, so I'm certainly not going to cross him in death," Red laughed.

Vaughn O'Dell made his way to their table and sat down.

"I haven't seen the sheriff around, Red, isn't he coming?" he asked.

"I don't think he's gonna make it," she replied.

———————

On Sunday morning, Red and Mary Jean accompanied Julie to scatter Ray's ashes.

The old fishing boat was now named the *Wandering Star.* It was small and weathered by the passage of time, its single diesel engine belching black smoke as the captain pushed the throttle forward, and the boat slowly chugged its way from the dock. Fifty years ago it was named the *Dolce Maria,* the Sweet Mary, when Ray's father had scraped together the money to buy it.

"He would have liked this," Julie said as she stared out to sea. "Taking his last ride on the boat he worked on with his father."

The ocean around Crescent City was usually rough in the summer, the onshore wind whipping up long rolling white-capped three to four foot high waves. Today it was mirror glass smooth, almost like the sea was paying its last respects, also.

It took an hour and a half, and they were back at Ray's home before noon. The three of them spent the rest of the day together. Quiet conversation, a little wine, telling Ray Silva stores.

———————

Red was up at 5:00 Monday morning. It was a work day, and there was still a massive amount of paperwork to do.

It was already light by the time she finished her run. She would miss the mornings on the North Coast, when the sun came up early, and the twilight lingered until close to 9:00 in the evening.

Moving up on the Highway Patrol meant promoting, and promoting always meant moving, she thought to herself. Wherever they sent her when she promoted to captain, it was a certainty it wouldn't be as pretty as this, she realized.

The newspaper was lying on the driveway. Idly she tore away the protective plastic bag and flipped open the paper as she walked toward the front door, scanning the headlines.

Jesus, she said to herself as she walked and read. Front page, a story about a woman in Crescent City with fifty cats. Another story about new limits on the amount of crab commercial fisherman could take.

Opening the paper she scanned page two, checked out the five day weather forecast and the police log from the previous week. The small article on page three stopped her in her tracks.

Ray Silva was as prophetic in death, as he had been in life, she thought to herself. The local paper really was a rag.

The article was only nine lines and really didn't say much. Sheriff Jerome Williamson, it seems, had accidentally killed himself at his residence while cleaning his weapon.

As she walked back in the house, Red Wolff had a half-smile on her face.

ACKNOWLEDGMENTS

Writing a good book, or a bad one for that matter, is a function of having a vivid imagination and a bunch of good friends. I've been blessed at least with having an abundance of the latter.

A special thanks to Candy Stiesberg for being my biggest cheerleader. Chet and Tish Hunt for their help with spelling. Ilene Angel, for taking her valuable time to read through one of the early drafts and providing her candid comments. Thanks to my pal and former co-worker, Nancy Herrera, for her assistance with punctuation, and again to Nancy, and her sister, Alice Paige, for changing the graphics on the badge which appears on the cover. I'd of been lost without the help of Dawn Wooten, whose computer skills formatted everything and prepared the map. Also, thanks to Steffani and Taylor Angel for lending their names to create a character. And special thanks to Donetta Walker, the best comm-op at Los Angeles Communications Center, for her input on dispatch operations, and for watching out for unit 15-70 so many years ago.

A word about commas. Judy, my wife, and best friend, is my number one supporter and was my number one proofreader. She is a product of Catholic school, and puts a comma every other word, whether it's needed or not. Conversely, I only put in commas when it feels right. In the interest of marital bliss, I did it her way.

She did all she could to make it perfect. So, at this point, any incorrect grammar, punctuation, or misspelled words that remain, and too many, or not enough commas, are operator error.

A big MAHALO to each of you for your help.

LaVergne, TN USA
25 May 2010
183826LV00002B/14/P

9 781602 645639